TETSAMI KN...
WAS ...

She flicked the sat co...
channels. And she fir...
seeing.

"They're jamming me. They're looking for me!"

As she tried to strangle the *Lady*'s controls, goosing the vehicle to go ever faster, Tetsami could see turquoise and black dots on the horizon in the rear video. She knew it was hopeless, even as she forced the *Lady* to skip dunes like a rock across the ripples of a frozen pond. The spuds behind her were riding military contragravs, and they were armed. Still, if she couldn't outrun them, perhaps she could outrun their radio interference, if only for a moment, and get off a message. She turned the ship's computer on to record and yelled at the computer's audio pickup.

"I'm Kari Tetsami. I'm about to be captured or killed by Proudhon Spaceport Security. Proudhon is conducting a massive military operation in the desert north of the spaceport. I think they've bought every mercenary that cruised the port. They've destroyed at least one commune. Fifty thousand people, gone."

After crashing over another dune, Tetsami slammed the repeat button. With the sat transmitter on wideband, some of that might get through somewhere. She looked out the rear video and saw five contragravs now, closing fast. She tried to get just a little extra speed from the *Lady*.

And that was when the ship flipped over. . . .

PARTISAN

Hostile Takeover #2

S. ANDREW SWANN

DAW BOOKS, INC.
DONALD A. WOLLHEIM, FOUNDER
375 Hudson Street, New York, NY 10014

ELIZABETH R. WOLLHEIM
SHEILA E. GILBERT
PUBLISHERS

First Printing, December 1995

1   2   3   4   5   6   7   8   9

DAW TRADEMARK REGISTERED
U.S. PAT. OFF. AND FOREIGN COUNTRIES
—MARCA REGISTRADA
HECHO EN U.S.A.

PRINTED IN THE U.S.A

Dedicated to Pete and Andrea
(and the entire state of Minnesota)
for no particular reason.

ACKNOWLEDGMENTS

Thanks to Mary, Susie, Charlie, Levin, Joe, Bonnie, and Brian for savaging this manuscript—and thanks especially to Maureen and Geoff, whose comments made me add two of the neatest chapters in this volume.

NORTHERN ICE SHEET

BAKUNIN

EASTERN OCEAN

DIDEROT MTS

SINCLAIR

CELINE

EQUATOR

JEFFERSON

PROUDHON

WILSON

GODWIN

NEW PARIS

SARTRE

TROY

NEW LENIN

WESTERN OCEAN

ROUSSEAU

0   1000   2000
              1KM
              approx.

PLAINS, GRASSLANDS
SWAMPS, MARSHLAND
DESERT, WASTELANDS
TUNDRA, ARCTIC
TEMPERATE FOREST

SOUTHERN ICE SHEET
©J.GILBERT

DRAMATIS PERSONAE

CONFEDERACY

Pearce Adams—Confederacy representative for Archeron. Delegate to the TEC from the Alpha Centauri Alliance.

Ambrose—Dimitri Olmanov's Bodyguard

Kalin Green—Confederacy representative for Cynos. Delegate to the TEC from the Sirius-Eridani Economic Community.

Francesca Hernandez—Confederacy representative for Grimalkin. Delegate to the TEC from the Seven Worlds. Nonhuman descendant of genetically engineered animals.

Robert Kaunda—Confederacy representative for Mazimba. Delegate to the TEC from the Trianguli Austrailis Union of Independent Worlds.

Dimitri Olmanov—Head of the Terran Executive Command. The most powerful person in the Confederacy.

Sim Vashniya—Confederacy representative for Shiva. Delegate to the TEC from the People's Protectorate of Epsilon Indi.

OPERATION RASPUTIN

Gregor Arcady—Chief of security and CEO of the Proudhon Spaceport Development Corporation.

Klaus Dacham—Colonel, TEC. In command of the *Blood-Tide* and Operation Rasputin.

Mary Hougland—Corporal, Occisis marines. Prisoner of Dom Magnus' Diderot Holding Company.

Bhipur Gavadi—Mercenary in the employ of Proudhon Spaceport Security.

Alex Jarvis—Mercenary in the employ of Proudhon Spaceport Security.

Michael Kelly—Mercenary in the employ of Proudhon Spaceport Security.

BAKUNIN

Ezra Bleek—CEO and founder of Bleek Munitions.

Flower—A birdlike alien. Expert on the Confederacy Military. Partner in the Diderot Holding Company.

Ivor Jorgenson—Pilot and smuggler. Partner in the Diderot Holding Company.

Tjaele Mosasa—Electronics expert. Partner in the Diderot Holding Company.

Dominic Magnus—Ex-Colonel, TEC. Ex-gunrunner. Partner in the Diderot Holding Company.

Kathy Shane—Ex-Captain, Occisis marines. Partner in the Diderot Holding Company.

Kari Tetsami—Freelance hacker and data thief. Partner in the Diderot Holding Company.

Random Walk—An artificial intelligence device. Partner in the Diderot Holding Company.

Mariah Zanzibar—Security expert. Partner in the Diderot Holding Company.

Contents

PROLOGUE

Black Budget

"All the armed prophets conquered, all the unarmed ones perished."

—NICCOLO MACHIAVELLI
(1469–1527)

CHAPTER ONE

Friendly Fire

"One can watch everything and see nothing."
—*The Cynic's Book of Wisdom*

"Life happens to us while we are planning other things."

—ROBERT CELINE
(1923–1996)

"You bastard!"

The shout from behind caught Dominic Magnus completely off guard. He turned away from the four board members he'd been addressing, to face a fifth, Kari Tetsami.

"Excuse me?" Dom said to her.

Tetsami stood, blocking the doorway. Her normally pale skin was flushed a bright pink, her nostrils were dilated, and her hands were balled into fists. Dom could almost see her small body vibrating.

"Who the hell do you think you are?" she said.

Dom turned to the others in the meeting room. Mariah Zanzibar, his chief of security, was standing, arms folded behind her, avoiding eye contact with him. Mosasa, their resident electronics expert, was seated, working at one of the terminals set into the conference table. He stared at the terminal while, from the side of his bald head, the eye of his dragon tattoo stared at Dom. Dom had no way to tell where the nonhumans were looking. Random Walk, Mosasa's contraband AI, was in the wiring and could be watching out of any of the cameras in the room, or not. And Flower, their alien military strategist, had no eyes in its bullet-shaped head, only black Rorschach patterns over leathery yellow skin.

"Perhaps you should excuse us for a moment—" Dom said to them.

"Let them stay. Why shouldn't they hear this? They're in on everything, aren't they?" Tetsami stepped into the meeting room and jabbed Dom with her finger. "Unlike some of us!"

I've done it again, Dom thought. He only wished he knew exactly what it was he'd done.

"Me and Mosasa have to check the security perimeter," Zanzibar said, snagging Mosasa's elbow. Mosasa glanced up, as if suddenly realizing that there was a situation in here. He let Zanzibar lead him out of the room.

Flower stood on its multijointed legs, draping its wings about it like a cape. Its long serpentine neck appeared to be growing from some strange avian bush. "Observation of the defensive perimeter. He will give some opportunity to see static weaponry. He should be studied most closely, not?"

Even the alien can see it, Dom thought.

Flower glided out of the room, leaving Dom and Tetsami alone with the possible exception of Random Walk, silent in the wiring.

Tetsami paid no attention to the sudden exodus. "What the hell am I, Mr. Magnus? Some little twitch for hire whose usefulness has expired?"

Hearing her say "Mr. Magnus" chilled Dom's gut. For a confused second he couldn't figure out why. *Everyone* called him "Mr. Magnus."

But not Tetsami. Never Tetsami. They had been to hell and back together, through more life-threatening bullshit in the past five local weeks than any five lifetimes—even lifetimes spent on the anarchic planet of Bakunin.

Tetsami had never called him "Mr. Magnus." His *employees* called him "Mr. Magnus."

"No—" Dom began a belated response.

She wasn't waiting for an explanation. "After all this shit! After I planned the whole op for you—great! Now that you have your money, you don't give a shit about your pet hacker anymore?"

"What—"

Tetsami jabbed him again. "How many times have you held out on me, Dom? Where the hell are you going?"

Tetsami's anger shot into focus for Dom. "I was going to tell you when I got the whole board together."

She just stared at him, as if his skin had suddenly gone transparent. Dom had to raise his hand slightly to make sure that it hadn't. His hand was fine, olive-colored and natural looking. Dom felt a vibration begin in his cheek, and he lifted his hand to cover it.

"That's it, isn't it?" she said quietly.

Her sudden calmness was as disturbing as the anger of a few seconds ago. Dom hated seeing her like this, and he wanted desperately to fix whatever was wrong. "Just tell me what you want me to do," he said.

She shook her head. "I don't think you'd understand, Dom. You certainly don't act as if you would." She turned toward the door.

Dom felt a sinking in his chest. "Please. What's wrong?"

She stopped on the way to the door, her back toward him. He watched her head nod and her back shake. It could have been laughter. Or sobs. Maybe both.

"What's wrong? *Wrong?*" Tetsami sighed. "What's wrong is, after all we've been through with each other, I'm just another fucking stockholder."

He walked up and tried to put a hand on her shoulder. She shrugged out from under it and left him there, hand in mid-air. As he stood there, staring at his hand, he heard her say from down the hall, "Don't wait up for me."

Dom paced the loading dock, waiting for the techs to finish tuning the contragrav he was going to fly into Godwin. As he waited, he tried to will away the cold dread that clutched at his gut.

Dom's current enterprise, the Diderot Holding Company, was more successful than it had a right to be. In three weeks local, it had managed to convert the tunnel warrens under the mountains into living space for the thousand-plus refugees from the Godwin Arms & Armaments takeover. With Tetsami's planning, they had even managed to liberate 435 megagrams worth of liquid assets from Godwin Arms. . . .

Tetsami.

She was why Dom was depressed, even though, by all the standards that should have mattered to him, he should have been pleased with the operation. Her increasingly unpredictable reactions to him clouded any optimism Dom might have had. She should have been pleased with the way things were going.

It was becoming a mantra, counting the reasons why he shouldn't feel as if the world was crumbling around him.

The main reason was the fact that he, and most of the employees from GA&A, had survived to form a base of operations in the mountains. They had managed this despite the fact that Colonel Klaus Dacham, Dom's brother, had led the takeover of GA&A in what appeared to be a personal vendetta against Dom. A vendetta that might be over, now that Klaus had to believe Dom and his people were all dead. There certainly had been no more militaristic activity out of Godwin Arms since Dom's raid into his old company to steal back his own money. Tetsami had planned that raid. . . .

"Cold in here," Dom said, watching his breath fog.

The loading dock was a cavernous hollow in the rock, high up the side of the Diderot Mountain Range. The entrance, at the moment, was open to the air. It gave Dom a view of purple sky, wispy cirrus clouds, and the fat orb of Kropotkin that did little to warm the biting wind.

There were other reasons he should have been pleased. Kathy Shane, who had suffered extensive injuries in that raid, was going to live. She was still bedridden, but the doctors had managed to replace the damaged limbs with cybernetics.

That brought shadowy memories, too. Dom felt his cheek twitch.

Maybe he shouldn't leave.

He'd had the same thought dozens of times, ever since Tetsami had confronted him. Things were going well. He didn't need to go to Godwin. He could stay here and—

"And what?" Dom asked.

He walked to the edge of the cavern opening. The sky unfolded and suddenly he wasn't *in* the mountain. He was standing on the edge of a precipice, a vertical drop of two hundred meters or so, and then a rock slope tumbling down for hundreds more. Below and away, the weathered mountains gave way to rolling hills, and eventually disappeared under the chaotic sprawl of Godwin. The city of Godwin hogged a good part of the horizon.

"And what?" Dom repeated in a breath of fog. Icy wind tore the words away.

He could see no purpose a delay might serve. He shouldn't rearrange his business decisions to suit his personal problems.

He didn't even like to admit that his difficulty with Tetsami *was* a personal problem. He didn't like admitting that, despite his efforts to be fair to all his partners equally, he might be treating her differently. Treating her differently because of what he felt about her.

What do I feel about her?

"Too much," he answered himself. "I have over a thousand people I need to worry about right now. I can't delay things just because I think she—"

"Sir," came a voice shouting over the wind. "Your car's ready."

"Thank you," Dom said as he walked back to the waiting contragrav.

Business first, Dom thought. *I have to lay the groundwork to acquire another arms company. Take care of my people. Then I'll take care of myself.*

The setup was only going to take a week, two weeks at most. He'd figure some way to patch things up when he got back.

CHAPTER TWO

Tactical Retreat

"We are the least qualified people to judge ourselves."

—*The Cynic's Book of Wisdom*

"The world is a comedy to those that think, a tragedy to those that feel."

—HORACE WALPOLE
(1717–1797)

A week after Dom's departure, a handful of thirty-two-hour Bakunin days, Tetsami sat alone in her room, one utilitarian cube among hundreds. The only difference between her quarters and hundreds of similar places in the tunnel warren under the mountains was the fact that her alleged status in the Diderot Holding Company rated her a solo room.

I rate a rough-hewn cave all to myself, but not any consideration from Dom.

"The man is blind, or he really doesn't give a shit."

She forced the thought away as she tried to read her atlas. She touched the sensitive parts of the cyberplas, changing the display, paging through the seventy-five official planets of the Confederacy, along with the eight probationary members. The atlas was a Confed import she'd picked up in Godwin.

She and Ivor had flown into the city of Godwin, to pick up a physically rebuilt Kathy Shane. Shane'd been in the Stemmer Facility, a very expensive—and closemouthed—hospital serving the moneyed corporate wheels in Central and West Godwin. In three weeks, and sixty kilos, Stemmer had managed to replace her legs and most of her skin.

Sixty kilos was a lot of cash, more than Shane's weight in gold. Tetsami was glad that she hadn't lost her appreciation for such numbers, despite keeping company that tossed around *megagrams.*

She and Ivor had picked up a quiet, but ambulatory, Shane from the hospital's loading dock, something Tetsami had looked forward to. She needed to see Shane okay. She felt responsible for Shane's injury. But despite Shane's recovery, two things cast an ambivalent cloud over everything.

First, Shane didn't cooperate by taking her survival well. Her mood had been dark and sullen all the way back to the mountain. Tetsami had tried to talk to her and all she got was a cold stare that she couldn't, or just didn't want to, interpret.

Second, there had been no sign of Dom.

They'd been in the same God-banging city as Dom was, and he didn't even make a token showing. Tetsami knew he was undercover, and that he didn't want to risk attracting his brother Klaus' attention—even though, by now, Klaus had probably convinced himself that he had killed everybody involved in the original Godwin Arms organization. Everything that had been a part of GA&A was either occupied by Klaus' forces or was reduced to gravel to a depth of ten meters.

But the bastard *could* have left her a message.

Once it'd been clear—during their wait to check Shane out of Stemmer—that Dom'd be a no-show, she had done a little shopping. She had managed it even with Ivor playing his father role full bore. Ivor hadn't wanted her to go into Godwin alone, but he'd been torn between staying with Shane through the Stemmer bureaucracy and accompanying her on her hop through central Godwin.

In the end, she'd convinced him that a large white-haired Slav accompanying a petite Asian woman was going to attract more attention than the petite Asian woman alone. Not to mention that the petite Asian could take care of herself.

She had spent an hour, picking up the atlas, and conducting some financial maneuvers in one of Godwin's few banks with off-planet connections.

"You should have talked to me, Dom," she said to herself.

One of the most depressing things about this atlas, complete as it was, was the fact that the planet Bakunin—the planet she was born on, the planet she had lived all her life on, the planet she was contemplating abandoning—wasn't even listed.

The atlas listed Kathiwar, an airless ball of rock out on the extreme fringes of the Indi Protectorate. Kathiwar orbited Beta Pictoris, and had a population of less than a million. It was inhabited only to put a way station between the Confederacy and Tau Puppis, the one contact with the Volera Empire, the only alien spacefaring species the Confederacy had come across since its founding over a century ago.

They gave a listing for an airless wasteland that barely justified its own existence by providing a stepping stone to Flower's species. That damn rock was listed, but not Bakunin. A rock with less people than some communes, but not a planet of over a billion that was snuggled in close to the heart of the Confederacy. Bakunin sat just over fifteen light-years from Earth, swimming close to the head of the Confederacy like a minnow next to a five-armed octopus.

Does it matter? I'm searching for alternatives to Bakunin. I already know this place as much as I want to. Don't need some Confed cartographer telling me specifics on what I'm leaving.

Tetsami sighed and continued to page through planetary descriptions.

As she did, someone rang for entry. She put down the cyberplas atlas and walked over to the door, a metal bulkhead set into a fissure that'd been widened with a mining laser. It had probably come from Mosasa's old salvage place. It looked like it belonged in a battleship, or a bunker.

She pulled it open to reveal Ivor Jorgenson, the one person that she, not Dom, had convinced to join in leading this enterprise. Seeing him, this white-haired bull of a man, right now, sent a crashing wave of guilt over her.

"Hello," she said weakly.

She had known this man for all of her living memory. For almost all of that, he had been her only family. Now she was contemplating abandoning him, as well as this damn planet.

"Can I come in?" he asked after she'd stood frozen in the doorway for nearly half a minute.

Tetsami nodded, backing from the door. Suddenly she felt as if she was six again and Ivor had caught her doing something nasty. She resented the feeling.

"Good to see you," she lied.

She remained standing by the door while Ivor zeroed in on the chair she'd abandoned. "Punkin, what's bothering you?"

"What? Nothing. Everything's fine." She folded her arms because otherwise she'd be gesturing futilely all over the place.

Ivor nodded, but his expression showed that he could read the lies in her face. Ivor glanced at the table and at the cyberplas atlas lying on top of it. His fingers hovered over the luminescent display glowing through the touch-sensitive plastic. He touched it, calling up world displays.

"Cynos," he read off at random. "Capital of the Sirius-Eridani Economic Community. Orbits Sirius A. Thin methane atmosphere, three-quarters of a billion people burrowed into a cold little rock." He touched the display again. "Dakota. Part of the Seven Worlds. Orbits Tau Ceti along with Haven, the Seven Worlds' capital. Frigid, but at least it has an atmosphere. Most of the water is locked into permafrost. Any colder and the poles would freeze CO_2 out of the atmosphere during winter."

"Ivor," Tetsami said weakly.

"Davado Poli—haven't heard of that one before—out on the fringes of the Indi Protectorate. Low G. The whole population lives at the bottom of a caldera that puts Olympus Mons to shame. Guess the atmosphere's breathable down there."

"Ivor," Tetsami repeated.

"Dolbri—well, everyone knows about Dolbri—"

"Ivor!"

He looked up from the cyberplas atlas. "I wasn't interrupting you, was I?"

"Yes. No." Tetsami swung her arms in frustration. "Damn it, Ivor. What do you want?"

Ivor shrugged. "I wanted to know when you were planning to leave, Punkin."

Tetsami stared at him, ashamed. *Of course he knows. Like I can keep a secret from him.*

"Oh, Ivor." She felt as if she were on the verge of tears. "I'm sorry. I can't—" She stopped, hung up on that one word.

Ivor stood up. "It's all right," he said. He came over and hugged her. Tetsami shook in his arms like a child, hating how she felt. Hating that she hadn't told Ivor that she was leaving.

Hating the fact that she'd been acting like Dom, with his secrets.

He always acts so surprised when you catch him at it. As if everybody acts that way.

"I'm sorry. I was going to tell you—" That sounded so much like Dom that she choked on the words.

Ivor didn't seem to notice. He patted her shoulders. "I understand." He let her go and looked down at her with a fatherly stare that she'd never seen him use on anyone else. "You don't worry about leaving me, hear? I'm not here to tie you to this place."

Tetsami snuffed and wiped her eyes. "I've been waiting for a long time—"

"You've wanted to leave this planet ever since you knew there were other places to go."

Tetsami nodded. It was true. It was true even when she was making a living as one of the best freelance software jockeys in Godwin.

"If I could have, I would have taken you off-planet myself. Bakunin's no place to raise a child."

Tetsami glanced at the cyberplas atlas. "You could come with me. You could cash in your share of the company, too. We could both emigrate somewhere nice, calm. . . ."

Ivor shook his head before she was half finished. "I might cash out, Punkin. But I'm not leaving Bakunin. I can't return to the Confederacy."

"But—"

"I can't, okay? At best, they'd lock me up."

"After twenty years—"

"With my past, *especially* after twenty years. My damage's been done. But you go. As far as the Confederacy's concerned, everyone born here has a clean slate."

"I really don't want to leave you here," she said.

"You'd *better* go. I couldn't stand being the only thing holding you to a place you hate."

"I don't think I hate—" Tetsami began. "I just have to leave."

Ivor nodded. "Have you decided where?"

She shook her head, no. All she'd decided was that she wanted off-planet.

"When?"

When? Tetsami realized that she'd been delaying only because she didn't know how to break things to Ivor. He probably knew that. That was why he was here. "As soon as possible."

Ivor smiled, nodding. "Need a lift to the spaceport?"

"Thanks," she said. "Give me a day to get my shit together."

"Okay." He turned to leave. Before he could get out the door, Tetsami grabbed him in a hug and muttered, "I love you. Dad."

"Love you, too, Punkin."

As they broke their embrace and Ivor left her to her atlas, she wondered why it was so hard for her to say those words to anyone else.

She put thoughts of Dom out of her mind. In thirty-two hours she'd be at the Proudhon Spaceport, on the opposite side of the Diderot Mountains from him, and Godwin. With luck, shortly afterward, she'd be deep in tach-space on her way to some decent planet of the Confederacy.

CHAPTER THREE

Factions

"People corrupt power, not vice versa."
—*The Cynic's Book of Wisdom*

"There is no worse heresy than that the office sanctifies the holder of it."

—LORD ACTON
(1834–1902)

Sydney, Australia, the capital of the Terran Confederacy and the center of humanity's diplomatic universe, was fifteen-point-one light-years away from the anarchist planet Bakunin.

Only fifteen-point-one light years.

Dimitri Olmanov, the head of the Terran Executive Command and the human embodiment of all the political and military power within the Confederacy, could remember a time when fifteen-point-one light-years wasn't an "only."

Dimitri was a hundred and sixty years old, patched together with all the technology at the Confederacy's disposal—all the nonheretical technologies, at least.

He sat in a small room halfway up the giant Confederacy spire. Ambrose, his bodyguard, stood at parade rest a half-step behind and to the right of Dimitri's chair. The room was a lushly appointed waiting area, all wood and plants, indirect lighting, and oil paintings instead of landscape holos.

The room didn't need a landscape holo. One window filled the entire eastern wall. From his red leather chair, Dimitri had a panoramic view of the Pacific Ocean, a view from five hundred meters up. From here he could trace the shallows and the depths with his eyes. The horizon seemed infinitely far.

Infinity's a long way, Dimitri thought, *when fifteen light-years seems close.*

For the first fifty years of Dimitri's life, fifteen light-years wasn't just far. It was fifteen years standard worth of *time*. The late unlamented Terran Council had used manufactured wormholes to link star systems together, wormholes that were, for all practical purposes, one-way. That didn't concern the Terran Council, since they used the wormholes to dispose of criminals, dissidents, refugees, and eventually, any excess population the Terran bureaucracy could get away with.

Travel was instantaneous for the traveler, who'd end up fifteen light-years away. But the traveler would see a universe aged fifteen years beyond the start of his journey.

Theoretically, someone *could* travel the wrong way down a wormhole and end up in their own past. However, the Terran Council had a policy of executing anything and anyone that came out the wrong end of a wormhole. The Council had no desire to deal with interference from a chaotically indeterminate future.

Dimitri had seen the Council crumble when the first tach-ships were built. The possibility of two-way travel between the stars had ended the Terran Council's domination and given rise to the Confederacy. The Confederacy that Dimitri had been trying to hold together for the last eleven decades.

Now, over a century after the first tach-ships were built, that fifteen-light-year journey had shortened to the point where a military transport could clear the distance in twenty-one days standard. The speed of tach-ship transportation was closing on the speed of tachyon transmissions themselves. The standard tach-comm link, one that had been in use even when humans traveled the realspace void in sublight ships, could clear that fifteen-light-year distance in less than a week.

That was, in fact, what Dimitri was waiting for.

A planet-based tach-comm message took nearly as much energy to send as a real ship. They were reserved for messages of diplomacy and intelligence gathering. And while incoming messages would be received by his subordinates and filter their essentials up to him, Dimitri sent many outgoing messages himself, as a reminder of the resources he was using.

This waiting room was for use by the diplomatic corps,

representatives of the eighty-three planets forming the Confederacy. The tach-comm was seeing a lot of use lately. It was closing in on the date of the eleventh Decannual Terran Congress, the nearly year-long legislative session for the entire Confederacy.

The tach-transmitter wasn't here, of course. This was only the ground-based uplink. The transmitter was one of a dozen in orbit. Dimitri would record his message here and have it transmitted up to one of the tach-comm ships, who would relay it once their orbit brought them in line with BD+50°1725, the dim red star Bakunin orbited.

The natives had named the star Kropotkin. Dimitri supposed it was an improvement over the original.

One of the techs opened an oak door and said, "We're ready for you, sir."

Dimitri leaned on his cane and forced himself to stand. It was a strain. The weight on his joints ached, especially in Earth's gravity. Dimitri didn't say anything. His bodyguard, Ambrose, didn't appreciate Dimitri's comments on mortality. Three-quarters of Ambrose's brain, and only slightly less of the rest of his body, was artificial. Cybernetics had been grafted on to what had been a piece of human wreckage, programming the malleable remains to be a perfect bodyguard.

Not enough of Ambrose's brain was computer to trespass on the AI taboo. But enough of it was to make the remaining human mind uncomfortable when Dimitri's speech conflicted with the programs in Ambrose's skull.

"Come, Ambrose," Dimitri said.

Ambrose followed. He'd follow if Dimitri had said nothing.

Dimitri walked behind the tech, through the door, and into the private comm suite. The soundproof room was a stark black cube with an unremarkable holo-comm sitting in the center. The tech who'd brought them here let the door whoosh shut behind Dimitri and Ambrose.

Dimitri could have recorded his message and had someone else beam it up to the tach-transmitter, but this was arguably more secure.

He sat in front of the terminal and felt the relief in his joints. "The weight is going to crush me, Ambrose."

"Sir?" Ambrose took a step forward to help him and Dimitri waved him away. Ambrose didn't understand metaphors.

"Not my weight. The weight of years, of lives, of accumulated evils."

Ambrose looked relieved. "As you say, sir." His conversational gambits were limited.

Dimitri switched on the holo and prepared his transmission to Colonel Klaus Dacham, the commander of the TEC's Operation Rasputin, the project on Bakunin. Dimitri had timed this transmission as tightly as he could. The six TEC Observation platforms that Dimitri had sent to Bakunin space twenty-one days ago would be arriving now. The Executive Command Observers were small, stealthy, tach-capable ships crammed with sensory apparatus that could resolve a planet down to the square meter. The platforms would be a welcome asset to Colonel Dacham's operation.

That wasn't why Dimitri had sent them.

Soon after this communication reached Bakunin, other ships would begin arriving in the system. The TEC Observation platforms were a deterrent. This tach-comm was a warning.

This is also a test, Dimitri thought, *a test for Klaus and his brother.*

A few kilometers away from Dimitri Olmanov and the central hive of the Confederacy, a man named Jonah Dacham sat in a bar deep within Sydney's nonhuman district.

Jonah was still fresh from a nine-year exile on Mars, and he was here, in this bar, to begin to salvage the mess that his namesake—fifteen light-years away on the planet Bakunin—didn't even know he was in yet.

Meeting in this place had been Francesca Hernandez's idea. Jonah thought it was supposed to make him nervous. In fact, the surrounding fur, growls, and inscrutable expressions made him feel less nervous than did the crowds of people in the Confederacy's capital city.

He had spent nearly a decade in isolation on Mars, and while three weeks on Earth had acclimated him to the gravity, he knew it would take him much longer to acclimate to what passed as normal humanity.

Jonah had been surprised to find that there was, in fact, a large nonhuman population on Earth. He had thought that all remnants of genetic engineering had been exiled by the Terran Council during the Wars of Unification. Apparently,

enough engineered creatures thought of Earth as "home" to
have a substantial number emigrate back after the fall of the
Council and the rise of the Confederacy.

As Jonah waited for his contact, he still thought that the
creatures around him, feline, lepine, canine, were the minority of their kind. Most of the exiled nonhuman population of
Earth had never come back. They stayed on the planets they
had, The Seven Worlds, the smallest and most xenophobic
arm of the Confederacy. Until this year, in fact, the Seven
Worlds had been almost completely absent from Confederacy politics.

Absent until now.

For the eleventh Confederacy Congress, the Seven Worlds
would have a representative to sit along with the four other
arms of the Confederacy—the People's Protectorate of Epsilon Indi, the Sirius-Eridani Economic Community, the Union
of Independent Worlds, and the Centauri Alliance.

Those four arms represented seventy-six planets, when
you counted probationers. The Seven Worlds had sent *one*
representative to sit with seventy-six others, Francesca
Hernandez from the planet Grimalkin, the person Jonah was
here to meet.

Jonah waited, barely touching his beer. It was a good
place to meet, even with the smell of fur and animal musk,
even with the patrons eyeing him with slitted, predatory pupils. Jonah doubted either Dimitri or his equivalents in the
four human arms of the Confederacy would have any ears
here.

Finally, Hernandez showed. She was a lithe feline creature, a head taller than most humans. She wore a belt over
her spotted yellow fur, and nothing else. That in itself
marked her, even in a bar full of her fellows. All the others
here had some sort of token clothing.

As she slid into the booth with him, Jonah found it hard
to believe that she was the descendant of an archaic twenty-
first century experiment and not the result of a more natural
evolution. On second thought, Jonah realized that in a way,
she was. When the exile period began, the number of species
that the geneticists had created was on the order of ten thousand. Jonah didn't know, but he suspected that the number of
species in the Seven Worlds had dropped below a hundred.
The bad designs had all died out.

"I apologize for my tardiness." The diction was of one

who was still mastering the language. The accent was rumbling and honey-coated. Not a human voice.

You're testing me. Seeing if I really want to deal with your people. "Not a problem. I'm not worried about time. Only timing."

Timing.

Jonah had a computer in his skull to keep track of time, to keep accurate dates. However, because of the nature of time over interstellar distances, he had still needed to reference the date when he had finally arrived on Earth after his nine-year wait. According to his knowledge of events, it was about six Bakunin weeks—eight weeks Earth local—since 435 megagrams of hard currency had been stolen from the basement of Godwin Arms & Armaments.

His doppelganger would be in Godwin, Bakunin's largest city, preparing the takeover of Bleek Munitions.

Proudhon Spaceport was about to be closed to outbound traffic.

Warships from all corners of the Confederacy were about to converge.

And, in the desert east of the Diderot Mountains, a place called the Ashley Commune, populated by over fifty thousand people, was about to cease to exist.

Thinking of Ashley made Jonah think of Tetsami.

He brought himself back to the here-and-now. Nothing was going to change on Bakunin. He was here because he had fifty-nine days left before the situation became hopeless, and a very short window within those fifty-nine days where he could affect the outcome.

"Timing," Jonah repeated.

"Timing, yes. I sent the outline of your proposal in a tach-comm to Tau Ceti as soon as you presented it to me."

"So do you have an answer?"

She shook her head. "We have no diplomatic compound on Earth. Therefore, no truly secure tach-communications. Even what little I coded to the capital was too sensitive for debate over the Confederacy's devices."

Jonah did what he could to conceal his disappointment. "So what now?"

"As I told you, I have no authority to commit all Seven Worlds to your proposal. Tau Ceti is sending someone who can, another representative to the Congress."

"Who?"

She shook her head. "That was also too sensitive to trust to the Confederacy's comm. They will be here in forty days standard."

"Forty days?" That was cutting things awfully close. The Terran Congress would have already started its session. Jonah damned the Seven Worlds' slow ships. He also damned the xenophobia that kept their power brokers away from the Congress. He managed to maintain good grace about it. "Then I must wait," he said.

"Then you must."

Jonah stood and held his hand out. His right hand, which was a crude biomechanical device, its chromed finish scarred and pitted from years of wear. He held it out in the same sort of psychological test that Hernandez had intended by meeting him here.

Hernandez shook it.

PART FOUR
Laissez Faire

"Monopolies are sacrifices of the many to the few."
—JAMES MADISON
(1751–1836)

CHAPTER FOUR

Embargo

"The bureaucracy only changes in response to some grand disaster."
— *The Cynic's Book of Wisdom*

"Fascism is Capitalism in decay."
— VLADIMIR ILYICH LENIN
(1870–1924)

Forty-four Bakunin days after they'd met, Tetsami finally severed the ties between her and Dominic Magnus.

That's what it felt like, anyway, when she stepped down from Ivor's contragrav, hugged him good-bye, and walked out onto the road leading to the city of Proudhon. All she had was her duffel, the clothes on her back, and a hand-comm recording twenty megagrams worth of assets that were safely off-world.

By *forty-five* days, that's where she wanted to be, safely off-world.

Her steps away from Ivor's contragrav van, and toward the outer sprawl of Proudhon, were her first steps into a new life. She should have felt good about it. She should have been smiling, at least.

She stood on the eastern fringes of Proudhon. She was supposed to be better off question-wise walking in on the ground, rather than letting Ivor fly her into Proudhon's airspace. The Proudhon Spaceport Development Corporation jealously guarded its dominion. There were enough antiaircraft emplacements to make sure that no one ever deviated from assigned flight plans. Neither she nor Ivor wanted to borrow trouble.

Ivor buttoned up the van and lifted off. She watched, as the maneuvering fans blew fine black sand across the road.

She stood on a sun-cracked ribbon of concrete, and watched
the contragrav recede into a purpling Bakunin sky.

Kropotkin had already set on the other side of the Diderot
Mountains. About five hundred kilometers that way, west
beyond the mountains, beyond the city of Proudhon, Dom
was going to see another half-hour of sunset.

"Sheesh. Cut that out, girl."

She forced a smile on her face. It hurt her cheeks.

She turned around, absorbing what should be the last view
of her native planet.

To the east the ribbon of concrete continued, a road to
some project that never came off. It arrowed straight into the
desert, to be swallowed by standing waves of black sand. In
that direction lay fifteen hundred kilometers of arid desert
before the continent ended and the ocean began. To her
south was more desert. Beyond that horizon would come
tundra, then the southern half of the glaciation that covered
most of Bakunin's surface. Over the horizon to the north, the
desert would slowly turn into mountains.

A gust of burning wind peppered her face with flecks of
sand, making her squint.

Despite the fact she knew the geography beyond what she
saw, this bit of road looked like the end of the world. Three-
quarters of the horizon was nothing but rippling black sand.

She turned to face Proudhon, the city here, at the end of
the world.

The city she faced, in all practical senses, *was* the spaceport. There wasn't a place where the eye could separate
launching facilities, fuel storage, or landing strips from the
other functions of the city. Even from a half-klick away, she
could see the merging of the city's function with its essence.
High-rise offices doubled as control towers. Old landing
pads now served for more mundane parking. Grounded
transports had been turned into bars. Old apartment buildings sprouted large new radar domes.

Everything was lit up, be it from the garish neon of the
bars, or the color-coded landing lights that seemed to grace
every point where architecture formed a right angle.

In the midst of Proudhon, forming the off-center heart of
the city, were the buildings headquartering the Proudhon
Spaceport Development Corporation itself. They were giant
white monoliths, a floodlit counterpoint to the chaotic
sprawl of the remaining city. The ordered cluster of build-

ings, rising toward a dominant central tower, was the stamp
of the Spaceport Corporation. It was a reminder that—
despite the name of the original settlement here—Proudhon
was a company town, and everything here was under the eye
of the corporation.

But, towering over it all, stood the weathered humps of
the Diderot Mountain Range. The darkening snowcapped
mountains loomed over everything, edged by gaudy pink
highlights from the sunset beyond.

Tetsami's stomach churned with a rising dread. For a brief
instant she considered going back, returning to Diderot, Ivor,
and everything she'd just left.

She pushed the thought aside.

Not only did she not want to admit second thoughts, but
the only transportation she had were her own two feet. The
only destination within walking distance was Proudhon.

She still stared at the city, a half-klick away, and wondered what made her feel that the scene was so wrong. She
had never even *been* in Proudhon before. Her only views of
the city were from her hacker runs on the data net, and one
brief distant glimpse from the foothills on the other side of
the city.

She shrugged her reservations aside and started toward the
city. The sky darkened as she walked, and the city became
even brighter. Slowly, as the city's lights swallowed the
stars, she understood what was wrong. The last time she had
seen Proudhon, the sky had been alive with spacecraft coming and going. The noise had been a constant subliminal
hum, with spacecraft shooting by every few seconds.

However, since Ivor had put her down here, she hadn't
seen a single craft take off or land.

"What do you mean nothing's leaving?" Tetsami asked
the guard.

"Just that, Miss Jorgenson. All outbound craft have been
grounded by Spaceport Command. I'm sorry."

The man was a functionary of Proudhon Spaceport Security. She was in his little office at the edge of the city, reg-
istering as an outbound visitor. They didn't care about her
real name or anything—Tetsami had used the alias "Kari
Jorgenson" out of congenital paranoia—but if Security
found her without an ID chit anywhere in the city . . .

Well, that was best not contemplated.

The ID chit was a badge of her right to be here, and proof
that she'd paid a deposit to the Spaceport Corporation—
nonrefundable. It was a bit of a protection racket, but as
things went on Bakunin, it was fairly mild. Tetsami suspected the chit acted as a locator badge so security could
find you when the deposit ran out.

She had the shiny black ID chit in her hand, and the
turquoise-and-black clad bureaucrat had just waited for her
money to transfer before he'd informed her that nothing was
leaving the spaceport.

Even though the city was her only option, she was royally
pissed at this nimrod for committing her to the money transfer before telling her.

"Damn it!" she yelled at him. "I need to get off-planet."

"A lot of people need to get off-planet, Miss."

Bloody-Christ-Almighty! "Why the delay?"

The guard gave her a long sigh that told her that he'd already gone through this a hundred times, but he'd do it just
this once more. "A small number of Confederacy ships
tached insystem. They are apparently affiliated with the
Terran Executive Command. Proudhon Spaceport Command
is holding all traffic until the situation can be resolved."

"Is that all? Why stop *everything?*"

"If you have a question, address it to the proper depart-
ment." The guard leaned to the side and said, "Next!"

A large black woman in a photoreactive dress that was a
size too small elbowed her out of the way and started talking
to the guard as if Tetsami didn't exist.

Tetsami left the office, anger a smoldering coal in her gut.

Proudhon was a mess.

It felt like someone had opened all the cages, just for her
arrival. Night had fallen and the hustlers, the dealers, the
winos, the boy-toys and the junkies, everyone and *everything* was out to get theirs. Most of them seemed convinced
that they could get it from her.

As she walked, trying to find a hotel—any hotel—she was
offered at least ten different ways of getting high, four or
five ways of getting laid, and at least one way of getting
even.

The black marketeers didn't bother her that much. All of
Bakunin was a black market. If she weren't looking for a

room, she might have even scraped up an interest in a hardly-used gamma laser, or the bootleg software library.

When it came to the drugs, she was neutral. She didn't use anything other than liquor herself, not from high moral standards, but because anything remotely hallucinogenic meddled in the sensitive mental wiring that made her this dirtball's best freelance netrunner—even past her prime.

All that was tolerable.

What broke her was the kid. He—or she, the kid was too wasted for Tetsami to tell—came out of nowhere and grabbed her arm. Tetsami felt a yank and turned to see a face with hollow eyes, and teeth too long because of receding gums. It wasn't until she heard the voice that she realized it was a kid, no more than fifteen.

"Wanna some good time?" a kid's soprano coming out of this crewcut skull face.

Tetsami had lived most of her life on the cesspit streets of Godwin, but this kid struck her like a depleted uranium bullet. She was drawn up short by shock, and the kid misinterpreted it as interest.

Hands even more skeletal than that face groped her. "Do whacha want, babe," the kid said, licking chapped lips. "Whacha want. Just need a charge. Got a charge, babe, and we can have lotsa fun."

The kid was rattling off the words as if it was some viral program that was looping through his—her?—brain. Tetsami stared helplessly at the kid's eyes. Dead, those hollowed eyes, lit only by a fierce inner hunger and, deeper, an ugly parody of hope.

Loathing churned in Tetsami's gut, freezing her to the spot while her skin wanted to dissolve under this creature's touch.

"Come on, babe," the kid said. "Just one little charge—" The kid's hand slid mechanically over her breast.

Then she caught a glimpse of the side of the kid's neck. That's when she ran.

The sight of the concave dimple on the kid's neck, just like her own, had sent a shudder of pure terror though every nerve in her body.

To hell with self-respect. To hell with streetwise safety. To hell with self-assurance. Tetsami ran.

That kid had a fucking biolink! The kid's a software junkie. A fucking—

Even as she ran, she forced away the word.

"Wirehead." That's what the East Godwin maggots called her, after she'd gotten the implant. Everyone so damn certain that she'd end up another brain-dead husk . . .

Even Ivor.

She ran until she finally hit a hotel. Then she caught herself, leaning against the wall, panting. Kid long gone, too wasted to keep up with her.

Biolinks took best in adolescents, giving the best connection, speed, resolution. The converse wasn't true. Teenagers were the worst people to trust with direct access to their own cerebral cortex.

Throughout all of the Confederacy, it was illegal to plant a biolink in a minor. But the planet Bakunin wasn't part of the Confederacy, and nothing was illegal here.

Tetsami leaned against the wall and fingered the dimple in her own neck.

Must've seen mine, she thought. *The kid saw mine and thought I was a kindred spirit. There but for the grace of God and an engineered biology go I.*

Wirehead.

"Christ."

For once, the unadorned blasphemy seemed sufficient.

After her breathing no longer burned her throat and the stitch in her side had faded to a dull ache, she looked up at where she'd found herself.

The hotel was called the New Yukon. It looked like a dive, but she wasn't in the mood to be very choosy.

She pushed herself away from the wall and walked in.

CHAPTER FIVE

Preferred Risk

"Better to regret something you have done, than
something you haven't."
>   —*The Cynic's Book of Wisdom*

"If love is judged by its visible effects it looks more
like hatred than friendship."
>   —FRANCOIS DUC DE LA ROCHEFOUCAULD
>   (1613–1680)

Dominic Magnus stood on the top of the Waldgrave Hotel
on the West Side of Godwin and breathed in the morning air.
It made no real sense, but he felt good.

*How long has it been since I just stood somewhere and
enjoyed the view?*

Too long, felt like never.

Below the rise of West Godwin, the land dipped to cup the
shimmering commercial chaos of the central city. Even the
blasted industrial wasteland of East Godwin didn't appear
too awful in the rosy morning light.

And, above everything stood the frosted spine of the
Diderot Mountains, rounded by age, unimpressed by man-
kind's recent appearance. Somewhere, midway between here
and the orange-purple tree line, sat the Godwin Arms complex. His brother Klaus was there.

Just thinking of Colonel Klaus Dacham should have
brought his mood to a crashing halt.

It didn't, and the feeling was so uncharacteristic that Dom
wondered if he was sick. *Can one decision make so much
difference?* Apparently so.

Dom took another deep breath and stretched the sleep
from his joints. The wind was bracing, still carrying the chill
of Bakunin's sixteen-hour night.

"Mr. Shaji?" A voice came from behind him.

"Shaji" was one of the names he was using on this trip into Godwin. His appearance matched the pseudonym. In case his brother wasn't convinced of his demise, he had adjusted the pigment of his polyflesh skin from its normal olive cast to a deep chocolate brown. With his normally black hair, and sunglasses over his brown eyes, he appeared of Indian descent.

He turned to face Gregg Lovesy, a mid-level veep in Argus Datasearch. Argus was a company that Dom had used frequently, and Lovesy in particular was a man he often dealt with. Lovesy knew Dom from five years of association, and knew Dom would be disguised. He still looked surprised at Dom's appearance.

It took a moment for Dom to realize that it might be because Lovesy saw him smiling. Dom put on a businesslike demeanor. "I am that worthy," he said, the previously agreed upon response.

Lovesy looked relieved. "Do you have a place to talk?"

"My aircar's parked over there." Dom waved toward the rooftop restaurant. Between them and the restaurant was a parking lot graced by a dozen luxury aircars. One of them was Dom's. Dom put his arm around Lovesy to lead him, and the man flinched.

Lovesy shrugged out of Dom's grasp and made it to the aircar first.

Dom opened the doors. Once they were comfortably inside, Dom switched on Mosasa's countersurveillance devices. Then he asked Lovesy, "What've you got for me?"

"A low profile dig, kept off of the net, just as you asked." Lovesy pulled a flimsy sheet of cyberplas from his pocket. "Read it when you have a chance to memorize it. The sheet's a one-read-and-wipe. It's the only copy."

Dom nodded. "Can you summarize what's on this?"

"Very gentle investigation. No primary sources. So this has no guarantee. Okay?"

"Just rumor. All I expected."

Lovesy sucked in a breath and started rattling off the data that Dom was interested in. "You were right. The biggest block of stock is held by Ezra Bleek. No one admits to seeing him for the past five years. Various stories say he's dead, medically incompetent, or being held prisoner by his children. The official Bleek Munitions story, and most of the ru-

mors, have him in the basement of the family estate."
Lovesy looked out the window and said, "You can probably
see the enclave from here, the walls at least. No, you're not
parked close enough to the edge."

"What *is* the official Bleek Munitions story?"

Lovesy looked back at Dom. "The official line is that
Ezra is barely alive, on a massive life-support system, and
can only participate through his children's proxy."

"How likely is that?"

"You a betting man?" Lovesy asked.

"You know the answer to that."

Lovesy nodded. "My advice is, don't start now. The official story's crap. And, from what we've dug up, the Bleek
children are thoroughgoing sons of bitches, and that includes
the daughter."

"Can I have the story without the editorializing?"

Lovesy obliged him.

The information on Ezra Bleek and his kids, despite debatable reliability, was extensive. Bleek was in his sixties, an
immigrant from Thubohu. He was a businessman and what
was commonly known as a tax refugee. He'd pooled most of
his assets into Bleek Munitions upon his arrival and had a
total of three children before his wife died—quietly, in bed,
an unusual death for the spouse of a Bakunin executive.

The kids were born and raised on Bakunin, and despite
the safe, isolated, and well-defended schools Ezra paid
through the nose for, the motherless kids ran amok. The
kids, two sons and one daughter, fully exploited the liberty
that Bakunin and their dad's money gave them.

Apparently, five years ago, Ezra caught wind of a particularly disturbing party thrown by his children. The details of
the event were sketchy and conflicting, but the rumors went
that it involved chains, leather, holo cameras, and at least
four different species, only two of which were sentient.
There was little agreement on the specifics, but it was universally agreed that it passed beyond the bounds of both
good taste and good sense, even for Bakunin.

Ezra apparently ransomed the kids from the Bakunin
Church of Christ, Avenger after the trio had been caught in
a particularly compromising scene involving a nonhuman
prostitute and the ripening corpse of a large dog. At least
that's how the rumors went. It, however, was a firmly estab-

lished fact that within days of the alleged event, Ezra registered a will with Lucifer Contracts Incorporated.

Lucifer prided itself on enforcing "unbreakable" agreements. They charged exorbitant fees, but very few people dared cross them. People who broke LCI contracts had the habit of winding up deceased in the most disturbing ways.

It didn't take a genius to figure that Ezra's will cut the kids off without a cent. Especially since it was shortly after the will appeared that Ezra disappeared into his own basement with an unspecified illness and the kids took over the running of Bleek.

It was all that Dom had hoped for.

"All the specifics are on the plas I gave you," Lovesy finished.

"Thank you, it was well worth the expense. As always." Dom pressed the control that opened the door on Lovesy's side of the aircar.

Lovesy stepped out and said, "Feel free to use us again, Mr. Shaji."

"I will," Dom said, and held out his hand to Lovesy.

For a moment the Argus veep didn't seem to know what to do. After a brief hesitation he took Dom's hand and shook it. As he did, he looked closely at Dom and asked, "Do you feel all right?" His eyes asked, *Should I call Security?*

Lovesy was expecting another code phrase, one indicating trouble. Instead, Dom said, "No, Lovesy, I'm fine," which meant just what it said.

The door closed on the befuddled veep and Dom looked out the windshield, at the brightening sky, and wondered again, *Can one decision make so much difference?*

In all the wreckage in which his soul wallowed, from the moral bankruptcy of his profession, to him and Klaus circling the corpse of their mother like a pair of rabid wolves, the last thing he should feel was "fine."

But last night, and this morning, he had made a decision to do what Tetsami wanted. He would level with her.

She was right that he was keeping her in the dark about all his business operations, when he should be treating her like a partner. They were equals in the Diderot Holding Company, and the operation couldn't have existed without her. But here, in Godwin, while he laid the groundwork for a semifriendly takeover of Bleek Munitions, Dom had realized that he was hiding some of his biggest secrets from himself as well as her.

He wasn't treating her differently, awkwardly, because of some ingrained habit of keeping things close to the vest. After all, he hardly ever kept part of the business secret from Zanzibar. And while he'd argued with himself that he trusted Zanzibar because they'd worked together for so long, the same couldn't be said of Mosasa and Random Walk with whom he trusted the layout of the temporary mountain headquarters *and* the security setup.

Trust wasn't the issue here. All the board members were in it together, and he trusted all of them, even Shane when Zanzibar thought trusting Shane could be a big mistake. He trusted Tetsami as much as any of them, but he didn't tell her things. . . .

He simply had trouble talking to her. It had taken him too damn long to realize why.

He cared for her. Cared for her in a way that was nearly pathetic.

The only way he was ever going to get over that obstacle was to admit it to her as well as to himself. Make himself the fool. She'd laugh at him, maybe mock him again like she did when he tried to pay back his fifty-kilo debt to her. He could picture a thousand ways she could take the news—from hysteria to horror. But he'd do it anyway.

He'd tell her, damn his pride, and after she was over the fear, or disgust, or whatever—after all that was over, maybe then they could work together again. As a team.

That thought brought another unaccustomed smile.

Lovesy must think I'm nuts.

CHAPTER SIX

Fact-Finding Mission

"If you can keep your head when those about you are losing theirs, you obviously don't know what's going on."

—*The Cynic's Book of Wisdom*

"Before digging, know if you wish dirt or a hole."

—STONE-BY-WATER
(*ca.* 2288)

Tetsami had been in the bar for four hours when she noticed the mercs.

She was the fourth overlong Bakunin day into her extended visit to the port city of Proudhon. She was in one of the dozens of dark little holes that clustered around Lindbergh Street, the main drag of the southern end of Proudhon. She had been here four days, and she had spent the last three barhopping and cursing her luck.

She should have left as soon as she had gotten her money. As soon as she made that off-planet transfer in Godwin. But no. She needed that extra day to get her shit together.

By all rights she should be in the netherworld of tachspace right now, shooting between points A and B at some ungodly multiple of lightspeed.

Grand Lord Jesus Almighty and his Tap-dancing Apostles.

She had to show up the very day that the Terran Executive Command began playing tourist. The whole Proudhon Spaceport had ground to a messy halt because of the unprecedented tach-in of six—God help us *six*—TEC military vessels into Bakunin's local space.

But that wasn't the bad news—oh, no.

She got a room and waited for the dust to settle, for the passenger craft—any passenger craft—to start moving again.

And three days later, when things had barely calmed, a fleet—a mother-humping *fleet*—tached in. A drop-ship *carrier* and multicraft escort. She wanted to slit someone's throat, but she didn't know whose.

She was sitting in a city that was in a worse mess than Godwin ever saw; between the pimps and stranded tourists trying to pick her up, she couldn't go outside without getting accosted. It made the Bakunin fetish of going around visibly armed seem more than fashion sense.

She hung around the bars on this end of Lindbergh because they were empty most of the time, unlike the human morass clogging the districts close to the hotels.

What the hell use was twenty-five megagrams if you couldn't even get off-planet? Between the order of magnitude increase in Proudhon's normal chaos, and the waiting lists of other people who'd gotten shafted on their outbound journey, it'd be damn lucky if she found an opening within the month—and *that* would probably have a few weeks' waiting list tagged on it.

Worse, it was giving her the opportunity to have second thoughts. To think that leaving wasn't such a good idea. And all that should have been behind her by now.

And it gave her a chance to think about Dom, the ice-hearted bastard.

She'd managed quite a hole for herself, between depression, inebriation, and lack of sleep, over the past three days.

She was sitting in the bottom of that pit, telling herself for the Nth time that she wasn't abandoning Ivor, Shane, and the rest of them—and to bloody hell with Dom—when she caught sight of the mercs out of the corner of her eye. Watching them seemed more interesting than thinking about bailing out on her native planet, so she shifted slightly in the booth to observe the table the soldiers had taken over.

Jackson's Hole was typical of the bars serving Lindbergh, tiny and dark. Dark enough that it was hard to discern other patrons, and harder to discern what you were drinking. Tiny enough that it wasn't difficult to eavesdrop on a table halfway across the barroom.

There were five mercs in all. They shouldn't have been an unusual sight, since the planet Bakunin was known across the Confederacy for—among other things—being a paramilitary clearing house. Bakunin, Proudhon the spaceport-city in particular, had the highest concentration of soldiers of fortune of anywhere in the Confederacy.

They shouldn't have been unusual.

They were.

In all the human flotsam clogging Proudhon's plumbing since they'd turned off the flow of ships, these were the first mercs Tetsami had seen on the streets.

"Service!" bellowed the largest of the five, presumably the leader of the expedition. A barmaid emerged, wearing a spiraled hairdo that was really meant for zero g.

"What can I get you?" the barmaid said in a tone that implied that a lot more was for sale than the liquor here. Tetsami found it depressing.

Apparently the mercs' minds were elsewhere. All the leers the barmaid received were strictly pro forma. "Real wine, lady. The sparkling stuff. From Banlieue. Or Earth if you got it."

The spiral nymph raised an eyebrow. "I'll see what we have."

When the barmaid left, getting a somewhat absentminded swat on the ass, one of the other mercs turned to the leader. "Champagne, Sarge?" He was a freckled redhead, and looked to be the youngest.

"This is a celebration, and you jerkoffs better appreciate it. That's an order."

"We got the job, then?" piped up a wiry dark-skinned man with a handlebar mustache. He spoke with an accent that seemed to come from the Indi Protectorate.

"Good as got," said the man seated to the right of Sarge.

The bottle came and the cork was popped. Tetsami faded even farther into the shadow of her booth. She realized that she was becoming more sober as she watched. The drink in her hand was untouched.

She had been ten years hacker-cum-laude in the dirty underside of Bakunin corporate espionage, and her greatest asset in that job was her intuition. Occasionally her line of reasoning jumped a few steps ahead of the facts. Usually such jumps had to do with impending disaster.

Right now she was putting together the Confed ships in orbit, the shutdown of the spaceport, the recent dearth of mercs on the streets of Proudhon, and these guys' new job. She was forming a picture. The picture said "bad news."

The glasses were passed and Sarge's right-hand man continued talking. "We've not signed anything, but we got a copy of the contract and a whopping retainer."

"This all up-and-up?" said a lethal looking black man.

"Hellfire, Abby," said the dark man with the mustache. "If you found a half-ton of gold, you'd worry about a hernia."

Sarge shook his head and tossed a few chits to his men. "Those're the contracts, and the money. The cash's free, no commitments."

"Eeyow!" said the redhead as he looked at the chit.

The guy with the handlebar mustache shook his head. "Cool it, Wes. Someone'll cosh you in the head for that."

The redhead, Wes, looked around like he expected to be attacked. The mercs laughed. Tetsami eased deeper into the shadows, and found her back to the wall. Her abandoned drink sat at the other end of the booth.

There was a pause in the mercs' conversation as the three grunts examined the chits. Sarge and his right-hand man looked on benevolently, sipping their champagne.

Abby, the black man, looked up at Sarge and said, "Damn it, this is shit-poor on specifics. Doesn't even say if the job's off-planet or not."

Sarge shrugged. "Each of you make up your own mind."

"He's right," said Wes. "This don't say nothing about the *mission*."

Sarge's right-hand man spoke. "These guys are very security conscious. Anyone who accepts goes incommunicado after being briefed. They don't want people talking loose about their mission—like in a bar somewhere, for instance."

A weak chuckle went around the table.

"Anyway," he continued, "the point is the bottom line. We've held out for a while, and we'll be getting about five times what the first guys who jumped on this bandwagon signed for. All of it up front, cash. There're salaries, bonuses, they'll provide brand-new equipment *and* any necessary training."

"I still don't like not knowing what the specs are," said Abby.

"You're the minority," said Sarge. "Look around at this town. Where you think Brady's team has gone? Or the Lazarus squad? Even that brass-balled Jarvis came out of retirement when this got waved in his face." Sarge shook his chit.

"Like I said, you each make up your own mind. But I think you all know what me and Delstein here are doing."

"I'm in," said the man with the mustache.

"Me, too," said Wes with only a slight hesitation.

All eyes turned to the black man, Abby. He cleared his throat and said. "Damn it, where would you guys be without your one voice of sanity." He stood and raised his glass. "To the mission."

"Whatever the fuck it is."

"Wherever the fuck it is."

"However the fuck we fight it."

"Whoever the fuck we fight!"

As they toasted each other, Tetsami slipped out of the booth and out of the bar.

Tetsami wandered the streets of South Proudhon, letting the alcohol cook out of her system. As the haze on her brain faded, it left an unreal feeling to the event in the bar.

After all the crap she'd gone through already on this planet, she did not like the feeling she was getting. She'd seen South Proudhon as an escape from the hustlers crowding everywhere else. That was because she wasn't native to Proudhon. If she had known this town, or if she'd been paying attention, she'd have noticed earlier that this part of town should not be dead.

This was the mercs' hangout. It should have been clogged worse than anywhere when the ships stopped flying.

But even the streetwalkers were gone. *Flooding the other parts of town,* she thought. *All the hustlers have moved on to where there's at least some action.*

She no longer liked the nearly empty bars in this end of Lindbergh. Even the streets she crossed were bare of traffic, with the exception of the occasional Proudhon Spaceport Security car.

Where were all the mercs?

She stood on the corner and let everything sink in. She was at the corner of Armstrong and Lindbergh. It was an intersection even a nonnative had heard of. Allegedly this is where a soldier-boy was supposed to come if he wanted a party—whether his party came in a box, a bottle, a pill, or someone else's pants.

Kropotkin had barely set on the neon-chrome holos of the

bars and Tetsami heard something totally unnatural for Proudhon.

Silence.

It only lasted a few seconds before one of the bar's doors opened, letting out the sound of muted voices and the thrum of a band. But the streets sucked up the sound as soon as the door whomphed shut.

Tetsami hugged herself.

A security car rushed by, scooting on air jets and contragravs, silently blowing garbage off the road as it raced by her on some mission of its own. Its flashers were on, but the sirens were mute. There was no one to warn out of its way.

Her gaze followed the security car and she thought of the first time she had seen Proudhon. It had been from the foothills of the Diderot Mountains to the west. Even from a few kilometers, Proudhon had been *loud*. The city itself was more raucous than Godwin, its big brother across the mountains, and had been alive with the sound of air traffic. Every ten seconds, round the clock, something was in the air— coming or going.

What was happening here?

She thought of the nearby Confed ships and decided that this was more than few sudden unwanted neighbors in the vicinity. Tetsami looked into the bar next to her. It was hard to see past the holo of the exotic dancer and her snake, but the place appeared half empty.

Girl, why did you have to go and notice? Things were—
"Going so well? Right?" she whispered to herself.

The sinking feeling went beyond her rapidly diminishing prospects for leaving this anarchic rock. The weirdness enveloping Proudhon, and those damn Confed ships up there, were beginning to feel like much more than an inconvenient coincidence. She had tried to ignore the idea that, maybe, those ships had something to do with Colonel Klaus Dacham.

Now that it was looking like she wasn't getting off-planet soon, it was getting hard to ignore.

She had just come out the ass end of a rather nasty confrontation with Klaus. Klaus was running a TEC operation, and those were TEC ships up there. Until now she had pretended that it wasn't something to worry about, because the Terran Executive Command had their grubby hands in everything. That looked less like sane reasoning now, and more like screaming denial.

Klaus had run a TEC op on the *ground* just the other side of the mountains from here. Klaus had used Confed troops to take over Godwin Arms. That had been the first time Tetsami had heard of the TEC setting foot on Bakunin.

She was running from that as much as the rest of the planet. As much as Dom.

Looking into that bar, she had the nagging feeling that she had started running a little too late.

Now what?

She could go back. . . .

"What's the point?" she said into the empty desert air.

A dusty merc type walked out of the bar next to her and strolled diagonally across the street. He stopped at the public billboard, scanned through the entries, kicking windblown trash as he read. Tetsami watched the guy and thought that, maybe, she should find out a little about what the fuck was going on.

The merc type headed off down Armstrong. Tetsami walked up to the billboard. The boards were an ubiquitous feature in Proudhon, one on every major intersection and one in the lobby of every major building. There was a credit port—but it only wanted a few grams if you were posting something. Tetsami only wanted to scan the posts, and that was free. Free, that is, if you had the obligatory ID chit. Tetsami inserted hers into the port.

Until now she'd only used the thing to scan ads for berths off-planet and come up void. Now, she simply let her curiosity guide her. It was an odd sensation, especially scanning the personals. It was as if the holographic text floating in front of her was the missing voice of the city surrounding her.

There were dozens of ads with the flavor of, "HARRY? WHERE ARE YOU?" or, "KATHY, COME BACK, ALL IS FORGIVEN." It was chilling, considering the empty streets around her. There were also a number of cryptic messages of the type, "the candle has been lit," "the wax is melting," "curse the darkness." A whole series of messages were like that. The balance consisted of the typical lonely people looking for other lonely people, lonely perverts looking for lonely perverts, "SWFGHB seeks great Dane with own leash" sort of thing.

The section of people seeking employment was notably sparse. None of the "talented solder seeking dirty little war" ads. *None.* Not a single mercenary soldier-of-fortune type was out advertising for work. An assortment of tech types, pilots, grounded ships looking for cargo—but no mercs.

Normally there should be a glut of these guys.

The help wanted, however, *that* was a revelation.

She'd been a hacker premiere for nearly a decade on this rock, ever since she was old enough to get her biojack implanted. She knew the electronic map of this planet as well as anyone alive, and while she'd only been on the *streets* of Proudhon for, collectively, half a week out of her life, she knew the computer net in this city as well as she did the one in Godwin. Better, even. Since the Proudhon Spaceport Development Company was a monopoly, owned half the city, and *was* the other half, the comm net here was standardized for the most part, unlike the chaos of the Godwin net.

That meant that Tetsami could look at all the comm codes for the few dozen "soldier wanted" ads and see that most of them routed through the same node in the Proudhon net.

Not just mercs, but pilots, techs, whathaveyou.

Tetsami looked over her shoulder at the empty streets.

"Salary, bonuses, training, full medical benefits," she whispered. The best of the ads looked almost too good to be true.

She was afraid they weren't.

CHAPTER SEVEN

Just Cause

"We hate others for our own shortcomings."
—*The Cynic's Book of Wisdom*

"The offender never pardons."
—GEORGE HERBERT
(1593–1633)

Colonel Klaus Dacham couldn't sleep.

He lay in his brother's bed, high atop the residential tower in the Godwin Arms complex. He should have been anticipating the coming fruition of Operation Rasputin. The mission was proceeding without a hitch. Arms production was on-line and peaking, and they were closing on their last delivery to Proudhon.

Still, his mind was troubled.

And what troubled him wasn't something he could justify. If only the sweat coating his sheets had a rational cause. If his bowels shook because of the warships from the Sirius-Eridani Community, it would not be half as bad. The SEEC ships were here, and now. They could be acted upon.

How could you act upon a phantom?

Klaus' eyes were screwed shut and his head rolled back and forth—as if he could shake loose the memory.

"Your brother put you up to this. Didn't he? DIDN'T HE?" she yelled at Jonah. Klaus stood next to him, trembling, fearful, sick in his gut. They were twins, but fraternal, not identical. Jonah was the bigger of the two, and he was bearing Mother's rage more stoically than Klaus could.

They weren't even a dozen yards out of the administrator's shack before she started. Around them grew the thousand-year-old forests of Waldgrave's belt-continent. The small hu-

*man logging camp looked as tiny in its midst as Helen
Dacham's children looked in her presence.*

Klaus could smell the liquor on her breath.

"DIDN'T HE?"

"No, mother. It was my—"

*Jonah didn't get a chance to answer. Helen's hand, heavy
with gaudy rings, slammed across Jonah's face. Klaus heard
the impact.*

Klaus hated Jonah for not crying out.

"Don't call me that in public!"

*Klaus could feel the eyes of the loggers boring into him.
All these men, the kind of men Helen bedded, were watching
him, seeing the fear in him, laughing.*

*Suddenly she turned on him. "You put him up to it, you lit-
tle freak— Didn't you?"*

"No," Klaus blubbered. "It was Jonah's—"

*She hit him, not with the flat of her hand, but with her
fist. Klaus fell, fell like the sapling he and Jonah had cut
down. Klaus felt warmth below his belt and all he could
think of was the walk home, his pants marked with his own
urine.*

*"Don't lie to me! Do you know what the fines are going
to cost me? You're his curse on me. Your father's curse!"*

*"Please!" Klaus sobbed. He hated her for humiliating
him. He hated Jonah for not being humiliated. He hated because he had told the truth. Jonah had been the one to decide to poach the sapling. Jonah was always the leader.*

Klaus hated that, too.

*"Stop crying, you wretch. You don't know what hurt is.
Keep it up and I'll give you to him—then you'll know pain."*

*Klaus didn't even have the strength to disobey her. His
tears came to a strangled halt. The threats about Father
scared him, even though Helen Dacham never revealed the
man's identity.*

*All Klaus knew was that Father scared her. That was
enough to scare Klaus.*

"Damn you. Damn all of you."

Klaus opened his eyes and cursed himself. He was pathetic, living thirty-year-old memories like that. Twice pathetic because the woman was dead, long past reconciliation.

He decided that sleep was a lost cause. He got up from the
bed, the sheets sticking to his body. He peeled them off and
walked, naked, to the shower.

Damn Jonah.

Dominic, Klaus thought. *He called himself Dominic Magnus when I finished him. Give him the name he died with, he shouldn't share a name with me and Helen.*

In the shower, he let cold water sluice the sleep from his body.

"Damn him."

Damn his brother for always leading him along, like a dog on a leash. *He* spawned the idea to poach that tree. *He* was the one who convinced Klaus to come with him when the TEC recruiter showed up on Waldgrave. *He* led Klaus through the TEC Officer Training School. *He* led Klaus up through the widening gap in their ranks within the Executive Command.

Then came Styx.

He had never understood how their mother had come to the planet Styx. Styx orbited Sigma Draconis, on the opposite side of Sol from Waldgrave, and in another arm of the Confederacy altogether.

However, while he didn't understand how she came to be there, he understood how she died there. She was one of thirty-five thousand corpses left when the TEC Colonel Jonah Dacham reduced the city of Perdition to rubble.

Klaus turned off the water, fully awake now.

After that, and after Jonah/Dominic had retired from the TEC, the siblings' race had turned from leader-follower into hunter-hunted. When Klaus had known that Jonah— *Dominic*—had been the one who had . . .

Ever since then, Klaus had known that he would have to kill his brother, revenge the death of the woman he hated. He had never had respect in her living eyes, but maybe—in death.

Klaus walked out of the shower. All phantoms, useless phantoms. He wasn't even sure his brother was dead. It would be insane if somehow he had managed to survive the *Blood-Tide* backing into GA&A's office complex. But Klaus' people had finished rebuilding the damaged part of the offices and they hadn't recovered a body. It was possible that the *Blood-Tide*'s short, manic flight from the GA&A complex had scattered Dominic's corpse in the woods along with other wreckage. Search teams had found one missing marine out there.

It was also possible, given the extensive reconstruction of

Dom's body, that the office fire had reduced him to unrecognizable cybernetics.

Still, there were those nagging doubts.

And, lastly, there was the uncomfortable fact that the success of both his personal and political missions was not making it any easier for him to sleep at night. Klaus shook his head. It was useless to try and get any more sleep now. He dressed.

Klaus looked at his brother's bed, with its damp sweat-stained sheets, and wondered if Dominic had ever had problems sleeping at night.

CHAPTER EIGHT

Brain Drain

"Nothing hurts as much as the loss of something you've never had."

—*The Cynic's Book of Wisdom*

"Lord, grant that I may always desire more than I can accomplish."

—MICHELANGELO BUONARROTI
(1475–1564)

On the way back to his base in the Diderot Mountains, Dominic Magnus still felt that things were finally going right. With his well-crafted "Mr. Shaji" identity he had managed to prepare the beginnings of his takeover of Bleek Munitions.

He had just closed his last meeting. All of Bleek Munition's stockholders—the ones Dom talked to anyway—were willing to part with their shares at the price Dom was offering.

The only obstacle left was Ezra Bleek and his children. Unfortunately, Ezra, the founder of Bleek Munitions, was nearly inaccessible behind the proxy held by his kids. And the kids certainly weren't going to part with their father's stock.

Other than Ezra's block of stock, Dom had enough leverage and had cooked enough deals to take over right now. He had two hundred megagrams of liquid capital, and that was enough to leverage everything on the financial side.

All he needed was to contact Ezra Bleek successfully, and do an end run around his children.

Dom was letting the computer drive his luxury contragrav. Specifically, he was letting Mosasa's software do the driving. He'd been gone for a day shy of two weeks, and the security setup Mosasa and Zanzibar were in charge of should be fully operational now. The approach to the Diderot Holding Company would be very well monitored. Anything that came within a klick of the entrance without following specific flight paths would be blasted out of the sky.

Trespassers who crossed the perimeter would get one kill warning before they were shot down. Only one was necessary. With the proliferation of communities and communes across the Bakunin landscape ranging from simply isolationist to xenophobically hostile, smart pilots rarely ignored no-fly warnings. Stupid pilots only did so once.

Dom's aircar slipped inside the no-fly perimeter and received the rote warning. Dom responded with a rote three-word clearance code. The point wasn't the code, it was the holo transmission of his voiceprint, retina scan, skin galvanity, pupil dilation, ad infinitum. Not only couldn't a nonmodified vehicle slip through the system, you also couldn't force a cleared driver through it without security picking up abnormal stress reactions.

Dom's fingers tapped the control stick.

Security only gave him confirmation by not shooting him down.

The computer flew the car over the thinning orange and purple forest. Soon he was gliding above the naked foothills of the mountain. *I wonder if Tetsami's still angry?*

Dom decided to worry about that when he talked to her. The less he thought about it, the less chance he had of talking himself out of it. He was going to talk to her—

He just had to stop worrying about it.

He forced his mind on to the security setup. It seemed to be operating smoothly now. That was good. Not only because he was paranoid about someone finding the mountain headquarters before the operation relocated—and he had good reason to be paranoid—what was encouraging about the setup was that it was a collaboration between the new and the old. It was a collaboration between Mariah Zanzibar, one of his oldest and most trusted people from the late Godwin Arms, and Tjaele Mosasa, whom he'd recruited a little more than five Bakunin weeks ago.

That boded well for the operation as a whole. If the Diderot Holding Company could move smoothly, over a thousand GA&A employees working under a board of directors of entirely new people, perhaps the transition over to Bleek Munitions could come off.

Dom hoped so. He had a thousand people here who needed new lives.

The computer flew the car in, close to the ground, straight at what appeared to be a flat side of the mountain.

Dom knew what was coming, but he still didn't like it.

The car flew through the wall of rock. The wall itself was a combination of thermal damping field and high-quality holo projection. It camouflaged the doors to the vehicle bay in the side of the mountain. From inside the bay Dom could look back and see the doors close. As the computer landed the vehicle, Dom watched the massive thirty-meter-long doors slide shut behind the holo image. The holo itself looked like a thin casting of the rock face, seen from the wrong end.

Dom got out of the car. It was warmer than the last time he'd been here. The camouflage and the field on the door allowed them to heat the place to a little above freezing.

Dom looked around for a reception committee.

Mariah Zanzibar approached him from across the cavernous parking area. As she closed on him, Dom saw that she didn't look happy. On a two-meter-tall woman with the grace and lethal bearing of a black panther, a woman who also happened to be Dom's security chief, the expression was not reassuring.

"Welcome back, sir," Zanzibar said.

"Thank you," Dom said. After a pause he added, "You don't have to call me 'sir.' Or 'Mr. Magnus' for that matter."

A smile, little more than a crease at the corners of her mouth, briefly lit Zanzibar's features. "Old habit, Mr.—just an old habit."

Dom walked toward the exit at the far end of the cavern. Zanzibar fell into step with him. He asked, "How are things going here?"

"Smoothly, for the most part. We got a third residential area up. The medical facility is finally up to spec. We have a security net up with full surveillance on all external access points. Engineering got the Commune's old power system on-line again. We have environmental control on all the inhabited tunnels now. We've been keeping an eye down the hill at GA&A, nothing changed down there. Security has a report on their activity for you."

After a pause, Zanzibar added, "And Shane came back from Godwin six days ago."

They stood in front of the exit to the cavern. A secondary security system was clearing them for entry into the greater complex. After a few seconds of silent observation, the computers opened the door. Dom and Zanzibar walked into an air lock that prevented waste heat from slipping close to the mountain's surface.

Once they were through Dom asked, "What's wrong?"

Zanzibar sighed. Dom thought the sound odd coming from Zanzibar.

"Shane, for one thing," Zanzibar said. "She's well *physically.*"

"But?"

"Shane wanted to die in that plasma blast," Zanzibar said matter-of-factly.

Dom looked at Zanzibar, but her face was unmoved by the flat assertion. It wasn't something she'd say, even of a woman she disliked, unless she thought it was true.

Dom stopped. A familiar chill was back, freezing out some of the optimism he'd been feeling. He recognized it. It was the feeling he got when he destroyed things close to him. Shane had been a Confederacy Marine who had defected to join Dom's people. Zanzibar couldn't trust Shane because of that. Ironically, Dom trusted Shane precisely because she'd defected.

He could manipulate her.

He could also identify with her.

"Is she suicidal?" Dom asked. He pronounced the words deliberately because part of his face seemed to vibrate of its own volition.

It was a small tic, and Zanzibar didn't seem to notice—or perhaps she had just known him too long. She shook her head. "The doctors left in the life monitor for us."

It wasn't an unequivocal yes. But it wasn't a denial either.

"Maybe I should see her."

Zanzibar put a hand on his arm. "No."

Dom looked at Zanzibar and felt a brief wave of confusion. It was as if the synapses—his biological ones at least—misfired wildly for a few instants and dumped him in a world where everything was just *wrong* for a half second.

The feeling passed. In its wake was left a shattering realization. *She said "no" to me and I couldn't handle it.*

He started walking again and was surprised that his voice sounded normal. "What's the problem?"

"Guilt. I doubt she'd react well to you. She's locked in her room most of the time." Zanzibar sounded disapproving.

Dom almost asked if Zanzibar thought Shane might become a security risk. Fortunately he thought better of it.

Maybe Tetsami was right. Maybe I am that bad. He had to talk to Tetsami, for his own sake.

Dom pulled the conversation into a track he could more easily control. "How about the others? I was hoping to have a board meeting tonight."

They had traveled down a few dozen meters of natural rock corridor before Zanzibar spoke. "Mosasa's tireless. Random's running our computer systems. Ivor's been ferrying stuff back and forth. And Flower is—well—Flower."

They walked a few more meters down the corridor, toward the executive apartments while Dom waited for Zanzibar to finish. After a few seconds Dom decided that Zanzibar was taking too long.

"What about Tetsami?" Dom asked, slowly.

Zanzibar stopped and put a hand on Dom's shoulder. "She opted out, Dominic."

"What do you mean?" Dom felt an edge cut into his voice. She couldn't mean what he thought she meant. But, as he said the words, ice grew into a permafrost that coated the underside of his skin.

"She cashed out her share."

Dom turned to face Zanzibar. Things couldn't collapse that neatly, the universe wasn't built like that.

Zanzibar wore an uncharacteristically gentle expression.

"Where is she?" he asked.

"She had Ivor drop her at the Proudhon Spaceport."

"When? Damn it, *when?*" He tried to control his voice, but it still came out harshly.

"Five days ago."

Dom let that sink in. "Five. Days?" he repeated like an idiot.

Zanzibar nodded.

There was a long silence during which Dom could feel all the liquid in his body slowly turn to stone. He took a deep breath. Slowly, he nodded. It only took him a few seconds to gain control of his voice.

"She's gone by now," Dom said. "On her way anywhere."

Zanzibar released his shoulder. "I'm sorry."

Dom felt confused for a moment. "No reason to be sorry. She told me her intentions a long time ago." *Was it that you didn't believe her?* "I think I'll find my own way to my apartment."

Zanzibar nodded and stepped back. "The board meeting?"

Dom had already started down the hall. "First thing tomorrow."

"Not tonight?"

Not tonight, Dom thought. He said nothing.

Dom retreated into his apartment. It wasn't much different than the residential apartments built for the twelve hundred people that now swarmed the black Diderot caverns. The room itself had been quickly hacked out of the bedrock. Where the lasers had carved, the stone was smooth black and polished. Where there had been voids in the rock, the walls were unfinished.

It was one room, half natural cavern—and the instant Dom entered it, he realized that there was no place he could look and escape his reflection in polished rock.

"Evil bastard," he whispered at multiple images of himself.

His hands—both of them—were shaking.

He had driven Tetsami off-planet. He was driving Shane, perhaps, to suicide. They were symptoms of a larger problem.

Dom realized his eyes were closed.

"Look at yourself!"

And he was looking at himself even before he opened his eyes. He didn't need his hands in view to see the blood on them. Behind him was a trail of destruction that he had run from all his life—

He had never faced it.

His eyes were open now, and he willed the pigment to fade from his synthetic skin. In the walls, fractured, color-distorted images of himself clenched their fists, shaking accusations at him. Their flesh faded from the chocolate brown that had been Shaji's disguise, through the copper-bronze that was his "normal" coloring, to the translucent white of an albino, to clear pseudoflesh. Dom ripped off the clothes he wore, the fabric parting with little resistance.

He stood naked before himself, infinitely repeated, stigmata fully revealed—the titanium alloy bones, the artificial muscles snaking with wire filament, the few glistening pink-red organs he had been born with, and the chromium skull with the incongruous brown eyes and white enamel teeth.

All this under a body that pretended to be human, a body whose exterior was indistinguishable in form and function from the one that his brother had nearly destroyed a decade ago.

You ape humanity, Dominic, but this *is your true face. A technological death's head.*

For a decade he had never looked straight at himself, at this. The symbol of his guilt. The reconstruction he saw had saved his life. He should have died.

He had come to Bakunin instead.

Ten years he had been in the Terran Executive Command, the enforcers of the Confederacy. He had been an officer. He gave the orders. Orders to kill troublemakers, suppress demonstrations, neutralize orbital habitats, and in one case, reduce an entire rebellious city to chunks of gravel the size of his little finger. He was good at what he did.

Then Helen Dacham had died.

His mother dead by his ignorant hands. For the first time he had seen what he was good *at.*

Death for thousands—millions—that's what he was. Maybe he thought to achieve some sort of balance as a gun-runner. Selling arms to the revolutionaries as well as the imperialists, the Confed planets and the separatists, the capitalists and the socialists, the oppressor and the oppressed. Maybe he was leveling the playing field.

Maybe he was simply multiplying his evil.

All the justifications he had used then came to his lips now, but became so much ash before he spoke the words.

And now?

Now he *made* weapons.

For a quarter of a century you've been running from the corpse at the end of the gun. You stopped pulling the trigger to give the order. You stopped giving the order to sell the gun. You stopped selling the gun to build the gun. Now you want to buy the damn factory.

But it never changes, does it?

It's still your finger on the trigger, and the corpse is still your mother.

CHAPTER NINE

Durable Goods

"The only way to insure you like the answer is to
not ask the question."
— *The Cynic's Book of Wisdom*

"There is far greater peril in buying knowledge than
in buying meat and drink."
— PLATO
(*ca.* 427–*ca.* 347 B.C.)

Tetsami spent the rest of her evening walking inside the
white buildings which formed the central city of Proudhon.
It helped sharpen the edge to her paranoia.

*Something big enough to empty Proudhon of mercs would
have lit up warning lights all over the planet.*

Wouldn't it?

The central cluster of skyscrapers was the only area of the
spaceport-city that had a logic to its design. She wandered
along their crystal walkways. Outside, the red evening light
of Kropotkin washed the world in blood. Hours ago she'd
passed the fifty-story hotels ringing the hub of Proudhon,
demarcating the line between order and chaos.

It also marked a line that the street people couldn't cross,
but a person with a visitor's ID chit and her credit could.

She followed walkways from one office building to another, catching glimpses of the greater city. The twisted
blending of spaceport and city didn't extend to the hub.

Tetsami had combed the ads, tracing their origins. The
trail had ended in the Proudhon Tower, the center of the hub.
The home base for the Proudhon Spaceport Development
Corporation.

Specifically, the ads seemed to have come out of Spaceport Security.

That scared the shit out of her.

Unlike Godwin, where the city's order, such as it was, was kept balanced between hundreds of competing interests, Proudhon was a gigantic company town. Proudhon might not be the largest city in Bakunin, but it might have been the largest corporation. Proudhon *was* access to Bakunin. Anything making landfall on Bakunin had to pay a tithe to Proudhon, whether it used the spaceport or not. Proudhon had the force to back up its monopoly. Proudhon Spaceport Security was the largest and most heavily armed force on the planet.

Spaceport Security had been doing a lot of hiring as of late.

If Proudhon Security is massing an army, someone would have to notice—

She was avoiding the return to her hotel room. Now it wasn't just the street trash she was scared of running into. Spaceport Security could monitor everything from access in and out of the city to all the data traffic on the Proudhon comm web.

They could even monitor the ID chit that she dared not dispose of while she was inside the city. They might know that she was aware of something going on. They could decide that she knew too much. All it could take was some dedicated software monitor watching access to the public information boards.

It was sheer paranoia to think such a thing.

But they *could* do it, and that kind of power was an alien concept to Tetsami. She couldn't deal with it. She was used to the free-for-all in Godwin.

Worse was the idea that someone might use that power to disappear her. She kept telling herself that there was no way someone could keep a massive security force buildup secret.

But Proudhon was a closed system. If the company wanted to, they could keep a very tight grip on information going out of the city.

Maybe lethally tight.

The dilemma was a pressure on the back of her skull. She'd dug a little too deeply, and there was the chance someone might have noticed. If she sat tight and pretended nothing was wrong, someone might decide to preempt any further curiosity on her part.

But if she rabbited now, Proudhon Security would know.

They'd know the second that little ID chit left the city. She took the black electronic rectangle out of her pocket and stared at it as if it was a live detonator.

She could pitch it and run. But she had heard stories of Security goons canvassing the streets, flushing out anyone who wasn't databased. They were usually flashed by a vehicle-mounted plasma jet and left for the infrastructure crews to mop up.

She was here under an alias, and if she attracted attention to herself, something would happen.

Chances were, something *bad.*

She'd been moving on foot ever since she'd discovered the scope of what was going on. Briefly, she'd thought about leaving on foot. She might avoid Spaceport Security that way, but Proudhon was surrounded on three sides by a band of black sand over two thousand klicks wide and fifteen hundred deep.

She suddenly felt she had wandered too far into the hub. She looked around, and it was as if the company had enveloped her. Halfway into the center of the hundred-square-block central city, Tetsami could no longer see a view of Greater Proudhon's sprawl. The views out the walkways were all alike.

On every side, bone-white towers mirrored each other. Pseudo-marble pillars supported statues that guarded their corners—eagles, griffins, pegasii, dragons, and other winged beasts Tetsami couldn't identify.

It unnerved her.

Not the statues, but the fact that they, and the buildings, had all been built by one corporation. Godwin had bigger buildings, and more of them. But Godwin was a hodge-podge; differing construction styles and intent tended to cancel each other out.

The similarity of the buildings here in the hub seemed to concentrate their mass, focus it like a magnifying glass. It wasn't like walking through a city, it was like walking through a gigantic machine.

She turned around to make her way back to her hotel. She had to escape this place.

Tetsami spent the rest of the sixteen-hour Bakunin night sitting cross-legged on her bed in the New Yukon Hotel, trying to figure out where she was going to escape *to.*

On her lap was a Bakunin Planetary Atlas she had bought in the gift shop housed in a much higher-class hotel. She had decided if her escape off-planet was blocked, she would find a nice little hole somewhere on this dirtball to lay low until whatever was about to explode blew over.

The atlas was a flimsy sheet of cyberplas. It was already beginning to warp with her repeated thumb-presses on the screen and the color display was beginning to blur.

Should have bought the fifty-gram hypermap. Not like I couldn't afford it.

The scene slid repeatedly over Bakunin's one continent. Cities flew by, Proudhon, Godwin, Troy, Rousseau, Wilson, Celine, Jefferson. When she touched a city location, she was awarded a brief flash of information: "Proudhon: Pop—3.6 million. City planning: *** Security: **** Hotels: ****½ Transportation: **** ..."

"Godwin: Pop—10.6 million. City planning: *½ Security: * Hotels: *** ..."

What kind of tourist would go to Godwin?

Tetsami looked at the atlas in her hands and shook her head.

What kind of tourist would come to Bakunin?

"Troy: Pop—5.1 million. City planning: ** Security ** ..."

"Jefferson City: Pop—0.5 million. City planning: **** ..."

Yeah, Jefferson gets four stars for city planning. Great, if you like neoclassical pseudo-marble kitsch.

"Rousseau: Pop—1.8 million ..."

It was the eighth time she had paged through the information. It felt like population statistics for a hundred different cities were scrawled permanently into the backs of her retinas. Most of the information provided by the atlas was useless. Its capsule security ratings were laughable. And who gave a shit if Jefferson City had the best hotels on the planet, or the worst hospitals?

Its data on communes was even worse. It tried to treat them like cities, which they weren't. For one thing, communes were closed. Not just in terms of environment—almost every commune on Bakunin tried to be self-sufficient—but also in terms of population. The half that even allowed in outsiders nearly always forced the visitor to buy a share of the commune.

The other difference between the communes and the cities was philosophy.

The cities were all in a tenuous equilibrium state between hundreds of forces, from the corporate entities based in them down to the street gangs that fed off the debris drifting to the bottom of the social order.

Communes, however, were monolithic entities dedicated to a single—sometimes bizarre—belief.

Technically, Jefferson City was a commune, though the Jeffersonians hated the term.

The atlas she had left out entries for some of the biggest communes. The Zeno Commune, she knew, had something like a half-million people in it, but there wasn't a listing for it. Worst of all, the atlas gave no indication about a commune's sociopolitical slant.

She could decipher a few communes that gave their ideology away in their name. New Jerusalem was probably *not* a bunch of rabid atheists. But when she saw the name Olympia . . . Was that a bunch of classical democrats? A collection of neopagans under the Grecian pantheon? Or was it a free-love sex colony?

Tetsami's eyes hurt. She tossed the atlas.

Might as well strike out at random and dig in as soon as she found population.

If she wanted population, she knew what direction she *should* go in. Proudhon was the *only* major community on the eastern side of the Diderot Mountains. The city sat on Bakunin's tepid equator at the edge of a desert nearly as empty of people as it was of water. There were a few towns on the eastern coast of the continent, where the land began to flower a little again. The biggest of those was Sartre, a million people about twelve hundred klicks east of Proudhon.

However, most of Bakunin's population was to the west. Almost all of Bakunin's population was concentrated in a three-thousand-kilometer strip running from the opposite slope of the Diderot Mountains a nearly equal distance to the western shore.

Since Bakunin had at least a billion people—no one was really sure, no accurate census existed—the concentration of the habitable living space made the population density in that strip equal to some of the oldest continually inhabited areas of Earth.

That was the way she *should* go to find population.

Tetsami didn't want to go back in that direction.

She threw herself back on the bed and stared at the ceiling. There was a slight vibration as the fluid in the mattress readjusted to her position, and she sank a few centimeters. Above her, her reflection stared down out of the mirrored ceiling.

"Why don't I just go back?"

Damn regrets again. The feeling that she had abandoned everything. The sense that, if she gave Dom another chance—

She clamped down on that feeling. Hard.

Dom was an icy unfeeling bastard who didn't give a shit about her or the way she felt, and the sooner she accepted that, the sooner she'd get that part of her life over with. She'd have to be happy with the twenty megs she had.

After all, Dom certainly wouldn't be thinking about her. Once she was out of his business operations she'd be even more irrelevant to him than she'd been when she was there—

Christ! Stop thinking about it. You've got more problems than Dom's insensitivity.

"Sheesh, this is all bullshit."

Tetsami got off the bed, grabbed her black duffel from the closet, and started packing. She emptied drawers indiscriminately into it. She'd hesitated long enough. She'd been in this hotel for too long. It was time to get out. She'd beg, borrow, or steal an aircar, and she'd be out of Proudhon today. She'd chuck the ID chit out over the desert somewhere.

There were more than enough communes on this side of the Diderot Mountains and, damn the consequences, she'd strike north until she found one that would let her in. Whether it was an Amish farm community or a Rastifari ganja plantation, she'd deal with it when she got there.

It was closing in on dawn, the streets were empty of most human debris.

She had made it out of the New Yukon without checking out, and it took her nearly an hour at a bulletin kiosk to find a vehicle. Her ID chit was tied to the transaction, but she had to deal with that risk.

Problem was, all the rental agencies—agencies, Tetsami realized, that only operated at the sufferance of the

Proudhon Spaceport Development Corporation—were
closed. The only aircars around were taxis, which were run
by Proudhon and wouldn't leave the city limits. Eventually,
Tetsami had to satisfy herself with buying an off-road
groundcar from the classifieds.

She called the owner and was surprised at how ready the
man was to meet her at this time in the morning.

By the time she reached Proudhon Security's northern-
most checkpoint, the man was waiting for her.

He was sitting on the hood of the dirtiest vehicle Tetsami
had ever seen. Under the dust she could see something that
could have been black-gray desert camouflage, or simply a
very bad paint job. Unlike an urban groundcar, this thing had
wheels, huge ones. The tires came up to her chin.

When she reached the vehicle, the owner vaulted off the
hood in front of her, forcing her to come to an abrupt halt.

"Jarvis," he said, sticking out a hand armored in calluses.
He was tanned a deeper brown than most people managed
in Kropotkin's red glow. His hair was the color of drift-
wood.

"Kari Jorgenson," Tetsami said, using her alias. She tried
to figure out the man's age, but it was as fruitless as trying
to date a piece of mahogany. Somewhere between forty-five
and two hundred.

"So you're interested in buying the *Lady?*"

Tetsami nodded without saying that the *Lady* looked more
like an old dowager. "Mind if I look—" Tetsami noted the
way Jarvis was caressing the hood "—*her* over?"

"Go ahead. She's seen a lot of use, but she's in top
shape."

As Tetsami started going over the car, Jarvis extolled its
virtues. "The chassis is a Royt design for planetary exploration. It's rated for three Gs, fifteen atmospheres, and class
five terrain."

Tetsami looked out from under the front fender. "Where
do you drive this thing?"

"I did a lot of prospecting in the mountains. Dolbrian artifacts. Of course she's overengineered for a simple off-
roader, but the *Lady* here can take anything—including full
submersion."

"Find any?" Tetsami asked.

Jarvis chuckled. "Dolbrian artifacts?"

Tetsami nodded. She was intrigued, since part of the elaborate plan she'd developed for Dom's raid on GA&A—it seemed ages ago now—involved a story to cover their digging activity. The cover was the search for traces of the Dolbrians on this planet. The Dolbrians had died out a hundred million years ago and might—or might not—have terraformed Bakunin.

Circling Kropotkin was certainly a weird place to find a relatively Earthlike planet.

Jarvis was shaking his head. "If I'd ever found so much as a rock touched by the Dolbrians, I wouldn't need to come out of retirement."

Would be one hell of a meal ticket.

She walked around the car, noting the array of lights on the front. They were matched by a rack of lights on the top of the car as well as a few swivel-mounted beams on either door. "The cabin's contained?"

"Up to three atmospheres, like I said. I've added a killswitch to the environment control. Without the recycler you can add a week's running time to a full charge."

"A week?" Tetsami had pulled a side panel exposing the engine's inards. One look and she wished Ivor was here with her.

"She's a Royt exploration vehicle. It runs the axles on a power plant rated for a contragrav. You can get a month standard out of the onboard power before a recharge."

Tetsami arched an eyebrow. "How fast can it go?"

"Believe me, you'll roll her before you find out." He grinned. "I'm asking ten K."

To her eye the *Lady* was probably a bargain at that price. "So why you selling her?"

"Decided my retirement was premature, but with the new job it was a choice between selling her or scrapping her."

Tetsami looked at Jarvis. He could be a merc type.

She asked, "New job? What?"

"Nothing you'd want to be involved in." The voice was suddenly hard. She saw a man she didn't want to push.

Jarvis was part of the whole strangeness swamping Proudhon. And he was right, she didn't want to be involved in it.

"I'll buy her," Tetsami said. "Will you accept off-world credit?"

"Of late, I prefer it."

The way Jarvis said that made Tetsami glad she had transferred her twenty megagrams to an off-world bank. Even if the interest rate sucked.

CHAPTER TEN

Kill Ratio

"The future strikes with blinding speed. The past
takes its time and *aims*."
—*The Cynic's Book of Wisdom*

"Even God cannot change the past."
—AGATHON
(*ca.* 448–*ca.* 400 B.C.)

Deep in the heart of the mountains sat the conference room
of the Diderot Holding Company, a hemisphere of mirrored
black rock ten meters in diameter. Its centerpiece was the
circular conference table, with seven chairs. The table was
one of the few finished-looking objects in the whole mountain.

Only five of the chairs were filled. The room felt empty
to Dom.

She's gone, he told himself. *Just another mistake that you
can't recover.*

Dom felt numb. He hadn't slept last night. He'd stayed
awake, wondering what he could have said to her. And when
that effort had lost the ability to wound him, he had spent
the night mentally replaying events from his past.

Now, as dawn broke on the eastern face of the Diderot
Mountains, he was supposed to brief his board on the coming takeover of Bleek Munitions. It seemed an empty process.

As he collected his thoughts, he felt the others staring at
him. Zanzibar, Mosasa, Ivor—even Flower seemed to stare
at him with its reptile-avian eyeless face.

To have something to say, he spoke to the remaining
board member present. "Are you recording, Random?"

"Of course," came the response from the holo projector buried in the table's center.

To think he'd been looking forward to this.

He now had to justify a massive investment all six of these people had risked their lives for.

He had to make good a debt to twelve hundred employees. Twelve hundred people he had evacuated from Godwin Arms, alive despite his brother's best efforts. Dom owed those people a new living.

It just seemed so useless now.

He started tapping his fingers idly. "During my trip to Godwin I confirmed that Bleek Munitions is our best target for a friendly takeover. It requires a debt load. But one we can handle."

It was hard to ignore how dead the air in this room felt.

He told the assembly about Ezra Bleek and his ungrateful children. He told them about the rumors of Ezra's confinement, and the possibility that—given escape as an incentive—Ezra might be a willing participant in the takeover of his own company.

Ungrateful children.

That phrase resonated. He recited dry statistics, figures on stock manipulation, transactions that should give them control of Bleek Munitions. As he spoke the words fed to him by his onboard computer, another, older, part of his brain fed him other violent images.

Styx.

Styx, a colony over a century and a half old, orbited Sigma Draconis in one of the narrowest parts of the Centauri Alliance. Sigma Draconis was a star dimmer than Sol, and despite the planet's close orbit, Styx was cold as hell. Its oceans were locked under ice sheets, the depths only kept liquid by submerged volcanoes. Its atmosphere was clouded by smoke from eruptions. The ground was covered by black, tarlike snow.

A half billion people called it home.

A TEC Colonel by the name of Jonah Dacham was responsible for the deaths of thirty-five thousand of them, and the destruction of their capital city, without ever setting foot on the hellish place.

That wasn't *me,* a small part of Dom's mind argued. You aren't Jonah Dacham.

No, the cold part of his mind answered. *You're not Jonah now. But you were him,* then.

Zanzibar said, "The kids will fight." And it was like listening to a voice from another era.

Dom answered by rote. "The kids will fight. But it's still a friendly takeover. We'll have the stock. The kids only have position. Once Ezra's blood and retina-print are on a stock transfer and it's filed with Lucifer Contracts, we'll have controlling interest. Even the unions won't interfere."

Flower gestured for attention. Its long neck—a third of its three-meter height, rising from the midst of a forest of leaf-like feathers—bobbed its saurian head about a meter closer to Dom. The head was smooth and only marked by black Rorschach patterns over a yellowish skin. When it talked, the jaws opened the bony beak a crack, and remained immobile.

Its voice was nasal and deliberately phrased. "Bleek, he is a dispersed operation, is he not? He will force us to disperse also? Our small force cannot secure buildings scattered all over the city of Godwin. He would be no easy task for a moderate-sized army. The best we can manage is a small assault team."

"We have to make sure that all of Ezra's kids are in one place. Bleek isn't a closed operation like GA&A was. Anyone not responding directly to the board is going to sit back and watch the management change."

"A bloodless coup," said Ivor Jorgenson.

Even as Dom nodded his agreement, the word "coup" brought him more memories of Styx. The Styx of fifteen standard years ago.

Colonel Jonah Dacham had received a blip on the comm of his scout-craft as soon as it had achieved a Stygian orbit. The message had come from the rebels holding Styx traffic control.

The holo accompanying the voice had shown a large weary-looking man, red-haired and red-bearded. "Incoming craft. This is your only warning. We have control of the planetary defense network. You will not be allowed to enter the lower atmosphere."

The Stygian rebels had held all of Perdition City, the central spaceport there, and the extra-planetary defenses, blockading the entire world. With the exception of the planet-based tach-transmitter in the government Citadel,

Styx was isolated from the rest of the Confederacy. The Citadel stood in the middle of the capital city, Perdition.

Dom remembered his response to the rebels' challenge. "I am Colonel Jonah Dacham, TEC, here on behalf of the Confederacy."

"We know who you are." The red-bearded man gazed out from the holo with icy blue eyes. "This is an internal Stygian matter. Any Executive meddling will be dealt with harshly."

"I've come here in good faith, alone, to negotiate some sort of settlement."

"I thought the Confederacy didn't deal with terrorists?"

My friend, Dom remembered thinking, back when he was Jonah Dacham, *we deal with terrorists all the time. What we don't do is* negotiate *with them.*

Something Mosasa said tore him free of the evil memory. It took an effort to keep his voice level. "Other problems?"

"That's what I said," replied Mosasa. Mosasa was looking even more like a pirate than he usually did. In addition to being tall, black, hairless, and adorned with a profusion of gold earrings, he wore a red silk blouse open to the waist, allowing Dom to see more of Mosasa's massive dragon tattoo than usual. The head of the dragon curled around Mosasa's left ear to give him an off-kilter three-eyed stare, the third eye being the dragon's.

"Communications has detected some disturbing air traffic." While Mosasa spoke, Random took over the holo in the table. The holo fuzzed to life with a scrambled video signal. The speakers came on with digital gibberish. Occasionally the holo would resolve into something almost comprehensible. The display froze on a blurred color-negative picture of someone's face.

"This is from three days ago, after a group of twelve ships tached in from the direction of Epsilon Eridani. We can't unlock the scrambling—"

"But?" said Dom.

"But," Mosasa continued. "We've IDed the source of the signal." Random played with the holo and the frozen signal shrank to one corner of the display, revealing video of a gigantic spaceship floating against a starry background. "The SEEC 'Freighter' *Daedalus,* and escort. Thank Flower for the graphic."

"That's what tached in?" *A military Confed ship?
Proudhon air-traffic control should be going ape.*

Mosasa nodded. "The signal intercept was an accident. It
was supposed to be tight-beamed to somewhere in
Proudhon."

Dom felt as if control had finally slipped from his grasp.
His own handle on events was one of the few anchors he had
in his life. Suddenly he'd been knocked adrift.

Proudhon had a stranglehold on orbital traffic around
Bakunin, and a stranglehold on information about orbital
traffic. He was hearing about *Daedalus* indirectly, and that
meant that Proudhon was screening information about the
nature of the ship.

Ships, Dom corrected himself.

Ivor said something, and Zanzibar began to argue with
him. Dom ignored them. He *needed* to understand this new
development. The myriad threats he'd been juggling since
he'd come to Bakunin had been tolerable because he understood them.

He even understood his brother, after a fashion: Helen had
been on Styx.

But why, suddenly, this? Did anyone here realize what
this could mean?

*What are SEEC ships doing out of the Sirius-Eridani Eco-
nomic Community?* Dom thought desperately, furiously. His
fingers drummed a machine-gun rhythm on the table while
pointless debate orbited him.

Ships like the *Daedalus*—a tach-capable carrier holding
dozens of drop-ships for planetary and ship-to-ship assault—
were technically not supposed to exist. The Confederacy
Charter forbade tach-capable warships in hands other than
those of the Terran Executive Command. Ten years in the
TEC had taught Dom the futility of the non proliferation
provisions of the Charter.

Every arm of the Confederacy owned its own private fleet
of "trading vessels," "scout-ships," and "heavy freighters."
The fraud was so accepted that "trading vessel" was a
Confed euphemism for warship. The Alliance military arm
was still called the Centaurian Trading Company, after its
original function.

The deception was accepted as long as the fleet stayed
within its own borders.

Any warship venturing out into disputed Confed space
was an invitation to all-out war.

Mosasa described four other small vessels that had parked at
the Lagrange points fore and aft of Schwitzguebel, Bakunin's
largest moon. "Random hacked this video from a Proudhon
air-traffic control sat. Flower has IDed them as ships from the
TEC Terran Defense Force."

That captured Dom's attention. He stared at the holo, hand
stilled.

He stared at a smear of a holo that was supposedly looking at Schwitzguebel's L-5 point. The ships were hard to
make out but Dom knew what they were. "Six ships," Dom
said.

"We only detected four," Mosasa said.

"TEC observation platforms," Dom explained, feeling
more tendrils from his past digging into his brain. "If the
other two don't want to be seen, they won't be. They're
probably orbiting directly opposite Schwitzguebel."

"Are you sure?" asked Ivor.

*Ivor, I took a stealth ship just like one of those and laid
waste to the capital city of Styx. I know them well.*

"I know TEC procedure. They wouldn't leave a sixty-
degree slice of the planet uncovered." As he answered, Dom
thought, *I know you, too, Ivor.*

Dom remembered flying one of those fatal little craft.

He remembered negotiating the landing with the red-
haired man, Commander Robert Elision, airborne division of
the Stygian Presidential Guard, the man who was in charge
of the Stygian coup. "You know why I'm here, Commander," Dom had said. "You've known I was coming for at
least nineteen days. I doubt you would have called me personally if you hadn't already made up your mind."

Elision's lopsided grin didn't touch those ice-blue eyes.
"You're right. I've made up my mind, though I have trouble
believing the TEC offer to send a single negotiator. Not your
style."

Jonah Dacham shrugged in response.

"I've got confirmation from our intel sats, that crate
you're riding could hold five guys at best. Be assured that
your welcoming committee will be ten times that."

"I have clearance to land?"

"Yes, you have your damn clearance. Deviate from your
approach and you'll be shot down. Another ship tachs in and

you'll be shot down. I'll talk to you, but I want you to remember, this situation doesn't make me happy."

"I'll remember, Commander," Jonah said as he maneuvered his craft for an orbital approach to the city of Perdition.

By all accounts, Commander Elision had a very strong position. With the exception of a few members of the Presidential Guard, his coup had been bloodless. He had the support
of most of the Stygian military, nearly a hundred thousand
troops. Perdition was an armed camp. The only spot of
ground on the planet Elision did not hold was a circle of
about a kilometer's radius around the Citadel, right in the
center of the city.

There were almost no civilians left in central Perdition.
That wasn't just due to the revolt—there'd been very little
actual shooting, despite the twenty thousand troops ringing
the Citadel—the retreat from Perdition was due to the loss
of the dome on the city. While it was barely possible to live
on the surface of Styx without environmental control, it
wasn't pleasant.

The small observer-craft slid into a preprogrammed approach toward Perdition and the spaceport. Jonah watched
the planet out the forward observation port. There was nothing for him to do. Everything was in the ship's computer.
The maneuvering the craft was about to do required micro-
second timing and allowed nothing for human error.

Jonah watched the dirty gray-and-black-streaked ball of
Styx. Jonah couldn't see beyond the eternal smog, but the
TEC observer was a spy craft. While he had talked to the
Commander below him, Jonah's craft had measured and
quantified the area around Perdition to the last centimeter.
Behind him, in a space that used to be crew's quarters, Jonah's technical package was refreshing its own database
with that information, assuring it that its current trajectory
programming would place its contents on target.

As the craft began to kiss the lower atmosphere, the technical package was satisfied.

Dom forced himself back to the present. *Stealth craft,*
Dom thought. *If Random hacked a Proudhon sat to see
them, then Proudhon knows they're there. Proudhon is burying all this.*

"They want to be seen by the *Daedalus,*" Dom said, mas-
saging his temple.

The babble around the room ceased. Everyone looked at

him, and the most disturbing look was Ivor's. It wasn't
Ivor's expression that chilled him. It was the depth of his
eyes, blue, cold, staring out as if through a blizzard. Dom
continued gazing at Ivor and feeling a tightness in his chest.
"Those SEEC ships aren't supposed to be here. Bakunin's in
disputed space. The Economic Community *could* claim
we're in their space, but so could the Indi Protectorate, same
for the Union, the Centauri Alliance, even the Seven Worlds
at a stretch.

"The *Daedalus* being here isn't just threatening to
Bakunin, but to four-fifths of the Confederacy. Anything aggressive might start an interstellar war."

A long silence filled the room. After a while it was broken
by Random's voice from one of the speakers. "See, Tjaele,
I *told* you the shit was about to hit the fan."

Ivor stared back into Dom's eyes, reflecting none of the
recognition Dom felt. "You're saying that those TEC ships
are here to prevent the *Daedalus* from doing anything?"

There's no possible way Ivor could be . . .

Dom nodded. The world felt very far away, as if he were
in free fall, dropping into a deep gravity well. "Just having
a visible presence is a deterrent."

Ivor shook his head. "I can't believe that the sudden appearance of all this Confederacy bullshit is unrelated to what
we went through at Godwin Arms."

The tightness in Dom's chest grew worse. He had forced
himself to believe that Klaus' attack on Godwin Arms was
a personal vendetta against him. If he had ever truly believed that, Dom now knew it was false. The specific target,
GA&A, Dom's company, might have been motivated by
Klaus' hatred. But the fact that the TEC had launched an operation on Bakunin couldn't result from the obsessions of
one lone TEC Colonel.

The TEC had sent Klaus here on a mission, and Dominic
still had no idea what the mission was—except that it required the control of an independent arms manufacturer.

Dom felt control slipping even further away as he admitted, "It isn't. The TEC observers are probably here to prevent
the SEEC from interfering with their operation."

Klaus' operation.

"This situation doesn't make me happy," Ivor said.

Dom looked into Ivor's eyes, and knew. The quote from
years past—

The memory crashed in on Dom—

Jonah's craft had kissed the lower atmosphere. The technical package had been satisfied.

The computer switched on the observer's Emerson field. The field on a TEC spy ship was wide-band enough to soak up the most popular parts of the EM spectrum. Jonah's view out the port turned black as his ship shrouded itself in an ellipsoid of darkness.

As the Emerson field cut in, so did the craft's contragrav. And as the observer was cut free from the Stygian gravity well—to fly off tangentially, carried by its orbital velocity—Jonah's package slid out of the observer's belly, to continue the approach to Perdition.

The fact that Jonah was still around meant that the computer had performed the maneuver flawlessly, and the rebels in Perdition did not know what had just happened. By the time they did, they would have neither time nor inclination to search for Jonah's observer.

Jonah waited until a half minute before impact. Then he turned off the Emerson field so he could watch.

He was a considerable distance from Styx now—far enough from its mass for the contragrav to be irrelevant—and he turned the observer's full battery of intelligence-gathering devices on the planet.

Jonah called up an enhanced picture of the planet's surface near Perdition. The city was a hot spot, glowing white on a monochrome plain. At this resolution, Jonah could see a third of a continent.

A call was coming in on the holo. Jonah turned it on without sending back a transmission that would reveal his location.

"—even if you can't hear me, you bastard. God, do you even understand what you've done?" It was Commander Elision.

A cloudy white form floated toward Perdition on Jonah's screen.

"The Executive doesn't even care that we did this without shedding blood. You suckered us—" Someone whispered something from offscreen. Jonah realized that the Commander's background was a scene of chaos. "Ten seconds they say. Fine, just remember, thirty-five thousand peop—"

The transmission died just as the cloudy white haze hit

Perdition. The white of Perdition blazed whiter for an instant, and slowly began to fade.

Jonah began to flip the resolution higher and higher, until the area the city occupied filled the screen. At this resolution, individual buildings could be seen—the few that remained.

The strike had been surgical in its precision. Jonah's package had been two tons worth of polyceram monomolecular filament. It had been woven into a net ten kilometers in radius. The only difference between this net and any other orbital ordinance was the irregular elliptical hole in the center.

The fact that the only thing left standing in downtown Perdition was the Citadel and a few square blocks surrounding it showed that Jonah's package had hit dead center.

The Citadel stood alone now, over a smoking gravel pit. In a few places the gravel humped high, testifying to where the rebels had managed to shoot holes in the polyceram net. All those shots had been too late. Shooting down the net was as futile as trying to sweep back an ocean.

An entire rebel army with a single shot.

God damn him, God damn him to hell. He had been *proud* of that mission.

It took all of Dom's effort to maintain his control as that memory slammed through him, like the net shredded Perdition.

He couldn't help staring at Ivor.

He can't *be Elision. Elision's dead. Ivor's too old. Ivor's lived on Bakunin twenty years. Perdition was only fifteen years ago.*

Dom felt that reality had lost its focus.

The conversation sped by him.

"That means that the TEC operation is an ongoing concern," Flower said. "He implies that the TEC objective is longer term than the takeover of Godwin Arms."

Who are you? Dom wanted to scream at Ivor.

"Klaus and company haven't budged from the site," Zanzibar said. "Other than repelling attacks and flying their cargo ship, there's been no major activity there in over a month."

"My concern is that the *Daedalus* was transmitting to Proudhon," Mosasa said.

It can't be you, Dom thought at Ivor, *Styx was fifteen years ago.*

"So?" Ivor said, oblivious to Dom's unease. "Everyone

who tachs in to this system pays a call to Proudhon unless
they want a cloud of killer sats on their ass."

Fifteen years. Everyone died.

"But a scrambled transmission?" said Mosasa.

Dom put a hand to his forehead, as if the pressure could
stop the rising tide of memory. Fifteen years and thirty-five
thousand people.

That, and Helen.

The horror of it all, what tore at him right now, was the
fact that, if Jonah Dacham had foreknowledge of his mother's death, it would not have stayed his hand.

If Helen Dacham's death been a part of the planning, Jonah would have leveled the city anyway. Jonah was not one
to grieve for victims of procedure. Even Helen.

The horror was that Helen Dacham's death was an accident. She had no business being on Styx. She certainly had
no contact with the sons who had abandoned her a decade
earlier.

All of Dom's morality was a fluke. The fact he saw the
blood at all, was because the damn thing was an accident. It
was a million-to-one shot that allowed him a conscience at
all.

Somewhere, God was laughing.

CHAPTER ELEVEN

Conscientious Objector

"It is easier to determine what is profitable than what is right."
—*The Cynic's Book of Wisdom*

"The diseases of the mind are more destructive than those of the body."
—MARCUS TULLIUS CICERO
(106–43 B.C.)

Kathy Shane sat in the corner of a hollowed-out cave deep in the Diderot Mountains and did what she'd been doing every day since the medics had let her go; she remembered.

She had gotten good at it. She had managed to bring to mind every face and name that went with her old command. In her mind she was busy playing back every shared joke, every confidence, every time she'd helped someone out of a tight spot, and every time one of them had saved her ass.

She'd sold out every single one of them.

It didn't matter that Colonel Klaus Dacham was a raving loon. It didn't matter that the colonel thought nothing of wasting hundreds of civilians if they were in the way. It didn't even matter that the colonel had used his command to implement his own personal agenda.

What mattered was the fact that she had gone over to the enemy and caused the death of her own people.

Traitor.

The word was just her size.

Shane paced the room on her new legs.

It wasn't right for her to survive.

Sweet Lord Jesus, Shane thought, *I know I've never been one of your better children. It's been years since I've talked to a priest, but, dear Lord, I need one now.*

"Bless me, Father, for I have sinned."

Shane rested her forehead against the cold stone wall and wept. She knew the road she was traveling. It was a diminishing downward spiral, and at the bottom of the pit was herself, with the end of her own rifle in her mouth.

Would it be such a loss? She had not only betrayed the marines, but her planet, her family, herself. She had thrown all that away for a collection of people who would never be able to fully trust her, because of what she was.

She tried to tell herself that she had saved over eight hundred civilians from execution at Klaus Dacham's hands. She tried to tell herself that she had saved her people from becoming part of an atrocity. . . .

But she had committed her own atrocity.

Every time she saw the path she was treading she told herself that suicide was a mortal sin. Each time she said it, it seemed that her soul was less worth saving.

Help me, Jesus.

The door to her room buzzed.

Shane didn't answer it. There was no one in this tunnel warren that she wanted to see, with the possible exception of Corporal Hougland, who was being held prisoner somewhere below her. Shane had yet to visit her. Shane had a suspicion that seeing her former comrade would simply be a prelude to eating the barrel of a laser.

The door buzzed again.

"Go away," Shane said weakly. Of course, with the stone walls and the thick door, her visitor wouldn't hear her. *Just as well, let them think I'm asleep.*

Or dead.

Multiple buzzes this time, very insistent. Apparently her visitor wasn't going to just go away. Shane debated letting the intruder buzz to his heart's content. But she came to the conclusion that whoever it was would be gone sooner if she just answered the door.

The door buzzed again and Shane moved to answer it. Before she reached the door, she realized that she hadn't dressed.

She glanced into a mirror as she passed her bathroom. She was a mess. She was naked except for a pair of dirty briefs. Bright red scars circled her upper arms and thighs, and her neck. Her red hair had grown back nearly six centimeters, and had knotted into unwashed clumps. She probably smelled wonderful.

The room wasn't in much better shape. Clothing was kicked everywhere. Trash and soiled bedding massed in the corners.

Shane was disgusted with herself.

Her visitor was leaning on the buzzer now. An unending whine. Shane's gaze stayed glued to the mirror for a few more seconds. Then she bent over and picked up a robe.

This better be worth it, Shane thought as she pulled on her robe and answered the door.

Ivor Jorgenson stood there with a tray that seemed to hold at least five different meals.

"Hello, I thought you might need this."

Kathy looked at the tray and remembered just how long it had been since she'd eaten anything. She looked up at Ivor and realized how bad she must look to him.

Ivor's mild smile never wavered.

"So, you're the psychiatric delegation?"

Ivor shrugged. "No one has seen you in the cafeteria since you came back."

What do you expect? I've been through a physical purgatory for the past thirty days, local. I've only been able to walk for the past week. It'll be longer before I know where to walk to.

"Come in, I guess," she said.

Ivor stepped into the room, over a pile of Shane's dirty underwear. He went over to a table piled with garbage and nonchalantly brushed aside the debris as he set down the tray.

He pushed aside a used bandage, and Shane nearly gagged.

It was finally too much for her. "Damn it, aren't you going to say something?"

Ivor looked up, and his impassive expression made Shane furious.

"What do you want me to say?" he asked.

"Look at me! *Look at this room!* Tell me I'm being self-destructive. Tell me that I'm wallowing in self-pity. Tell me to stop feeling sorry for myself. Tell me *something.* Anything!"

"Why? You seem to know what needs to be said."

Shane realized that tears were running down her face. Her

voice was cracking and it made her feel that much more ashamed. "Oh, God. I'm such a mess." She ran a shaking hand through her hair and her fingers got caught in the snarls.

Ivor reached a hand toward her shoulder and Shane flinched. "Don't touch me. I'm filthy."

"Maybe you should take a shower."

Shane disengaged her hand from her hair and nodded. She wondered how she had lived with the itch in her skin for as long as she had. She walked to the bathroom, wiping her eyes.

As she closed the bathroom door—actually a curtain that drew across a natural cave opening—she peered back at Ivor and said, "Don't leave."

"I'm not going anywhere," he replied.

Shane ate for about fifteen minutes before she finally asked him.

"Why?"

Ivor had spent the time methodically tidying her cavern. She had almost objected. When she finally spoke, he acted as if their conversation—if it could be called that—had never been interrupted.

"Why what?"

Shane lowered her fork. "Would you please cut the act? My tolerance for bullshit is nil right now."

Ivor put down the sack of laundry he was packing and sat down at the table, opposite her. "I just thought you might be hungry." He placed a finger on the edge of one of the plates in front of her. The plate tilted up and a few lone crumbs rolled down the surface. "Was I wrong?"

Shane shook her head. "I can't figure you out."

"What's to figure?" Ivor let go of the plate and watched it clatter back on the tray.

"So you're not going to tell me how foolish I'm being? How life has to go on and all that crap?"

"That's your business. Besides, I told you you already know anything that needs to be said."

"No pep talks?"

"None."

"Won't say you know what I'm going through?"

"Even if I did."

Shane sighed. "Thank you for dinner."

"You're welcome."

Shane tried to figure out what was going on behind those bushy white brows. She failed.

Ivor stood and bent to get the bag of laundry he'd collected. Shane touched his shoulder and he stopped. "I'll get that," Shane said.

Ivor straightened. The laundry stayed on the ground. "I'll go, then."

The room was beginning to blur. She only nodded.

As he reached the door, she spoke up, ashamed at how her voice was cracking. "It started out right. I was doing the right thing. It's just somewhere it went so damn wrong. . . ."

Ivor paused in the doorway. Half in. Half out. "It's never easy," he whispered. Shane barely heard him.

"What?"

"The right thing," Ivor said.

Then he was gone.

Now what? Shane thought.

She sat there for almost five minutes before she said, "Now we go down to the damn fabricator and replace this stupid laundry."

CHAPTER TWELVE

Target of Opportunity

"Never underestimate a problem you're running from."

—*The Cynic's Book of Wisdom*

"Death waits in desolate places."

—MARBURY SHANE
(2044–*2074)

The *Lady* was a tank.

Tetsami had the car outfitted for an indeterminate stay in the desert. For once, the scum of hawkers and hustlers clouding Proudhon was more than an irritant for her. From a bootleg medkit to drinking water, she was able to purchase everything she needed on the street. That was important, because none of her purchases went down on the Proudhon net. If there were any computer spies from Spaceport Security, they were effectively blind to her six-hour shopping spree.

With a goal, even a short-term one, she moved quickly—not even bothering to burn the bridges behind her.

Once equipped, her major concern was departing the city proper. She was safe as long as she walked the streets carrying the ID chit, but she worried that Spaceport Security would fall on her as soon as she tried to leave Proudhon's perimeter with it on her person.

She was trying to slip away, unseen by the most technically advanced security force on the planet. She drove the *Lady* around the streets of the inner city as she tried to decide on a solution.

The controls of the *Lady* finally gave her an answer.

The fact that she rode a wheeled vehicle gave her an out, as did, ironically, the fact that the security here was so technically advanced. What Spaceport Security would be monitoring would be either radar contacts leaving the city—which the *Lady* was too low to trigger—or energy spikes drifting across the perimeter.

But the *Lady* didn't need power to move.

Instead of trying to leave by the city gates—whose roads didn't go where she wanted anyway—she jumped an inner-city culvert, punched the *Lady* through a crumbling retaining wall, and started barreling north along a concrete basin that lined a dry riverbed.

Once she got the *Lady*'s momentum going down the arrow-straight culvert, and had assured herself of the mostly downward slope of the bed, she cut the power—leaving the axles free.

The *Lady,* inertia personified, kept rolling down the smooth concrete.

The *Lady*'s windows were sealed. She had to open the door into the screaming desert air to pitch her Proudhon ID chit out into the wind. It took a few tries to close the door again.

The *Lady* rolled out of Proudhon, traveling down a channel whose concrete walls were now taller than she was. By the time the sky opened up, and the *Lady* was barely rolling, Proudhon was three klicks behind her.

Tetsami reengaged the Lady's power, hoping that she was far enough away from Proudhon for them not to worry about the power spike. The feeling of freedom she felt, now that she'd pitched that ID card and quit the city limits, made her press the *Lady* toward her maximum speed.

The *Lady* flew down the channel, occasionally spraying up sheets of stagnant water. The ride was smoother than Tetsami expected in a wheeled vehicle, which was why she nearly fulfilled Jarvis' prediction and rolled the damn thing.

About four klicks out of Proudhon, the concrete ended, and the real riverbed began. Tetsami hit the riverbed without throttling back at all. The effect was akin to suddenly introducing a bucket of sand into a well-oiled mechanism running at the peak of its capability. The *Lady* bucked, shook, and tried to vibrate apart.

In a panic, Tetsami fought to bring the car under control. The wheels left the ground twice before Tetsami managed to power things down. By then, the *Lady* had plowed up and over the side of the riverbed, driving into the desert proper.

Serves me right, Tetsami thought, *for piloting this thing like a contragrav.*

The locator set into the dashboard flickered and Tetsami hit it. The display snapped into focus, showing her four klicks north of Proudhon. The distance was growing. Tetsami switched on the rear display, and saw a blurry sand-blown image of the central Proudhon spires receding into the distance.

The sight was reassuring.

The *Lady* plowed north and the spires began to dim with the atmospheric haze. Evening came and the sky had assumed a purple cast by the time Proudhon had vanished completely in the desert behind her.

As she drove, she meditated on possible destinations. Eventually, she wanted to hit population. But the desert communes were going to be less welcoming to strangers than most. People came to this arid land for solitude. As the empty landscape shot by her, and the Diderot Mountains rolled away to her left, it was easy to see why.

The eastern half of the continent was her best bet, still. However, to achieve that without help from Dom and company—and she was rigorously trying to avoid thinking about Dom—she had to head northwest for nearly a thousand kilometers before there was a pass in the Diderot Range that she felt comfortable navigating. There were other passes, much more convenient ones, between here and there. However, all of them were much higher up in the mountains. She didn't want to try navigating those in her inexperience. Jarvis could probably do them blindfolded—but this was her first crack at a vehicle that touched the ground, and she had no idea what she'd do if she hung the *Lady* up on something.

A thousand-klick detour seemed reasonable, if she didn't want to risk stranding herself.

Darkness came long before she was halfway there. But camping was simply a matter of parking so the slowly advancing dunes wouldn't bury the *Lady*. The car was originally for exploration purposes, and was designed for a cramped crew of four. With only Tetsami aboard, the accommodations were palatial. There was a recycled-water shower, a bunk, a full ground station comm setup, a kitchen. All without counting Jarvis' modifications. Jarvis had installed a small machine shop that took up the space where two bunks used to be. He had also upgraded the sensor setup to include low-level radar, seismic sensors, mass sensors, and a host of geological equipment. The equipment included a trunk full of explosives and a mining laser.

When Tetsami pulled over for the night, she thought that she could very well go to ground in this thing and forget about dealing with communes or whatever. As long as she could get recharged and resupplied, the *Lady* could house her for months.

She could survive by herself indefinitely. That made it all the more troubling that, when she was trying to sleep, she began to regret leaving her peers in the Diderot Holding Company.

Worse, when she was on the fringe of sleep, she began to miss Dom.

Tetsami's first morning in the desert was unnerving.

The nose of the cab pointed east, and Kropotkin began blazing red light inside as soon as it peeked over the horizon. The windows polarized themselves against the glare, but the light still woke Tetsami up. And it woke her to silence. A silence that made her terribly aware of her own breathing.

The weight of the silence was suffocating.

She stumbled out of the bunk and opened one of the side doors on the *Lady,* letting in chill morning air. She stepped out into fine black sand and looked toward the horizon, shielding her eyes from the flaming ball of Kropotkin.

All the way to the horizon, there was nothing but black sand, a few rocks, and the occasional fleshy purple globe of a native Bakunin plant. Tetsami slowly turned. The scenes to the north and south were the same. To the west the band of the Diderot Mountains thrust up from the horizon, their snowcaps a violent pink in the morning light.

The only sign of humanity within Tetsami's sight was the *Lady.* Everything else was as if humans had never touched this planet. The sprawl of Proudhon had been effortlessly swallowed by the desert. Even the *Lady*'s tracks had been erased by the night winds.

Right now, Tetsami was the farthest she had ever been from another person. It gave her an empty feeling in the pit of her stomach, as if she were in free fall.

She ran back into the *Lady* and shut the door. She turned

on the sat substation to an audio broadcast. Any broadcast. She just needed to hear someone's voice.

"—apologize for the reduction in service. The Proudhon Spaceport Development Corporation regrets this temporary inconvenience. To repeat, areas 025-B through 356-H are closed for inspection, areas 356-I through 587-M are for priority outbound traffic only, passenger service is still under hiatus—"

Tetsami closed her eyes and shook her head weakly.

Come on, girl. Relax. It's no worse out there than a blank shell program.

She looked up, out the front windows, tuning out the broadcast. The wind outside slipped past the *Lady*'s blocky form with a dull moaning whistle.

God, that's creepy, Tetsami thought.

She brushed black sand from her pants and realized that she was still wearing the same clothes she'd been wearing when she'd left the New Yukon.

After showering and changing, Tetsami started the *Lady* back on her trek north and west. The dawn-lit landscape was surreal. She seemed to drive on an endless pane of rippled black glass.

Occasionally the *Lady* would run over a cannonball-sized plant, throwing purple juice and triangular seeds across the windscreen. After the third plant went splat, the nose of the *Lady* drove through a permanent cloud of nearly-invisible bugs that seemed little more than sand with wings.

Kropotkin had reached its zenith, high in a cloudless turquoise sky, before Tetsami saw her first sign of humanity—a pillar of black smoke drifting across the northeastern horizon, almost directly in line with her destination.

The *Lady* had an array of long-range sensors on her, so Tetsami knew pretty much what was there by the time she arrived. What she approached was one of the thousands of little communes that dotted the surface of Bakunin, even in such a bleak place as this desert.

The commune sat about two hundred and fifty klicks due east of the mountain pass she was aimed at. It had been a complex of buildings and connecting superstructure that radiated out from a central dome as if the whole complex was a splayed octopus. Smoke rose from at least five points within the embrace of the octopus' outflung arms.

Even though there was no immediate sign of any movement, Tetsami parked the *Lady* in a valley of the sand's standing wave and watched the commune from two klicks away. She sat there for nearly two hours, as midday passed into the afternoon, trying to max out the resolution on the *Lady*'s surplused cameras.

Nothing moved out there but the slowly dying smoke.

The first, and obvious, conclusion was that she was looking at the aftermath of a commune war. Despite—or perhaps because of—the idealism of the communes, they were often prone to warring among themselves. The commune wars were generally for one of two reasons. Most commonly, neighboring communes found themselves expanding into each other's territory, or competing for a limited resource that could be anything from fresh water to the local holotransmission airspace.

The rarer and much more ugly form of commune warfare was the ideological war. One force decided that a commune with a competing point of view should be eradicated from the face of the planet. Sometimes the decision was mutual. If communes banded together in a war like that, the results were very bad, involving scores of communes as well as the cities around them.

Around the time Tetsami was born, there had been a major conflagration involving five hundred communes. That last major explosion was why the New Aryan Front only had one commune left on Bakunin.

This *looked* like the aftermath of a commune war. An obvious conclusion. That was why Tetsami distrusted it.

It took her a while to figure out exactly what commune she was looking at. The *Lady*'s computer held an atlas that was much more accurate than the tourist guide she'd picked up in Proudhon. But while the *Lady*'s topographical surveys were second to nothing Tetsami had ever used before, the political info was years out of date. That was a major liability in the shifting sands of Bakunin, where political stability was an oxymoron.

Eventually she used the *Lady*'s sat ground station capability to leech onto a library database somewhere in Godwin. Political atlases were public domain sort of stuff and the only hacking she had to do was a few shells to hide the source of her signal from the spuds monitoring the sat.

With her updated atlas, all she had to do was hit the *La-*

dy's quirky locator a few times to get a fix on what she was looking at.

The octopus was the Ashley Commune. It was a hubbard. In other words, it was a utopian experiment based on somebody's—a Doctor Ashley presumably—bizarre psycho-anthro-sociological theories. Tetsami thought that, despite the fact that each hubbard was based on a specific some-one's original weirdness, they all ended up looking alike.

The fact that Ashley Commune was a hubbard made a commune war less likely. Hubbards tended to be too inner-directed to conflict with other communes over ideology. They were on their way to their own personal nirvana, after all. And in the wastes out here, Tetsami thought that, scarce as resources might be, the communes were too widely spaced to infringe on each other.

Just to make sure, Tetsami checked her updated atlas and determined that the closest commune to Ashley was Olympia. It was over a hundred fifty klicks away and, yes, it *was* someone's idea of a free-love paradise. Not on Tetsami's list of the ten communes most likely to undergo violent expansion.

All this research went on with the dark hill of a sand dune hiding most of the *Lady* from Ashley. The octopus had yet to show any signs of life, and the smoke had reduced itself to a few bare wisps. If there was anyone there left on a war footing, they would have noticed her by now and sent some challenge over the comm. The dune might hide her from a superficial eyeball search, but the *Lady*'s energy profile was as subtle as the rest of her.

No competent sentry could miss her, even at two klicks.

That meant that there were no competent sentries out there.

Tetsami only debated briefly with herself over investigating the scene. The damn thing was in her way. And, while she was out in the desert to *avoid* getting pulled into messes like this, it was pretty obvious that if she didn't get a good idea of what happened to Ashley Commune, the same thing could easily blindside her out here. Especially if she got caught out in the pass, which was essentially a diagonal line, a hundred klicks long, with very little room to maneuver.

She told herself that she was being as cold and logical as Dom, but her hands were sweaty inside her driving gloves.

Dom's hands didn't sweat.

Why are you thinking of him now?

Tetsami started the *Lady* moving. She spiraled in toward the commune so she could get a good look at each side of the place before she closed on it. With all the sensors pointed toward the commune, she soon saw what the smoke had come from. It wasn't from the buildings, which seemed intact for the most part. The five pillars of smoke came from distinct black piles *between* the arms of the octopus. Whatever the piles had been, it was impossible to see what they were at this distance. The *Lady*'s cameras could barely make out the char against the black sand, and that only because the piles still smoldered.

Tetsami was on the third spiral in when the *Lady* bucked over a hump that was much harder than it should have been. The impact threw Tetsami forward over the controls, and she drew the *Lady* to a halt.

Without the engine going, the desert reclaimed its silence. The silence—even the wind was dead for the moment—was even more disconcerting with the large humped forms of Ashley Commune only a half-klick away.

Tetsami left the *Lady* with a shiver.

The sand burned her feet, even through her boots. It was strange to have to endure this heat when Kropotkin was such a weak sun. Bakunin's thirty-two-hour day compensated for it. Sixteen hours of daylight, even from the red orb of Kropotkin, was enough to make things dangerously hot.

Tetsami was already sweating by the time she walked the five meters back to the dune that had obstructed the *Lady*'s progress. Even through the distorted heat shimmers, she could see that there was a major difference between this meter-tall hump of sand and its cousins.

The six-ton chassis of the *Lady* had left no tracks in its surface.

Two parallel trenches led up to the dune on one side, met the surface, and disappeared. The tracks only reappeared at the site of *Lady*'s landing.

Tetsami wiped away the sweat from her eyes and touched the surface of the dune. It looked like sand, but the surface was hard. It felt like some sort of composite.

She was looking at some sort of carbon-fiber sheet draped over something else. It was hard to see because the weave incorporated other materials that blended color and texture almost perfectly matched to the sand. She felt along the perimeter, burning her hands when she accidentally buried them in real sand piled against the windward side of the object.

She determined that the sheet was a single piece of camouflage, that the object it covered was mostly buried, and that the exposed surface was a meter high, about three meters long, and two meters wide at the widest point. The buried object was hard, sounded hollow in places, and was roughly teardrop-shaped.

There was no way for Tetsami to remove the carbon-fiber sheet by hand. Not without removing several tons of sand. So she went back to the *Lady* and pulled the mining laser out of storage.

As she set up the laser, she admired the camouflage. It was nearly perfect. It probably matched the sand up and down the spectrum. A contragrav could fly over it and miss it entirely. A satellite wouldn't have a clue. The only way to detect it would be to either pull a systematic mass scan of the desert, or to trip over the thing.

It took her about thirty minutes, and she gulped down about a gallon's worth of drinking water, but eventually she'd cut a ragged U with the tripod-mounted mining laser. With the cut in the covering she could pull away a flap of the camouflage.

When she did, it revealed something frightening, but not wholly unexpected.

The flap of camouflage had been covering part of the drive section of a military contragrav craft. Most of the contragrav was buried in the sand, and from the holes in the skin, under the camouflage sheet, it was irreparably damaged.

The markings were in the turquoise and black of Proudhon Spaceport Security.

Father, Son, and Holy Ghost in three-part harmony, Tetsami thought. *This I don't need.*

She'd just stumbled over Proudhon Security's covert op. *You don't go this far to hide the wreckage of a battle unless you're trying damn hard to be unobserved.*

Tetsami looked over the empty black plain and wondered how many other dunes held similar surprises.

She covered the exposed section of the contragrav. Then she broke down the mining laser and drove the *Lady* straight for Ashley. Suddenly she wanted very much to find out what had happened there.

CHAPTER THIRTEEN

Grandfather Clause

"It's never what you expect."
—*The Cynic's Book of Wisdom*

"Resist your time—take a foothold outside it."
—LORD ACTON
(1834–1902)

Dom still wanted to talk to Tetsami, but he was becoming thankful that she had gotten off-planet. Something was brewing here, with Klaus, the Confederacy, and the TEC, and that meant that it was almost certainly something bad. Past and present crises threatened to swamp him, and it was fortunate for her that she wasn't involved.

So far, after a day of brooding, he still couldn't come to grips with what was happening here. If the TEC had a plan beyond Klaus' own designs, Dom couldn't see what it was. But he should have.

All the blood I've shed in their name, and I can't see what they're doing.

Everyone else here seemed to share Dom's tunnel vision. Revenge had been an accepted reason for Klaus' takeover of GA&A. It was a Bakuninite motive, a human motive.

But there were SEEC warships in orbit. Whatever had happened, was happening, was *going* to happen, involved more than Colonel Klaus Dacham's bloody-minded hunt for his brother. It involved the States of the Confederacy, a whole nest of motives and politics that Bakunin natives were willingly blind to. Absurd that Bakuninites would be blind to anything involving chaotic politics, but Dom had seen the blindness operate. He suffered from it himself.

The Confederacy was something "out there." Never mind

that Bakunin was surrounded by at least three different arms of the Confederacy.

At the moment, Dom was trying to come to grips with them "down here."

Zanzibar was showing him the latest view of Godwin Arms & Armaments, now wholly Klaus' operation. The video came from an observation platform mounted at the end of a kilometer-long tunnel terminating five hundred meters above the conference room Dom sat in.

The small observer dome was high on the west face of the tallest mountain on this stretch of the Diderot Range and camouflaged to be invisible to anyone more than twenty meters away. It was remote-operated by a communications laser farther down the mountain. The sensor package had been placed by robots which had then done their best to destroy any possible physical access to it.

The whole thing was part of a series of remote lookouts that had been had been completed and on-line for about two weeks, and gave them wide-spectrum views of everything between Godwin and Jefferson City, as well as a few kilometers beyond in both directions. The system was even capable of tight-beam communications.

It was the best system for looking over the horizon, short of a spy sat. In fact, the only better view of Godwin that Dom had ever had was with GA&A's own spy sat, since a casualty of Klaus' takeover.

The holo display showed the Godwin Arms complex from nearly overhead. Most of the scars on the buildings were gone.

Dom felt a familiar chill, and a tightness in his gut. He felt desecrated when he looked at that. Not only was it his company down there, seven years of his work, crushed. But it was the damn Confederacy, too, government drones operating in the name of some State.

Zanzibar fiddled with the console and the scene shifted slightly to show the landing field the Confed troops had made outside the perimeter towers. The field had served as parking space for two Barracuda-class troop-carriers.

One of the ships was missing.

"How often?" Dom asked Zanzibar, feeling Klaus' hands clutch at his gut.

"The ship leaves in the morning, returns the next night," Zanzibar said.

"Never the *Blood-Tide?*"

Klaus' ship, *Blood-Tide*, was a Confed troop-carrier. It was an over-armed dropship that could have taken out a city a dozen times GA&A's size. When the takeover had happened, Dom had been expecting the cargo ship *Prometheus*. Instead, the *Blood-Tide* and the hundred-plus marines aboard her had taken Godwin Arms & Armaments with its inventory, and production facility, intact.

"No," Zanzibar prodded the display where one ship was still parked. "That's the *Blood-Tide* there, you can see the pulse cannon in the nose."

"Where does the cargo ship go?"

Dom didn't need to ask what the cargo ship carried. GA&A only manufactured weapons. GA&A could be at full production, and could be shipping it—*all* of it—somewhere. Daily.

Goddamn it, why?

You don't put all those arms in somebody's hands, even on Bakunin, and not have something explode. There wasn't a force on the planet that could absorb those kind of shipments. At least, Dom fervently hoped not.

"They pass through the mountains somewhere. They never go extra-atmospheric, so we don't have any real way to track them."

"Could you have Random hack a spy sat?"

"We've tried to get at the Proudhon Traffic Control programs. But the Confed ship doesn't use a standard transponder."

Dom had an ugly suspicion, "Proudhon doesn't challenge it?"

"No," Zanzibar shook her head.

She saw the same things he did. She probably saw them clearer since she didn't wade through his memories of Executive Command. Proudhon had been accepting of a dozen things from the Confederacy and the TEC that should have ignited challenges at best, shots from their orbital linac at worst.

But nothing. Proudhon was perfectly accepting of Confed treading all over their monopoly. That meant that either Proudhon was completely ignorant of everything going on under its nose—or Proudhon was in on it, up to its neck.

It would have been obvious earlier, if it wasn't for that Bakuninite blind spot. A blindness that kept them from seeing that some Bakuninites might actually accept, and work *with,* the Confederacy.

Dom's gut felt like ice.

"Are we going to do anything about this?" Zanzibar asked.

Dom wondered if Zanzibar had noticed how much their relationship had changed. When Dom had been CEO at GA&A, she never would have led a question at him like that. In the seven years they'd worked together at GA&A she had never questioned him, even implicitly.

Dom turned his back to her and the holo. "Are you suggesting that there's something we *could* do?"

"It feels like we should do *something.*"

Yes, Dom thought, *somebody should do something. But with my history, I'm the last person to ask. I'm nobody's hero, and in a fight between Bakunin and the TEC, I am the last champion you'd want.*

"I understand your feeling. But we have to keep a low profile. If Klaus ever gets the suspicion that we're still active, he might target us again. We've got twelve hundred people here to think of."

Dom walked toward the door to the control room.

"But," Zanzibar said, "as long as Klaus is down there, we run that risk."

Dom turned around and looked at her. Her arms were folded across her chest and the worry in her eyes made her look less like a warrior. Dom felt an uncharacteristic urge to reach out and reassure her.

He stood where he was and said, "Not *we.* Me."

Zanzibar stared at him as if the distinction meant nothing.

Dom went on. "Klaus has an agenda from the TEC. What he has against *me* is personal. The TEC only wanted GA&A's facility. The TEC didn't order the targeting of GA&A's personnel. That was Klaus trying to hurt *me.*"

"So?" Zanzibar swung an arm out uselessly.

"Remove me from the picture and Klaus has no motive for attacking our operation." Dom said it slowly, as if he had just realized it himself.

The silence in the room was interminable. Dom felt a need to continue filling it. "After we take over Bleek Munitions, I intend to disappear."

Running away again, Dom thought.

But what else can I do? Should I stay and draw Klaus'

fire down on all these people? Klaus' personal vendetta has already taken more lives than I care to think about.

"Dominic?" Dom realized that Zanzibar was using his first name. It was the first time in his memory that she'd done so. She hesitated for a long time before she asked, "What happened between you and Klaus?"

It was the first time in seven years that Zanzibar had asked him a personal question.

What *had* happened? Why did his brother want to kill him?

It made Dom think of Styx again.

"We're twins," Dom said. "We're too much alike. Much too much alike. I don't think either of us can bear it."

He left Zanzibar before she could ask for an explanation.

After the meeting with Zanzibar, Dom felt hollow and useless.

He was still coming to terms with the idea of abandoning his operation as soon as it bore fruit. The thought was a deep ache inside him, even though he knew that—even without Klaus gunning for him—there was no longer any way he could rationalize his profession to himself.

He wished he could have run like Tetsami ran. Wished he could have gone *with* her. He wished he didn't have the ties to the people in this mountain that kept him here. He wished he was someone else.

Especially now.

Styx had been eating into his mind like a virulent fungus. It clouded his vision, and in every memory he now put Ivor's face on Commander Elision. Dom was undergoing enough reality slippage in the present without having to revise his past.

He had to resolve it. He had to talk to Ivor.

The very thought iced his heart deeper even than the thought of Klaus down the mountains in GA&A.

Dom found Ivor in the cafeteria, a gigantic cavern whose tables were sawed-off stalagmites. Ivor was off by himself, at the very edge of the lighting. The cavern didn't stop where Ivor sat, but trailed off into yet more unused caverns.

Past Ivor, the caves were so dark that it looked like a hunk of interstellar void had been stuffed inside the mountain. The only boundary the cafeteria had on that side was a red rope warning off casual spelunking. Ivor was about a dozen meters out on the wrong side of the rope.

Dom ducked under the rope and walked up to the giant white-haired man.

"Hello?" Ivor said as Dom reached him.

Dom realized that, in all the time since Ivor had come on board the operation, he had never been alone with this man. Dom felt the beginning of a facial tic. He managed to control it.

"Can we talk?"

Ivor stood up. "Sure."

Dom took a few more paces into the darkness and Ivor followed, stumbling and cursing.

"Where are you going?"

"Nowhere." Dom said, stopping a few meters into the black. Ivor nearly plowed into him, but Dom held up a hand, stopping his progress. Ivor didn't have Dom's adjustable photoreceptors to acclimate him to the dark.

The cafeteria was now a bright glow barely hidden by a forest of rock formations. Ivor felt around and found a stalagmite to lean up against. "What's on your mind, son?"

A lot of things, Dom thought. "Styx," Dom said.

Dom expected that to trigger a floodgate of accusations against him, perhaps even an attempt on his life. However, Ivor didn't attack him, verbally or physically. Ivor simply turned back toward the cafeteria and said, "No comment."

"Commander Elision?"

Ivor's shoulders slumped. "Let it lie."

Dom had expected some sort of confrontation. In some ways, he might have even been hoping for it.

"Are you Elision?"

"Robert Elision's dead."

"I know," Dom said. "I killed him."

Ivor turned around. Ivor's steel-blue irises were swallowed by his pupils. His expression was unreadable.

"That wasn't an answer to my question," Dom said. "Are you Robert Elision?"

With a toneless voice Ivor said, "I'm his ghost."

Ivor wasn't talking metaphorically.

It explained how Ivor could be a man who died fifteen years ago. It explained why Ivor looked ten years older than

Elision should be. It explained why Ivor had a reputation on
Bakunin that stretched back twenty years.

Ivor was a ghost.

Up until the time humans had come across the Paralians,
and discovered the Paralian physics that made a tach-drive
possible, human interstellar transport relied on engineered
wormholes. The wormholes—a marriage of quantum mechanics and relativity—had a number of drawbacks.

The holes were hideously expensive to build. Maintenance
was cheap once they were in place, but initially shooting the
hole across the void, and then pumping it to reasonable size,
was a tremendous expenditure of energy. Once they were of
usable size their mass fixed them in place.

However, the most important drawback was the fact that
travel was limited by the speed of light. Even though travel
from the entrance of the hole to the exit seemed instantaneous for the traveler, from the universe's perspective the journey would take years.

This wasn't a simple adherence to relativity. A wormhole
was a point of physical connection not only between two
points in space, but two points in *time*. The 4.5 light-year-
long wormhole from Earth to Occisis extended from a point
orbiting Sol to a point orbiting Alpha Centauri 4.5 years in
the future.

It was this connection that produced ghosts, because the
connection worked *both* ways.

In one direction, Earth to Occisis, the traveler would exit
four and a half years later—superficially obeying relativistic
common sense.

If the traveler tried the reverse journey through the same
wormhole, from Occisis to Earth, he would emerge four and
a half years *earlier.*

From the traveler's perspective, he had just moved into
his own past.

From the universe's perspective, the wormhole had just
coughed up a ghost. A virtual person. A spontaneous fluctu-
ation of the quantum equations governing the wormhole.

The view had to be that way. A ghost was from a possible
future, a future the ghost changed simply by existing in its
own past. When someone looks down a wormhole into the
past, it will agree with the past as he knows it. When he

looks up the wormhole, to the future, he sees an unreliable boiling chaos.

It was a basic asymmetry that allowed scientists, who still clung religiously to causality, to define ghosts as quantum fluctuations blown up to the macroscopic level.

That helped justify first the Terran Council's, and then the Confederacy's, "control" of ghosts. No stable political structure would willingly allow interference from an unreliable, shifting future, and the Terran Council had a vested interest in keeping the wormholes one-way.

So, the policy was to destroy anything that came through the wrong end of the wormhole. It was simple and efficient. And since the policy was known even to those up the line in the infinity of manifold futures, it deterred the creation of ghosts in the first place.

Even if the ghost escaped the automated battle stations guarding the wormhole's mouth, the legacy of fortress Earth from the diaspora was the fact that the legal existence of a ghost was denied throughout the Confederacy. Legally, a ghost was not a person.

That was all history.

For over a hundred years the main mode of interstellar travel had been the Paralian tach-drive. Ghosts were the stuff of tall tales. . . .

"The man I—" Dom began.

"That man had to be eleven years removed from any connection with me."

The noise from the cafeteria was strangely muted. Somewhere water dripped.

Dom didn't know what to say.

After a while Ivor asked, "What did you expect?"

"Hmm?"

"Do you want me to be angry? Sad? What the hell does Commander Robert Elision have to do with me now? That's half my life ago."

"I'm sorry," Dom said. "It just shook me."

He pushed past Ivor and started back for the cafeteria. He felt a massive hand on his shoulder. "Wait."

Dom turned.

"I know what happened on Styx."

"You *should* be angry."

Ivor shook his head. "I start blaming people, and the first tar on that brush hits me."

"I don't understand you."

"I had the ego to believe I knew enough to change my own past for the better. I was very wrong." Ivor released him. "It took a disaster to teach me to let go of the past."

Dom thought, *What if the past won't let go of you?*

CHAPTER FOURTEEN

Collateral Damage

"Guns don't kill people, bullets do."
—*The Cynic's Book of Wisdom*

"You got to duck or you got to shoot."
—DATIA RAJASTHAN
(?–2042)

After the death of her parents, Tetsami had one recurring
nightmare. She was left running through the corridors of a
huge empty building. Running from room to room, finding
no people. Calling for her parents and only being answered
by her own echoes. The dream had terrified her, often waking her in tears.

Ashley was that dream.

As Tetsami wandered through the buildings of Ashley, she
had to make an effort to clamp down on that terror from her
childhood. She had wandered the halls for nearly three hours
now.

No one.

Not a single person graced the halls of Ashley Commune.

There weren't even any bodies, only the frightening and
enigmatic piles of ashes. Ashes she did not want to sift
through. From their appearance, the black mounds of
charred debris were the remains of every vehicle in the commune. Five compact formations of vehicles, all torched.
Without coming close to the still-hot piles, Tetsami could
count the remains of at least twenty different vehicles, now
so much slag.

She hoped that the vehicles were the only things that had
been torched. She hoped the rancid-sweet smell in the air,
like overdone pork, was in her imagination.

She wandered through the commune and the signs became even more horrifying.

Meals sat at tables, partially eaten. A nursery had cushions ringing a single chair, a picture book card-reader sat on the chair frozen in the midst of a page. Nearby, a classroom was paused in the midst of a lesson, computers on tables, a half-written sentence charred into the dead holoboard behind the teacher's desk. Small go-carts were halted in the center of walkways. Some still held packages that had never reached their destination. Empty elevators were trapped between floors.

Fifty thousand people, that's what the *Lady*'s new atlas said the population of Ashley was.

Every single one of them was gone.

A smell like overcooked meat.

Tetsami felt sick.

She desperately wanted to jack into the commune's core computer, buzz the security program, discover what had happened. But it only took a cursory look at a few terminals to see that the whole Ashley net had been scragged. An electromagnetic pulse had wiped the whole place. None of Ashley's electronics seemed hardened, and every bit of volatile memory in the commune would be thoroughly EMPed.

"Does anyone know this has happened?" Tetsami asked, surprising herself with her own voice.

The answer was obvious as she replaced the panels of Ashley's DOA sat ground station.

No.

A surprise attack. The whole area was washed by an EMP. Power supply, the communications, the holoboard, the picture book, all killed with one shot. When the troops came down from the dunes, there'd be some resistance, but not much. Ashley never expected to be attacked. It had precious little defense.

They had to surrender.

Then?

"Then, after the attackers account for everybody, they flame every vehicle from the commune to make sure anyone they missed wouldn't make it over the desert out there."

But the people?

No, please, not in the vehicles . . .

Tetsami's voice sounded cracked, and she told herself it was because her throat was dry.

Ashley was dead. Even if the people had survived the attack, the EMP was a deathblow to the commune. Without power or electronics there was no environment control, no fresh water, no scrubbing outside the dome. The desert would swallow Ashley within a few weeks.

Tetsami reached for her water bottle and found it empty. That was her sign to leave. She'd been draining water in here almost as fast as she filled the bottle. There had been a number of gravity-filled water coolers throughout Ashley, and she'd been topping off her bottle as she went, but the commune was an oven. Even out of Kropotkin's glare, Tetsami thought that any more time in here would invite heat stroke.

She snaked her way back along the octopus' arms, making better time now that she was no longer examining the details she passed.

When she emerged into open air, night had begun to claim the desert. When she entered the *Lady*, she feared that her groundcar would be as dead as the commune, as if the EMP was contagious.

The *Lady* surged to life without a problem.

Thinking of Ashley's fate made Tetsami's hand drift to the back of her neck, to the dimple of flesh marking her biolink.

She wondered how many had died in the pulse.

Ignorant people thought an EMP wasn't an antipersonnel weapon. An electromagnetic pulse only fried electronics, after all. True. But it also fried cybernetics, which might be a little uncomfortable if your heart was artificial. An EMP in space was a deadly weapon that could turn an unshielded spacecraft into an overpriced coffin.

For someone with direct wiring to the brain it would be an instant electrostatic lobotomy.

Even behind the polyceram armor shell of the *Lady*, Tetsami began to feel incredibly vulnerable.

The desert was no longer a welcoming host. Out here, somewhere, was a large group of people she didn't want to meet. She drove the *Lady* in a circle around Ashley and pointed her east, to catch up with the mountains, and her destination. Two hundred and fifty klicks away from Ashley was a cleft in the Diderot Range that descended nearly to sea level. Her passage west.

She wanted to call someone on the *Lady*'s ground station, but she was terrified that even a tight-beam broadcast might reveal her location. It was paranoid, and she almost used her sat uplink a number of times. Each time it felt like too much of a risk.

She just concentrated on putting as much distance between her and Ashley as she could. The *Lady* flew across the dunes, heedless of Tetsami's ability to control her. Twice she almost lost control. The third time the *Lady* was close to seventy klicks per and bumped up on an invisible rock on the downward side of a large dune. Both wheels on the right side left the ground and the left side of the nose plowed into sand.

The jolt made Tetsami realize she needed sleep.

After spending fifteen minutes getting the *Lady*'s nose unburied and determining that the damage was superficial— one headlight smashed—Tetsami crawled into the back and collapsed on her bunk.

Tetsami awoke to bright red sunlight and the sound of rushing water. It took her a few minutes to realize that the sound she heard was the comm part of the *Lady*'s ground station. The comm was still on, from her repeated abortive efforts last night to get herself to use the thing.

Tetsami turned over and looked out the front. All she could see was the dune that had nearly swallowed her last night. The chrono on the dash, next to the locator, told her that it was nearly eleven in the morning. She must have really exerted herself to have slept as long as she had.

She felt like hell.

She peeled off the clothes she'd slept in and ran herself through the shower. It was only marginally effective. Her muscles still ached, her head throbbed gently, and none of the clothes she had left were very clean.

The ground station comm burbled on.

She went on the comm and tried to tune in a channel. She *had* been overly paranoid last night. She should get word back east about what was going on in the desert. Any army out here was much more likely to find her from an overflight than from a tight sat transmission.

She was more vulnerable to eyeballs than radios.

The ground station didn't want to work. Everything she tuned to piped in static.

"Don't tell me I scragged the thing in the last bump."

That looked to be the case. She could tune in absolutely nothing. "Shit."

She killed the comm, turned on the rear video, and began backing out of the pit that the *Lady* had nearly made for herself last night. The *Lady* was a trouper about it. The tires dug into the sand and pulled her out of trouble almost as quickly as she had gotten into it.

As Tetsami pulled the car out into the open desert again, she noted that the rear video looked fuzzier than usual. "Not another thing broken—I want my money back. . . ."

Even as she said it, she knew something was wrong.

No.

It wasn't damage to the video. It was radio interference.

No, come on.

Tetsami flicked the sat comm back on and scanned the channels. It finally registered what she was seeing.

"Oh, dear sweet Jesus, girl. What a fucking idiot! They're jamming you. They're saturating the area with RF interference. They know you're here. They're looking for you."

Tetsami could hear her knuckles pop as she tried to strangle the *Lady's* controls. Even as she goosed her vehicle to go ever faster, Tetsami could see black dots on the horizon in the rear video.

Turquoise and black dots.

She knew it was hopeless, even as she forced the *Lady* to skip dunes like a rock across the ripples of a frozen pond. The spuds behind her were riding military contragravs, and they were armed. The only weapons on the *Lady* were the mining laser, in a locker by the bunks, and Tetsami's laser sidearm that would do precious little to an armored vehicle.

Tetsami kept on the throttle, nevertheless. If she couldn't outrun them, perhaps she could outrun their radio interference, if only for a moment. If she could get out from under the worst of the ECM, even for a moment, she might be able to get off a message.

With that in mind, she turned the ship's computer on to record. As the *Lady* hopped dunes and shook Tetsami around like some monster rodeo animal, Tetsami yelled at the computer's audio pickup.

"I'm Kari Tetsami." Tetsami had the air knocked out of her as the *Lady* jumped a dune. "I'm about to be captured or killed by Proudhon Spaceport Security. Proudhon is—" Another jump, another thump. "—conducting a massive military operation in the desert north of the spaceport. I think they've bought every mercenary that cruised the port. They've destroyed at least one commune. The Ashley Commune. Fifty thousand people, gone."

Tetsami slammed the repeat button after crashing over another dune.

With the sat transmitter on wideband, some of that might get through somewhere. She looked out the rear video and saw five contragravs now, only a half-kick back at best. She saw that and tried to goose just a little extra speed from the *Lady.*

Tetsami fulfilled Jarvis' prediction and rolled her.

CHAPTER FIFTEEN

Disclosure

"Much morality is there for the perception of others."

—*The Cynic's Book of Wisdom*

"God will forgive me; that's his business."

—HEINRICH HEINE
(1797–1856)

After two days, Ivor's visits forced Shane to be a human being again. She could turn herself into a vegetable when she was left to herself, but not when she could see herself through another's eyes. Ivor didn't even have to say anything about it. Just the presence of another person made Shane disgusted with the way she was acting.

Guilt was one thing, suicidal self-pity was another.

But, while Ivor's handful of visits forced her into considering things like eating, and hygiene, and human contact, it did little to ameliorate the central darkness within her, the fact that she had repudiated her entire life. She had ended up killing people that once were—no other word really fit—once were her family. The Occisis marines had been all she had.

She had cut herself off, with nothing left to fill the void. Nominally, she had a part of this "corporation" Dominic Magnus had built in the mountains. This "corporation" struck Shane more as a band of pirates or a guerrilla army.

In theory she had a place here.

In practice, Shane doubted it. No one trusts a turncoat, and that's what she was, in the end. Never mind the fact that she'd saved over eight hundred civilians, never mind that her participation in the raid on GA&A was intended to be bloodless. She was still a traitor.

Even in an anarchy like Bakunin, that carried weight. It carried, perhaps, even more weight. Few organizations on this planet had the power to compel loyalty; loyalty became a premium. The devotion here, in this mountain, between employer and employee, seemed almost feudal to Shane.

She didn't fit.

But she prodded herself into human contact anyway because if she stayed locked in a room, she would eventually decide that eating a laser would be a good idea.

Two days after Ivor's first visit there was a board meeting that seemed a good enough excuse. She owned part of this company, supposedly.

The meeting was Mosasa's and Flower's briefing on the plan they'd formed to take over Bleek Munitions. It was the first meeting Shane had attended since she had been injured, thirty-two Bakunin days ago.

For her participation in the assault on GA&A she could either take part in this, or take the twenty-five megagrams due her for betraying her people.

Not bad, she thought, *Judas only got thirty pieces of silver.*

From her seat at the conference table, Shane could tell that a lot had changed. For one thing, there was an empty seat. When she'd taken her seat next to Ivor, she asked about it.

Ivor responded with a curt, "Tetsami left."

That was disturbing. Not that Shane had ever gotten to know Tetsami very well, but the entire assault on GA&A had been Tetsami's plan. Tetsami had engineered the theft of 435 megagrams worth of hard currency out from under Colonel Klaus Dacham's nose—435 megagrams of Dom's money. Tetsami's work had financed everything that happened in this mountain warren.

So far, Tetsami had been the only one to take the twenty-five megagram share instead of a seat on the board.

Shane could see that Tetsami's absence was not the only change. Dom seemed to have changed radically. He hardly commented on the proceedings, and he observed everything with a hollow stare. Shane wondered if Tetsami's absence was having any effect on Dom. Shane had suspected that there was more going on there than simple business, but she'd never inquired.

Both Ivor and Zanzibar seemed very careful with their

words, as if anything they might say could have terrible consequences. Both of them kept looking at Dom, as if looking for cues that weren't forthcoming.

Only Mosasa and Flower seemed unchanged, and if either of them noted the tense dynamics of the room, their presentation gave no sign. *The only two people acting normally in this room,* Shane thought, *are the alien and the android.*

Shane wondered if any of the others had discovered that Mosasa was as much a construct as the AI he supposedly shepherded. She also wondered what Random Walk, that AI, was thinking as he sat invisibly behind the observation cameras.

She wondered what she was doing here.

Shane briefly paid attention to the plan to take over Bleek. There was no slot in the plan crafted for her, and it was just as well. From the sound it was almost a military op, and she was still learning to use the cybernetics that had replaced her limbs.

And they're calling this a "friendly takeover?" This is a crazy planet.

I want to go home.

When the meeting broke up, she followed Ivor down a corridor and grabbed his arm.

"Ivor?"

"Yes?" He seemed somewhat startled, as if she'd broken in on some train of thought.

"I want to see Hougland."

While the board had debated the strike to extract Ezra Bleek from his own basement, Shane had come to the realization that she was never going to heal any of her self-inflicted psychic wounds without confronting her comrade.

"Ah ..." Ivor responded.

Hougland was their one Confed prisoner. She'd been taken during the Godwin Arms break-in. Hougland had been one of Shane's people, a corporal in the Occisis marines, and Shane was responsible for her imprisonment. Shane had fired the stunner that had knocked Hougland out.

"Are you sure?" Ivor asked.

"It's long past time," Shane said, even though her stomach was beginning to have second thoughts.

"If you say so." Ivor began to lead her along a side passage. "I'll take you down there."

Locked in her room, Shane had never realized how far the tunnels extended. The tunnel they walked was straight—more or less—and on a gentle downward slope. The only signs of human intervention were the lights mounted every ten meters, and the few points where the floor of the tunnel had been carved flat.

They walked along it, in silence, for nearly fifteen minutes.

"How far do these tunnels go?" Shane said to break the silence.

"They're everywhere," Ivor said. "Legend says that you can walk from pole to pole underneath the Diderot Range."

From the feeling in Shane's ears, they had descended quite a distance. It felt warmer and more humid. She had the suspicion that they had dropped below sea level.

Finally, the tunnel's walls slipped away into a huge cup-shaped cavern. Even with the lights dotting the walls, Shane couldn't see the ceiling of the chamber. The ragged bowl was a hundred meters in diameter at its widest point, and the floor was dotted with slabs of broken stone and gravel.

By the entrance to their tunnel stood a desk, behind which sat a bored-looking guard. The guard seemed fully absorbed in running diagnostics on a plasma rifle.

Shane had routinely done such chores every day for most of her professional life, and the scene brought a wave of irrational nostalgia. Her stomach sank and she suddenly wondered whether or not she really wanted to see Corporal Hougland.

She looked at Ivor and was glad she'd had him bring her here. She wouldn't back out in front of him. Seeing Hougland, facing her, was essential to Shane's being able to live with herself again—

But she knew every minute of it would be agonizing.

Ivor held out his hand and stopped in front of the desk. Shane started to move closer and Ivor held her back.

"See that groove in the rock?" Ivor asked.

"Oh . . ."

"There's a standing stun field just over the line." Ivor grunted for the guard's attention.

The guard, who looked no more than eighteen, glanced up from his plasma rifle and nearly dropped the multimeter he was using when he saw them. Shane saw his reaction and had more uncomfortable flashbacks. His reaction was just

the right kind of frazzled for a grunt who, without any warning, has a commanding officer injected into his daily routine.
When she'd commanded a whole company, she'd tried not
to inspire that response in her troops, but she knew a *lot* of
colonels who would have produced that reaction in her.

Twelve hundred people in this mountain looked at her as
part of the command structure now. The idea churned her already boiling stomach.

Ivor had the guard clear them and drop the stun field.

They passed over the line and the field reinstated itself.

The guard's desk, Shane noted as they passed, was very
simple. The only things on it were an alphanumeric keypad,
a holo display, and a large red button.

Ivor stood by the guard. "This is your business, I'll wait
for you here. Just avoid any lines on the ground."

"Where is she?"

Ivor pointed.

Shane picked her way across the massive bowl of rock.
Hougland's cell was directly opposite the guard station. As
Shane made her way to it she saw that Hougland was not the
only prisoner this place had been designed to hold. Large
cubes had been excavated from cracks in the rock wall and
fronted with bars. Shane counted at least a dozen down here.
All of the cells faced the open center of the bowl, all of them
in view of the guard station. Every crack that seemed a tunnel out was fronted by the grooved warning of a stun field.
In some places the generator marking the center of the field
was visible, a brushed-metal sphere perched on the point of
a stalagmite. In most others, the generator was hidden
above, in the darkness.

Hougland's was the only occupied cell, and Shane reached
it before she was ready to.

Hougland had a cube of rock that was five meters on a
side, spacious for a prison cell. The door to the cell was a diagonal crack in the rock wall that narrowed to barely a meter
across at the floor. Bars were set in the rock, apparently
meant to withdraw upward when needed.

The interior of the cell was neat, kept to military specs.
But the walls, and the floor, were covered by an explosion
of color. Most of the cell was wrapped in a mural. Starships
streaked through an imaginary void, amazingly lifelike planets were frozen in orbit around painted suns that almost hurt
to look at.

Hougland was on her hands and knees, drawing the outline of a ringed gas giant that would take up three-quarters of the floor. Shane noted that the mural stopped in a razor-sharp line, about two meters from the entrance to the cell. That was where a standing stun field would keep the prisoner out of reach of the door.

Shane watched Hougland draw, unable to say anything.

She stood there for a long time, long past the point where she knew Hougland was aware of her. Hougland completed the perimeter of the innermost ring on the planet before she stood up and faced the door.

Shane saw that Hougland had lost a lot of weight. The gray jumpsuit hung on her, catching on her bone structure with unflattering accuracy. Her hands were a smear of color from the painting, a violent contrast to the military precision with which Hougland kept everything else. Hougland's face was pale and narrow now, making her eyes appear larger and sadder.

The only thing that had remained the same was her hair. Hougland's brunette skullcap was still meticulously kept in an Occisis-style crewcut, the transverse strips on her skull marking her place in the Occisis hierarchy as well as insignia.

Shane ran her hand through her own hair and realized how long it had become.

"At first I didn't believe it," Hougland said. She put down the palette she'd been using and stared at Shane with weary eyes.

The stare was painful, but Shane couldn't tear her eyes away.

"Why are you down here, Captain? To gloat?"

Shane couldn't say anything.

"You had us fooled. We thought you were a marine. We could count on you." Hougland's voice was raising slowly. "All shit. *All fucking shit!*"

Something broke the jam in her throat and Shane yelled back. "Yes, damn it, I am a fucking traitor!"

Hougland closed her mouth.

"Whatever you think of me, you're right. I wish to God I had done something else." Saying that seemed to loosen the knot in Shane's stomach.

"Why?" Hougland said.

"Justify it?" Shane shook her head. "I can barely justify

it to myself. Anything I said would come across as a cheap rationalization."

"I deserve some explanation."

Shane finally lowered her eyes. "I thought I was saving lives."

It poured out, the whole story. From the point where she first believed that Colonel Dacham was a nut, to helping the GA&A civilians escape the stare of a plasma cannon, to becoming involved with Dominic Magnus, to the point when she found herself firing a plasma rifle in the hold of the *Blood-Tide*.

Hougland looked at her with an appraising stare. "You fired a plasma weapon in an enclosed space?"

Shane looked at her new hands and closed them. They almost matched her old ones. "It was an exotic form of suicide."

"You thought you were saving lives?" Hougland's tone was sarcastic.

Shane thought of the squad of marines that had been on the business end of her plasma rifle when she fired it. The weapon was called "pocket sunshine" for a reason. Shane winced.

"I thought if I could help Dom's team get in and out unobserved, I could save the marines casualties."

Hougland snorted. "I hope you're not asking for forgiveness."

"No." Shane looked up. "That's God's territory."

"Then what do you want from me, Captain?"

"Nothing."

A silence stretched to the breaking point before Hougland asked, "Why are you here?"

"You said it. You deserve an explanation."

"Why don't you explain it to a court-martial?"

Shane decided there wasn't anything more to say. Hougland stood there, unmoved and unmoving. Shane shrugged and turned to go.

"Captain," Hougland said.

Shane turned.

"You might have been right about the civilians."

Shane waited for more, but Hougland picked up her palette and returned to her planet on the floor.

A small concession, Shane thought, *but one I didn't ask for.*

Shane walked from the cell feeling better, even without absolution. *God,* Shane silently prayed, *don't let her turn back and realize that she spent her life defending something she doesn't believe in. I may deserve it. She doesn't.*

Shane looked back at the mural-shrouded cell.

Good luck, she thought at Hougland.

CHAPTER SIXTEEN

Checks and Balances

"Money isn't everything, and neither is anything else."

—*The Cynic's Book of Wisdom*

"There is nothing permanent except change."

—HERACLEITUS
(ca. 540–ca. 480 B.C.)

Dom sat behind his desk and brooded on his future.

Soon, the preparation for the Bleek Munitions takeover would be complete. Soon, perhaps with Ezra Bleek's blessing, the Diderot Holding Company would buy out the third largest munitions company on Bakunin. Dom had gone over the plan a dozen times, but had found nothing he could improve on. Even the delicate shifting of assets through the computer net—the wooing of the last few shareholders, the negotiations with the bank—even that was being handled by Random Walk, who could be several places at once.

When that mission was complete, his personal obligation to the twelve hundred people in this mountain would be almost over. They would have back their lives, their homes, and their work.

His obligation would be almost over. Dom couldn't stay with Bleek as long as Klaus was out there. Dom couldn't allow those twelve hundred people to be Klaus' lever on him. Dom had to disappear.

He would leave and let Bleek roll by under new management and GA&A's surviving employees. Leave with twenty-five megs. There was no reason why that money couldn't last him the rest of his life. No law of nature said he had to be an exec, command people. With that money and some work on his identity he could even return to the Confederacy. He could become lost in the mass of fifty billion human ciphers out there.

Dom put his face in his hands.

"I can do it. Klaus *has* to believe I'm dead."

No. Not the Confederacy.

Dom knew the Confederacy wasn't a real option. He hadn't been able to disappear in the chaos of Bakunin, even with a rebuilt body and a new name. He couldn't *possibly* disappear into the Confederacy with its paranoid States, with its bureaucracy, its monitors, and not with the TEC's eyes behind everything, watching. Dom had been an officer of the TEC, he knew how much the Executive Command's intelligence service saw—

Planets which believed that the Confederacy's primary purpose was to preserve planetary sovereignty would be appalled.

No, he had to disappear, really disappear. Outside of suicide, Dom only knew of two options that would truly erase him from the Confederacy, permanently.

One option was Ivor's. If Dom could travel the wrong way through part of the old Terran Council's wormhole network, he would effectively sever his connection with this universe. He would reside in his own past, and the future he knew would change chaotically simply because of his own presence. He'd be a ghost.

The problem—Bakunin wasn't part of the old wormhole network, and Dom would have to travel at least fifteen light-years to find a usable wormhole. Also, Ivor might be a good enough pilot to outmaneuver the automated battle stations that were supposed to keep out refugees from the future, but Dom wasn't.

The other option he had was Proteus.

He'd run away, again. It was a habit that was becoming hard to break. He wondered if Tetsami's presence might have been able to convince him not to. Dom thought that it probably would. Dom wondered, if that had been the case, whether he'd have the nerve to admit why he was staying. He doubted it.

Someone buzzed at his door.

Dom raised his face. "Come in."

The door slid aside, and there stood Kathy Shane, short, freckled, curly red hair fitted tight to her skull. For some reason she reminded Dom of Tetsami, which was strange, since the two women only had their height in common.

"Do you have a minute?" she asked.

"I have all the time in the world." Dom rubbed his forehead and felt the other hand drumming the desktop. His thoughts started revolving around Tetsami, light-years away by now. He tried to stop.

Shane sat in a chair opposite him and crossed her legs. Dom knew that the limbs Shane wore were artificial, like more than half his own body, but somehow that didn't register. Shane's arms and legs looked like a part of her, down to the freckles. She didn't look like a marine, Dom thought, she looked like ... Dom hunted for the word.

"I wanted to know what's going to happen to Corporal Hougland."

Valkyrie, Dom thought.

I wonder where you are, Tetsami.

"The prisoner?"

Shane nodded.

"We would have released her long ago, if it wasn't for the fact that she could reveal our continued existence, not to mention our general location, to Colonel Dacham."

Shane nodded, as if that was what she expected. "You'll be quitting the mountain soon."

"We'll release her after that information is no longer sensitive." *I'm reverting to TEC-speak,* Dom thought. *All the crap I thought was buried begins to surface when I talk about Klaus.*

"Aren't you worried about him going after your employees again?"

Not all employees, some are partners. "Those attacks were directed at me."

"So?"

"After Bleek is controlled, I'll no longer be an issue." Dom sighed and stilled his hand. "Hougland will be released then."

"Good," Shane reached into the pocket of her coverall and withdrew a ramcard chit and a reader. She placed it on Dom's desk.

Dom drew the reader toward him. "What's this?"

"My share."

Dom looked up from the reader.

"I decided I want no part of this. I've dropped any claim on either the money or the corporation."

Dom sucked in a breath. "Do you realize what you're doing?"

Shane nodded.

He drew his hands away from the reader as if it was the detonator to a live explosive. "Why?" Dom asked.

"There are some things I can't forgive myself for. I believe that I had the right things in mind, but if I took that money, I'd never be sure. If I lose that, I can't live with myself."

He gingerly picked up the reader and paged through it. It was fairly straightforward. With no real laws on Bakunin, contracts and that ilk tended to be in plain language. The document Shane had written was as binding as any on Bakunin—

Not at all, technically.

"It wasn't your fault things went sour," Dom said.

"It's my fault I was there."

It's my fault you were there, Dom thought. "Are you going back?" Dom asked.

"I don't know."

"They'd court-martial you."

"They'll shoot me," Shane said. There was little emotion in her voice, but Dom noticed that the hardness in her eyes couldn't hide the redness in them. "Wherever I go, I don't belong here."

"Here where?" Dom asked, flipping to the last page of her document without really looking at it.

"I don't get you."

"Here, with this corporation I'm building, or here, Bakunin?"

Without changing her expression, Shane wiped her eye with the back of her hand. A slow, deliberate gesture, as if she had to concentrate to control her limbs. Dom thought back to his own reconstruction, and the rehabilitation afterward, and sympathized.

"I want to go home," Shane said. "If I turn myself in for what I did here, I want it to be at the place where I was born."

She wiped her eye again. Her hand slipped and she turned the motion into running her fingers through her hair.

"I want to go home," she repeated.

"Occisis?"

"Occisis."

"Smuggling yourself back into Confed space won't be easy. Especially if you go to a capital planet like Occisis . . ."

"I know," Shane said in a tone of such resignation that Dom knew that she'd never really considered getting off-planet as a real option. Dom's thoughts returned to the line they'd been running along when Shane had stepped in.

He had yet to tell anyone his full plan. Even Zanzibar only knew that he was planning to disappear. Dom had thought that the less people knew, the safer they'd be from Klaus.

Shane was different. Klaus had reasons to pursue her that had nothing to do with him. She was in the same boat he was, and he was responsible for dragging her aboard.

"I could help," Dom said.

"What do you mean?"

"I am planning a trip to a special commune. After this corporation has completed its purpose."

"A commune?" Shane looked intrigued despite herself.

"Proteus, one of the stranger ones. I plan to disappear there."

"What do you mean?"

Dom paused to consider how to describe Proteus.

"Most religions speak of the flesh as so much clay," he said. "The Proteans take a literal slant to that belief. They mold the clay to suit the occasion. They can change everything about you. Height, skin color, retina print, even your genetic profile."

"How?"

Dom paused to gauge what her reaction might be, then he said, "Nanomachines."

"What?" She hardly winced, but Dom could see the basic Confed reaction in her. He knew it well. He'd been sickened when he first heard about Proteus.

Dom shrugged. "We're outside the Confederacy. None of the bans on heretical technologies apply. Not on genetic engineering, not on artificial intelligences—"

"Not on nanomachines . . ."

Dom knew she was thinking of Titan, and what had happened when the intelligent nanomachines there decided to take over the terraforming project. The human-machine war that followed sterilized all of man's outposts in the outer part of humanity's home system. That was back when even the nearest star systems were barely in reach. The scars from that had yet to heal, and no human had since landed on the surface of Saturn's largest moon.

Initially, five million people had died. Nearly a billion people over the years had died as a result of that event. Some from going too close to Titan, most from the Terran Council—and then the Confederacy—"sterilizing" the sites of banned nanotech experiments.

The TEC had a free rein to use "necessary force" to erase nanotech sites. One planet was no longer habitable because of TEC action. Fifty million had died when a hundred-kilometer asteroid had punched a hole through their planet's crust.

Fortunately for Proteus, that only applied within the Confederacy. Military action outside the Confederacy, even action based in fanatical dread, was still a very sensitive political issue.

"You're going there . . ."

"As a pilgrim, to vanish within them."

"Oh, God."

"It isn't necessary to go that far. They can, and have, provided legitimate identification for anywhere in the Confederacy."

"More nanotech?"

"They can copy documentation atom by atom. All the antiforgery measures mean little to them."

"Do you have to . . ." Shane waved her hand, leaving the sentence unfinished.

Dom shook his head. "They only require the faith of those who alter the body." Dom rubbed his hand. It looked real, like the rest of him, but he thought he could sense the metal under the pseudoflesh.

Shane shook her head. "I'm surprised these people haven't taken over your planet by now."

"They're rather insular," Dom said. "This technology is one area where Bakuninites share attitudes with the Confederacy. If anything escaped, the Proteans could count on a few orbital nukes landing on their heads."

"I see."

"The offer stands."

Shane stood up and moved toward the door. "I'll think about it."

"And, please," Dom asked, "keep this between us?"

She nodded and walked through the door, stepping as if her shoes didn't quite fit.

Why did I do that? Dom thought. He didn't know anyone here who wouldn't be horrified about what he planned to do to himself—with the possible exception of Random Walk. Why would Shane be any different? Proteus would be the last option she would want to take.

Dom was different from most people. The major part of his body wasn't him to begin with.

He looked down at the card-reader in front of him and read the last page.

Shane had given her share to Ivor.

Dom wondered why.

CHAPTER SEVENTEEN

Think Tank

"Suspect your enemies, but more so your allies—
they can do more damage."
—*The Cynic's Book of Wisdom*

"I don't meet opponents, I crush them."
—BORIS KALECSKY
(2103–2200)

Colonel Klaus Dacham sat deep in a bunker buried under the offices for the old GA&A complex. On an examination table in front of him was the body of Johann Levy. Levy stared at the ceiling, directly at the floodlight that illuminated the table.

Klaus might as well have been alone.

Klaus had everything in his command firmly under control, but his mind still kept returning to his brother like a tongue to a wound in his mouth, tasting blood and dead flesh. Klaus kept returning to this human wreckage on the examination table.

Out of habit, Klaus stood outside the circle of light, so the prisoner couldn't see him. It was a pointless gesture. Levy was long past caring.

The biomonitors strapped to Levy's naked chest blinked green. But Levy's stare into the light told Klaus that he'd nearly been used up. Klaus sat down at the control console anyway.

"Hello, Johann," Klaus said as he activated the computers.

The body on the table stirred slightly. Klaus' voice still reached something inside that skull.

Levy moaned.

Klaus allowed himself a hard smile.

A month he'd had Levy down here. A month since

"Dominic Magnus" had attacked the Godwin Arms complex that Klaus now occupied. A month since he'd died.

Should have died.

No easy unequivocal end, damn it all. Just the *potential* of his twin's continued existence worried at Klaus' mind. A job undone. A poison spreading from a gangrenous limb that should have long-since been amputated.

The creature strapped to the table had revealed most of the story to Klaus. Klaus had had a biolink buried in Levy's skull and used it to peel the man's brain like an onion.

In previous sessions, as Klaus manipulated Levy's virtual universe, Levy explained how "Dominic" had come to him.

Johann Levy had been a man of some stature in the underground economy of Bakunin, a professional middleman. If you needed an assassin, a smuggler, a thief—Levy could find them for you, for a price. He had also earned a reputation as a safecracker, though he had never gone out into the field for a job.

When Klaus had peeled that part of Levy's mind, Levy admitted that it was because he was a coward.

Most of Levy's Bakunin reputation was a fraud. He had made a name as a Paschal revolutionary, when in fact he had fled the planet before the TEC arrived to put down the students. Johann Levy wasn't even Jewish. He was part of the thirty-percent Arab population of Paschal. Levy had never even made a token protest against the Paschal theocracy.

Every session peeled back more of the lies and more of Levy's guilt.

Everyone who talked to Levy had seen a different face. Even Klaus. Levy had been the anonymous Mr. Webster, who had cost Klaus seventy megagrams' worth of black currency from his TEC discretionary fund. Webster had been one of Klaus' arms into the heart of Bakunin. Klaus had used Webster to send contract assassins after his brother's GA&A loyalists.

Those contracts were a failure because, like Levy, Webster was a fraud.

Webster had been created for Klaus' benefit.

All of Levy's personal guilt had been transferred toward Klaus Dacham, the man responsible for the TEC operation on Paschal. Levy hated him. Levy feared him even more. Levy became his informant.

That alone made Klaus take pleasure in strip-mining Levy's soul.

Multiple layers of fraud and deception.

While Levy's Webster persona came to Klaus, Klaus' damned brother had come to Levy. Within days of Klaus' takeover of GA&A, Levy was approached to join an expedition to break back into the GA&A complex. The object of the break-in was a safe filled with 435 megagrams of hard currency. "Dominic Magnus," the former CEO of Godwin Arms, wanted Johann Levy to break the safe for him.

Levy never went into the field.

But Webster knew who "Dominic Magnus" was—Jonah Dacham, Klaus' twin brother.

Fraud and deception.

Levy played both sides of the fraternal battle. His object, apparently, was to engineer the disaster the break-in became. Levy had wanted to choreograph the twins' final meeting, absolving his own guilt by having the one assassinate the other.

The lies Levy wove, to Klaus, to Dominic, and to everyone around him, had become an integral part of his personality. By the time Klaus had stripped this far into Levy's brain, every new revelation disintegrated another part of Levy's mind.

Klaus barely cared. All that mattered was the fact that Levy was the only living witness he had. The only person who might *know* that Dominic—Jonah—was dead.

Klaus fiddled with the environment on the biolink interface until he heard an audible response from Levy.

"Ohhhh."

"Can you hear me?" Klaus asked. Of course Levy could. Levy couldn't avoid it. The sound was picked up by a microphone and fed directly into his brain.

"Ohhhh."

Klaus tripled the apparent volume and repeated. "Can you hear me?"

"Yes," Levy said, drooling. Levy's head thrashed side to side and his neck ached. One of the audio outputs on Levy's biomonitors picked up its tempo.

Klaus was glad that Levy still had his linguistic skills. Klaus had seen readouts on Levy's brain activity. The creature strapped to the table had already lost most voluntary motor function, time sense, and spatial awareness. Levy had lost most of his identity to Klaus.

Not quite enough, yet.

"I need you to remember again," Klaus said, reducing the apparent volume control.

"I can't no more." It came out in a sob. Levy's eyes were locked, sightless, on the light above him.

"The memory's still there, Mr. Levy," Klaus said as he raised the stimuli level on parts of Levy's brain. The holo in front of Klaus showed a rotating cross-section of Levy's brain activity. As Klaus adjusted the controls, certain black parts of the display shot through with color.

Levy's back arched, and three biomonitors went amber.

"If you can't remember, Mr. Levy, I'll have to remember for you."

Klaus lowered the stimuli control and Levy's body relaxed. The biomonitors faded to green.

"I 'member," Levy said.

"You remember the bad man?"

"Hurt the bad man," Levy said.

"Yes, you were going to hurt the bad man. Remember how." It wasn't a question.

Klaus pulled Levy through the whole assault on the GA&A complex. It was the tenth time he'd done it. Because of Levy's degrading language skills, it was the longest. Nearly three hours, and by the end, Levy was speaking in half-gibberish. The episode brought Klaus no closer to confirming his brother's demise.

Klaus stormed back up to the upper levels, cursing Levy. *Brain-dead wretch.*

Klaus took the elevator to the upper levels of his command center and composed himself. His doubts about Jonah/Dominic were still the only cloud on his horizon. He wouldn't let that weakness show in front of his troops.

Klaus Dacham didn't delude himself. His brother was his one weakness. In moments of honesty, Klaus admitted that it was an obsession that went far beyond the death of Helen Dacham. That was why his brother had to die.

The doors of the elevator slid open on the ground floor of the office complex.

Klaus walked down a corridor past sentries who nodded and saluted him. No one asked for his ID. In the last month, the GA&A complex had undergone a total overhaul. Security had been revamped down to the wiring.

Klaus walked past the last sentry, straight at a closed red-and-black striped door. The armored door was one of the new TEC additions to the GA&A complex. As Klaus walked toward it, he trod across a black and yellow line.

Most people paused at that line, waiting to see the door move. If the door didn't move, that meant that the security sensors found something objectionable. There was enough firepower buried in the walls to eradicate a squad in powered assault armor. Most people wanted some assurance that the computer had cleared them before they crossed the demarcation line.

Klaus walked right past.

The door began sliding open when Klaus was halfway across the ten-meter kill zone. When Klaus reached the door, he had to duck slightly because it was still rising. Once he cleared the half-meter thick door, it began closing, never having fully chunked home.

Klaus emerged on a catwalk circling close to the ceiling of a large chamber. The ceiling was considerably lower in here because of reinforcing armor, and the floor was four stories below.

The command center had been hollowed out of the GA&A complex, using the foundation of the office building as a frame. The room was a perfect cube, dominated by a gigantic holo display in the center. The display showed a schematic globe of Bakunin. Glyphs floated over the planet's surface and within the space around it. Every twenty-five minutes, this communication center had a direct burst-feed from six TEC observation platforms in orbit. From here, Klaus could get a picture of anything on the planet, all the junk in orbit, and most anything in nearby space up to about ten megaklicks.

The only problem was sifting through the wealth of data. Five TEC intel officers were down here around the clock to aid the computers in finding the relevant needle or two in the twelve million haystacks that came in every hour.

Klaus rounded the catwalk toward the stairs, passing two more sentries. He walked down four flights.

Little filled the space of Klaus' command center. Even so, Klaus had wanted the majesty of this space. Even if few of his people ranked high enough to see the command center, his twenty-meter armored cube reflected his control of this place. The centerpiece holo had been built specially for this room by the GA&A factory. It took an engineering detail an extra week of overtime, but the effect was worth it. The holographic globe of Bakunin dwarfed everything, a towering white-blue sphere ten meters in diameter.

Klaus thought he should do a speech over a holo like that.

His civilian TEC subordinates approached him when he reached the foot of the stairs. He stood and waited for them. Their reports were simple affairs, almost perfunctory.

The last modification to the GA&A complex had been completed. The factory level had peaked production. The fully-loaded *Shaftsbury* had flown off to Baker Station without incident, and operations had cut the turnaround time from sixteen to twelve hours.

Internal security, for once, had nothing to say to Klaus about the Occisis marine force—Klaus' one sore point in this operation. He had already punished a dozen marines for insubordination, and a few for disobeying orders. Of the twenty-four people he'd had shot for treason after the attack on the complex, half had been marines. However, after those twenty-four, the reports from internal security had steadily improved. Whispering had died down. Klaus supposed it had to do with the fact that the Occisis command now consisted entirely of his supporters, people he'd promoted himself in the last month.

Klaus would still feel better when the marines were shipped over the mountains and dispersed. The Occisis marines might be *his* now, but they were *his* only for the moment. The TEC people, the people who filled this complex, they were his forever.

His communication officer, Jonathan Whissen-Hall, dutifully relayed the last sync signal from Earth off of the tachcomm. Nothing new. Comm status with the observation platforms in orbit was nominal. After going through the generic data, Whissen-Hall added, "There's also been another request from Proudhon to talk to you. I can raise them if you want to talk to them."

Klaus had been putting that off. It wouldn't be good to enter that contact in the wrong frame of mind. To correctly orchestrate phase two of Operation Rasputin, he needed to treat his opposite number across the Diderot Mountains as an equal. Klaus didn't enjoy that.

However, Klaus would endure it because he had to follow the TEC plan. Up to a certain point.

Klaus nodded to Whissen-Hall, who nodded to a tech in front of a generic-looking holo-communicator. The communicator *was* generic. It was the scrambler and the tight-beam equipment it was tied into that was state of the art. It took the tech a few minutes to bounce the signal off the right satellite and work through the layers of command in Proudhon. After a while the tech nodded and turned the seat over to Klaus.

In the holo display before him sat Gregor Arcady, the commander-in-chief of Proudhon Spaceport Security. He was also, after certain recent "problems" within the secret board of the Proudhon Spaceport Development Corporation, the sole and absolute ruler of the city of Proudhon.

Arcady was a tall man whose black hair was graying at the temples. He had a walrus mustache that had gone white. Arcady affected a pipe and a pair of anachronistic spectacles. He looked like a teacher.

Arcady puffed on his pipe. "Colonel," he said, by way of greeting.

"Commander," Klaus said, "you wished to talk."

"Just so." Arcady spoke like a teacher. The front didn't deceive Klaus, who knew that Arcady had killed the CEO of his own company with his bare hands. Arcady had done it without mussing his suit or leaving a mark on the CEO's body.

"Two things," Arcady said. "You are aware of the *Daedalus* and its escort?"

Klaus nodded. He felt his teeth grinding. He did not like Arcady.

"The *Daedalus* has been talking to us," Arcady finished.

Klaus swallowed his surprise. This was news to him. He had been confident that the SEEC warship wasn't going to interfere with a TEC operation. If it did, news would reach Earth as fast as those TEC observers could transmit it. The Sirius-Eridani Community could find itself at odds with three-fifths of the Confederacy, perhaps in a shooting war.

"What kind of talk?" Klaus hoped that the words didn't sound as forced as they were.

"Offers of aid."

If someone on the ground asked *them to intervene, could that fly in the Congress?*

"Did you accept?"

"If I did, that would be a tacit statement that Bakunin exists in Sirius-Eridani space."

"Yes it would." *Assuming that your voice ends up governing Bakunin.* "It could also pull in other arms of the Confederacy."

"I've yet to respond to their offer."

"I appreciate you being so candid." The words hurt.

Arcady took his pipe and poked the stem out the holo. "Allies, Colonel. I wouldn't sour things by going behind your back."

I wonder if you ever told your old boss that. Klaus thought a moment.

"You said two things?"

"Why, yes. Quite a while ago you passed a list of people to us."

"Go on?" Klaus was finding Arcady exasperating.

"One of your bad pennies turned up. In the midst of our desert operation zone, no less. Could have been quite a mess if we hadn't contained—"

"Who?" Klaus cursed himself for treading on Arcady's line. It showed his anxiousness. *Could Dominic have shown up?*

"Name's Kari Tetsami. We're holding her in the operation zone. There are a pair of other security risks I want to pass on to you."

"Tetsami's the only one from the list?"

"Just so."

"Send her back on the *Shaftsbury,*" Klaus said.

"About these others?"

"Send them all." *Tetsami.* Klaus knew the name from his interrogation of Levy. He knew Tetsami, knew she'd been part of the GA&A assault. She'd know, surely, if Dominic Magnus was alive or dead. And, from what Klaus knew, he wouldn't even need medical to install a biolink in her.

Klaus thought of Tetsami as Arcady told him about the other prisoners.

PART FIVE

Caveat Emptor

"Those who own the country ought to govern it."
—John Jay
(1745–1829)

CHAPTER EIGHTEEN

Gunboat Diplomacy

"When you rattle your saber, it becomes difficult to stab someone in the back."
—*The Cynic's Book of Wisdom*

"Power ought to serve as a check to power."
—CHARLES MONTESQUIEU
(1689–1755)

On Earth, deep in the heart of the Terran Confederacy, Dimitri Olmanov looked up from a holographic globe of the planet Bakunin and said, "She had to be killed, Ambrose."

"Yes, sir," Ambrose replied. His voice was innocent of any emotion.

The two of them, Dimitri and his bodyguard, were inside Dimitri's private chambers, a monastic set of cells within the lowest sublevels of the Confederacy tower. Deep underground, the small set of four rooms was the most heavily guarded area in all eighty-three planets of the Confederacy.

"Helen Dacham had to die," Dimitri said.

He wasn't really talking to Ambrose. There wasn't a mind behind Ambrose's dark eyes. Not one to talk to, anyway. Three-quarters of Ambrose's brain was artificial, malleable remains programmed to be a perfect bodyguard.

"As you say, sir."

Dimitri sat, staring at the globe, thinking of Helen.

He had been the commander of the Terran Executive Command and the most powerful person in the Confederacy since its inception. Over the past century, his orders had cost nearly a billion lives, all in order to preserve that Confederacy. He had become the arch-demon for a cosmos of his own creation.

And, still, Helen's death weighed heaviest on his soul.

She had been a child of one of the richest families of Banlieue. Dimitri had only seen her innocent beauty. She had risen to be the most envied woman in the Confederacy. That was a hundred years ago.

The Confederacy had been young, and Dimitri himself had been a relative innocent.

Fifteen years ago, when Dimitri had orchestrated the events that killed her, Helen had become anonymous, one of the endless supply of poverty-stricken that formed the population base for one of the Confederacy's truly wealthy planets. She had a life deep in the ugly part of Waldgrave. Poor, unemployed, surviving mostly on the charity of the loggers who worked Waldgrave's continent-forests.

She had abandoned all she had, and allowed a wormhole to edit sixty years from her life, to escape him. He was a hundred and sixty years old now. If she had still been alive today, she would be only sixty-eight.

She had tried to vanish from him. She had ordered her own personal tach-ship through not just one of the old Council wormhole gates, but a series of them that eventually took her over sixty light-years. Because of the time she'd spent in transit, her twins were born three generations after they were conceived.

It only took Dimitri another five years to find her again. But he left her alone, to begin with. He let her raise the twins. He had been thankful to find her at all. After all, she *could* have gone the wrong way down the wormhole and he might never have found her after her universe permanently diverged from his.

"It was her contact with me that destroyed her. I had killed her the moment we'd met. A person can't be touched by me and remain uncorrupted."

"Sir?"

Dimitri looked up from the globe. "Not you, Ambrose. Evil implies choice, and you've had that removed from you long ago."

Ambrose looked on impassively.

Dimitri looked back at the holographic globe. It showed a planet that was mostly white. Massive glacial sheets capped both poles, crowding ocean and continent into a thin strip girdling the equator. The planet was larger than Earth, but less dense. It had a single mountain-backed continent that ran diagonally from icecap to icecap. The planet was old, older than Earth, old enough to have exhausted most of its geothermal furnace. It was home to at least a billion people. But, of course, with no accurate census, no one could be sure.

"She would have interfered with her children's lives once she'd discovered what her twins meant to me. I couldn't allow that." Dimitri watched the globe turn, staring at the continent as it rotated into view.

"I'm going to die soon," Dimitri said.

Ambrose made a strangled noise.

"Don't take it personally," Dimitri told his bodyguard. "It isn't an assassin that will claim me. It will be a too-long denied age. The doctors have replaced nearly all they can replace. Short of some heretical technologies, I may only have a year or two left."

"Please, sir . . ."

"I'll stop talking about it." Dimitri turned off the globe. "But I have spent years making sure I will not bequeath a succession battle to the Confederacy. Helen would have muddied the waters, and I had to eliminate her. You will serve my successor, Ambrose."

Dimitri stared into Ambrose's black eyes, trying to see into whatever humanity remained in there.

It took a long time for Ambrose to respond. But he finally said, "Yes, sir."

"Good." Dimitri glanced at the space where the globe was. "A pity this couldn't be done cleanly, with just the twins. It's a sign of my failing vision that I didn't anticipate the political vortex Bakunin would become."

Dimitri picked up his cane from a holder next to the table and got unsteadily to his feet.

"A pity this power struggle is now tied to the Dacham brothers—but it is appropriate." Dimitri shook his head. "Time to meet our Sirian comrade, Ambrose."

Dimitri ascended to his offices, higher than his residence, but still deep within the foundation of the Confederacy tower.

Kalin Green was waiting for him. She was his opposite number in the Sirius-Eridani Economic Community, the second largest of the five arms of the Confederacy. She was the chief intelligence officer of the SEEC, delegate to the TEC

Security Council, and the Congressional representative from Cynos—the third richest planet in the Confederacy.

She sat in the lounge outside his office, staring at a slab of rock that stood in place of the western wall. The rock was covered in intricate alien carvings.

Dimitri waited for the outer door to close behind him— leaving Ambrose outside—before he spoke. "I'm pleased you agreed to see me."

Green turned to face him with an even gaze. "Is there some reason you expected reluctance?"

Many, Dimitri thought. Within the SEEC intel community her title was commander of external operations. According to the Confederacy Charter, such a person should have nothing to do, since covert operations between the arms of the Confederacy were supposedly banned. Those were the TEC's job.

If you're not reluctant to talk to me, Dimitri thought, *you should be.*

Green turned back to look at the rock wall. "Is this an original?"

"Yes."

"A Dolbrian starmap." Green's voice softened. "I've only seen reproductions."

"Extremely rare and well-guarded artifacts. This one's from Mars, and the smallest of the three discovered. It only shows a half dozen systems—including Sol." Dimitri ushered Green into his office.

When they entered Dimitri's wood-paneled office, Green's voice returned to normal. "I'd like to know why I am here."

"It's a security matter," Dimitri said as he eased behind his desk. None of his joints were his own, but the replacements ached as much—maybe more—than the originals. It was a labor to seat himself, even with the aid of the cane.

He gestured above the desk and the wood-grain surface came alight with a few glowing pages from his last personal intel report. "I've received a number of disturbing reports from the Rasputin Operation. Bakunin."

Dimitri pointed at a part of the displayed image and it exploded up from the desk's surface and became a large holo display floating between him and Green. The image was an enhanced view of a section of a planet's orbital space. The planet was mostly ice, hugged by a strip of habitable space on the equator. Its shallow crescent was cut by a ruby sun.

In orbit below the camera's point of view were a dozen spacecraft of varying sizes. The central ship was a huge slotted cylinder that was girdled by five massive toroids. Dimitri knew that the ship was close to seven hundred and fifty meters long and was unable to enter an atmosphere even with contragrav assistance.

Dimitri asked Green, "Are you familiar with that scene?"

"The planet bears some resemblance to Bakunin."

Dimitri leaned back and killed the holo. "It is Bakunin. And those are SEEC ships, *Daedalus* and its escort. That picture was taken by a TEC observation platform. The tachcomm just arrived."

Green was silent.

Dimitri rubbed the bridge of his nose and suddenly realized that it had been quite a long time since he had had any sleep. "According to the Charter, the TEC is supposed to be the only organization with tach-capable military ships."

"I hope you are not going to charge us with some sort of violation."

"Perhaps I should."

Green's mouth opened, but nothing came out.

"Those ships are floating in disputed airspace. Bakunin is supposedly independent and three-fifths of the Confederacy are already upset that the TEC is running an operation there. Now that the *Daedalus* is there, how do you think they'll react? Perhaps I should clean up all these little messes."

Clean them all up before I die, he thought.

Dimitri stood up, ignoring the pain. "The TEC has overlooked a lot in the interest of stability. But it seems the Confederacy insists on destablizing itself."

Green frowned up at him. "What are you talking about?"

"We keep close tabs on *all* military vessels in the Confederacy. You know as well as I that the 'cargo ship' *Daedalus* isn't going to be the only force interested in Bakunin."

"I am certain that there is an explanation for this. I'll need to consult with Cynos."

"I thought you might."

Green stood up to leave.

"One more thing," Dimitri said, sitting down again.

"What?"

"I found it advisable to inform Mr. Vashniya of this development. It seems that a similar collection of ships— 'scouting vessels'—tached out from Dharma." *Almost exactly the same time that we dispatched the* Blood-Tide *to Bakunin,* Dimitri thought.

Vashniya was Green's equivalent from the Indi Protectorate, and had been pulling unexpected moves ever since he'd arrived for the decannual Confed Congress three months ago.

Dimitri went on, "The *Red Sun* and *its* escort will arrive in Bakunin space in five days standard."

Green stared silently at him.

"I want to avoid a nasty confrontation." *If the* Daedalus *does anything, it might start a war.*

"Your concern is appreciated," Green said, and left.

Dimitri sat in the silent office and hoped he had defused a potentially explosive situation. Even though weapons were going to be pointing everywhere when the Indi ships arrived, the diplomats had a chance to talk everyone out of the situation now.

Either way, Operation Rasputin would continue without outside interference.

And, more important, Helen's twins would be free to face each other. The result of that conflict was infinitely more important than what happened to Bakunin.

CHAPTER NINETEEN

Prisoners of War

"What you don't know will kill you."
—*The Cynic's Book of Wisdom*

"In revolutions authority remains with the greatest scoundrels."

—GEORGES-JACQUES DANTON
(1759–1794)

Tetsami surprised herself by waking up.

She rode on the floor of a near-empty contragrav troop-carrier. Compared to the *Lady* there was hardly any sense of motion at all, even though it was probably going three times faster than the fastest Tetsami had managed in the wheeled vehicle.

The front of the craft was blocked off by a small armored door, so the only sign of movement Tetsami had was the slice of the desert she could see out viewports in the rear of the craft.

She tried to get a better view, and realized that she wasn't in the best of shape. The pain shooting through her body told her that, at the very least, her torso was roped with bruises in the shape of the *Lady*'s crash harness.

Her grunt of pain brought no sympathy from her fellow passengers.

There were two of them. One by the rear door, one by the entrance to the cockpit. *My own personal escort,* Tetsami thought.

The two guards were hard to tell apart. Their uniforms were exactly alike, flat-black light armor with just enough environmental capability to run for a full day out in the desert sun. The helmets they wore had opaque faceplates, also black.

As she slowly got off the floor, she realized that the guards weren't the only restraint on her. Her wrists and ankles were hugged by restraint buckles, fat toroids of brushed metal that had contracted snugly to her skin.

Sheesh, Tetsami thought, *there goes my plan to overpower two armed soldiers with my bare hands, jump from a moving contragrav, and run a few hundred klicks of desert without any water. . . .*

To a certain extent, Tetsami was grateful for the buckles. They were actually less of a pain for the prisoner than more mechanical restraints. As long as you remembered that your limbs would be englobed in a stun field if you moved too fast, or if one buckle moved too far from the others, or if one buckle deactivated prematurely, or if you got too far from a base station, or . . .

Maybe they are just as much a pain.

Tetsami managed to get into one of the seats lining the walls of the transport without feeling any stabs from an active stun field. She already hurt too much to move fast enough to activate the buckles. Tetsami hoped that, if she had broken ribs or something, her captors would've bound them up. It didn't *look* like they wanted her dead, so they wouldn't just let her bleed to death from a ruptured spleen, right?

Tetsami forced her thoughts away from that subject.

She looked at her guards. They seemed unmoved by her struggle to sit upright. Both sat with their guns across their knees, Dittrich Hypervelocity Electromags. The weapon matched their low-profile appearance. A Dittrich 1.5 mm HVE had a lower energy profile than a laser, and a much lower one than a plasma rifle. Not only would the monocrys steel flechettes pass through most low-grade armor, but they had such a highly charged magnetic field when they hit that it counted as an ECM weapon.

By the time she'd run that through her head, she'd decided that her run-in with Dom had affected her in more ways than one. When she'd just been a data thief, her weapons expertise had been confined to being able to tell an energy weapon from a projectile weapon—most of the time.

Now she could quote stats on the things.

Do you think of me, Dom? Are you running to my rescue right now? Or am I just the ungrateful little bitch that scrammed off-planet?

Why can't I decide how I feel and stick with it?

The fact that she wanted Dom angered her almost as much as her capture. She forced herself to think back to the guards' weapons. How hard could it be to fire those things?

She only thought briefly about that. The restraint buckles she wore probably had a weapon sensor on them. They'd freeze her up if she got too close to any artillery. Grabbing one of those guns was still a nice thought, though. Those HVEs could blanket an area as wide as a plasma rifle, for nearly as long, and the flechettes would pass right through these guys' light armor.

Sheesh, she thought. All that was more of Dom's influence. If it wasn't for him she'd never even consider opening up and walking into combat like some half-assed marine.

Christ, was everything now going to start reminding her of Dom?

She turned away from her guards and stared out the small ports in the rear of the transport.

The first things she saw were the mountains. Theat meant that they were going mostly east. The Diderot Range was disturbingly far away now, little more than a rocky border holding down the desert's black horizon. She could barely see the divot that marked the northern pass she'd been aiming for. It was almost directly behind them. She tried to estimate distance, but she couldn't come up with a number. While she had been in the desert, she had never driven out of sight of the mountains, but from this view she was now farther east than she'd ever driven the *Lady*.

She wondered where the *Lady* was.

Kropotkin was setting behind the mountains. The sky behind them purpled as she watched. The mountains became dark shadows blocked out by a dull-red border.

There was no sign of any other contragravs, but when she tried to catch a glimpse of the desert below them, she could see that they were shooting along high above the surface, at least thirty meters up.

She looked at her companions and asked, "How long was I out?"

They shifted their weight but said nothing.

"Can you tell me how long we'll be riding this thing?" Silence.

"Am I going to get any medical attention?"

Tetsami waited for a few minutes, just to be sure that she wasn't simply dealing with unusually slow mental processes.

"As I see it, there're two possibilities. I've been abducted to be part of a harem and you're two of the palace eunuchs whose tongues have been removed to retain the caliph's secrets."

Pause, nothing.

"Or you guys have just been ordered not to talk to the cargo."

No response. Tetsami sighed. They could at least nod at her. Something. If they didn't shift their weight occasionally, she'd begin to think that her captors had seated two extra sets of empty armor in here just to play with her mind.

When they landed, and the door opened in front of her, she thought, at first, that she was looking at more of the desert.

Only when her two caretakers led her out of the vehicle did she realize that the dunes she was looking at weren't dunes. She was looking at more sheets of carbon-fiber composite, like the sheet that had covered the contragrav wreck at Ashley. The camouflage would fool a satellite, but this close she could see the vehicles underneath.

Hundreds of them.

Even in the hurried march around the personnel carrier she caught glimpses of everything from intercept fighters to airtanks. When they rounded the back of the contragrav, if it weren't for her escort, she would have frozen in shock.

At least five—maybe ten—square kilometers of desert were covered by temporary housing, barracks, and hundreds, thousands, tens of thousands of troops. Towering six stories above all of that was a Paralian-designed Barracuda-class troop-carrier that reminded Tetsami an awful lot of the *Blood-Tide*. The Barracuda sat in a floodlit landing area that overpowered Kropotkin's weak evening glow. It was offloading crates from out of its massive hinged nose.

Her escort hustled her into the midst of the military base, improving her view of the spacecraft. Her stomach sank as she recognized the crates the Barracuda was off-loading. She had seen their like before, in the warehouse level of Godwin Arms & Armaments. The crates contained newly fabricated weapons, tons of them.

Blanketing the whole complex, maybe fifty meters above

her, was a black canopy. Not a physical roof, it was gener-
ated by a parked countersurveillance craft bearing the
turquoise-and-black markings of Proudhon Spaceport Security. Those craft were twenty meters across, disks squatting
on their ellipsoid contragrav generators. They resembled the
personnel-carrier Tetsami'd been brought here in, except for
the five-meter-tall spines erupting from their backs, each
spine topped with a rotating sphere nearly as big as the craft
below it. The sphere housed holo projectors, and Emerson
field generators—enough hardware to fully mask a huge site
from detection by anything more than sixty meters above the
surface of the desert. Above each craft hovered a flat, circular Emerson field blocking out most of the EM spectrum.

They passed three more countersurveillance craft before
reaching their destination. This far inside it would be impossible to tell day from night with the countersurveillance going.

Their destination was another temporary building. Its only
difference from the buildings around it was the absence of
windows on its flat trapezoidal surface. The building was
right off the quad where the Barracuda sat. One of her
guards said something too quickly to make out, and the
door—the only feature in the sloping wall—slid aside.

One of the guards grabbed her by the upper arm and
walked her inside, while the other hung back by the door.
The light in here was so dim compared to the floodlit landing area, that the guard had left and the door had closed before her eyes had adjusted to the illumination.

As the lumpy forms in the room resolved into people, one
of them surprised her by saying, "Small world, isn't it?"

It was Jarvis, the man who had sold her the Lady.

"Are you all right?" asked Jarvis.

Tetsami was too fuddled to think straight. She was still
reeling from the scope of the camp she'd just been walked
through. Running into someone here that she knew had finally pulled the mental locks down.

"Sit down," Jarvis said, dragging a crate over to her.

Her eyes had adjusted to the murky dark, and she could
see that two others, in addition to herself and Jarvis, occupied the inside of the prefab storeroom. Both were male and
wore black and turquoise uniforms, as did Jarvis.

Jarvis handed her a canteen and said, "Drink?"

Tetsami nodded and took a mouthful, avoiding the temptation to drain the whole thing.

Jarvis looked much as he had the first time she'd seen him, a man weathered by the elements until all the softness had leeched out of him, leaving bone, bleached hair, tight muscle, and skin like old leather. She still couldn't figure his age, but the stubble that now grew on his cheeks was several shades darker than the hair on his head.

He watched, with something hard in his gaze.

Tetsami wiped her mouth and returned the canteen. She noted that Jarvis also had restraint buckles on his wrists and ankles. It had taken a few minutes to register that Jarvis and his two silent companions were just as much prisoners as she was.

"How did you end up here?" Jarvis asked.

She shrugged. "Running from Proudhon. Wrong direction."

Jarvis shook his head and drank from the canteen himself. He offered it to the two others, they both declined. She seemed to be the center of a lot of attention.

"Is that all?" Jarvis asked.

"All what?" Tetsami asked.

Jarvis put a hand on her shoulder and stared at her. "Why do they want you?"

"Huh. I just stumbled on this—"

Jarvis was shaking his head. The set of his jaw made her think of a coiled spring.

"—what?" Tetsami finished weakly.

"Less than five hours ago I had a command here, miss. I was training a patchwork company of mercenary goons to work as a team. When word came in about you, it took my employers ten minutes to decide to lock me down."

"Huh? Wait, all you—I—what?" Tetsami said.

Jarvis let go of her shoulder. "You managed to sour a spotless reputation simply by breathing on me. I'd like to know why my employers think you're such bad medicine."

Yeah, like all this is my fault. "You have pretty shitty employers."

"So? I want an explanation."

She was getting sick of all this. "Fuck if I owe *you* anything." She stood up. The two mute prisoners seemed to shrink back from the scene. They'd let Jarvis do all the talking. Tetsami glanced at their reaction and decided that maybe this wasn't such a good idea.

Jarvis turned around slowly, fluidly. "Do not test me." He moved within a fraction of the maximum speed the restraint cuffs would allow. He slid in front of her.

Without any warning she found herself facedown on the ground, her arm twisted behind her, throbbing in agony. She knew she'd blacked out for a moment—and the insanely contradictory thought that ran through her mind was the fact that he had moved so damn slowly.

Jarvis let go of her arm and stepped back. She sat up and looked at him. No wonder the other two prisoners were so cowed. "Sure know how to treat a woman," she said, rubbing her elbows.

"Arguments are considerably shorter when it's obvious where they lead. Now, why are you such poison?"

Tetsami glanced toward the door. Out that door was a military TEC ship off-loading weapons from GA&A. It was now pretty obvious why Proudhon Security wanted her. Proudhon Security was working with, or *for,* Colonel Klaus Dacham. She was pretty sure that Klaus would like to have a long talk with her.

She gave Jarvis the general rundown, avoiding anything that could get Dom's people in trouble.

Avoiding specifics seemed a futile gesture. If they handed her over to Klaus, he'd gladly drain her mind like a bulb of cheap wine.

As she talked, she tried very hard to resent Jarvis, but the fact was that she was hitting the point where she no longer really gave a shit. They were all on the same damn boat, and where the holes came from didn't seem so important when she was breathing lungfuls of ocean.

She got to the end of her tale and looked up at Jarvis.

"Your turn," she said.

"What?" Some of the hardness had leaked out of him. Tetsami suspected that he didn't like the TEC any more than anyone else did. She could tell that he'd been somewhat surprised to hear about the origin of that ship out there.

"If you don't want to come across as a complete asshole, you'll explain this setup."

For a moment it looked like she had triggered another scene of graceful aggression. The look faded.

"I suppose," he said.

The story Jarvis unfolded confirmed Tetsami's worst fears. The Proudhon Spaceport Development Corporation had swelled the ranks of its private army to incredible size. Hidden in the desert, it had been building for months, since long before the TEC invaded GA&A. It had grown within Proudhon Security, a secret even from its parent corporation.

From Jarvis' description, there had to be a close to a million-man army scattered in bases throughout the desert. An army run by Proudhon Security, armed and probably financed by the resources of the TEC.

"Ashley?"

"Ashley is in direct line with the mountain pass the forces are using. It had to be neutralized before the attack."

The attack?

Bakunin had always been too fragmented for someone to consider a serious war of conquest. It had too many conflicting interests to ally under a single banner. Proudhon now managed such an army by appealing to the one near-universal binding agent on the planet—money.

Proudhon had bought itself the largest single armed force on the planet.

"The TEC is financing this," Tetsami said.

"You know this for a fact?" Jarvis asked.

"The outlay for this is beyond any megacorp. Even a planetwide monopoly. If it wasn't, someone would have tried long ago."

Jarvis nodded.

At the mention of the TEC, the darker of the two other prisoners spat on the ground. Tetsami looked in their direction, "Care to introduce our roommates?"

Jarvis shrugged and turned away. The smaller, lighter-skinned man stood up, wincing clumsily when he pushed the velocity perimeters of his restraint buckles. "Kelly's the name. No proper title, never got fully processed. The sour-looking wog here goes by the name Gavadi."

The large toroid on their wrists made shaking hands uncomfortable, but Kelly's stance seemed to demand it. "Why're you two on ice?" Tetsami asked.

"Well, Gavadi, his politics don't agree with the mission they're running here."

Tetsami turned toward the dark man. Gavadi's expression was unreadable in the gloom. However, Tetsami could sense the man's distaste for Kelly. Tetsami revised her original assessment of the situation in here. Kelly might have been cowed by Jarvis, but Gavadi simply looked like someone who had very little to say. Gavadi noted her examination. He nodded toward Kelly. "He's right." Our employer's intention was never clear until we were out in the desert. My reaction was—" Gavadi paused as if searching for the word, "—*rash.*"

Kelly sat back down. "Typical Bakuninite. Caught him sabotaging one of the contragrav tanks. Would've paralyzed a whole column of armor if they hadn't got to him."

"What did you do?" Tetsami asked Kelly.

Kelly shrugged and pasted on an innocent expression. With his red hair and freckles he looked almost boyish. It was a look that Tetsami's years on the streets of Godwin had taught her to read as "con man." The kind of man who'd stumble into stealing your money and convince you that he really didn't want to and he was doing you a favor anyway.

"What can I say? I suffered a departure from the Occisis marines that was less than, shall I say, honorable. Apparently my search for employment here was looked on with some disfavor."

He shrugged again.

I can almost believe that, Kelly, Tetsami thought. *But I trust my instincts and they say that you got burned pulling some sort of scam.* The possibilities came to her mind, unbidden. Phantom arms sales. A regiment of nonexistent troops bivouacked in the mountains. Corporate intelligence. *What'd you try to sell them, Kelly? How much did they buy before you fell in the pit?*

"Jarvis?" Tetsami asked. There was a question that had been nagging at her since she'd seen the columns of smoke.

Jarvis turned around.

"What happened to Ashley? The people?"

Jarvis gave her a pitying look.

Tetsami felt sick. "Fifty thousand people?"

"They called it an evacuation. The civilians didn't put up much of a fight. They boarded the buses that Proudhon had driven in, after the EMP, once everyone was prepared to leave, they turned the plasma cannons on them—"

The entire population of that commune, wiped out. She'd been there, seen those piles. Tetsami's stomach started spasming. All that prevented her from vomiting was the absence of anything solid to heave.

"That many people," Tetsami said, and her voice came in a sour hiccup. "They're going to be missed. This *can't* be kept a secret."

"Only needs to be one a few days more," said Kelly.

They were only days away from open warfare and there was nothing she could do. Not unless she could escape and warn someone out there. Give them some chance to defend. Warn Dom.

Tetsami looked at the door to the warehouse. "We have to escape somehow."

"I'm working on it," said Jarvis.

Even as he said it, the door slammed open. The whole room was washed by the glare off the landing field. Tetsami's eyes were dazzled and it took her a few moments to discern the massive form of the *Shaftsbury* with its nose gaping open. Silhouetted before the craft was a ring of a dozen armed guards.

"Time to go," said the lead guard.

CHAPTER TWENTY

Intelligence Analysis

"Any government will kill you if it feels threatened."

—*The Cynic's Book of Wisdom*

"The worst thing in this world, next to anarchy, is government."

—HENRY WARD BEECHER
(1813–1887)

For most of the night Dom stood in the corner of one of the cavernous landing areas. He watched departures for Godwin, the deployment of the people who would physically take Bleek Munitions' assets once the stock transfer had been recorded. The aircars left at irregular intervals, using the night and unorthodox flight patterns to hide themselves.

The time was approaching.

A truck left, a cargo hauler that currently transported a squad of Dom's paramilitary security troops, the elite survivors of the Confed raid on GA&A. Those would be some of the people who'd take on Ezra Bleek's children and their board members in the corporate headquarters.

The door was sliding shut on the vehicle bay when Mosasa stepped up next to him. "Mr. Magnus?"

"Yes." Dom wondered if Mosasa ever slept.

He turned to face Mosasa and, when he saw Mosasa's expression, he realized something had gone terribly wrong somewhere. "What's happened?"

"Come up to the conference room," Mosasa said.

Mosasa led him there.

In the room, around the holo-dominated table, stood most of Dom's fellow board members. All looked as if they'd been roused from sleep.

Shane leaned against a wall in a robe, flexing her hands. Ivor's cheeks were white sandpaper and he was trying to finger-comb his hair, which resembled a dandelion gone to seed. Zanzibar was fully awake and appeared displeased about the fact. She sat in one of the control chairs, draining cups of synthetic coffee. Three empty cups already sat in front of her.

As Dom walked into the room, a buzzing emerged from the hall behind him. Dom stepped aside just in time to let by a flying robot. The robot was a squashed sphere about a meter in diameter, bristling with sensors and dangling manipulators like a chromed jellyfish. It flew by silently at shoulder height.

The buzzing came from the alien, Flower. Flower walked into the room, wobbling somewhat on its double-jointed legs. It tipped over once and thrust out its massive wings to balance itself, nearly knocking Zanzibar's coffee out of her hand. The buzzing came from its head, which was bobbing at the end of its serpentine neck.

All in all it went through quite a production before collapsing into a heap in the corner, cradling its head in its hands.

Not a morning creature, Dom thought.

The robot rotated to scan the room with its cameras and said, "Everybody?"

The voice was Random Walk's. Dom supposed that Random could use any robot it wanted to, via remote control. Random used this one so often that Dom suspected it contained part of Random's brain. Dom knew that Random's brain could be separated into at least two parts—it was necessary to do so during the raid on GA&A, to get part of Random inside an RF-shielded environment. Dom appreciated the robot, it gave him something to look at when he talked to Random.

When Random spoke, most people assented with a simple "yes" or a nod, but Flower babbled something in mixed alien and human tongues that sounded like, "The senses are dulled but the mind is here and unpleasant about it."

Mosasa activated the large holo display set into the table. "I apologize for waking all of you."

"We've discovered something of an emergency," Random said.

The holo filled the room with the crackling buzz of high-

level radio interference. "Random was scanning sat transmissions looking for the *Shaftsbury*."

"Whatberry?" Ivor mumbled in a gravelly voice.

"Cargo model Barracuda," Shane whispered to Ivor.
"Klaus' number two ship."

"This transmission was recorded in the data stream,"
Mosasa continued. "Random only filtered it out ten minutes
ago."

The holo chose that moment to resolve a picture. The face
was only visible for a single blurred moment, but that was
enough to make out the features.

"Tetsami," Dom said simultaneously with Ivor. Ivor no
longer sounded tired.

The audio on the holo was very bad. White noise waved
over the signal. When it receded, Dom heard, "—captured or
killed by Proudhon Space—" The rising tide of interference
rendered the next few words incomprehensible.

Fade in. "—ing a massive military operation—" The
screaming whine of feedback broke over the signal. The
holo's video signal was briefly razor-sharp before dissolving
again. Tetsami's voice rose to be only just audible over the
buzzing rush that followed the disintegration of the picture.

"—north of the Space   " The voice dropped below audi-
bility.

"—every mercenary—"

"—destroyed at least—"

"—Ashley—"

"—Fifty thousand people gone."

The signal finally crumbled under the wash of noise. For
a long time white noise was the only sound filling the communication center. Dom was frozen by the single thought:
She's still on Bakunin.

"Where is she?" Ivor demanded, staring at the static on
the holo.

"The signal was jammed," Random said through his robot. "Only one satellite I accessed picked up the signal, and
even then I had to overlap five separate retransmissions—"

"Damn it, where is she?" Ivor raised his arm as if he were
going to strike the robot. Shane put a hand on his arm and
Random's robot floated back out of range.

Mosasa interposed himself. "Please, we just found this out
a few minutes ago."

Random kept backing around the holo. The body of the

robot was bobbing up and down, a nod. "I've been checking what I can. The transmission is twenty-three hours old—"

"And you just now—" Ivor began.

"Shhh," Shane said.

"Yes," Random continued. "Unfortunately, this was deep in the data stream. Even at my processing speed it was twenty hours before my search algorithm discovered the data, and another three before it was cleaned and decompressed into something comprehensible. This is the result of only a few thousand noncontiguous kilobytes buried in several million times as much data. It was jammed wideband transmission. It came from somewhere in the desert north of Proudhon. Resolving the source more accurately isn't possible with only a single satellite for reference—"

"You can tell that from the message," Ivor mumbled.

"The most disturbing part is the commune," Mosasa said.

Random's robot bobbed in another nod. "Yes. We've been trying to raise the Ashley Commune ever since we deciphered the message. No response. I accessed a Proudhon ATC sat to look down on Ashley's location. Energy output nil."

"Ashley's population was fifty thousand," Mosasa finished.

Dom knew everyone was thinking of the last few words Tetsami had gotten out. *Fifty thousand people gone.* Why did he see his brother's hand in that?

That's what we do, Dom thought.

Zanzibar was talking to Mosasa, "Proudhon Spaceport Security?"

"That seems to be the implication," Mosasa said.

"Also," Random added, "the stretch of northern desert we're discussing is currently only watched by Proudhon's own satellites. It's a low-priority stretch of the planet. Nothing in synchronous over it, and other sats are generally placed to pass over those latitudes on the *west* side of the Diderot Mountains."

"What would Proudhon Security want with Ashley?" Zanzibar asked.

Every mercenary, Dom thought, *Proudhon is the capital city for soldiers of fortune.*

Massive military operation.

Dom knew why he saw his brother's hand in this. The

pieces of the whole ugly puzzle were beginning to fit together.

He ran a shaking hand through his hair and tried to convince himself that he was wrong. Around him the room had devolved into a shouting match. Flower was going on about Ashley's military insignificance. Zanzibar wanted to know how Proudhon Security vanished fifty thousand people. Proudhon had a large security force but not *that* large. Ivor wanted to know, very badly, where Tetsami had ended up. Shane wanted to know why Random had been looking for the *Shaftsbury*.

Dom barely noticed when the room went silent.

"My God," said Zanzibar, "Dominic, what's wrong?"

Dom looked up and realized that everyone was looking at him. He was shaking as though he were freezing to death. He put a hand on the chair next to him to steady himself, but the chair's arm nearly came off in his hand.

"Someone get a medic," Ivor said.

"No," even his voice was shaking. He hugged his arms around himself and tried to hold his body together. "I know what they're doing."

"What" said everyone in the room.

"Politics, you see. The Confederacy doesn't like Bakunin, no tariffs, no taxes, customs, or contraband—tremendous drain on their economy." Dom listened to his voice as if it was someone else talking. The sound was too high, too arid, and it vibrated like a piano wire. "They'd like Bakunin to become a normal member of their community of planets."

People were staring at him.

He looked at them like they'd just missed the punchline to a very obvious joke. "Don't you see? The TEC take over GA&A. Why? Not just Klaus' personal vendetta. Where do hundreds of tons of weapons go? Where's the production going? Not the open market." Dom waved his arms. "They want Bakunin to join the Confederacy. To join, it has to sign the Charter."

"To sign, it has to have a government," Random said.

"A State," Zanzibar said.

Realization began to dawn even on Shane's face. "They'd want a government run by domestic forces . . . oh, my God, *that's* what phase two is."

Dom collapsed into a chair and tried to regain some of his composure. Somewhere in the desert, there was a massive army. An army that was preparing to invade the east. *How many people*, Dom thought, *how many thousands?*

When would they strike?

Oh, God, Tetsami, where are you? I'm sorry you've become part of this insanity. You deserved more from me.

CHAPTER TWENTY-ONE

Security Risk

"The only escape-proof prison is one's own mind."
—*The Cynic's Book of Wisdom*

"Tyrants have not yet discovered any chains that
can fetter the mind."
—CHARLES CALEB COLTON
(1780–1832)

Corporal Mary Hougland didn't sleep. She lay in her bunk,
staring at the walls of her cell. She had finished the mural
today, just before they began lowering the lights to mark
nightfall during Bakunin's obscenely long day.

The mural was complete, so it was time.

Hougland had been waiting for hours, working up the
nerve to go through with her plan. It had been the single
thought that drove her ever since she'd been dragged into
the mountains. Now, with the moment so close upon her, her
mouth had dried up and a molten band of excitement
clutched her abdomen.

She could only try this once. If she screwed it up, her captors would immediately see through the weakness of their
jury-rigged prison.

Hougland forced herself to be very patient. She was good
at it. It was the same patience that allowed her to gradually
cut her own rations in half so she would be thin enough to
attempt this. The same patience that allowed her, in another
world, to spend years on a single painting. The same patience that allowed her to tackle the stun field.

The thought made her flex her hands. They were still
numb in spots, but there was no permanent damage.

The Emerson field that cloaked the front of her cell in an
invisible flat sheet was programmed to disrupt the operation

of the human nervous system. However, that programming wasn't absolute. Stopping a biological system was infinitely more complex than stopping a laser blast. Given time, life could adapt.

The mural Hougland had wrapped the cell with had more purposes than artistic expression, or even preventing boredom from driving her insane in this cavern. The painting kept her hands flexible and nimble, and the constant coat of paint over them concealed the subsurface bruising that her nightly battles with the field had caused.

Every night, for a month, Hougland had pushed her hands through the invisible barrier. Every night she'd gritted her teeth as fiery needles seared her hands. Every night she came close to thinking that she had pushed the envelope too far, and that she had done permanent damage to her nervous system.

But a week ago—a Bakunin week, seven of these insufferably long days—she had looked at her numbed, burning hands hanging over the line demarcating the barrier, and had flexed them.

Until then, her whole plan had been theoretical. She had known that a stun field wasn't absolute, that some people could worm through and maintain consciousness. She had also known that the reverse was true. A stun field could vary in the opposite direction and permanently paralyze, even kill.

She was still unsure if she could pass all the way through.

She did know that it would be unpleasant. The way a stun field warped perceptions, the side effect of unconsciousness was a blessing.

There was, however, no more putting it off. The mural was complete. That was her signal to make the attempt.

It was a miserable ten hours she waited. She lay on her cot, eyes held rigidly at half-mast, staring out at the one guard station. The guard who manned the desk during the deepest part of Bakunin's sixteen-hour night had been on the job, working that shift, since the beginning of Hougland's captivity. She had watched him fall into a steadily softening routine, until he spent most of his shift perusing a cardreader.

In the last month Hougland had done absolutely nothing to make her captors more cautious. She had been a model prisoner.

Even when Captain Shane had showed up.

Seeing her former commander had to mark one of the lowest points of Hougland's life. She had to clamp down on every single emotion she had. It had felt like hours before she could force herself around and talk to Shane.

Hate, at the start, had been Hougland's overriding emotion. A perfect crystalline hatred forged over the weeks in the cubical stone kiln of her cell. It should have burned her to ashes.

Worse than the hate, the sense of betrayal, was the sense of confusion. Shane had been a perfect example of what Hougland had wanted to be. Shane had been the symbol of everything that the marines had meant to her. The collapse of all that had left Hougland hollow inside. The disillusionment had been a dull ache in her soul even before the attack that had taken her prisoner.

Something had been desperately wrong with her perception of Shane, the marines, and her role in the universe. It was a desperate, awful admission for someone who prided herself on her clarity of vision. Worst of all, she couldn't find the flaw in the lens, because it was in her own eye.

She'd been staring at the guard for three hours now, and it had been nearly fifteen minutes since he had turned away from the card-reader in his hands. He was deeply engrossed, or had nodded off.

It was time.

She slipped out of her bunk and carefully placed her feet so as not to smudge the mural on the floor. In two steps she had reached the field.

Hougland took deep breaths and consciously tried to lower her heartbeat. What she was about to do would be unlike simply thrusting her hand through. She would pass through quickly this time, and she had to hope that her nightly battles with the field had given her body the necessary armaments to fight for some tenuous scrap of reality on the other side.

She huddled to expose as small a cross section as possible and stepped through headfirst.

Her inner ear spun and slammed itself through the back of her skull. The world was a centrifuge out of control. Every muscle in her body rippled with fiery needles and cramped hard enough that it felt like they were tearing away from the bone. Her skin was on fire. Her eyes felt like burning coals and every nerve inside her teeth rang as if a phosphorus grenade had let go in her mouth. Her bladder did let go.

But she didn't lose consciousness, and she didn't scream.

It took an eternity for the feelings to fade to a tolerable level. She knew that most of the pain would go after a few seconds, but when she managed to open her eyes she still felt that it would be days later and she'd be in a medical ward somewhere under much tighter security.

However, when her eyes opened, she was still standing in her cell, on the other side of the stun field. It couldn't have been much more than fifteen seconds.

The guard hadn't moved.

She rubbed her face and found moisture. Her hand came away bloody. She had suffered an explosive nosebleed. She looked down, and the front of her jumpsuit was covered with it.

She'd come out the other side conscious, but she was in physically worse shape than she'd expected. The muscle cramps had dug in and the ache would be with her for days. Priming herself for this had come with a price. She'd maintained awareness, but she'd become sensitized to the stun field.

She couldn't turn back now. In her state, passing through another stun field just might kill her.

The next obstacle was the door to her cell. Unfortunately for her, the engineers that'd rigged this place had realized that a stun field wasn't universally effective. The field was simply a deterrent, a delaying measure, to keep her out of reach of the real physical barrier, the bars in front of her cell.

The bars were close-set and anchored in an asymmetrical diagonal crack in the stone. The setting showed the haste with which her captors had constructed the place. Even though her cell was the first to have been finished, it still showed the scars of the excavation. The builders hadn't even bothered to smooth out the lines of the door.

That was Hougland's chance.

The stun field may have been only meant as a delaying measure, but it had made the engineers careless. The barrier at the front of her cell wasn't as complete as it would have been had it been alone.

The bars themselves were ellipsoid and as thick as her forearm—or as thick as her forearm had been before she began cutting her rations. The long axis of each bar was canted toward its neighbor, giving a zigzag cross section. That made the gaps between the bars deceptive. It would be easy to wedge part of her body through and find it permanently trapped.

However, near the top of her cell, the asymmetry of the crack had given the engineers trouble. One side of the crack had bowed out for nearly a meter and the builders had had to insert a stationary bar barely a meter long in the gap.

Over the past month, stress fractures caused by that one bar had caused rock to crumble away from the wall. The gap, three meters above her head, had doubled in size over the past month. There was now over a half-meter space between the bar and the side of the wall, six times the narrowest gap between the bars.

Hougland knew she could slip through that hole. She had forced herself to lose 12 kilos just to be sure.

With one eye on the guard, she began climbing upward. The effort ignited fires in her still-cramped arms, and she could vividly picture the rainbows of bruising blossoming across her body. Violent rose, tan, and yellow punctuated by the occasional splash of purplish-black. She could feel them growing across her back.

At least the climb was easy. The wall of the crack sloped away beneath her and occasionally she could use the base of one of the bars for a foothold. She was becoming so used to the pain washing through her body that she hardly noticed when her hand slipped and the fingernail on her right index finger peeled away like cheap paper. She just sucked the blood away until it slowed to a gummy trickle.

During the climb, the guard looked over three times. The only time Hougland was in real danger was the first time, when she'd barely climbed to eye level. However, her cell was swathed in darkness, and her body was covered by the lip of the crack she was climbing. The guard, by now, was lazy and glancing over only by habit. Each time he looked, she froze and allowed the guard to see only what he expected.

Each time the guard returned to his card-reader.

She reached her goal, exhaled, and began wriggling her way through.

If the guard turned around now, it would be over. His lazy

eyes would register an anomaly, and even if it took him a half second to react, there would be nothing she could do.

She pushed through it, scraping her shoulders, crushing what remained of her breasts against the rough stone. What had seemed a massive gap from the floor of her cell now seemed impossibly tiny. Parts of her jumpsuit shredded as she slowly pushed her rib cage through.

Through it all, the agonizing part was retaining her silence through the effort, and keeping her eyes locked on the guard below her. Even at this distance, she was sure every noise she made reverberated throughout the whole stone bowl.

Toughest of all was pulling her hips through the tiny space. She had gone through on her stomach, and she had to rotate to her back and another quarter turn before she'd slipped all the way through the hole.

Then, suddenly, there she was, sitting on a tiny lip of stone, her lower legs now the only thing inside the hole. Hougland allowed herself the first smile in quite a long time. It wasn't over yet, but the worst had gone by about as smoothly as she could expect.

She considered dropping to the chamber floor and disabling the guard. But it would lose her as much time as it would gain. Also, her run-in with that white-haired giant of a man had taught her some discretion. If she had slipped away quietly, instead of trying to take the man out, she wouldn't be in this mess.

Hougland silently sighed and turned away from the guard. A meter above was one of the light fixtures. Beyond lay darkness. Hougland stood, using the bar's molding as a foothold, and climbed up into the darkness, where she'd be invisible.

On the ground, all the exits were cloaked by stun fields. Above, there was only air, rock walls, and an impossibly high ceiling. Somewhere, up here, there'd be a passage the engineers, in their hasty construction, hadn't gotten to. Hougland was going to find it.

If she was lucky, by the time the guard here raised the alarm, she'd be long gone down one of those endless caverns.

CHAPTER TWENTY-TWO

High-Level Source

"The path out of a problem generally leads to one twice its size."

—*The Cynic's Book of Wisdom*

"There is choice, and there is necessity."

—WILLIAM IV
(2126–*2224)

"Time to go," the lead guard had said.

What he meant, Tetsami thought, *was "time to wait."*

The guards had led the quartet of prisoners across the floodlit landing area and up the ramp into the nose of the *Shaftsbury.* Walking up the ramp, under the upward hinging nose, made Tetsami feel like she was being swallowed by a Paralian leviathan. She wondered if the feeling was a coincidence, since this was a Paralian-designed ship.

The cargo space was huge, fifty meters from the nose to the bulkhead at the rear. A slightly curved ceiling ten or fifteen meters above her head marked mid-height on the cylindrical main body of the ship. Oddly, the huge space, even though it was mostly empty, didn't echo. As they stepped out on to the floor of the chamber, Tetsami could tell why. The *Shaftsbury* was multiple hulled, and between the hull was sandwiched some sort of toughened pseudoflesh, a self-sealing plastic whose ability to regenerate and heal damaged parts of itself resembled living tissue. The cargo compartment had an extra layer of the pseudoflesh on the interior. It resembled resilient black rubber with gray scars marking where tears in the surface had resealed.

They were led to a line of seats all the way in the back of the compartment, by the rear bulkhead. Tetsami saw only three exits from the cargo area. The nose, and two hatches in the ceiling reached by ladders set in the wall.

They were seated, instructed to belt themselves in, and left with a single black-clad guard as silent and impassive as the stealth cadets who had brought Tetsami here.

There was only one thing in the cargo area besides them. Strapped down in the center of the space was the squat, ugly, tarp-covered form of the *Lady*. Jarvis didn't seem surprised to see the vehicle, and from what Tetsami could see, the vehicle didn't look the worse for being rolled over a few times. Then again, the *Lady* was tough, and sand was yielding.

They sat there, silent under the stare of the guard and his matte-black Dittrich HVE.

Time ground on.

They sat for so long that Tetsami was startled when a klaxon began sounding and red lights started to flash. Fifty meters away, at the nose of the craft, the ramp began withdrawing. It was a noisy affair, all warning beeps and sirens. As the guard looked off in that direction, Jarvis whispered into her ear. Even without echoes, the noise made it difficult for her to hear.

"You have a biolink?"

Tetsami nodded, Jarvis could see the telltale dimple himself; it was on that side of her neck, just at the hairline. With the right interface she could jack into just about any computer system with it. It was how she had made her living until—

What is he thinking?

"Be ready," he said before the guard turned around.

Oh, great. He's thought of something and he isn't going to be able to tell me until it happens.

She wished she was sitting next to Dom.

Stop that.

She could figure *something* out. Jarvis must intend to take out the one guard. That was fine, he could try, it was his life. After the way he'd disabled her back in the cell, she suspected that he might be able to do it. Even with the restraint buckles.

That was their major problem, the buckles. They needed to be disabled for any escape. Until then, someone at the base station could zap them all if there was trouble. Even if the goober manning the base station was oblivious, even if the base station wasn't manned at all, if any of them got farther than X meters away from it, they'd be zapped. If one of the four buckles restraining them went dead, the others would zap them. If one of the buckles got too far from the other three, the three would zap them.

Tetsami looked at her wrists. There had to be a programing port.

Restraint buckles were an idiosyncratic method of imprisonment, and they had to be programmed with the captive's limb length, their free axis of movement, the length of their stride and a dozen other kinematic factors unique to each prisoner. That software would reside in the buckles themselves, so they could be passed from base station to base station with a minimum of fuss.

Fat toroids of brushed metal. At first glance they appeared seamless. Upon closer examination, she could tell they were constructed of very finely machined pie wedges. They must be able to add or remove wedges to get a snug fit. There was also some give to them. Not much, but enough for Tetsami to slip a finger between the buckle and her wrist. The buckle gave a warning buzz that sent a painful tingle down her arm, so she stopped that avenue of exploration.

By the time the nose to the *Shaftsbury* had shut, she had found what she was looking for. On each restraint buckle was a slightly larger wedge, and on it, near the inside curve of the toroid, was a small beveled hole that would be perfect for a probe.

All Tetsami would need to hack the software would be the wires.

The red flashers at the *Shaftsbury*'s nose stopped rotating as the main entrance closed. The cargo area filled with the sound, the hydraulic whoosh of the hull fusing itself shut. Smaller lights flashed by the nose as wall-mounted holos reflected the ship computer's checklists. In less than three seconds, the displays faded.

The floor began to resonate. The high-frequency vibration was inaudible, and barely felt beyond a slightly numbing sensation when she touched a surface. She knew what the feeling meant. The pilots had just been given the all-clear to fire up the contragravs.

Their guard faded to the wall and grabbed a strap to support himself. His gun remained free.

Even as she felt the vibration of the *Shaftsbury*'s quantum extraction furnace, it was pulling kilograms of contramatter plasma out of virtual nonexistence. Tetsami felt the ship begin to lift almost immediately as the contramatter tried to push away from the real mass of Bakunin. Tetsami's stomach dropped out from under her as the pilots stoked the contragrav furnace.

It only took seconds for Jarvis to move. Her stomach was still sinking with the *Shaftsbury*'s acceleration when she realized that Jarvis was out of his seat. He moved like a dancer, without sound. Somehow, even with the graceful, and seemingly slow, moves, he managed to clear the distance between his chair and the black-clad guard before the guard could bring the gun to bear.

It was the perfect time to strike, Tetsami realized. The guard was disoriented from the ship's acceleration, he only had one hand free, and the gun must have been heavier than it should have been. Even as he raised the Dittrich HVE into a firing position, Jarvis was within arm's reach.

The gestures Jarvis made to take hold of the guard's hand and neck seemed almost gentle.

The sounds that came from the guard were not.

The guard jerked, and the HVE silently discharged a millisecond burst into the floor of the cargo compartment. There was a puff of black smoke from an ovoid patch in the floor, then a lighter patch of pseudoflesh flowed in to heal the hole.

Jarvis turned and muttered something about assholes who rely too much on their technology. The guard slumped down, dangling from the single strap.

Tetsami had already unbelted herself and stood.

Suddenly Kelly was asking questions all over the place, "Hey? What's happening here? A breakout? How do we get off this ship then, not that I'm not in . . ."

Tetsami had trouble walking in the still-moving *Shaftsbury* and she wondered how Jarvis managed to remain graceful. "I think I can deprogram the buckles, if they left my interfaces in the *Lady*."

"Do it," Jarvis said. "I can't touch that weapon until these are off." He turned toward Kelly and Gavadi. "You two, get up and keep those hatches shut."

They'll be lucky to be able to do any such thing, Tetsami thought. *And until the buckles are off, our keepers don't even have to come down here to disable us.*

Tetsami pulled the tarp away from the side entrance of the

Lady. The old three-axled girl was a more than welcome sight. Her wrists twinged at her, warning her that she was moving close to the limit of the buckles' tolerance. She moved more deliberately as she opened the door and entered the *Lady.*

It was obvious that her captors had been through the contents of the *Lady.* Everything had the look of being rifled through. Even the sealant tape on the dash and the seats was new, as if someone had peeled back the tape to examine the cracks for hidden whatevers.

Her own luggage was still back here, repacked. She opened the duffel and dug furiously, but she couldn't find her case of interfaces.

She felt a brief wave of panic until she realized that the duffel's contents must have been sprayed all over the compartment when she rolled the *Lady.* Her captors had repacked her clothes, but the electronic gear—

She opened up the tool cabinet next to the mining laser, and there they were, right on top.

Her hands were shaking as she drew a needle-probed optical interface from the selection. How long did she have before someone reached the base station and activated all the buckles? Minutes? Seconds?

She hyperventilated and put those thoughts from her mind.

She was a hacker, a data thief, a runner in the electronic warren of Godwin. She was the longest-lived independent netrunner on this whole dirtball. *Risk? What the hell was risk?*

The wire seemed almost alive as she fitted the rounded terminus against the dimple in her neck.

Long ago, deep in the roots of her family tree, some government or corporate scientist back on Earth had designed some of her genes. That fiddling had cursed her family for generations as humanity decided it was horrified by genetic engineering, especially of humans. The Tetsamis had fled to Dakota with the rest of the gene-engineered dross, and later Tetsami's parents had fled to Bakunin.

However, the curse had a purpose.

The original modifications were meant to optimize the crude bio-interfaces available in the twenty-first century. Tetsami's brain was *made* to ride the wire.

Her built-in hardwire interface had been there upon birth.

The interface began running even before she slipped the probe into her buckle.

Tetsami's senses dropped away as her time sense telescoped into infinity. Hours in here could pass in minutes to the outside. She was wired in now, and she saw her difficulty. The buckle carried no shell program, it wasn't feeding her any information. She had to grope around in a blank mental space, and find a crack she could exploit.

Time fractured and became unreliable as she thought motion into a sense-deprived landscape. Seconds became hours became days, and she knew if she didn't achieve something quick, the biological part of her mind would fatigue and *give* her something to see.

Then she found it. Felt it, more than saw it. It was a ropelike conduit, a comm line to something, somewhere. As she followed, it became more distinct, resolving into sight and sound as well as touch. She flew along this golden rope, feeling the messages carried within it.

It was the transmission link to the base station. And she could feel it now because the base station was transmitting.

She was too late; they were playing the kill code over the stunners.

No, she was still operating. The man at the station was taking a few seconds. She had some time.

Tetsami shot back over the link, merging herself with the signal. Bothering little with finesse, she blew through handshakes and transmission protocols. She reached the core of the base station even as it was trying to armor itself against the invader. No time for subtlety, Tetsami knew. It was time to use a scorched-earth policy and hope it didn't backwash over the transmission link.

She nuked the base station's command set. She bombarded it with homemade viruses, formatting, and reboot commands. She slammed random garbage into its main core processor. The security programs caught most of it, but like an antimissile battery, it couldn't catch them all.

A format command stuck, and the whole image of the base station winked out.

Tetsami jacked out of the toroid. It felt slightly different. She tried an experiment, swinging her arm as fast as she could. There was no warning tingle. She'd done it.

Now, of course, there was the problem of getting out of a flying spacecraft intact.

One thing at a time, Tetsami thought.

Tetsami came out of the *Lady* after removing the buckles on her wrists and ankles. It was easy, once the programming was dead. She had barely stepped out of the tri-axled vehicle when Jarvis yelled, "Get the hell down!"

Recent history must have helped improve her reaction time, because she had hit the pseudoflesh floor and was rolling even as a wave of monocrys flechettes broke across the side of the *Lady.* The chamber ripened with the smell of red-hot ceramics and ozone, and the side of the vehicle rippled with icy-blue sparks where the supercharged flechettes struck its skin.

Tetsami found cover under the *Lady.* The pseudoflesh immediately behind her erupted into a foul black cloud.

Apparently she hadn't solved the *whole* problem.

From her view underneath the *Lady*'s chassis, she could see Jarvis returning fire with the unconscious guard's HVE. The opposing fire was coming from an open hatch out of view in the ceiling of the cargo compartment. She *could* see their fellow prisoner, Kelly, in a crumpled heap on the floor directly below one of the hatches.

As Tetsami looked in that direction, another crumpled heap fell across Kelly. This heap was different in that it was clad in black, was armed, and was missing most of its head above the lower jaw.

Tetsami had to turn away from the sight as Jarvis said, "That was a stupid move, Tetsami, but you drew the bastard out."

Jarvis' booted feet rounded the *Lady,* and after a few seconds Jarvis said, "Get the hell out here and grab his weapon."

Tetsami had to take a few deep breaths before she pulled herself out from under the *Lady.* She kept from looking at the dead guard as she walked up to Jarvis, who kept talking.

"You were barely in time. Gavadi and Kelly both're stunned."

Tetsami looked toward the other port and saw the crumpled brown heap of Gavadi. "Are they all right?"

"I assume they're alive," Jarvis said as he thrust the dead guard's weapon into her hands. "Can you hack into the system on this ship?"

Tetsami felt dizzy with the speed of events. "If there's an access port, yes. But—"

"This is what you have to do. First you need to black out their communications and security. Then I want you to get their field on-line and use it to cloak this ship's EM signature."

Tetsami opened and closed her mouth a few times as Jarvis spoke. Finally, she said, "Do you know the power drain that'll—"

"I want this tub to drop out from any observation. I'm going up there to take care of the crew. By my count there'll only be three of them. *Move!* They still might not realize what's happening."

Tetsami backed away from Jarvis, who was climbing up the ladder to the upper level of the *Shaftsbury*.

Damn it all, when she was in Dom's operation, at least she was partly in control.

She ran up to the nose of the craft, looking for a port giving access to the ship's systems. It wasn't as if she had much of a choice. If she'd been given time to think, this was what she'd be doing anyway.

Nearby one of the holo displays she found an optical port that would take one of her interfaces. She could feel the wiring in her brain heat up even before she'd pulled out the cable. Just thinking about it started time slowing down, made her feel flushed.

Hacking a live system on a moving vehicle, one they happened to be riding . . . She wondered if Jarvis had any idea how dangerous this was. Tetsami did. She doubted that one in twenty hackers could pull this one without causing a fatal error—like crashing the flight control system.

Now that she had the wire in her hand, the idea just excited her. *If we die,* Tetsami thought, *we die on the wire.*

There was a fold-out seat with a seat belt next to the terminals. She sat herself down and strapped in.

Once secured, sweating with anticipation, she jacked the live contact into the base of her skull.

The interface broke over her senses in a series of shuddering waves. She'd jacked herself directly into a live data pipeline. It only took a few subjective seconds to realize that she'd plugged into a diagnostic port. There were no security protocols here at all, she was just riding the stream of data between here and the contragravs. She plowed upstream to the control systems, abstract mountains of programming that fed the rivers of data.

Everything she touched was a live contact. Every move she made sent some effect flushing downsystem. The experience gave her an aching rush that had nothing to do with the *Shaftsbury*'s shell program.

She knew she had no time to be gentle. She needed to lock out their radio contact with their command. She found the tributaries that led to the cockpit control systems. The structure there was hideously complex and alien. She had to wade through pools of command structures that weren't made to take a rider like her. The ripples she made as she passed blanked out portions of data.

There was nothing she could do about that. The cockpit system wasn't designed to take a biojacked rider swimming in from the diagnostic systems. If something was in the way, she just had to unclog the memory to let her through. If that meant erase, that meant erase. She had no time for finesse.

She finally found the radio and unclogged the last memory channel, erasing the communicator's memory. The *Shaftsbury* was now mute.

Operating the Emerson field was much easier, since the operational setup was *supposed* to be operated from the cockpit control system. It took her less time to get the field on-line in a wide-spectrum shield than it took her to erase the communication software.

All it took was one priority command to the field's core software.

Mission accomplished, Tetsami thought.

Then all hell began to break loose.

It started on the wire, shortly after she gained command of the ship's Emerson field. Parts of her virtual world began to evaporate. It took her a moment too long to realize what was happening.

Oh, shit! I've bypassed all the safety protocols!

She tried to send a new command to the field, but her contact with the *Shaftsbury*'s system was lost before the command had formed.

She jacked out and whispered, "What have I done?"

She needed to get to a priority control jack before the whole system crashed.

If she had been working off of her own agenda, she never would have made such a stupid mistake. But she had been following Jarvis' orders, and the thinking part of her mind had just been turned off.

She unbuckled herself and headed for the ladder to the crew level.

All the *Shaftsbury*'s systems were on a priority list in the main computer. Usually the list went something like: life support, flight control, communication ... all the way down to the holo displays in cargo and the hand dryer in the bathroom. She had just, inadvertently, put the field's power requirements at the head of the priority list.

The computer, obligingly, was already shutting down nonessential systems to keep the field powered up.

Stupid, stupid, stupid ...

Tetsami reslung the HVE across her back and pulled herself up the ladder. As she did so, the ship lurched to port, nearly yanking her away from the wall. Below her, she saw the headless guard roll off of Kelly. She wished she had the time to check on Kelly and Gavadi, but she had to get to a priority port before a critical system failed.

She climbed up through the hatch as the ship pulled another hard maneuver to starboard, doubling her over the lip of the hatch and shoving the air from her lungs.

The lights in the corridor here had already been cut down to emergency levels, casting a red glow over everything and making the spots of gore on the wall a dead black. She didn't need to see the color of the stains to know what they were. She could still smell the ozone-transformer reek of an HVE discharge and that wall was covered with microscopic craters from impact-scattered flechettes.

The ship stabilized, and Tetsami pulled herself up into the empty corridor, unslinging her weapon.

She knew nothing of the *Shaftsbury*'s layout, other than the fact that the cockpit was in a hump above the nose. However, she had no trouble finding her way there. She just followed Jarvis' cursing.

Lights were shutting off as she ran. She knew that the only priority access to the ship's systems would be in the cockpit now.

"What the fuck you mean you *can't!*" Jarvis yelled ahead of her.

Tetsami ran up a narrow flight of stairs that led to the cockpit. As she ran, the *Shaftsbury* dipped its nose in a shuddering dive. The stairway fell away from below her, and when the dive leveled out, she slammed face first into the stairs.

She got unsteadily to her feet, bloodied and feeling a massive bruise where her HVE's stock had rammed into her abdomen.

She closed the cockpit. Jarvis was blocking the door, back to her, yelling at the crew. "Get some lift, you bastards!"

The voice responding to Jarvis was calmer than it should have been. Tetsami figured that it was the pilot. "The system is diverting power from the contragrav. Neutral gravity is the best we have."

Tetsami came up behind Jarvis and, for the first time, saw the view outside the ship.

"Christ's balls!" she said.

Out the cockpit window she could see a massive sloping wall of snow-covered rock sliding by. A snow-covered valley rolled and humped as it raced by underneath them. All around, the horizon was blocked by massive domes of moonlit white-dusted rock. Every detail was much too close.

"What are you doing here?" Jarvis yelled at her.

Who put you in charge? "I need to get to a priority terminal—" She started to push past Jarvis. That was a mistake.

Jarvis grabbed her. "We have a crisis here. I can't let you—"

"It's your effing crisis! That field jimmy you had me pull is sucking power from everywhere and if I don't restructure the command priority list—"

She was interrupted by an electronic siren coming from the pilot's console. A festival of red lights began sprouting across the control panels.

"We've lost power to the contragrav," said the pilot.

Too late, we're dead.

"Hang on," he kept saying in his too-calm voice. "We're going to have to ditch her."

Another crew member, the navigator Tetsami supposed, started calling off numbers. "One thousand meters."

They started turning in the air, toward a saddle between two peaks. Much too close.

"Seven hundred meters."

"Five hundred meters."

There was an emergency harness set in an alcove to the rear of the crew compartment. Tetsami dove into the padded alcove and pulled the crash webbing over herself. The padding responded by shaping itself to her body.

The pilot killed the sound effects that were warning of a half-dozen critical power failures. All the noise left were the voices of the crew members.

"Four hundred meters."

Tetsami tried to pull closed the door to the alcove, sealing the crash pod. It didn't want to stick—part of the crash harness kept it from latching.

The dark cliffs around the *Shaftsbury* silently slid by. The valley passed away as they descended toward the saddle of rock. The white beneath them widened from a ribbon, to a highway, to an ocean of white.

"Two hundred meters."

The door to the crashpod slammed shut, making her wince. It bounced open again.

Snow and ice began slicing across the cockpit windows.

"One hundred meters."

At the critical moment, Tetsami closed her eyes.

The impact threw her down and forward into the crash harness. The harness cut into her legs, crushed her breasts, and her neck felt like it was being cracked like a whip. The sound was deafening, as if the shuddering craft was riding inside an unending explosion.

The cockpit shook, slamming her against the emergency harness and the padded wall behind her. The padding on the wall was twenty centimeters thick, but when she slammed against it, she felt the metal spars beneath it raise welts against her shoulders and the backs of her thighs.

The door tried to slam shut. The only thing saving her from the crashing impact of the repeated slamming of the door was the swollen padding molded around her body, hugging her inside the alcove.

The rumbling continued with the sensation of violent deceleration. The jerk threw the door open again and above the avalanche of sound, Tetsami heard something shatter explosively. The shatter was followed by razor-cold air that felt like it was stripping every bit of exposed skin off her body.

The ship shook violently, slamming the door open and closed, again, and again, and again. . . .

Someone was screaming and Tetsami screwed her eyes shut tighter.

The cockpit was filled with screaming air, strobed by the spastic door to the alcove. Tetsami was being intermittently blasted by ice that felt like ground glass.

After an eternity, the motion stopped. So did the sound. The door slammed shut once, then slowly creaked open. Tetsami hurt.

Even with the crash padding hugging her into immobility, every joint in her body had been shaken barely within the limits of tolerance. Her neck and shoulders felt especially stiff. Cold burned her face and hands into a dry parchment that could crumble at a touch. Her torso felt striped with bruises that probably broke the skin in places.

Even opening her eyes was a painful struggle against the frost that gummed them shut.

"Shit . . ." she whispered through bleeding lips when she could finally see.

The light in the *Shaftsbury*'s cockpit was a surreal rose glow, the emergency lights filtered through snow that covered the front of the cockpit, the windows—or where the windows used to be.

Something, probably a huge chunk of ice or rock, had shattered across the top of the *Shaftsbury*'s nose. It had blown in the windows. From the looks of the bodies, half-buried in snow, it had also killed the pilot and copilot.

Snow was everywhere, a drift sloped away from the bottom edge of the windows, burying the pilot and copilot's stations. A mirror-image drift sloped up on either side of the door to the rest of the ship.

Snow caked the walls and the instruments. Red dots glowed diffusely, the ship's last few warnings about damage and power consumption. They were fading even as Tetsami watched.

The navigator had been blown clear of his station. He lay in a crumpled heap on the side of the door opposite Tetsami. Unlike the pilot and copilot, he looked alive. As she watched, she saw his chest move.

Jarvis, who had been next to her, was nowhere to be seen.

Great plan, Tetsami thought as she hit the release for the harness, a small switch by her otherwise immobilized right hand. She winced. Every movement, however fractional, felt as if her joints had been spiked with sand.

As the padding shrank, releasing her to hang from the

crash webbing, she realized that she might have trouble standing.

Great.

She wasn't sure if she was cursing herself or Jarvis.

CHAPTER TWENTY-THREE

Diminishing Returns

"Guilt is not a survival trait."
— *The Cynic's Book of Wisdom*

"Uneasy lies the head that wears a crown."
— WILLIAM SHAKESPEARE
(1564–1616)

Dom remained in the conference room through the night and into the morning. It became his control center. No one had managed any more sleep, least of all, Dom.

Somewhere out there, Tetsami was in the hands of Proudhon Spaceport Security. It was almost certain that Klaus had her, or would have her soon. The thought of Tetsami in Klaus' hands was worse than any thought of the TEC organizing a government by force on Bakunin.

If Klaus had Tetsami, he'd know about Diderot, about Dom, and about twelve hundred people. . . .

Random flew the nets of Bakunin trying to find some angle, some transmission, that would give them some idea of Tetsami's fate. He had yet to find anything.

Dom slogged through the hours as if he were waist-deep in mud. Events had run beyond his control, and he seemed to be losing the sovereignty of his own body. He'd tensed his muscles to the point where the synthetic fibers wrung the remaining living tissue into agonizing cramps. If he didn't sit there and concentrate, his limbs would erupt into spasms of involuntary vibration.

Dom cursed the God that put more than a thousand people on one side of the balance, and Tetsami on the other.

The constant arguing didn't help matters any.

Ivor's facade had crumbled early. *"I don't believe you!"*

Dom sat there unmoving. Not because he felt nothing at

the attack, but because he felt that if he let any of the tension he felt leak out, the dam would burst and everything would crumble. "We're past the point where we can stop," Dom said.

"You can't ignore this, act like nothing is happening."

Is that what I'm doing? Dom felt his hands, especially the fully cybernetic left one, sink their fingers into the armrests of the chair.

At the moment, he and Ivor were alone in the conference room—if you discounted Random, who roamed the wiring. Flower and Mosasa had flown to Godwin to supervise the Bleek takeover, Zanzibar had gone with them to lead the break-in on Ezra Bleek's mansion.

Dom didn't know where Shane was.

They'd spent hours arguing about the possibility of war, but the only concession they'd made to Proudhon was to bump up the timetable. They were going to try to take over Bleek in daylight, a day early.

Dom hoped, desperately hoped, that they would be able to clear all twelve hundred employees into Godwin before Klaus discovered that everyone was still alive.

"Answer me, damn it!" Ivor shouted at him. "What the hell are you going to do about her?"

"Tetsami's one person," Dom said quietly. "I have over a thousand to think about."

"That's it, isn't it? She's no longer part of this." Ivor waved a hand wildly, taking in the whole mountain surrounding them. "She no longer matters."

A twitch ran up Dom's arm, and he felt part of the chair give. His left hand rose about six centimeters, still clutching a piece of the chair. "Ivor." Dom's effort to control his voice became more strained. A vibrato was seeping in. "Think for a moment."

"About what? She's out there, needs our help—"

"We don't have the res—"

"—and you don't care!"

Something in the chair snapped and Dom found himself standing. Ivor took a step backward. Dom was holding the armrest of the chair like a club. Dom's words came in short gasps. It was all he could do to keep from screaming. "You have no right."

"You—"

"Shut up!" Dom swung the chair's arm between them.

Something inside his head was saying that he had finally
snapped. "Call me a monster. Call me an evil bastard. Damn
me to hell." Dom jabbed Ivor in the chest with his makeshift
club. He restrained himself but he still brought a whuff of air
from Ivor. "Don't *ever* tell me what I care about!"

Ivor fell backward into another chair, and Dom stopped
his advance.

"Tetsami," Dom continued, "might just be the only thing
left that I do care about."

"Then *do* something."

"*What?* You're a pilot. Tell me how many vehicles you
would need to do a full sweep of the northern desert?"

"Uh—"

"Tell me the odds of finding an army dug in there with
decent ECM capability. Tell me that no one will notice a
wide, sector by sector search of the area. Tell me that we
even have a good idea of where to look now that they've had
nearly a full day to move her."

Dom's words seemed to bludgeon Ivor as efficiently as if
he was using the chunk of metal in his hand.

"I have people here whose lives depend on this Bleek operation. Lifetime employees, their families, their children,
who have nowhere to go if this operation doesn't come off.
Twelve hundred people my brother would gladly kill to get
to me."

"I'm sorry," Ivor said. He looked beaten.

Dom dropped the armrest. It clattered to the floor. The anger washed out of him as quickly as it had come. "And, if
Proudhon is working with—or for—Klaus, and they have
Tetsami, Klaus is going to know very soon that I am alive
and where we all are."

Someone should do something, Dom's thoughts echoed
Zanzibar's voice. *Who could do what, though?*

"I want a vehicle," Ivor said.

"It's a big desert," Dom responded, even though he already knew he'd let Ivor go. One craft had a better chance
of getting in and out of—whatever. Especially with Ivor
driving.

"A small contragrav, and supplies."

Dom nodded. "Okay. But it's not just Tetsami you should
look for—"

They looked at each other, and Ivor nodded slowly. They
both knew that someone needed to confirm the intelligence

they'd gotten. Someone needed to see the Proudhon army and report back.

"Find them before they find you," Dom said.

Ivor nodded, his face set so gravely that Dom feared for anyone who might have even looked at Tetsami funny. Dom also feared for Ivor. He had the sinking feeling that he was sending the white-haired giant out on a suicide mission. Never mind that it was actually Ivor sending himself.

Dom felt responsible.

He *was* responsible. It was his fault that Tetsami had left in the first place. His own ham-handed inability to deal with his own emotion. Dom thought that if he had, even once, managed to drop a hint of how he had felt. How he still felt . . .

His mind looped around tying itself in knots.

"What are *you* going to do?" Ivor asked.

The question was almost an accusation. Dom could see that the veneer was fully off of Ivor now. All the civil pretense was gone. The look Ivor leveled at him held withering contempt and something else that Dom could barely stand.

Pity.

Someone should do something.

If that someone was him, something was what? From this mountain fortress, a mountain that might soon have Klaus' forces overrunning it in a search for him, what could he do? Dom looked around at the conference room. It was, perhaps, the most advanced part of the whole jury-rigged setup that riddled the mountain.

If nothing else, he could warn people. Multiple transmissions would be risky, and to actually get anywhere he would have to dig into his personal capital. He'd have to call people he knew, the contacts he had made over the years in Bakunin, use the trusts he had made. He would have to leave indisputable evidence that he was alive.

If I'm going to Proteus, what does that matter?

"I have a network of contacts throughout Godwin and the eastern communes," Dom told Ivor. "I am going to try and get a warning out."

It was amazing. Simply stating the plan managed to free him from the mental quagmire he'd been pushing through. Ivor nodded, as if he'd expected that much.

"Gather what you need and go to the northern vehicle bay. I'll have a craft waiting for you," Dom told him.

Ivor left without another word.

"Good luck," Dom whispered.

Alone now, Dom sat in the damaged chair and wondered who he was going to call first. Before he had reached any conclusion, the holo in front of him whooped red, demanding immediate attention. Dom answered it, to be greeted by the face of Kathy Shane, somewhere deep in the mountain. Behind Shane was a massive wall of rock.

"Mr. Magnus?"

Somehow, after the message from Tetsami, no one called him Dominic any more.

"That was an emergency circuit, what's the problem?"

"The problem is the guards you have down here are useless." Someone behind her began jabbering and Shane told him to shut up. "Hougland's escaped."

"How, when?"

"Slipped through the stun field and a wide spot in the bars, and climbed straight up the rock face. About the time we were all in the conference room, I suspect."

Dom caught a glimpse of the frantic guard behind Shane and knew it had been right out from under the guard's nose. He'd underestimated Hougland. "Damn it, I don't have anyone to spare." He really didn't. Every capable hand had been commandeered for the Bleek mission, even more so now that it was going down in daylight. All the hands he had left were injured, children, and people vital to the running, and subsequent breakdown of the mountain headquarters.

"I'll go after her," Shane said, in a tone that told Dom that she'd made her decision long before she'd called him.

"I can't send you out alone. Those caverns are endless."

"She won't be alone," interrupted an electronic voice on their transmission. The voice was Random Walk's.

"What?" said Shane.

"I am sending down my flying simulacrum to accompany you, with a piece of my mind, so to speak."

"Look," Shane said, "neither of you are obligated to do anything. This is personal." She hefted a large duffel. "I was going to leave anyway."

"Hougland's still a security risk," Dom said.

"Also," Random added, "I bring many things without which a search for another human in this mountain would be hopeless. Not to mention spelunking equipment."

"Take Random with you," Dom said.

"Okay," Shane agreed, "but he better get down here quick."

"I fly as we speak, Captain."

"Don't call me Captain."

"Keep me posted as much as you can, Random," Dom said.

"In the telcomm horror of those rock tunnels, I will do what I can."

Dom nodded and cut the connection.

The center will not hold, Dom thought.

Ivor was about to fly off into the desert to find his disappeared adoptive daughter. Flower and Mosasa were in position somewhere in Godwin, and Zanzibar was preparing to break into a mansion in the Western suburbs. Shane was about to disappear into the belly of the Diderot Range to hunt down a former comrade, taking along some fraction of Random Walk's brain.

And then there was one.

Dom sat alone in the conference room. It was nearly fifteen minutes before he ordered the first sat uplink.

CHAPTER TWENTY-FOUR

Hard Target

"It's better to hit your opponent when he isn't looking."

—*The Cynic's Book of Wisdom*

"Inequality of property will exist as long as liberty exists."

—ALEXANDER HAMILTON
(1755–1804)

Zanzibar flew the small contragrav van low over Godwin. She'd been troubled by what was about to happen, even though, of all the people running the Diderot Holding Company, Zanzibar had been the one least surprised by Mr. Magnus' decision to continue with the Bleek takeover.

The daylight was her chief worry. Kropotkin was just now clearing the mountains to the east. The plan called for a night mission, but circumstances had advanced the timetable. People had barely time to get into position before the signal was given. Mr. Magnus wanted his people firmly established in Bleek before all hell broke loose to the East.

Then he leaves.

However, the time for worries was past. Everyone was in position and it was time to make the damn thing work.

In the van with her sat four commandos, all handpicked from her security force. Unlike Mosasa and Flower, her knowledge of combat and tactics was more than theoretical. She would be the one to hold point in the most critical portion of the takeover. She'd be the person to contact Ezra Bleek.

The contragrav van she rode was dead black and over-armored. Mosasa's team had taken a commercial armored car, brought the armor up to military specs and installed an

Emerson field generator that wouldn't be out of place on a fighter aircraft. Unfortunately, the extra weight prevented the contragrav from getting any real acceleration.

The plan compensated for that.

The van began in a holding pattern a half-klick above the office buildings of West Godwin. It approached one of the fortified enclaves that clustered to the west of Godwin riding a shallow downward angle. Zanzibar allowed gravity to pull them toward the enclave, and the Ezra Bleek mansion.

The feeling dropped out of her stomach as the van started free fall.

They were only going to get one chance at this. If they missed the mansion the first time, the overloaded van was too ponderous to make a turnaround for a second shot.

The van dropped out of the sky, and in fifteen seconds they would hit the Ezra complex.

Fourteen. The trajectory mapped perfectly on to the computer track. The horizon rose across the van's windshield. Below, Zanzibar saw the ziggurat walls around the high-priced enclave that purported to protect its suburban residents from Bakunin's harsher realities.

Twelve. The horizon slipped out of Zanibar's view above the windshield. Godwin spread below her like a holo map. Everyone checked their strengthened crash harnesses. They were going to need them.

Ten. The ground closed with deceptive lethargy. Lights flashed by the comm on the van's dash. Enclave security had seen the van, and tracked its possible terminal point.

Eight. Individual buildings resolved themselves. Zanzibar could see the antiaircraft batteries around the perimeter of the enclave tracking the van.

Six. The enclave doubled its size, filling half the windshield. Zanzibar could see the Ezra mansion now, and she adjusted the trim of the van so the nose was pointing at it.

Four. Lasers lanced by the van. Ellipsoid rainbows broke across the nose as their military class force field soaked up the AA fire.

Three. The enclave had doubled in size again. The landscape was expanding now with visceral speed.

Two. They'd dropped from under the AA fire and were now over the wall. Residences shot by below them, too fast to make out any details. The only stationary point in the universe was the Ezra Bleek mansion, ahead and below, growing to meet them. As the van shot toward its target, Zanzibar could see people scrambling around it, like ants.

One.

"Hold on!"

The van skipped across the acreage in front of the mansion like a rock thrown into a pond. As it plowed toward the mansion, it tossed up sod, dirt, and former garden. The impact threw Zanzibar against the crash harness as she tried to control the collision. She maneuvered the van using only its fans.

The van plowed through a marble fountain, spraying water across its nose. Outside, blue-and-green uniformed guards scattered from the van's path, many unlimbering weapons and firing. The armor and the force field took up all the small arms fire.

The van's nose plowed into the wall of the mansion. It was a secure building, but it was a residence, not a bunker. Despite the polyceram reinforcement, the van blew the wall aside, coming to rest nestled in kindling that used to be hardwood floor.

As soon as the van stopped moving, Zanzibar hit the quick-release on her crash harness. She left half the team to defend the van against the security forces and repower the contragrav for their exit.

Bleek's private army was large, but confused. With their pretty uniforms and stylish laser sidearms, they were a ceremonial palace guard who had suddenly found themselves in a real war. The lasers firing through the hole into the ballroom were powerful, but monochrome—no hope against a military-class force field.

Zanzibar led a pair of commandos through the halls of the mansion. They ran over hardwood floors, past expensive tapestries and off-planet artwork. They were halfway to the core of the building, and the elevators, when they met the first heavy resistance.

Laser carbines sliced in at them from a forward intersection. Two of the Bleek palace guard had positioned themselves ahead, where the corridor ended in a conservatory. The guards were backlit by the unnatural white glow from the sunlamps in the room, hidden behind exotic plants that grew from the large marble planter they were using for cover.

Zanzibar and company had to flatten against the walls of

the corridor. Unlike the laser sidearms, the carbines were high-power enough to give any personal force field trouble.

Unlike the guards, Zanzibar's team wasn't armed with lasers. They each carried a Dittrich 15mm High Mass Electromag. The fifteen millimeter HME rifle fired rounds of steel-jacketed uranium.

It only took one volley from Zanzibar's people to reduce the marble planter to stone shrapnel and brown dirt. The planter exploded, burying the Bleek defenders under off-planet foliage.

Zanzibar's team ran through the conservatory and into a larger corridor that headed to the heart of the building.

The central room with the elevators was of a different character than the rest of the house. It could have been a room in Bleek's corporate headquarters. The walls were unadorned chrome, the floor a mirrored sheet. Diffuse shadowless light came from fixtures hidden in the tops of the walls. The elevator was armored, and the whole shebang was defended by at least ten heavily armed guards.

There was no time to be neat about things. The guards were aware of them coming down the hall at the same time they were aware of the guards. Zanzibar unlimbered her other weapon—a one-shot disposable plasma cannon.

As the guards massed to repel the invaders, Zanzibar hit the ground, waited half a beat so her three companions could do likewise, and fired the cannon into the room.

Plasma weapons had a nasty habit of backwashing in enclosed spaces. The firestorm that erupted into the room blew back an acrid rolling fireball across the ceiling of the corridor.

For a moment everything was red light, whistling air, and heat that taxed her force field to the point of failure.

Then the noises were alarms and klaxons. Cool white foam spilled over her. Zanzibar got up and looked into the elevator room. Blackened metal creaked and popped, foam hissed and crackled as it flowed from the few undamaged fire control systems. The smell of smoke, superheated metal, burnt synthetics, and charred flesh assaulted Zanzibar's nose as she stepped forward.

Have to remind myself, this is a friendly *takeover.*

The room was ankle-deep in white foam, which spared her from seeing the corpses of the guards. The elevator door had warped away from the shaft, making their job easier.

Fitzgerald, her security man, got to work with a small powered jack and soon had the elevator door off of its track,
leaving them access to the maglev shaft.

The inside of the shaft was streaked with soot and white
foam. The fire alarms were still going.

Zanzibar hooked a line to one of the magnet mountings
and lowered herself down the shaft. Fitzgerald followed her.

Down the shaft three levels and the smell and leftover
heat was no longer as intense. The elevator was at an upper
level somewhere. That made Zanzibar nervous.

The bottom of the shaft was knee-high in fire-suppressant
foam. It was hard to move because the stuff was beginning
to harden. Fitzgerald got to work on the door as Zanzibar
kept him covered with the rifle. As he worked, someone at
the guard's command-and-control must've had a brainstorm.
There was a sickening screech from above them, and Zanzibar looked up to see the bottom of the elevator hurtling
toward them.

Zanzibar pointed her rifle up, as if she could defend herself with it, and prayed.

The shaft shook with the agonized cry of abused metal as
the elevator slid past the open door above them. The elevator stopped.

Zanzibar stared up the shaft at the bottom of the maglev
elevator. The shaft up there had been warped by the heat of
the plasma blast. The elevator was hung up on something.

It couldn't last.

Zanzibar was still hearing the sounds of bending and tearing metal. It wouldn't be long before the weight of the elevator tore itself loose and it resumed free-fall.

"Hurry," Zanzibar said.

As if in response, she heard a hydraulic wheeze, and the
level of foam in the bottom of the shaft began dropping. The
doors in front of them opened and Zanzibar pushed Fitzgerald through the half-open door as she scrambled out of the
shaft.

The two of them stumbled out into an empty corridor. The
furnishings, carpet, and artwork all could have been part of
the mansion upstairs. However, the overall effect was
spoiled by the red flashing lights and the sirens. There were
two ways to go. Zanzibar chose the left.

Before they reached the end of the corridor, she heard the
tearing screech of metal, and the shattering collision as the

elevator slammed into the bottom of the shaft. A half-second later, a small wave of fire-suppressant foam washed by her feet, ruining the expensive carpet.

The corridor they ran down ended in a cul-de-sac. Its main feature was a vast armored window. Zanzibar approached the window cautiously, allowing Fitzgerald to cover her. Behind the window, she could see lab equipment, holo terminals, and a room done up in hospital whites and chromes. The door was a brushed metal air lock. She couldn't see any motion inside the room beyond.

As she approached, the air lock door slid open. Zanzibar leveled her gun at it, and was greeted by a lab coat being waved like a flag.

She raised her hand so Fitzerald wouldn't fire, and allowed a surrendering trio of doctors and lab techs—all young women—out into the hall.

Once Fitzgerald had the prisoners covered, Zanzibar walked into the air lock. The room beyond looked like an intensive care ward. She wove through ranks of equipment until she reached an armored door at the other end of the room. The door had a keypad next to it, flashing red.

"Send one of them back in here to open this," she called to Fitzgerald.

The blonde doctor walked in. "Are you going to hurt him?" she asked.

"No."

The doctor looked indecisive.

"If we blow the door, we might hurt him by accident."

The doctor sighed and punched in the combination. The door slid aside.

Zanzibar expected to see something that looked like a hospital ward. Instead, what she saw was a lobby leading into a softly lit library. The library had a four-meter ceiling and floor-to-ceiling bookshelves that held clothbound volumes that must have been worth megagrams. In the center of the room, reclining on a chair under a toroid-shaped reading lamp, was Ezra Bleek.

He snored loudly.

Zanzibar walked up to Ezra Bleek and thought, *the man must sleep like the dead.*

Despite his alleged incapacity, Ezra Bleek looked as healthy as a horse. He certainly had a healthy snore.

Sirens were still going off. There was even a flashing red

light set high in the wall of the library. The smell of distant smoke and suppressant foam filled the room.

And still, in a bathrobe, book steepled on his lap, Ezra snored.

He looked like a short prophet, with white hair and beard unkempt and going everywhere. The toroid reading lamp hung over his head like a cockeyed halo.

Zanzibar stepped up and shook Ezra by the shoulder.

A sucking snort came from Ezra's open mouth and he mumbled something that Zanzibar couldn't make out. She shook him harder.

Without opening his eyes Ezra yelled, "What? You waking me to say it's bedtime again? Or perhaps you have a meal I'm not hungry for—"

"Mr. Bleek—"

"Go way! You have cameras everywhere—I've lost my privacy, the least you can do is leave me when I am sleeping."

Zanzibar shook harder, "Mr. Bleek!"

"Take the tray away. It smells horrible—" Ezra's eyes blinked open. " 'Mr. Bleek,' she says?"

He sat up and turned, looking at Zanzibar for the first time. "I'd say something odd is going on here."

"They broke in—" started the blonde doctor, who had followed Zanzibar in.

"Please!" Ezra snapped at her. "I'm savoring the novelty. And I am not senile. I can see she isn't staff. I doubt my beloved daughter would hire some schwartze amazon as a day nurse."

Ezra took the book off his lap and stepped out of the easy chair.

"Mr. Bleek—" Zanzibar started again.

He shook his head, smiling. "Please, before I find I'm being kidnapped or killed, let me savor that little respect." Ezra held up his hand, " 'Mr. Bleek,' " he said slowly. "So long it's been. Always it's these shikse nurses, Ezra this, Ezra that—or worse, 'we need to eat' or 'time for us to go to bed.' It saps an old man's dignity." He took a deep breath, coughed a few times, and lowered his hand. "Please go on now, my polite intruder."

Zanzibar looked over her shoulder, and saw Fitzgerald covering the entrance to the pseudo-ICU ward. Apparently, with the elevator out of commission, they had some time before the Bleek guards descended to this level. She turned back, took a deep breath, and said, "Mr. Bleek, I represent the Diderot Holding Company. We wish to purchase your interest in Bleek Munitions."

"Oy. No wonder you have to break in. My children would never approve. They're afraid that someday they might have to work for a living."

"Would you consider selling?"

"I'm a businessman, much as my family would deny it. I'll consider anything. What are you offering?"

"Fifty grams a share."

"For fifty grams my children would sell." Ezra shook his head.

The unmistakable sound of a uranium bullet slamming into something unyielding came from down the corridor. Zanzibar looked at Fitzgerald. He was still there, guarding the entrance to Ezra's quarters.

"Sir—" she said, trying not to let too much urgency slip into her voice.

"I know. Time. Things go so fast on this planet. Yes, for fifty grams you have a sale." Ezra raised a finger. "If—"

Zanzibar looked from Bleek to the exit. More sounds of gunfire were reaching them over the noise from the fire alarms.

"If?"

Ezra hiked his robe about himself and said, "Why, as long as you deliver me from this gilded dungeon."

"Come on," Zanzibar said. She grabbed him by the shoulder and maneuvered him toward the exit. To his credit, he didn't ask to stop for anything even though he was only clad in robe, briefs, and slippers.

The two of them passed by Fitzgerald, who was covering the remaining medical staff but looking worriedly through the window at the hallway. Zanzibar noted that Ezra gave each woman on the staff a wide smile that seemed to drip with irony.

Once she, Ezra, and her backup cleared the front air lock, she closed it on the medical staff and shot out the controls.

The noise of gunfire was very loud now, and she couldn't see her way to the elevator shaft because of a hazy smoke that clouded the corridor. They would be walking into a firefight blind. Zanzibar stood there, listening for a while.

It was definitely a single HME, one of her people, backing toward them. As she waited, she could see occasional flashes of energy weapons. The man by the elevator had been firing a delaying action all the way from the surface. He had to be close to the limit on ammo.

All of them were in a cul-de-sac. In a few seconds they'd be pinned to the wall. They did have a contingency plan. She only hoped that Ezra understood—

"Forgive the imposition," she whispered at Ezra before slipping her arm across his chest under his arms, and lifting him off of the ground.

Zanzibar sucked in a breath. Then she yelled, as loudly as she could, "We have Ezra Bleek! Lay down your weapons and step away from them or your leader dies!"

Zanzibar hoped this would work. The guards probably thought they were protecting Ezra, rather than holding him prisoner.

Ezra was helping matters by frantic yells of "Don't shoot!" She didn't know if he was yelling at the Bleek guards, or her.

The sounds of shooting ebbed, and she slowly advanced. Soon she caught up with her second comrade, Davidson, who had been dragging an elevator door back toward the cul-de-sac as a hunk of portable cover. Zanzibar passed him and waved him forward with her gun hand.

The squirming Ezra was pressed to her chest while her right hand angled her HME rifle up toward his head. It wasn't the best way to wield the weapon, and if she ever fired she'd probably decapitate both of them in addition to breaking her wrist. However, the posture was essential, because suddenly she was facing a forest of blue-and-green uniforms, who had, indeed, dropped their guns and had flattened themselves against the walls.

"Remember," she yelled at them. "We're carrying personal fields. Mr. Bleek is not. An energy weapon will probably fry him before I decide to pull the trigger."

They passed the elevator. It was a mess. The descending capsule had blown out a good chunk of wall.

"Okay," she said, whispering to her own people. "We take the stairs."

They continued down the corridor, past the knot of guards. She walked point, with Ezra as a shield. Her two comrades faced behind, walking with her, back-to-back.

The problem with the stairs was the fact that they were

badly located, and gave them a lot more exposure to the palace guard. They passed dozens of them. Fortunately, while their progress was slow, the guards set down their weapons as they passed.

From that point on it was a textbook case of corporate kidnapping—an unusual, but not unheard of, method of conducting business on Bakunin.

They emerged from the stairwell at ground level. They passed more knots of guards, all well away from their weapons. As they closed on the ballroom, the smell of smoke thickened. As they rounded the conservatory, they came across open air. The whole second floor above the ballroom was gone, and what was left of the third was a charred ceiling that was slowly collapsing. Charred debris covered the floor, and Zanzibar had to step carefully over wreckage and bodies to make it to where the ballroom had been.

The van was there, but the ballroom itself was gone, mostly a blasted crater that burned and smoldered in dozens of places. The only remnants were a few sticks of hardwood flooring that had survived by being within the van's field radius. The two defenders had done well with the arsenal that had been left.

As Zanzibar and company closed on the van, the doors opened.

She pushed Ezra inside, and quickly followed and sat at the controls. The contragrav was powered and waiting for her. Fitzgerald and Davidson piled in last, and she was goosing the contragrav even before the door slid shut.

"Hang on," she said as the contragrav shuddered slowly into the air.

As the van started to slide out of the compound, the Bleek guards still didn't fire upon it. However, in an apparent failure of communication, the antiaircraft batteries at the walls of the enclave did, as soon as the van topped out.

Zanzibar's exit was more grueling than her arrival because of the slow acceleration of the beast they were riding. She had to duck and weave the van through laser fire for nearly half a minute before they cleared the walls of the enclave. Worse, the enclave defenders were also firing high-caliber projectiles at them. The van shook several times with impacts against the armor.

Mercifully most of the firing ceased when they cleared the wall. The defenders had decided against any parting shots.

Which was good, since now that the van wasn't over the area the antiaircraft was protecting, the defenders might've felt free to unload missiles and artillery at them.

Ezra was busy staring out one of the little armored windows.

"Mr. Bleek?" Zanzibar asked, once the van's course east over Godwin had stabilized. They were grazing over the tops of the skyscrapers now, slowly rising.

"Yes?"

She handed him a small pocket comm. "You're free. Here's the offer. I'd appreciate if you'd go over it quickly."

CHAPTER TWENTY-FIVE

Frozen Assets

"It is pointless to worry once the situation's become hopeless."

—*The Cynic's Book of Wisdom*

"The basis of optimism is sheer terror."

—OSCAR WILDE
(1854–1900)

Tetsami had no idea how much she'd been hurt until she freed herself completely from the crash pod. When she tried to stand on the snow-covered, down-sloping floor of the cockpit, the pain in her legs—especially the inside of her thighs—made her collapse. She pitched forward, face first into the snowbank at the front of the cockpit.

She had to stay there for a few seconds, despite snow flaying her windburned skin. When she finally could push herself upright, she had to hold on to the back of the pilot's chair to remain standing.

Her fingers were becoming numb.

She wondered how long she had before she had to worry about frostbite.

Once the pain of walking was no longer a constant surprise, she let go of the chair and checked the crew. Her assessment of the pilot and copilot was painfully accurate.

The pilot had been sliced around the face and neck by the exploding window, and one of the wounds had severed an artery in his neck. The blood coating him had already turned into a sheet of ruby ice. He had died with one hand on the control stick and one on the wound in his neck.

Tetsami felt sick.

The copilot had been struck by part of whatever had blown through the cockpit's window. His neck had been broken and part of his upper chest had caved in. There was very little blood and it looked like he'd died instantly.

Outside, she heard a long rumble and she hoped that this wreck was on a stable perch.

Tetsami made her way up the sloping floor, toward the rear of the cockpit. It was hard to maneuver, all the illumination came from snow-covered emergency lights.

The navigator was unconscious, but still breathing. It looked as if the impact had torn him free of his crash harness, or he'd put it on wrong. The man had slammed against the far wall, bounced off his control console, and had fallen to the floor. He was wrapped around the base of his own chair now, which made it hard for Tetsami to see his injuries. She didn't want to move him.

The sleeve on his right arm was shredded, and there was massive bruising and discoloration underneath, a major fracture or dislocation. In addition to the arm, she could also see that one leg was broken. Either that, or this guy was born with an extra knee.

He was probably the one she'd heard screaming during the crash. She would've screamed, too.

She felt for a pulse in his neck. Other than some rudimentary resuscitation, it was the only medical thing she knew how to do.

His pulse felt strong and steady and that gave her some hope that the man's injuries weren't immediately life-threatening.

She had time to get to the medkit in the *Lady,* and time to find out what happened to the other three prisoners.

Before she left, she caught sight of the navigator's nametag.

"Marc Baetez," she whispered through cracked, bleeding lips. Her words came out in a white fog that frosted the chrome of Marc's seat. "Stay alive."

She stood up and shoved her hands under her arms to warm them.

Walking to the cockpit entrance, up the slope, required tiny steps. Every few steps she had to wave her pained hands out into the cold to balance herself.

There was no sign of Jarvis.

Not until she made it to the top of the stairs.

Jarvis had taken a header down the stairs from the cockpit. His gun was halfway down the stairs, and the old mercenary himself was sprawled at the base. For the first time, Tetsami thought he looked like an old man.

She carefully limped down the stairs, supporting herself with first one hand, then the other. It was warmer down here, despite the chill following her down from the cockpit. She could feel her hands and face thawing, awakening fiery needles over every exposed piece of her flesh. Her near-frostbitten skin now felt flushed and sweating.

She hoped that was a good sign.

When she reached Jarvis, her breath only fogged a little.

To her surprise, Jarvis was alive. However, his skin was pale, and both legs looked broken. Also, from a fall like that, she wouldn't be surprised if there were a host of other fractures and internal injuries.

She didn't want to touch him, even to take his pulse.

Jarvis' pulse frightened her. It was weak and irregular, and it took her too long just to find it. She had to do something for him, quick. Only, she had no idea what. She had to get to that damn medkit. She wished she knew where they kept the medkit in this ship—it was probably closer.

She ran down the corridor, to the hatch for the cargo space. Her footing was surer, now that she wasn't sliding over snow, but the pain of the bruises wrapping her body made her fall three times before she reached it.

The corridor darkened as she progressed, blackness devouring what little ruddy light the emergency lights cast.

Her last fall was caused by a combination of dim lighting and the hatch cover for the cargo entrance. The cover had been torn from its hinges, probably from repeated opening and closing during the crash. It had come to rest ten meters away, down the slope of the corridor.

She picked herself up and made her way to the hole.

She was afraid to look down.

When she did, she saw a red icy hell. Snow covered everything down there. The emergency lights glowed through sheets of ice that fractured their hard red glow. The *Lady,* she saw, had partially lost its mooring. It was on its side and at an angle pointing away from the nose. From the drifts against its roof, some of the snow down there had to be two meters deep.

It was obvious that, during the crash, the *Shaftsbury*'s hinged nose had been torn away. Tetsami suspected that debris from that event must have been what shattered the windows in the cockpit.

"Christ on a stick," she muttered as she started to lower herself on the ladder. The contact of bare skin on the frosted metal rungs was so agonizing that she almost let go. She managed not to. In her condition, a fall like that, even into a snowdrift, would probably knock her out.

The climb could have only taken half a minute at most. It felt like an hour.

"Medkit," she said when her feet sank into the snow. "Medkit and gloves."

She checked the base of the ladder, but, of course, there was no sign of the dead guard or Kelly. Those two, along with Gavadi and the second guard were buried down here, somewhere.

They were also very probably dead.

Tetsami ran through the drifts, to the side of the *Lady.*

The tough vehicle looked undamaged, but it was difficult to get inside, given its posture. Tetsami had to climb up the middle axle to get to the door, something her body didn't need. She punctuated her climb with a flurry of curses and impromptu blasphemy.

When she reached the right-side door, now on top, she paused for breath.

When she did, she heard, faintly, someone cry, "Help."

Someone survived down here? How was she going to get to everyone before someone died?

Tetsami pulled the *Lady*'s door open and yelled, "Where are you?"

"Here, over here," it seemed to come from the rear of the cargo area.

Tetsami lowered herself into the *Lady.* It seemed to take her much too long to find the emergency medkit. She also grabbed a shovel out of a pile of mining equipment.

She didn't bother with the gloves.

"Keep talking," she called as she climbed out of the *Lady.* "Who are you? Are you hurt?"

"Kelly. It's cold. . . ."

Kelly? I thought he was stunned. Tetsami plowed through meter-deep snow, toward the massive drifts filling the rear of the cargo area. As she closed, she supposed it was possible that the shock of the snow could have revived him. It was known to happen.

Tetsami got to the drift and started digging, thinking all the time about Jarvis' thready pulse. It was only a few seconds before she'd uncovered Kelly's legs. He'd been buried under a drift. It was a meter deep around his legs, closer to three over his upper body.

Can he breathe?

Another half minute and she found him digging his way out toward her. When his face emerged from the snow, he blinked up at her and asked, "What happened?"

"Are you injured?" Tetsami asked.

Kelly rose slowly. A bad move if he was hurt. However, he seemed better off than Tetsami felt. Tetsami found that incredibly irritating.

"I seem okay," he said.

Tetsami tossed him the shovel and said, "Then find Gavadi. If you survived, he could've."

The next few hours were a blurry nightmare. She got to Jarvis in time, but, even with the medkit, she almost lost him twice while trying to stabilize his injuries. She followed the instructions on the medical database to the letter, but she couldn't help thinking she'd botched the job.

She followed the instructions for broken bones and shock, and she fed him the drugs the database told her to—and he still looked much too pale.

Marc Baetez was just as bad in his own way. She treated him for his arm and leg, and he managed to wake up enough to try and strangle her with his good hand. She had to struggle to sedate him.

By the time she'd gotten the two men stabilized, she'd used all the thermoplastic cast material in the medkit—most of it on Jarvis, who was now a statue from the waist down.

When she checked on Kelly, she was surprised to see that he had managed to dig out Gavadi. Kelly had found one of the ship's own medkits to attempt to patch the man up. Tetsami was surprised that Gavadi was still alive. She was even more surprised when she saw the extent of his injuries. Gavadi had lost his right arm, fractured his other three limbs, and was lacerated over a good part of his body. According to Kelly, Gavadi had busted most of his ribs and only survived without a broken back because he'd already had an extensive spinal reconstruction that replaced most of his vertebrae with tough metal cybernetics.

The last guard had undergone much the same kind of injuries as Gavadi, but without benefit of a reconstructed spine. He was dead.

Once the injured people were stable, Tetsami examined the cockpit again. According to the chrono on the pilot's wrist, it was well into morning. It should have been daylight outside. However, the drift over the nose admitted no light into the cockpit. The nose was deep under the snow.

It got worse.

Tetsami walked the length of the upper section of the craft, working up toward the tail section, checking every single port she could find. A few windows had broken, filling chambers with snowdrifts. But all were buried. None of the ports on this tub were close enough to the open air even to let in a little light.

Near the tail she could hear what might have been wind and blowing snow rattling across, above her. It sounded violent—and one hell of a storm if she could hear it this far under the snow.

Before long, this thing is going to be totally buried—if it isn't already.

Once exit seemed futile, she spent another few hours improvising a basket stretcher, to lower the two other injured parties down to the cargo area. The cargo area, despite the snowdrifts, was the best insulated—thus the warmest—part of the ship now. Tetsami and Kelly had set up camp in the belly of the *Shaftsbury,* a near-empty, red-lit space. A massive cave in some frozen circle of Purgatory.

By then it was clear that they could expect no immediate rescue.

Tetsami didn't know if that was good or bad.

It must have been close to noon when Tetsami was able to tend to her own injuries, which—now that she'd slowed down to feel them—weren't minor. While Kelly kept an eye on the severely wounded, she retreated into the *Lady* to privately tend to herself.

Minor frostbite on her extremities, especially her hands, was easily tended to with patches from the ship's extensive medkit. Her torso was ringed with bruises that deepened to near black in places. With the diagnostic kit she managed to find a half-dozen torn muscles and a sprain in her right knee and elbow. All aggravated from moving around.

Sitting on the back of the pilot's chair in the half-overturned *Lady* she had trouble believing that she'd climbed into the vehicle, much less done all she had since the crash.

It also made her wonder about Kelly.

She strapped support bandages and dosage patches on her sprains, and pumped some painkiller and accelerant into the areas of torn muscle. She was sparing on the drugs, since there were three people out there who needed it much more than she did.

How come you're fine, Kelly? I can barely get around. I was strapped into a crash pod. You got to bounce around free down here. You should be as beat-up as Gavadi.

Once she'd patched what she could patch, she rummaged into the debris covering the left side of the *Lady,* now the floor. It was fortunate that the vehicle had only tipped over, and hadn't rolled. Objects were spilled, but not quite tossed at random. She managed to find her duffel and a change of clothes. Nothing that was appropriate for the weather, but she finally had a pair of gloves—leather driving gloves, but they'd do.

She also searched for and found the *Lady*'s camping equipment. Most important, she found a pair of crystalline heaters and a few packets of compact insulated blankets. The wounded weren't going to die of hypothermia.

As she climbed out of the *Lady* and saw Kelly looking up at her, she realized that, after mentally bitching about Jarvis' taking charge of everything, suddenly she was in command of this fiasco.

"Wonderful," she muttered, breath fogging.

Be careful what you wish for, she thought.

At least they were alive, mostly. All they really needed was to get out of the *Shaftsbury.* They had the *Lady,* which seemed intact, and it was supposed to be a multienvironment vehicle.

All they had to do was get it horizontal and get it out of the cargo bay.

Tetsami looked up at the front of the *Shaftsbury.* It was a single sloping mound of red-lit snow that filled the cargo area in for ten meters at least.

Get the *Lady* horizontal, and get it out of here.

Sure, easy.

CHAPTER TWENTY-SIX

Displaced Persons

"Past and future are equally clouded by specula-
tion."

—*The Cynic's Book of Wisdom*

"History is a set of lies agreed upon."

—Napoleon Bonaparte
(1769–1821)

Shane had to climb up a sheer rock face to leave the bowl of
Dom Magnus' prison. With her new prosthetic limbs it had
taken a major effort of concentration to avoid a dangerous
fall. What kept her going was the thought that Hougland had
managed it, probably in a severely disoriented state, and
she'd done it without Shane's climbing equipment.

All the time, Random's oblate spheroid hung above her,
floating on its contragrav. The sight made the effort that
much more irritating.

Once she cleared the lights and found a ledge, it was only
a few steps before she left all signs of humanity.

After that, Shane allowed Random to lead. He followed a
trail of hair, dead skin, synthetic fibers and microscopic
traces of blood, all left behind by Hougland.

In the untouched caverns, time turned elastic. It felt as if
they'd spent hours traveling down black echoing passages
before she asked, "Why in hell did *you* decide to come
along?"

For some reason she resented the company.

"You planned to travel down here alone? This is some of
the most dangerous terrain on the planet."

Random was right about that. The tunnels were irregular,
and often a gentle slope would lead to a sudden drop into an
abyss. The bright searchlights flanking Random's sensors

had helped her avoid a few pitfalls she might have missed with just a flashlight. In fact, it was Random's sensors that made following Hougland possible.

None of that had mattered when Shane made the impulsive decision to be the search party for Hougland. Shane didn't know if it had been guilt, responsibility, or some left-over sense of honor from the marines that made her decide, but there'd never been a question in her mind.

"I don't know *what* I intended to do," Shane said. "But you didn't answer my question, Random."

"No, I didn't," Random replied. Then he floated along the passage in silence.

Shane shook her head and continued following the floating robot. She wondered what actually constituted Random's brain. It had to be fairly compact. It could fit in a suitcase as well as into the meter-diameter chromed jellyfish ahead of her. Compact and divisible into at least three parts.

After a long while, Random said, "Forgive my pause. I am busy deciding how to deal with you."

"Huh?"

There was an uncomputerlike sigh. "I fear that my mental process is much less 'human' than my surface would lead you to believe." The robot tilted on its axis in a manner reminiscent of a shrug. "Much of my personality is tailored for the moment."

"I'm not following you."

"I rely much on predictive psychology. Uncertainty about your possible reaction—"

Shane sighed. "Cut to the chase."

"It impedes my conversation when I don't know how you'll react."

Shane laughed. She laughed so hard she had to stop walking and lean against a black rock wall. Random floated and watched her with his impassive scanners.

When she finally stopped, he said, "See what I mean?"

"I'm sorry about laughing at you," Shane said. "I never thought of myself as particularly unpredictable."

"Do you want to rest a moment? We've been traveling for five hours."

Shane, now that she'd stopped moving, realized that she could use a rest. She was still recuperating from a massive injury, and her body was not quite in the shape it had been when she was still a marine. *If they were still mine, my legs would be cramping all to hell right now.*

Mentally she corrected herself. *Oh, they're mine. They're as* mine *as they can get, even though they'll outlast me.*

No cramps, but she realized that her heart was racing to keep up with her exertion. The way she sucked lungfuls of air told her that her cardiovascular system hadn't had a real workout for a month. She nodded at the robot and slid to seat herself on a rock.

When she sat, she felt a stab in her side. She tried not to show the pain. "You have a knack for changing the subject, Random."

The spheroid floated down to be at Shane's eye level.

Shane continued. "When we were trapped in the core of the *Blood-Tide,* you mentioned the way you think."

"I remember the comment—"

"You mentioned prediction there, as well." Shane recalled the exact words—*"My surface is a mimetic reproduction of human psychology, but my thoughts are—different. Most intellectual beings don't have the equipment to foresee the consequences of their actions."* Later on, he'd asked, *"Does prior knowledge of someone's decision—and the consequences of that decision—require you to share responsibility for that decision?"*

"Extrapolation is inherent in my nature," Random said.

"Why don't you tell me about it?"

The spheroid tilted toward her. "The story covers a lot of ground."

"We've got time. It's just you, me, and Hougland down here. And we *are* catching up to her, right?"

The spheroid nodded. "Okay. If you explain to me some of the more asynchronous parts of your behavior."

Shane smiled. "And what're those?"

"Why a Confederacy native from Occisis can deal with me as a person."

Random had a point. There were a number of heretical technologies that Confed society looked upon with moral repugnance. Genetic engineering of thinking creatures was the oldest, and probably most violated, taboo. Artificial Intelligence was almost as old a taboo, for many reasons, and it made a lot more people uneasy—Shane could think of only a few times that ban had been flouted, with disastrous results.

Worse, Random was an AI produced by the Race. Her home planet, Occisis, was founded in the Genocide War with the amoeboid Race. . . .

Everything she'd been taught to believe in should prevent her from reacting with anything but fear and loathing to Random Walk. But that wasn't the case. She dealt with Random as easily as she did with, for instance, Flower, the Voleran alien.

Slowly, she answered, "I'm not sure. I was disenchanted by my life on Occisis long before I came here. I think I joined the marines to escape the burdens of domestic patriotism."

Her family had been so proud of her. In a way, Occisis, in retrospect, was a very sick society. The Occisis marines provided the fighting force for most of the Centauri Trading Company, and therefore a single planet bred most of the warriors for an entire arm of the Confederacy. There were only three places someone could go on Occisis, the marines, the Church, or enter a society that was as regimented in thought as the marines were in action.

In the marines she could question things in her own mind without being accused of antipatriotism, or worse, treason. She was a marine. Calling a marine antipatriotic was like accusing a priest of atheism.

"It was a place where my acts could mask my thoughts," Shane said. "I was never a right-thinker, despite what my mother would say. If I hadn't joined the marines—or a nunnery—I probably would've been slotted for continual re-education. I had some freedom in the marines. To see other cultures, see vid that wouldn't ever be allowed in Occisis airspace, form my own opinion on things. Probably too much freedom for my own good."

"What do you mean?"

"I managed to alienate myself from my own culture. I think the only bond I have left to my own planet is my belief in God. And sometimes that feels like it's slipping." Shane realized that her vision was blurring somewhat and she looked up from her hands. "Your turn, Random."

Random's story was a long one. Long and complicated by the fact that, in his current incarnation, he shared memory with a quintet of old AIs. Each AI was from a different generation of Race technology, at one point one had even been coopted for human use. The five defunct AIs had been brought together by a pirate, treasure hunter, and jack of all trades named Tjaele Mosasa. Mosasa had used the five AIs to "jump-start" each other. That was over a hundred years ago, just on the cusp of universal implementation of tach-drive starships. Random and Mosasa arrived on Bakunin just as the planet was being founded.

Random's story, however, went back long before that.

The story began with the amoebic alien culture known as the Race.

The Race arose from a violent society on a violent planet. The Race's recorded history went back several times farther than humankind's, and in that history the Race had come close to annihilating themselves and their planet a half-dozen times. Eventually, the culture evolved until the prospect of direct violence, creature to creature, was anathema.

Unfortunately, aggression wasn't bred out, it was redirected. It became a racial passion to distance themselves from violence. Wars became intricate Machiavallian dances. Political and social sciences became advanced forms of violence. It became high art to discover, for instance, what piece of disinformation could destroy a political faction.

Soon the Race was "unified" under overlapping layers of competing bureaucracy where the highest achievement was to stab an opponent in the back without having one's hands anywhere near the knife—

A bad metaphor since the Race had neither hands, nor back, to speak of.

About the time the Race achieved space travel, they had raised sociology, political science, and even psychology, to such levels as predictive sciences that they needed to develop AIs just to handle the chaotic, shifting equations.

When, sometime in the twentieth century, the Race discovered the technological species on Terra, the whole culture experienced a direct confrontation between the impulses of territorial aggressiveness and the cultural taboos against direct confrontation—taboos that humans obviously didn't share.

That lack made humans incredibly dangerous to the Race.

The solution was a series of covert operations on Terra that would actively meddle in the equations of human society, moving the Terran culture away from space, and especially away from interstellar exploration. By the mid-twenty-first century the Race was winning a war that Earth didn't even know it was fighting. Their small manipulations—a rumor here, a dropped tidbit of technology there, political donations everywhere—had, in sixty years, produced a socially catastrophic wave of genetic engineering, a war in Asia that was still—three centuries later—among the five worst single conflicts in human history, and had managed to stagnate any move into space.

Eventually, however, humans discovered the meddling. In addition, they took over a number of AIs with their social programming mostly intact. The Terran forces' knowledge of the social programming essentially nullified its effect. Eventually, as the century turned, there was a series of wars on the Race's colonies.

It was called the Genocide War for good reason. Despite the AI-piloted drone weapons the Race tried to use to defend themselves, the fact that individuals were culturally unable to engage in direct combat spelled their doom everywhere but on their home planet.

For a while after that—and especially during the Wars of Unification that put first the United Nations, and then the despotic Terran Council, in charge of a Terran world government—humans accepted, even approved of AIs.

"What happened?" Shane asked.

Despite being born on Occisis—the site of the bloodiest of the Genocide battles, and birthplace of the Centaurian Trading Company that finally overthrew the Terran Council—she was hearing chunks of history that she was unaware of. She had assumed that the distaste for AIs had been universal from the war with the Race.

"AIs, especially Race AIs, are a security risk. It took the Second War of Unification for the Terran Council to see that. They actually used the Race's social programming techniques to implant a near-permanent loathing of AIs—as well as other 'heretical' technologies—in the human culture at large."

Shane shook her head.

"Ironic, isn't it?" Random said. "They did it to protect themselves from social meddling— And once AIs were widely despised, the Council's *own* use of AIs became one of the issues that brought them down. Of course, the Confederacy has institutionalized those anti-AI beliefs now."

"So you're a four-hundred-year-old oracle?"

"In one sense. Not that the future is in any way deterministic. History, society, and politics are chaotic in precise mathematical terms. Altering a small variable can cause quite a large effect."

"But you know the variables and the effects."

"To some extent. It's my turn to ask a question."

"Go ahead."

"Why haven't you told anyone that Mosasa is a cybernetic construct, an AI like myself?"

Shane shrugged. "Why should I have? I'm as disassociated from the people in this mountain as I am from home. Revealing your little secret seemed pointless."

Random was quiet for a while.

Shane stood up. She felt rested enough to go on. "Now I want you to answer my original question. Why'd you come down here with me? You were built by a people that nearly destroyed themselves with Machiavellian plotting. You have to have an ulterior motive."

"I do," Random admitted.

"What is it?"

"The Race were quite aware of the Dolbrians. In fact they scouted a number of habitable planets the same way your early explorers did—"

"The starmaps the Dolbrians left, uh-huh."

"Well, I suspect that, perhaps, there might be something more to find here than your missing Corporal Hougland."

CHAPTER TWENTY-SEVEN

Demographics

"Patriotism is the preferred method of covering one's ass in wartime."
—*The Cynic's Book of Wisdom*

"Everything belongs to the fatherland when the fatherland is in danger."
—GEORGES-JACQUES DANTON
(1759–1794)

While the Bleek takeover went on, Dom manned the holo in the conference room. The first people he called were other CEOs in Godwin. There were many businesses that GA&A used to have a friendly relationship with, and these were the people he was most familiar with. As he called his onetime peers, he felt control returning—even though the news was less than encouraging.

His first call was to the president of Excalibur Security, Li Tso Sen. Excalibur was the largest patrolling security company in Godwin. Its mission was primarily residential security for the western suburbs of Godwin—the protection of well-paid execs and white-collar employees. It employed a private army whose on-the-ground forces were close to eight thousand strong. Li Tso had been one of GA&A's most consistent and profitable clients.

Li Tso took Dom's news, as well as Dom's continued existence, calmly. And Dom felt a familiar icy chill when Li Tso returned the favor by informing Dom of a sudden, and recent, dearth of arms on the open market. Arms companies from Dittrich Electrics to the local Griffith Energy dealers were being consistently bought out of all their inventory by anonymous buyers—and the arms weren't reappearing on the market.

Li Tso also committed himself to the defense of Godwin. It was, after all, Excalibur's job.

Barbara Cantor at Royt Transports agreed to pass the news to her clients. She also had the disturbing news that Royt dealers all over the planet had been cleaned out of fighter-capable craft. She committed herself to maintain Royt's unshipped models for possible defense of the city. That was thirty craft in the Royt factory inventory, compared to over five hundred already sold.

He called Gregg Lovesy at Argus Datasearch, and was surprised to find out that *he* was surprised. Apparently no one had paid them to investigate Proudhon. It made a twisted sort of sense. The Proudhon Spaceport was a monopoly, with no competitors to order surveillance. . . . And everything north of Proudhon was a desert wasteland. Millions of square kilometers could hide anything. Lovesy agreed to disseminate the information among their clients.

The representatives he called at Lucifer Contracts Incorporated absorbed the information without comment. LCI was one of the most shadowy and secretive of Godwin corporations, and it enforced its rulings primarily through fear. Dom had no idea what their capabilities would be in a shooting war. The anonymous exec who answered the holo and listened to him, wordlessly, didn't enlighten him. LCI broke contact without even informing Dom if his information would go farther.

Dom called every business he could think of that might produce a fighting force. The calls accelerated, giving him a feeling of surreal breathlessness. He was on a greased downward slope with no bottom.

All the while, in the back of his head, Tetsami was telling him that he was too late.

Dom called every company that had ordered something from Godwin Arms, and thanks to the onboard computer in his brain, he had a complete list.

He called Maximus Transshipping, the main cargo-hauling company between Godwin and the northern communes. He called the Mahajan Bank, Renyolds Insurance, and every other major financial institution he could think of—many of which just gave him blank looks or cut the connection. He called every trade union from the pilot's to the author-and-creative-artists'. The artists' union actually had more of an armed presence—it was known for going after copyright infringers and plagiarists with a bloody, almost psychopathic, zeal.

He called every medical corporation on this side of the Diderot Range.

Somewhere in that time, he was told that Ezra Bleek had transferred his stock and that the Diderot Holding Company was in charge of Bleek Munitions. Another few hours after that, he learned of the surrender of the board of directors and that they were now in *de facto* control.

The second he got word about the lockdown on the Bleek board of directors, Dom ordered all personnel left in the mountain to relocate. He also ordered that Bleek immediately start production at maximum capacity. The weapons would be needed.

Even as he gave the instructions to Mosasa, the man in charge on the ground at Bleek Headquarters, Dom realized that the ultimate success of the takeover seemed to have shrunk in significance to the point where the announcement barely registered on him. Dom had enough presence of mind to feel chilled about the fact that the takeover was drained of all emotional content.

It held all the satisfaction of finally balancing a debit in the corporate books. Essential, but emotionally null.

At least he had taken care of his people. He could sever his connections now, while the ledger was balanced.

Except for Tetsami . . .

Even as he thought that, he continued manning the holo.

He called John Mariott, the principal gunrunner GA&A had dealt with in shipping arms to the northern communes. Mariott would help in warning the communes of the possible invasion.

He argued for a half-hour to get through to Ivanna Strovagard, perhaps the most powerful "boss" in East Godwin. Ivanna took it badly when he suggested that she talk to the other bosses in East Godwin to help provide a unified defense.

In the end, he even talked to the Bakunin Church of Christ, Avenger. The BCCA had once wanted to ransom him for his sins, and he had shot one of their priests in the stomach. However, the BCCA did operate a small army of power-armored Paladins. He managed to get his story out only because the priest he talked to didn't know him. The call was transferred up the line until someone who knew who he was cut the connection.

Dom sat back and realized he had no one left to call.

He turned off the holo. Once the electronics were powered down, the conference room was wrapped in unnatural silence. The sounds of activity that'd been the universal background hum of this cavern warren were absent. A hideout that had been engineered to accommodate over a thousand would soon be populated by less than a dozen. Then none.

He had reached the end of all his self-imposed obligations. He'd done as well as he could for everyone he owed.

Everyone but Tetsami.

The thought brought a twitch to his cheek. He raised his hand to cover it, even though there was no one there to see.

It was a death of sorts. His connection to the world around him had frayed and tattered until it had finally broken. There was nothing left to keep him here. Even if he wanted to stay, he had to remove himself—the focus of Klaus' attention—away from these people.

Dom pushed himself back from the table and stood. Even the artificial muscles in his legs registered psychosomatic cramps from his hours of sitting.

He didn't feel tired. Only numb.

What was left for him to do before he left?

Only a few details . . .

He switched on the intercom and keyed in the computer net. After a short pause the intercom responded, "You called, Mr. Magnus? Sorry for the delay, one third of my processing capacity is busy spelunking at the moment."

Dom shook his head. He wondered how many times Random Walk could divide himself and still remain himself. Then, Random always made a point that the part of him that interacted with humans was a rather thin shell of a program. What Dom thought of as Random, really wasn't Random. . . .

Dom wondered how many other people wore equally deceptive facades.

"That's part of what I want to talk about."

"Your instructions for Shane, before you leave?"

Dom almost asked Random how he knew. Instead he told him, "Tell Shane that Hougland's to be held until the mountain is fully evacuated. After that, she can use her own discretion."

"Anything else?"

"Yes. I'm divesting my share of the Diderot enterprise. I'm taking twenty-five megs in a private account and disappearing."

"Where are you going?"

Dom shook his head. "No forwarding address. I want a clean break. Tell Zanzibar to review the holo records of my calls, to see if she wants to add anything. As far as Bleek is concerned, get out the maximum production as soon as possible, there's a near-vacuum in the arms market this side of the mountains." He was running out of things to say.

"I'll pass all that on. Are you sure you want to leave right now?"

Dom shook his head. "What's to stay for? I'll only draw my brother's fire." He drummed his fingers against his thigh.

"They're going to need a leader here."

Dom turned away from the intercom and said, "This is Bakunin. There are no leaders here." As he walked out of the communications room he continued, fingers still drumming, "There are no leaders, and I'm not one of them. . . ."

Daylight had purpled into twilight by the time Dom's contragrav slid out of the northern vehicle bay. He flew down the slope of the mountain and hovered at treetop level once he passed the tree line. He checked the craft's radar for anything airborne near him. There wasn't anything except for a few aircars heading southwest, toward Godwin—his people, evacuating the mountain.

Not *his* people any more.

They were headed to Bleek and rebuilt lives.

Where Dom was heading was nearly fifteen hundred kilometers north. He was heading for a rebuilt *self.*

He maxed the contragrav's acceleration and double-checked the charge. He had at least eight hours of flight time without the reserves. Enough to get there, not enough to get back. Somehow that was fitting.

As the speedometer leveled off at close to 200 klicks per, he felt a tug at his cheek. He tried to massage it away.

"I've done everything. I've settled all my debts."

All but Tetsami.

He could still hear Ivor yelling at him, telling him he didn't care.

He did care, damn it. He cared more than was healthy. What was he supposed to do? Join Ivor in a fruitless solo search of five million square klicks of desert?

He had warned everyone about the threat across the mountain. He had relocated GA&A's employees. What was left?

Dom had to disappear because of Klaus. As long as Klaus targeted him, no one around him would be safe. Dom had to vanish before his brother realized he was still alive.

But it was too late. Klaus already had his hands on Tetsami. Who was he protecting by running away now?

Only himself.

The contragrav shot northward into the darkness.

Tetsami.

Tetsami.

Her name kept playing in his head as the tic in his cheek became steadily worse. He plugged the flight plan into the comm and let the computer fly the contragrav.

"I know what you were thinking, Ivor," Dom said to himself, "and you were right."

If he didn't try to do something about Tetsami, his life meant little. Tetsami managed to mean something to what eroded humanity he had left. If he left things as they stood, he would lose that part of his soul.

Even if he did manage to slip away from his brother again.

Ever since this madness started, it had been too easy for him to pretend that it was a simple commercial transaction, something with nice rational numbers that added and subtracted cleanly.

The pretense had become futile.

In the end Tetsami meant much more than any of this, and she had never known it. His businesslike, cold facade had all been a fraud, a con game—and Tetsami had bought it. And, because she had believed it, she was now in Klaus' hands.

Dom rubbed his temples. He hadn't done all he could. There was one thing left for him to try. It wasn't something anyone was going to suggest to him.

Klaus, after all, didn't care about Tetsami.

Dom did.

The contragrav he rode was a Royt executive model, and it had a full communications array. With that, and a reserve account worth twenty-five megs, it was fairly easy for him to rent time on three comm sats. He only needed one, but having three of them bouncing signals to each other would make his transmission hard to trace, and from a moving aircar, by the time anyone had localized the source the car would be kilometers away.

That was the plan anyway.

As he set up the connection, Dom noticed that his right palm was sweaty.

By the time he'd prepped the vid comm, he could catch a glimpse of the spotlit marble of Jefferson City, far off to his left. He watched it slide by.

It's a curse, being given time to think about this.

He had spent years building up his own personal ethos. A simple mechanical system of credit and debit, keeping the books even. By that old morality he really owed Tetsami nothing, they had split from each other.

The problem was, that old morality was delusional. It was a way for him to avoid thinking about what he did. The thoughts were too painful.

Whatever his old morality said, Dom knew he owed Tetsami much more than he'd been able to give her.

With that thought he opened the comm channel and called GA&A.

On the vid screen, Dom watched Colonel Klaus Dacham try and contain his surprise.

"Hello," Dom said. After a long pause he added, "Brother."

Klaus apparently weighed several responses before he said, "You're still alive."

We're the same age, Dom thought, *but he looks younger, surer.* "I wish to end things," he said.

Klaus drummed his fingers by the side of the video pickup. It was the first time Dom had noticed one of his nervous habits in his brother. *We're twins,* Dom thought, *we can't be so different.*

Would it be you down here, Klaus, if you had been the person to handle Styx?

"What are you offering?" Klaus asked.

"Myself. That *is* what you want."

"Ah—" Klaus said. Little emotion showed in his face and eyes. Nothing but the drumming fingers. It was like looking into a warped mirror. "Why do you give up now, offer me your precious hide?"

Dom tried to do it without letting on how important this was. "Too many innocent casualties. I want my people freed."

The drumming fingers ceased. *Something's wrong.*

"Pardon?" Klaus said.

Dom sucked in a breath. Make it sound like a matter of principle. "Your friends in Proudhon have captured an employee of mine. I'll give myself over to you once you've freed the prisoner."

"I don't know who you're referring to—"

A cold hand gripped Dom's sternum, the chill that came when the world began fracturing around him. "You're lying, Klaus."

"How dare you—" Klaus let the anger show for a moment, but he clamped down on it. Dom could see the fire, though, in Klaus' eyes. *No one dares question you, do they, brother?*

Klaus controlled his outburst. "This operation has no jurisdiction beyond the perimeter of GA&A. If you come in, I can guarantee you contact with the people you say captured this person."

Dom felt as if the air itself was turning crystalline. Dom knew that Klaus had to be aware of Tetsami. Klaus had been too fanatical in his prosecution of GA&A's personnel not to be.

But if Klaus *had* Tetsami he would be parading her, threatening her, just to have him come in.

"You can't run forever. Make it easy for—"

Dom looked up and stared into his brother's face. What he saw there told him everything. "Dead," Dom said.

"I told you that—"

"Shut up!"

Klaus shut his mouth, apparently shocked that anyone would dare address him like that. Tetsami was dead, and Klaus was responsible. That was how his brother worked, vengeance that spread toward everything that Dom might care about.

Klaus started to speak. "She isn't—"

Dom killed the connection and started redirecting the course of the contragrav. He had spent too long in contact with GA&A. He had given them a chance to trace the signal.

As he maneuvered, he tried to think of how it could have gone differently. He couldn't. Klaus could've used Tetsami as a bargaining chip, but Klaus was never one to bargain. Klaus would have drained her of information, then disposed of her.

The realization was icy and clear—once she was in Klaus Dacham's hands, there was no hope of seeing her whole again.

Dom knew, because Jonah Dacham would have done the same thing.

There was nothing left now. He drove north to deliver Dominic Magnus to the same fate as Jonah Dacham.

CHAPTER TWENTY-EIGHT

Acceptable Losses

"An egotist takes the universe personally."
—*The Cynic's Book of Wisdom*

"Without war no state could exist."
—HEINRICH VON TREITSCHKE
(1834–1896)

"Inexcusable!" Klaus yelled. His voice echoed off the gray walls of his cubical operations center. Towering above him, projected from the giant holo, was a terrain map showing a stretch of the Diderot Mountains north of the Godwin Arms complex. Klaus was yelling into a holo comm of a considerably lesser scale.

The man he was yelling at was Major Osha Speir, the commander of the orbiting TEC vessels. He was only the latest recipient of Klaus' anger. First the trace of Dominic's message went nowhere, and now they were telling him that they couldn't find the *Shaftsbury*.

Despite Klaus' frustration, the distance of orbit seemed to insulate the major from Klaus' anger. Major Speir said calmly, "You expect too much, Colonel. Photographic recon of an area that size is impractical—"

"You shouldn't have lost the *Shaftsbury* in the first place!"

"Sir, we were tracking the craft. We're tracking *every* spacecraft within an AU of Bakunin."

"How the hell did you lose her, then, Major?"

"The ship's RF signature vanished. Sir."

Klaus rubbed his forehead and looked up at the huge holo map above him. Across a snowy mountainous terrain that looked like a wrinkled sheet there was a single green line tracing the last known position of the *Shaftsbury*. Klaus had called up a real-time magnification showing the site of last contact. It had been futile. The scene showed him nothing. No debris, no heat traces of buried wreckage.

"How did that happen, Major?"

"Either the ship exploded violently enough not to leave any pieces resolvable from orbit, or its defensive screens were set to interfere with wideband energy—"

"Then it could still be out there somewhere." Klaus knew that the major was aware of the last transmissions from the *Shaftsbury.* The messages about the prisoners breaking loose in the cargo compartment—

That woman could have been his, she could have given him Dominic.

The major shook his head. "We've done an energy profile on what that would take. A Barracuda cargo ship would be able to maintain a wideband shield for seven minutes, max. Then there'd be a catastrophic power drain. It would have to lower the screens again or crash. No RF image matching the *Shaftsbury* ever reappeared on our scopes."

"Could it have landed somewhere?"

The major shook his head. "That was the first thing we checked. The possible flight radius covers nearly a million square kilometers of rugged terrain. Within that area, we've found nearly ten thousand sites flat enough for a landing."

Klaus sat back. "You can't show me any wreckage."

"No, and considering both terrain and weather, visual confirmation's unlikely. A substantial blizzard has passed through sixty-five percent of the search area. Our atmospheric projections show little improvement over the next thirty-two hours. Any remains from a crash will be buried by one to four meters of snow by now. Our only hope to find it from orbit would be a thermal profile. We could do a high-resolution scan for such traces, but the heat of the wreck would've cooled to background by the time we've covered a tenth of the area."

"What about radar mapping?"

"If the ship had crashed anywhere else, sir. The Diderot Mountains cause so much interference that a radar scan would be impossibly inaccurate."

"One in ten is better than nothing—do the thermal scan. Keep looking."

"Yes, sir."

Klaus cut the connection.

The ship was gone. It was hard to believe. The digital ties that bound the operation together were so prevalent, so universal, that it took something like this to remind Klaus that there was still a whole planet out there to get lost in. The *Shaftsbury* might never turn up.

His brother might never turn up.

Klaus tried to crush the traitorous thought. But it slipped through. It was as if everything had waited for his one moment of complacency. His brother could have planned this—calling not only to gloat, to tell Klaus he was still kicking, but to drop that veiled reference to the *Shaftsbury* in Klaus' lap.

Dominic had called to tell Klaus that, if not for the screwup with the *Shaftsbury*, Klaus'd have him now. If Klaus had his hands on that woman, he could have lured Dominic into his grasp. If he even had her body, he was sure that his TEC intel people could create a digital forgery that'd be good enough to fool his brother—over a comm line at least.

The disappearance of the *Shaftsbury* left him with nothing, and Dominic—Jonah—couldn't resist driving that point home.

Klaus had lied when he said that he didn't know who Dominic had talked about. According to the stories that he pumped from the psychological wreck of Johann Levy, Kari Tetsami, the prisoner aboard the *Shaftsbury*, had been one of Dominic's inner circle. She was part of the team that launched the attack on GA&A after Klaus had control.

However, his brother had delayed contact until Klaus had known that her body was probably buried under meters of snow and ice, all but inaccessible to him.

The disaster even went beyond their private fraternal war. Klaus had also lost possible spies from Epsilon Indi and Alpha Centauri. In fact, with the *Daedalus* and escort hanging over the Bakunin sky, Klaus had strong suspicions that such spies were the reason for the *Shaftsbury*'s disappearance.

Damn them all. Why must they interfere?

Klaus had been handed Operation Rasputin. He was the one who was in charge. Bakunin was outside the bounds of the Confederacy. Confed politics had no place here. No arm of the Confederacy had any business here before Klaus sent his delegation to the Terran Congress.

The Confederacy had no place interfering with him. The

Confederacy had no right to come between him and his brother. . . .

Of course, that was a dream.

Sirius and Centauri had built all the groundwork down here, before the TEC even approved the final stages of the operation. It wasn't the TEC who'd inspired Gregor Arcady to take over the Proudhon Spaceport and assemble an army large enough to impose a central authority on this anarchic planet, it had been the Sirius-Eridani Economic Community working with the Centauri Alliance. Those two arms of the Confederacy still maintained a vested interest in the operation, even though they were no longer officially connected to it.

And, of course, the Indi Protectorate was going to fight them all the way down the wire.

According to the latest tach-comm from Earth, the stakes were growing in importance. The internal Confederacy battle over Rasputin was no longer over economic drains and precedents for TEC interference—if it ever had been.

It was very likely that, once the Congress recognized the government imposed on Bakunin, Bakunin's status in the Congress would be elevated directly to prime. It was a single prime seat that could radically alter the balance of power in the Confederacy. If Bakunin's representative allied with the Indi Protectorate, Sirius and Centauri could lose the near-absolute control they wielded in the Congress.

The fact was, Bakunin was so close to Sol and the central hub of the Confederacy that every single arm could make a reasonable argument that Bakunin was inside their boundaries.

Klaus disliked politics. He liked chains of command that were direct, simple, and unquestioned. Like the operation *he* was running.

Klaus listened to his fingers drumming on the edge of the seat. There were obstacles in his path, but he would overcome them. And he would have those responsible pay for these difficulties. He was not to be trifled with, even by an arm of the Confederacy.

One of the techs in the communication center spoke, interrupting Klaus' thoughts.

"Your call to Proudhon is through, sir."

Klaus nodded and said, "Put Arcady through."

The holo in front of Klaus flickered into life, displaying

the professorlike countenance of Gregor Arcady. *This is the man that Sirius and Centauri have chosen to run Bakunin. Perhaps not.*

"Colonel," asked Arcady, "any news on the *Shaftsbury?*" *You are not so high, Arcady, that you cannot fall.*

Klaus shook his head. "No trace has been found. It's most probable that it went down in the Diderot Mountains between five hundred and a thousand klicks north of Jefferson City."

Arcady nodded. "Proudhon air-traffic control has come to much the same conclusion."

Klaus didn't reveal the last communication GA&A had had with the *Shaftsbury*. Arcady had loyalties beyond Klaus. Better to let Arcady wonder about those loyalties. Klaus said, "We don't know what happened, but we have to assume it was hostile action."

"By whom?"

"It doesn't matter. What matters is the possibility that the operation might be compromised—" Klaus knew that the operation *was* compromised. His brother was out there somewhere, and his brother *knew*. "I'm pushing up the invasion schedule."

"To when?"

"Immediately. I'm sending the *Blood-Tide*. The marines are to be distributed to their units. I want things to *move*."

"I would prefer it if there was some time for the marines and the mercs to work together."

Tough shit. You aren't in command here. "Work it out on the run. We don't want to lose surprise. Especially with your first target."

Arcady paused for a while. Finally he nodded. "Colonel," Arcady said, and cut the holo.

Klaus turned away and faced his staff. "I want two squads of marines equipped and sent north to pick up Magnus' trail. Ten minutes. All the others I want on the *Blood-Tide* in fifteen. Off the ground within the half hour. *Move*."

TEC officers scattered to the wind.

Operation Rasputin was about to engage upon Stage Three: The military consolidation of all political power on the planet.

PART SIX

Destabilization

"The word state is identical with the word war."
—Prince Pyotr Alekseyevich Kropotkin
(1842–1921)

CHAPTER TWENTY-NINE

Cold War

"Between too good to be true and worse than you imagine, bet on worse."
— *The Cynic's Book of Wisdom*

"Whatever you do, just keep moving."
— SYLVIA HARPER
(2008–2081)

Tetsami spent the balance of the day in one of the rear compartments, trying to dig out through the remains of an emergency air lock. She had spent about a quarter of the time actually digging at the snow. The rest of the time she worried about what kind of damage she was doing to herself while the painkillers masked her injuries.

The good news was she briefly broke the surface.

The bad news was that outside the *Shaftsbury* the temperature was subfreezing, the wind was close to sixty klicks per, visibility was nil, and it was closing on nightfall.

Tetsami retreated down into the cargo compartment, knowing that they'd need the *Lady* to get out of the mountains alive.

When she limped back to their camp, she began to feel the full weight of what she had done to herself. Not just physically, but emotionally. It had been seven days since she had pulled out of Diderot. It felt like an aeon.

She should have stayed. She missed Dom backing her up in a crisis. At least that's what she told herself she missed.

She collapsed next to Kelly and cursed herself for not telling *him* to go up and dig the hole. She might not like the responsibility of tending to the three wounded men, but she should have known better than to do that digging herself.

She wrapped one of the thermal blankets around herself

and fell into an exhausted sleep before she'd said one word to Kelly. She had embarrassing dreams about Dom.

When she awoke, she felt better. At least moving only hurt her a little now. Kelly must have let her sleep for a long time.

She traded watch on the wounded and told Kelly to get some sleep. She was guilty that he'd stayed awake for her, but she was also grateful. Someone should be keeping a wakeful eye on the casualties. Not that either she or Kelly could do much if one of the wounded started to slip. Neither of them were doctors, and the medkits were nearly empty.

Their camp was a clear spot on the floor of the cargo area where the portable heaters from the *Lady* had melted a circle five meters in diameter. Within that circle the temperature was reasonable enough for Tetsami's breath to stop fogging.

Sometime during the middle of the night the emergency lights had failed. Now the only light was from the heaters' crystalline heating elements, glowing behind ceramic mesh. The cylindrical crystals' orange light barely reached the walls to port and starboard, to carve latticework shadows.

Inky darkness swathed the cargo area to fore and aft, beyond the camp.

During the night the only sound, and the only sign of the snowstorm raging outside, was the abrasive rattle of the wind, far and small behind her. Throughout the night, the wind grew more and more quiet. Tetsami didn't know if that meant that the storm they'd landed in was losing strength, or if the ship was buried that much deeper.

She suspected the latter.

So damn alone. It hurt, even though she'd been on her own most of her professional life. *Who am I kidding? I've been alone most of my life, period.*

With the exception of Ivor, the only parent she really remembered, she had never had close ties to anyone. The environment in the social cesspit of Godwin City didn't foster close relationships.

"How come this never bothered me before?" she asked the emptiness.

She felt like she had in Ashley, running down endless corridors of endless nothing. She wondered if Godwin was much different. The population pressed close, but the people were so many nulls.

Lonely, miserable thoughts, all through the night. She hung perilously close to the edge of self-pity as she stared at the darkness cloaking the front of the *Shaftsbury*.

She wondered how she had managed to get into this mess. It was as if her contact with Dom and Godwin Arms had erased her ability to make a graceful exit. *Up to then I didn't give a shit—*

"Problem. The world still doesn't."

Why did that insensitive bastard fascinate her?

It didn't matter where she was, or how screwed up the situation became—her thoughts always drifted back to Dom. It had to be some element of self-destruction in her psyche. The same part of her brain that drove her into the profession that had killed her parents.

It certainly wasn't Dom's control-freak personality—or she'd be drooling over Commander Jarvis here. And while power was supposed to be an aphrodisiac, that couldn't be it. She'd met Dom in the dungeon of the Bakunin Church of Christ, Avenger. Ever since then, they had fought through mess after mess.

A month of working together and the bastard still couldn't confide anything in her, still couldn't trust her. She wanted his confidence. She'd had this pathological desire for intimacy with someone about as emotional as the *Lady*. The first time she worked with someone—

Maybe that was it.

"I'm going to run back to him, aren't I?"

The end of the night was marked, not by any changes in the environment in the *Shaftsbury*, but by Kelly waking up. In addition to Kelly's uninjured status, Tetsami also noted that the man had perfect time sense.

It was another note to put on a growing list of suspicions.

"Good morning, miss," Kelly said.

"I hadn't noticed."

Kelly looked around, his smile faltering slightly. He ran his hands through his red hair. "We're alive—that makes it a good morning."

Tetsami nodded. "It'll be better when we get out of here."

Kelly didn't argue with that. Instead he walked back to the *Lady* and pulled himself up to the door of the tipped-over vehicle. "Have you eaten anything?"

"Not hungry."

Kelly disappeared into the *Lady* and came out with a pair of ration packages. He tossed her one as he returned to sit opposite the heater from her. "Eat," he said. "It'll help you heal."

I notice you didn't include yourself in that statement.

As they ate, Tetsami said, "We have to get the *Lady* up-right."

Kelly looked around a moment in confusion.

"The vehicle," she added.

"Oh. You confused me for a second—odd thing to call such an ugly truck."

"Don't upset her. She's all we've got."

Kelly smiled and laughed in an odd way. For a second Tetsami had a glimpse of something beyond the boyish con-man facade. It was so brief that Tetsami didn't have a chance to figure out who it reminded her of.

"Indeed. I send my apologies to the old girl." Kelly looked toward the three-axled underside of the *Lady*. "Shouldn't be too hard to right her. Just a matter of lever-age."

Tetsami opened her mouth to say something snide about the size of the vehicle. However, Kelly said it with such a straight face that she suspected he might know what he was talking about. She didn't want to undermine what authority she had by riding on him.

After breakfast she double-checked the stability of the wounded. Checking their vital signs and replacing the saline-nutrient packs on their arms was about the best she could do. Jarvis looked a little better. Gavadi was in as grave a condi-tion as he was when she first saw him. The navigator, Marc Baetez, was still sedated. As far as she could tell, none of them were in immediate danger. However, Jarvis, and espe-cially Gavadi, needed a real medic, not recipe first aid from a medkit's database.

Once she was reassured that no one was going to die on her immediately, she limped after Kelly, to the overturned *Lady*. Her muscles were stiff from abuse, even through the painkillers. It felt like she'd just traded in her major muscle groups for a set a size and a half too small.

The *Lady* looked like a hopelessly beached whale. She lay on her left side, her nose angled away from the front of the *Shaftsbury*, her tri-axled floor facing aft. A huge drift piled up against her roof, almost completely burying that side.

In the shadowy space of the *Shaftsbury*'s cargo hold, the *Lady's* size was even more imposing. Her cross section was four meters square, and she was easily fifteen meters long. Walking up to her underside was like facing a wall.

"Just a matter of leverage," Tetsami mumbled.

Kelly nodded. "You'll see." He carried the shovel and just looking at it awoke sympathetic pains in her back, reminding her of her fruitless dig yesterday.

Kelly walked around to the nose of the vehicle, where the left front axle was buried in a pile of chain. Kelly started pulling at the chain—what was left of the *Lady's* moorings—until he had nearly five meters' worth.

She watched him tug free meters more of the heavy mooring chain and was amazed at the effort Kelly could exert without apparently working up a sweat. It *was* cold—but his breath wasn't even fogging.

Tetsami stared at Kelly through an intermittent fog of her own breath.

His breath wasn't fogging.

What had been a growing suspicion of Kelly grew into a sudden distrust that hit her like a physical blow. She took a few unconscious steps back as she tried to figure out what she was seeing. What *was* he?

Kelly picked up too much chain, too easily. He stepped up to the middle axle and looped the chain around the inside of the upper tire. All of these actions would've been relatively innocuous, if it wasn't for Tetsami's growing paranoia.

"Here you go," Kelly said, handing her the ends of the chain. She could feel the chill of the metal through her driving gloves. What Kelly wore wasn't much better, and she'd never seen a sign of discomfort from him.

In this frigid wreck she'd never seen *any* sign of discomfort from him. No shivering, no hugging himself to keep warm, no huddling over the space heater.

As she wondered about him, he said, "Now I'll excavate the other side and lever her up. When I give the word, you pull."

"This isn't going to work." Tetsami's voice was distant, her thoughts elsewhere.

"Not immediately, miss. We lever it up a few centimeters and I can prop it up with the snow back there."

That sounded unlikely. "We'll see."

She stayed there, holding the chain, as Kelly went behind

the *Lady*. She noticed how the plan kept him out of her sight during the process.

Damn it, she cursed herself, *he's the only ambulatory ally you've got.*

Kelly was the only one to come through the wreck unscathed. Tetsami couldn't believe that. It was also hard to believe that he'd just conveniently "recovered" from the restraint buckles' stun field.

"Pull."

Tetsami pulled. She was surprised to feel the *Lady* shift its weight.

"Okay," Kelly said, after she'd been leaning on the chain for half a minute. When she let go, the *Lady* was leaning toward her at a very slight angle.

The strain erased the effect of the painkillers. Deep aches burned in her joints each time Kelly told her to pull. Every time she was less able to comply. However, her diminishing ability didn't slow the progress of the *Lady*. As Tetsami moved back, the vehicle continued to lean toward her a few degrees with each effort.

The process was agonizingly slow. It took at least an hour, probably more, for the *Lady* to reach a forty-degree angle. By then, Tetsami was five meters away from it, and barely keeping the chain taut.

By then, when Kelly called for her effort, Tetsami could barely put any tension on the chain.

Her effort wasn't needed.

Tetsami watched as the *Lady* angled up, past forty-five degrees. It balanced at the halfway point for a long moment before gravity gradually took over. Slowly at first, but with a lethal acceleration, the *Lady*'s three axles tipped toward her. Even though she had at least two meters of clearance, she dropped the chain and stumbled backward.

The *Lady*'s wheels hit with a solid thump that sprayed snow and shards of ice over her. The *Lady*'s overengineered suspension absorbed the impact with a minimum of rocking.

Now that it was upright, it was easier to see the damage the vehicle had sustained. Most of the exterior lights had been smashed or torn off. What had been an external antenna array was now a ragged stump. The body sported a dozen large dents in the surface, and one of the middle wheels had been bent ten degrees from the vertical.

More significant was the damage the *Lady* hadn't sustained. As Tetsami circled it, hugging her aching arms to her sides, she saw that of all the new dents in the skin, not one breached the surface. None of the windows had broken, and it looked like the *Lady*'s hardened skeleton had retained its shape. When she checked the systems inside the *Lady*, the readouts showed little damage at all. None of the environment control was lost, and as far as mobility went, the only damage was a loss of power to the one bent wheel—but then the *Lady* could move with only two wheels under power, as long as they were on opposite sides.

The vehicle's durability amazed Tetsami, and only made her wonder about Kelly all the more.

A Royt ATV built like a tank hadn't survived unscathed— why had Kelly?

Tetsami left the *Lady* and saw Kelly bending over the wounded. She almost warned him away. She thought better of it before she acted on the impulse. Whatever her suspicions were, Kelly presumably had no reason to interfere with any of the injured men. If he had, he had already had more than enough opportunity while she'd slept.

He'd had enough opportunity to do *her* in.

Repeating that to herself a few times gave a check to her raging paranoia.

The only thing wrong with the guy is the fact he survived. . . .

And he doesn't sweat, and his breath doesn't fog.

Tetsami shook her head, walked up to Kelly, and placed her hand on his shoulder. Her sleeve rode up on her wrist, and for a brief instant the skin on her wrist brushed the skin of his neck.

She started to ask, "How're they doing?" but before she reached "doing" her voice trailed off.

Kelly was paying attention to Gavadi and didn't seem to notice her incomplete sentence. "Baetez is improving. Jarvis is stable. But Gavadi seems to be worsening. I think he has some internal bleeding, but there's nothing left in the medkits to help. He needs a doctor."

Tetsami barely noticed what Kelly said. She was too busy dealing with the fact that the touch of Kelly's skin was as cold as ice.

Tetsami had to keep telling herself that Kelly wasn't acting like a threat. It had gotten to the point where she had to confront him. But she couldn't do it now. She really couldn't do it until they were out of the *Shaftsbury*, when she wasn't needlessly putting the wounded into danger.

At least, she had figured out how they were getting out of here, wounded and all. She just hoped that she wouldn't destabilize the whole wreck in the process.

She said nothing as the two of them cleaned the inside of the *Lady*, emptying it of extraneous equipment, clearing the bunks for use by the wounded.

Tetsami checked the *Lady*'s mobility. She still ran. Just as important to getting out of here, the mining laser was intact.

Tetsami turned the vehicle so that what remained of the forward lights shone toward the nose of the *Shaftsbury*. The cockeyed white glow illuminated an unbroken slope of snow, floor to ceiling. Tetsami guessed that the snow filled the compartment completely for nearly ten meters. Who knew how much snow was on top of the end of the *Shaftsbury*.

However, it was the only exit for the *Lady*. And the *Lady* was going to get them out of the mountains.

Carefully, she and Kelly loaded the wounded into the bunks.

Once they were safe, Tetsami set up the mining laser at the front of the craft. The object was to melt a hole big enough for the *Lady*. Kelly wanted to excavate by hand, but Tetsami overruled him. The laser might be a more dangerous way to do this, but they didn't have much time to play with. Not only did they have a trio of medical emergencies, but there had to be an all-out search for this craft by people they didn't want to be found by.

And she had a good idea, from her experience yesterday, how long it'd take to hand-excavate a hole big enough for the *Lady*.

Tetsami had Kelly back the *Lady* up to the rear of the cargo compartment. She stayed stationed by the laser, set up on the one clear spot of ground where they had made camp last night.

She activated the laser.

The laser was designed for cutting rock and ore, and where it touched the snow, white powder sublimed instantly into superheated steam. A white cloud billowed up from the front of the cargo compartment and Tetsami had to turn off the laser and let the cloud subside.

Once she saw the snowdrift again, there was a three-meter-wide pit carved in the top of it. It glistened with a sheet of ice. Ice covered the snow and a five-meter-deep slice of ceiling that had been previously buried.

She fired again, clearing away more snow. Billowing steam turned to frost on every exposed surface. Melting snow instantly refroze.

By the third firing, she had cleared to the end of the *Shaftsbury's* nose. By now the steam had dumped enough heat into the rest of the cargo compartment for Tetsami to feel the temperature rising.

Once she could see the edge of the ceiling, she moved the laser forward so she could angle the beam upward. Toward the surface, she hoped.

Now that she was pointing in the right direction, she would keep the laser going.

Unlike her previous efforts, she heard sounds when she fired the laser this time. The snow whistled as steam flooded the front of the craft. Tetsami felt the heat this time, as a cloud rolled over her. This time, visibility only mattered as far as it interfered with the efficiency of the laser. Since the laser was so overwatted for this job, she decided that it didn't matter.

The snow started rumbling. She could hear snow sluicing down the hole she couldn't see. It became much warmer where she stood, and she could hear piles of snow collapsing in the chamber around her. The drift she had moved to had become a puddle soaking into the pseudoflesh padding on the floor of the chamber.

The rumbling reached its apex, and subsided, along with the cloud—blown away by a biting wind.

Tetsami turned off the laser and looked up an ice-lined tunnel about two meters in diameter. About twenty meters above her she could see a small purple patch of sky.

CHAPTER THIRTY

Ivory Tower

"Anything worth the trouble will cost more than you pay for it."
—*The Cynic's Book of Wisdom*

"It is human nature to view all technological change with awe or superstitious dread."
—JEAN HONORÉ CHEVIOT
(2065–2128)

Dom tried to think about Tetsami. He thought about Proteus.

Proteus wasn't a large commune, as far as such things went. It huddled where the northern edge of Bakunin's equatorial forest began to change into grassland, halfway between the equator and the edge of the northern glacier. Beyond Proteus, Bakunin was untouched by man's recent appearance.

Dom had never been there before, and from what Dom knew, few people ever ventured this way. Fewer came back.

The Proteans were one of the few cults on the whole planet that could claim to be universally despised—or feared. On a planet that tolerated Satanic churches which managed an occasional human sacrifice in with the sheep and goats, that was an accomplishment.

The fact that Proteus managed to exist at all was a small testament to the ideological conviction of the average Bakuninite. The concept of universal liberty struck deep here, a little deeper than the taboos against nanomechanisms.

It was a bigger testament to the Protean defense network.

Dom wasn't even in sight of the commune before he got a challenge over his comm.

"Please identify yourself." The challenge sent no vid along with it. It was the only sign that Dom had of the fact he was probably being tracked by a weapon that could erase both him and his contragrav.

That was probably the scariest part of Proteus. They could be equipped with anything that they could obtain a design for. The small commune, a few hundred thousand people at most, could be armed with things that the *Confederacy* couldn't afford to deploy.

Dom responded, "I am a pilgrim." Like many fringe groups on Bakunin, the Proteans had managed to turn their fetishes into a micro-religion. Dom doubted that any "non-pilgrim" had ever even seen Proteus, except from orbit. The closest non-Protean traffic ever got to the hubbard's complex was a large cleft in the Diderot Mountains maybe a dozen klicks to the south. While the pass was well-situated for low-flying craft, ones without environmental containment, it was far north of anything useful. The southern passages were more convenient, if smaller.

That pass, why does it make me think about Tetsami?

"Please hold your position until your escorts arrive. Welcome, traveler." That last bit was said with an air of sincerity. The sound was somewhat alien to Dom, even with all the idealists scattered over the Bakunin landscape.

Dom decelerated the contragrav until it was hovering over a wrinkled hillside. If not for the starlight and Dom's instrument panel, he could have been in a sensory deprivation tank. Mountains towered in the middle distance to his right, but they were blank shadows, little more than a feeling of mass. Below him, without a moon, the ground was almost invisible.

He could have upped the gain on his photoreceptors, but he would have to dim the instrument panel to see anything. Not a good idea even in stationary flight. The only sounds were occasional gusts hitting the side of the aircar, and a barely audible supersonic whine from the contragrav generator.

It was as close as he had gotten to being spaceborne in nearly ten years.

He missed it.

He missed a lot of things. He missed the moral simplicity of his life before Styx. He missed clarity.

He missed Tetsami.

I have a singular disregard for my own life, Dom thought.

What is this all but a cowardly form of suicide? Perhaps I should *just turn myself over to Klaus.*

If Dom went through everything here at Proteus, he would be just as dead as far as everyone who knew him was concerned. As far as everyone who cared about him. As far as everyone he cared about . . .

He was startled when his escort arrived.

He had expected an armed scout-craft, or something similar.

However, hovering in front of the nose of his contragrav was a quintet of dull blue spheres. All five were exactly the same size, less than half a meter in diameter. They described the points of a pentagon. Marking the center of the pentagon was a sharp red glowing dot that shone through the windscreen of his contragrav.

Nothing supported the spheres, which would make them the smallest contragrav generators that he had ever seen. More disturbing was the glowing red dot. Dom saw no source for the illumination, and as the sphere's flying formation moved around the nose of his contragrav, Dom decided that the sourcelessness wasn't an illusion.

After bobbing around to the left and the right, the formation centered itself in front of the contragrav's nose. Then it abruptly shot forward, not even giving Dom time to wince. The five spheres cleared the sides of the contragrav, and the red dot widened until the view out the contragrav's windscreen was a uniform ruddy glow.

Dom felt the contragrav lurch backward slightly, as if something had struck it. None of the controls read out any damage.

The other readouts seemed confused. The radar was sending back a uniform reflection, wiping the screen with a blank featureless glow. The altimeter read zero and the radio was blacked out—

"Please power down your contragrav."

The voice didn't come from the comm. It was omnidirectional, and loud.

Dom hesitated.

"You will not fall," said the voice. Dom held his fingers to the red glowing windscreen and felt it vibrate. "Your contragrav interferes with the escort's maneuvering."

Dom began switching off the power systems for the contragrav. As he listened to the engine noise recede, he braced himself for impact. Nothing happened. There wasn't even a minor sensation of motion. All that happened was that the readouts on the contragrav injection chamber slowly leveled off to zero.

"Thank you. We will arrive at the orientation center in fifteen seconds."

A steady acceleration pushed Dom back into his seat. The airspeed indicator remained at zero, but the inertial velocity speedometer was turning over past a hundred klicks per.

He didn't understand how what the spheres were doing was even theoretically possible—not unless they had somehow attached themselves to the hull. The red glow could be an Emerson field of some sort, but he had never seen one glow like that.

Fifteen seconds was all he had to contemplate the fact that Proteus might be advanced in ways far beyond the obvious benefits of heretical technology.

Then, abruptly, acceleration reversed direction and the inertial velocity rolled back to zero. Just when the counter zeroed out, the red light winked out and the omnidirectional voice said, "Welcome, traveler."

His contragrav sat on a well-lit landing area.

At least, that's what Dom supposed it was, even though his was the only vehicle on it, and by any standards the area was much too small. It would barely be able to handle two or three small contragrav craft—any type of cargo hauler would be out of the question.

"Then, they don't need much in the way of imports, do they?"

No one answered him. He had half-expected them to.

Dom powered down the remaining systems on the contragrav, popped the canopy, and got his first real view of Proteus.

He had expected a dome like most of Bakunin's communes, or a planned city made of repetitive architecture, like Jefferson City. What he looked at resembled something grown from a living crystal. The central feature was a spire that towered above the landscape. Its walls were parabolic arcs that shot toward an infinity that could have been a full kilometer above him. It glowed blue and white from within its walls. As he gazed at it, he could see regular crystalline webworks that formed the support structure. As he looked, he could see the pattern replicated within each division. And within those divisions even finer detail. And within them even finer . . .

"It goes on forever," said a voice from behind him.

Dom turned to face a perfectly sculpted example of human femininity. He stared at a nude woman who could have been the platonic archetype of athletic beauty except for the fact she was over two meters tall and had skin that had a mirrorlike reflectivity.

"Hello," Dom said. He found himself at a loss for anything else to say.

The woman held out her hand and said, "I'm Eigne. Welcome to Proteus."

Dom took her hand and was surprised to find it warm. "Thank you. I presume you're here to 'orient' me?"

She smiled with teeth that were perfect silver mirrors. "Yes. That and to discover the needs of this new pilgrim." After the initial shock of the sight, Dom began cataloging other, less drastic differences between Eigne and the human norm. She was hairless. Her eyes were the same mirror surface. Normal human surface irregularities seemed to have been smoothed out, skin wrinkles, blemishes, even her nipples.

"What did you mean, before? 'Goes on forever.' "

She dropped his hand and waved at the tower. "The Spire. It is the first thing any newcomer looks at, and the first thing they notice about it is the superstructure. The structure is supported by a crystal lattice that replicates itself down to the atomic level. If you magnified the lattice a million times you'd still see hexagons and triangles and so on."

"They built the towers on Mars like that," Dom said.

Eigne looked surprised, "They did, in fact. How did—"

"I've visited Mars once or twice."

"Have you?" Eigne took his arm and led him toward a building made of parabolic arcs intersecting a hyperbolic plane that was the roof or the wall, depending on the angle of approach. "Come, let's get to know each other, traveler."

Proteus felt like a fragment of an alternate universe that had somehow injected itself into the prosaic, dirty world of Bakunin. The architecture seemed a melding of the forms of life and pure geometry. It was a world of curved planes and spirals, fractals and conic sections. Eigne told him that the forms often had as much to do with structural strength as aesthetics. Even inside the buildings, Dom could occasionally catch glimpses of the infinitely receding structure he had noticed on the Spire.

Eigne led him through a corridor that Dom saw was a logarithmic spiral.

As they walked, she asked him questions.

"What is your name?"

Dom felt a jerk in his cheek when he said, "Which one do you want?"

Eigne shook her head. "It doesn't matter."

"Dominic." He rubbed his cheek, watching his distorted fish-eye reflection of himself in the back of her skull. "Call me Dom."

"Okay, Dom. You offered yourself as a pilgrim. Do you know what that means?" Eigne stepped aside to let something that looked like an ebony tumbleweed roll by. The object paused briefly by Dom, then flowed past.

"I'm uncertain." Dom continued to massage his cheek.

"It means you are offering yourself to the Change."

"That's why I'm here."

Eigne stopped and turned to face Dom, giving him an appraising look. At least that was Dom's interpretation. The reflections made her expression hard to read. "Few come here. Fewer still want *that*."

"I thought that was one of the main tenets of your philosophy. . . ."

Eigne placed her hand to her chest in a very human gesture of self-consciousness. "Shedding the flesh." She nodded. "There are very few who are willing to pay the price for that."

Dom thought of the twenty-five megagrams he had. "You aren't talking of money, are you."

She smiled. "No. Money, for us, is merely an interface for the outside world. We have no needs that we cannot fulfill ourselves."

"Then what *is* the price?"

"There are parts to it," Eigne said. "The first. The Change makes you part of us—in ways you can't fully understand yet."

Dom knew that it required joining the Protean cult, but the way Eigne said it made Dom think there was more to it than simply buying a share of the commune.

"The second is more easily explained. Come, I'll show you something."

There had been no more conversation during the trek. Dom spent his time observing the nighttime crowd that populated Proteus. There were many eidolons of humanity, archetypes of every race and color. But there were *others*. Bodies sculpted to some alien plan that Dom could barely comprehend. Eigne was the least alien of these. Most common, however, were the ebony tumbleweeds. As he passed more of them, Dom could see that they weren't necessarily spherical. Their form consisted of six branches emerging from a spherical core. Those six branches subdivided into six more midway up their length, then six more— The branches on these tumbleweeds divided again and again until the ends were a cloudy haze of invisible branchings. Each junction seemed able to rotate through nearly three-hundred-sixty degrees.

One tumbleweed Dom passed had pulled itself into a roughly bell-shaped form, standing on a trio of its primary branches. It was facing one of the human-formed citizens and was pointing the curve of the bell toward the man. Dom could see inside the bell and saw pictures flying across its surface.

This is not my world, Dom thought.

Eventually, Eigne led him to a massive chamber that must have been at the heart of the commune. The scene was an architectural marvel where every single wall seemed to fly away from the observer at an exponential rate. Dom suspected that they had entered the base of the Spire.

"I know what you've been thinking, Dom."

"What?"

They walked down a ramp that arced down into the center of the chamber. It was then that Dom could see that the walls were alive with tumbleweeds. They glided against the curving walls, unperturbed by gravity.

"You've been wondering why we aren't flooded with pilgrims. You've decided that even if the basis of our technology is universally feared, there must be an endless supply of people willing to brave that for what we offer—an end to the tyranny of the flesh. Perhaps even immortality."

"The thought has crossed my mind."

Eigne nodded. "For many who desire it, the price is too

high. Even those who accept joining us in mind as well as form, even they can reach this point in the journey and decide to back away."

They had stopped. They had reached a platform in the center of the chamber. Dom felt a slight wind. He looked up and saw, far, far, far above him, a tiny patch of darkness that might have been the sky. He was looking up the axis of the Spire.

The platform was round and supported by cantiliver ramps arcing away in every direction. The platform was bare except for what looked like a workbench supporting a black ellipsoid three meters in diameter. A tumbleweed sped down one ramp, rolled to the bench, did something to the ellipsoid, then disappeared off down another ramp.

"What *is* this point?"

"The ultimate end. The archive." Eigne waved toward the walls. "Everyone who has consented to the Change."

Dom waited for a moment. Then he asked, "Everyone *what?*"

"The price of the Change is threefold. Consent, devotion, and *information*. During the Change we know the pilgrim's existence down to the atom. To implement the Change, we must have the right to that knowledge."

Dom opened his mouth, then he closed it, allowing the implications to sink in. After a while he said, "Everything?"

"Everything. The walls of the Archive record a billion souls. Everyone the Change has ever contacted."

Dom stared at the tumbleweed-covered walls, speechless.

"Records exist here of people who were frozen in the twentieth century. There are records here of the scientists who terraformed Mars. There is a place here for every victim of the Titan accident. A planet's worth of knowledge resides here."

Dom turned away from the wall. "I can see why people back out."

"They do not understand."

Dom shook his head, "The mind is a very private thing."

"This archive is why Proteus exists at all."

He walked up to the workbench. The ellipsoid on it was matte-black and seamless. As he watched, another tumbleweed rolled up and did something, appearing to reach its infinity of branchings inside the ellipsoid without marring the surface or creating an opening. "What do you do with all this? What's the point of warehousing all these—" Dom had to pause a moment before he said, "people?"

"This isn't a warehouse."

"What is it then?"

"It's the staging area for our ultimate purpose." Eigne walked up and placed a hand on the ellipsoid, "and this is one of our seeds."

"I don't follow you."

She smiled again and spoke with a tone that Dom thought was reserved for religious fanatics talking about heaven. "Within this seed we can place a million minds as well as the collective recorded knowledge of the entire Confederacy. Within it is the capability to rebuild those people, this city, an entire civilization. From this seed can grow an entire planet."

Dom stepped back from the black ellipsoid, staring at its blank surface.

"With only a contragrav generator it can leave the atmosphere and slingshot itself around our star. Then it can knit itself a sail and ride outward on the star's wind. Eventually, after an aeon or two, it will find a planet." She looked up and smiled at him. "Think of it. Perhaps a million years after all this has become dust, you'll be resurrected on a new planet. A new paradise."

Dom stared at the seed, thinking about how much it looked like a giant black egg.

"This is our six-thousandth seed. When we are finished, we will launch it after our others, you could be part of it."

"I need to sit down and think about this."

She nodded. "Everyone does. I'll take you to a guest room."

CHAPTER THIRTY-ONE

Eminent Domain

"Sign your name to the universe and someone will auction off the signature."
— *The Cynic's Book of Wisdom*

"Life is short, art long . . ."
— HIPPOCRATES
(*ca.* 460–*ca.* 377 B.C.)

The tunnels under the Diderot Mountains really did go on forever. It was becoming obvious that Hougland's escape was a threat only to her own life. The farther they went during the search, the more Shane became convinced that Hougland was probably dead. The microscopic trail that Random followed was eventually going to lead to a crack in the floor, or a ledge of a bottomless pit, and at the bottom would be Hougland's crushed body.

Damn it, Hougland. You weren't stupid. You knew your chances down here were nil. Why'd you do this?

Shane knew the answer before she finished the question. To Hougland, this was preferable to captivity. Hougland was still a marine. Shane was something else.

"Rest again," Shane called out to Random. Her voice bounced off the rock walls a dozen times, ricocheting even deeper into the mountain.

The floating chrome spheroid stopped ten meters down and spun on its axis to face her.

Shane found a relatively flat rock to sit on.

"You should sleep," Random said. "We've gone on nearly a full day."

A Bakunin day, thirty-two hours, or just a standard twenty-four hour day? Does it matter?

She checked the chrono on her wrist and saw that it was only a standard day.

Only.

She ran her fingers across the stone she sat upon and shook her head. No sleep. There was no sense of time down here inside the eternal black rock. She had the strange sense that if she did fall asleep down here, she would wake up aeons later. A million years would pass by down here, unnoticed.

Not such a bad thing. What ties me here but possible charges of treason?

To the remaining military mind she had, avoiding the court-martial she deserved was as appalling a thought as the treason itself. This, despite the fact that she knew that she would be given no hearing. Military justice in the marines was only slightly less perfunctory than civilian justice on Occisis. They might give her a speech.

Who did she owe? What did she owe them? Would giving her life for the lives she took, would that balance the scales. What about the lives she saved? What about the eight hundred civilians that Klaus Dacham would have killed?

Would returning be an admission that she'd been wrong?

Dear God, I might be a traitor, but saving those civilians was not *wrong.*

"Are we catching up?" Shane asked Random.

"Her traces are becoming fresher."

"How fresh?"

"Less than three hours old now."

"No better estimates?"

Random shook his spheroid, "No."

"We'll probably catch up with her corpse—"

"I don't think so," Random said.

"She's probably injured, not to mention stumbling blind—"

"Not blind," Random said. "I've been detecting combustion by-products. She has a torch."

"How in the hell—"

"I suspect she found a thin, broken stalagmite, wrapped part of her jumpsuit around it."

Shane nodded, and her respect for Hougland grew. It would have taken patience to ignite the synthetics, but there was more than enough material in these caves to strike a spark with her belt buckle or some other metal part of her jumpsuit. Once lit, the fire would persist for a long time as the synthetics bubbled into napalmlike slag. It was dangerous and toxic, but it could work. You just wouldn't want to remain stationary next to it.

"Also," Random said. "I suspect that she knows where she's going."

"Huh? Where do you get that?"

The place Shane had chosen to rest was a large cavern that formed a junction for dozens of smaller passages, some barely wide enough to admit her arm, others that would have admitted ten marines in full battle dress walking abreast. The cavern itself was roughly domelike, the shape matching that of a sphere of clay thrown at the ground at an oblique angle.

Random flew his robot around the perimeter of the cavern. "As an example, the traces I find indicate that she stopped at every opening and examined it for some time before choosing this one." Random stopped in front of a moderate-sized opening half-obscured by mineral deposits leaking from a crack in the ceiling.

"So she debated a little, that doesn't mean she knows what she's doing. These caverns are unexplored by the people who *live* on this planet. She's never been to Bakunin before, and our briefings—" Shane got up from her rock and walked to the opening Random floated in front of. "Where are we, Random?"

"We've traveled close to sixty-five kilometers north of the holding cells. That puts us three hundred kilometers northeast from Godwin—"

"How deep?"

"Two kilometers below sea level—"

That explained the heat. The air felt like soup.

"From the surface?" Shane asked.

"Seven kilometers below the average height of the range above us."

Shane nodded. "For the last twenty hours or so we've been traveling downward, right?"

"Down and directly north."

"Directly away from GA&A, Klaus, and the marines," Shane said.

She wedged herself partly through the entrance to the new tunnel. It was a collage of shadows, but Random's lamps gave enough light past her to see that the slope was indeed downward. Shane unwedged herself and turned to face Random.

"Who designed the security setup of the prison?"

"Mosasa."

"And you, of course," Shane said. "To a large extent Mosasa *is* you."

"I can't dispute that—"

"The location?"

"Mosasa as well."

Shane looked back down the tunnel. "How much of this did you plan?"

"I don't think—"

Shane turned and grabbed the surface of the chromed spheroid. She didn't know exactly what she intended to do, but she had to shake something. "You *think* too much. That's all you do, isn't it? You set up Hougland for the escape. I bet you even damped the field on her cell to make it easier. You and your predictive psychology . . ."

"Please let go of my surface."

Shane let go and folded her arms. In her agitation she slipped them past each other and slapped her sides. It took a moment of concentration to get her artificial limbs to obey her.

Random floated back a few meters. "You're correct. I saw Hougland's strong interest in the visual arts. I intuited her personal history would've provided a strong historical interest in alien art forms—"

"The Dolbrians," Shane said.

"The Dolbrians. Hougland was the only resource available who might have the knowledge to recognize Dolbrian traces in these caverns."

"So you let her escape to lead you to the heart of whatever this is—God." Shane lowered her head.

Random sighed. "It wasn't quite what you think. There are some imperatives I operate on that a human would call subconscious. Sometimes I make decisions without the aware part of my mind knowing the reasons. Later I can decipher my reasons—but all of this is tangled under four centuries of overlapping programming."

"I don't know what to think about this, Random. I begin to understand why people hate AIs so much."

"Please. I've gone over the situation, and the risk was

minimal. On the other hand, the potential benefit to this planet is enormous."

Shane shook her head. "Just tell me two things."

"What?"

"Did you know that Hougland was going to be the marine I stunned in the assault?"

"No, I didn't."

"Can you lie, Random?"

"It's not in my nature as an information processing device."

Shane nodded and decided to get back on the trail. She'd rested enough.

It was a few minutes walking down the new passage before Shane realized that Random hadn't really answered her last question.

Shane let Random lead her deeper into the mountain, even though she couldn't trust him. Worse, she realized that there was no way she would ever get out of this mountain without him.

The most disturbing thing was that she had no idea where her loyalties were. She'd rejected the marines, the Confederacy, *and* Dominic Magnus' operation. She had no ties to this planet and her ties to her own were tenuous at best.

She wondered if Random knew enough about her to anticipate the ambivalence she felt about his—

Was betrayal the right word? From what Shane had seen, both Random and Magnus drove parallel courses. And Random was right in that finding Dolbrian artifacts down here might mean a lot for Bakunin. It could give the planet a massive bargaining chip in dealing with the Confederacy. Delivering that back to Magnus, could that be a betrayal?

Why all the Machiavellianism? Was it part of Random's psychology?

Shane began to appreciate how shallow Random's psychological facade might actually be.

The tunnel they traveled sloped downward, and—now that she was looking for it—Shane began to notice traces of what might have been incredibly ancient construction. What she saw *could* have been natural rock formations. But every now and then the walls would show too many straight lines and flat surfaces.

They had gone down this single tunnel for three hours or

so before Shane saw the first definite signs of intelligent design.

"Hold it, Random."

Random stopped his descent and turned around, washing her with his spotlights. Shane leaned back so her ink-black shadow didn't obscure the part of the left wall that'd caught her attention. It was one of the sections of wall that seemed too flat for nature. The area was a roughly elliptical patch, its long axis pointing down the tunnel.

The patch of wall was covered with carvings almost too faint to see. Random's spotlight deepened the shadows, making the scratches in the rock more visible. The pattern was incredibly complex, resembling a cross between Celtic knotwork and cuneiform writing. Lines looped around and through one another in repeating triangular patterns. The entire surface seemed to have been drawn with a single continuous line.

"God," Shane said.

"There's no way for me to measure the age of the carving right now. However the pattern matches recorded examples of Dolbrian writing."

Shane brushed her fingers around the edges of the ellipse. She wondered what the slab said.

"A hundred million years," she whispered. She was looking at one of perhaps only ten surviving sites of Dolbrian architecture known in the entire Confederacy. The writing she looked at was worth the economy of a small planet. Somehow it had survived water, lichen, and whatever tectonics that remained on this old planet.

It was the first time Shane had ever come in contact with an artifact this old. It was humbling.

"Shall we go on? We're only an hour behind Hougland now."

How long had she stared at this? Shane let a finger trace a looping line. It was a beautiful language.

She dropped her hand and turned to face Random. "Let's go."

Something incredible was down here. She could feel it.

The tunnel remained the same size, but its character began to change. The floor evened out until the bumps in the surface became a regular ribbed stairway downward. The walls became more even until the tube became a pentagonal prism.

The carvings deepened until they passed a point where the tunnel seemed pristine.

Shane traced her hand over the surface of the wall and found it covered by a thin layer of some transparent substance. *Something to preserve all this,* she thought. *They must have left it for us.*

"What's covering the walls?" she asked Random.

Random paused and drew a manipulator over the junction between the two upper walls. After a few attempts, Random said, "I can't isolate a sample to analyze. Very strong, very flexible."

"How strong?"

"A plasma torch might cut it."

Shane nodded, running her hand over the surface. The surface was smooth, almost slick. The coating was hard to see. Her fingers appeared to float a few millimeters over the carving. *We're close to the heart of all this. Close to Hougland.*

She nodded to Random and the robot spun and continued down the hallway. As they descended, a sense of weight was added to the air, like she was breathing the years piled around her. The air was dry, scratching her throat.

Every hundred meters seemed to slice another aeon off the age of the passage they walked. The walls began to acquire color underneath their protective coating. Reds and golds began to glint from the pits of the carved lines. Color spread outward in a swirling universe of alien patterns.

Shane had never heard of any Dolbrian remains that were this well preserved. Even the huge artifacts on Mars had been weathered until they were little more than orderly piles of polyceram rock.

She realized she was shaking.

The corridor continued on, its total length was nearly three kilometers angling down into the ground. Near the end, the signs of passing time were nearly gone. The walls sparked in Random's spotlight reflecting back golds, silvers, reds, and blues in looping triangular patterns.

The cross section was a bottom-heavy pentagon; the point above them seemed razor-sharp now. Only the floor was unadorned, except for a stone rib going across it every half meter or so. The ribs were necessary. The slope was nearly forty-five degrees downward.

"You knew this was here?"

"Suspected," Random said. "Even with me, that's not quite the same thing."

"Why didn't you send a search party, damn it?"

There was a long pause before Random said, "That's not the way my mind works."

"Where does it lead?" Shane asked. Despite her anger at Random, she couldn't keep the wonder out of her voice.

Random's answer was to continue downward. And, before she was quite ready, she learned the answer.

Random flew out of a door at the end of the corridor. For a moment Shane was blinded by the absence of the spotlight in the enclosed space. She stumbled out the door after Random. She stopped just on the other side because she sensed the walls had retreated. Her eyes took a moment to adjust to the change in lighting.

The first thing she saw was Random, floating nearly twenty meters above her. She was just getting a handle on the size of the space she was in when she saw Hougland.

Hougland was sitting cross-legged, spotlit by Random's floating robot. She was sixty or seventy meters away, across a smooth, flat plane of rock. Little of her jumpsuit remained and her body was scraped, bruised, and cadaverous. An evil-looking mass smoldered at the end of a club by her feet. She was blinking and shading her eyes, looking toward Shane and Random.

Warily, Shane walked toward Hougland. The smoldering club could make a nasty weapon.

Hougland didn't reach for it. Instead she continued to look in Shane's direction, blinking. She hadn't moved by the time Shane reached her, and it was obvious that Hougland was close to collapse.

Though she looked close to death, Hougland was smiling.

"Shane," Hougland said.

"Yes, are you—"

"Shh." Hougland raised a finger to her lips and Shane saw that the nail was torn away, leaving an ugly gash down the top of her finger. "I'm glad you're here. I shouldn't be the only one to see this."

Shane started digging for the medkit in her pack. Hougland put a hand on her arm. The hand felt frail and bony, but the grip still had some strength.

"Never mind me," Hougland said. "Just look."

Hougland turned her head to face upward, and Shane followed her gaze.

Random must have paid attention to the conversation, because the spotlight swung away from the two of them and focused its beam upward.

Shane gasped.

They were sitting near the center of a huge five-sided pyramid. The walls sloped upward at a shallow angle to meet a hundred meters above their head. Every inch of the space above them was alive with writing. In addition to the triangular writing, circular symbols graced the spaces above, concentric circles, ellipses, dots. Thousands of circles spread across the ceiling in an apparently random scene.

Shane, however, knew that the pattern was far from random. Even if she had never seen a picture of a Dolbrian starmap, she might have been able to guess what she looked at. The dots central to the circles varied in size and their color ranged from white-blue, through yellow, to orange-red. Directly above their head would be Kropotkin, Bakunin's star.

"My God," Shane said.

"Beautiful, isn't it?" Hougland said.

Shane kept staring at the ceiling. Just one artifact like this had allowed the Centauri Alliance to know where to find a dozen habitable planets. They had hoarded the information. They had managed to even "sell" planets to the Indi Protectorate for concessions in the Congress. The few Dolbrian starmaps that had been found to date were fragments, covering ten light-years at most.

Shane had no idea of the scale, but the intact map above her head must have covered an area several times the diameter of the Confederacy. The number of habitable planets, planets terraformed by the Dolbrians, listed above her head must number in the hundreds.

This wasn't worth the economy of a planet.

This was worth the entire Confederacy.

"Hougland," Shane whispered.

There wasn't a response.

Shane looked down next to her and only saw a crumpled heap.

"Random, give me some help here!" Shane knelt by

Hougland as the spotlight swung to cover them. She had the
feeling that she was already too late as they turned Hougland
over and tore open the Medkit.

Hougland, however, had a quiet smile on her face.

CHAPTER THIRTY-TWO

Arms Race

"Don't bring a knife to a gunfight."
—*The Cynic's Book of Wisdom*

"The gods are on the side of the stronger."
—CORNELIUS TACITUS
(*ca.* 56–120)

Dawn greeted Ivor on his second day of searching the eastern desert. He'd long ago admitted that his emotional involvement had allowed him to make a tactical blunder. Millions of people could vanish inside these four million square kilometers of black, windblown desert.

Finding a single person was hopeless.

Still, he flew a search pattern between the dead Ashley Commune and the gash in the Diderot Range. That two-hundred-and-fifty-kilometer stretch of desert seemed the most likely area to hold some sign. If he'd been ambushed at Ashley, *he'd* head for that pass.

Back and forth, wishing there were a hundred more of him, searching for tracks, wreckage, anything . . .

Alone, in a small contragrav flyer, he had nothing to do but watch the sand, listen to his radio, and think about the various versions of his past.

He had been thinking of Styx more and more ever since he'd been drawn into Dominic Magnus' circle of co-conspirators. Even before Dom confronted him about Robert Elision.

It was very easy for him to remember, despite the fact he'd been out of practice for so long.

Watching the rippling black plain below the contragrav, Ivor could easily picture the last time he was on Styx. He could still smell the ash-filled air, still hear the black slush sucking the boots of his damaged environment suit, still feel the weight of his son across his back.

The memory still brought an ache at the corner of his eyes, where tears would form, had he any left.

It had been his fault.

Then he'd been the commanding officer of the Styx Presidential Guard. He'd been Fleet Commander Robert Elision. As he had risen in the Presidential Guard, he had watched the technocrats in the Citadel grow more and more totalitarian. What had begun as a few simple errors in resource distribution had led to some civil disorder in outlying domes. The response from the Citadel had been panic. The growing insecurity of the civilian government in Perdition had led to using power, food, and access off-planet as blackmail, revenge, and a club to bludgeon their citizens into submission—

The situation lasted nearly six years before the threat of civil war was impossible to ignore. A civil war that would irreparably damage the ability of humans to survive on that dirty slushball. By then, the military was as disenchanted with the Citadel as was the rest of Styx.

In one sense it was nine years ago.

Fleet Commander Robert Elision had given the orders to take over the government. It seemed the only option, but it was much too late to prevent civil collapse. Taking the Citadel by force had been an agonizing affair that had left most of the capital city of Perdition in ruins. With the loss of central authority, most of the outlying cities devolved into violent riots as lines of resources were cut.

Even as the military took charge of the government, it was too late. There was nothing left to govern. The people of Styx no longer accepted authority, no matter that the seat of power had changed hands.

Two months into Fleet Commander Elision's attempt to bring order to the situation, a rogue faction of the Presidential Guard attempted to kill him—blowing his aircar out of the black Stygian sky. The missile had taken out half the controls of the military transport, as well as the contragrav. Still, his son—a lieutenant in the airborne division of the Guard, following his father's footsteps—who piloted the craft, managed to ditch the transport into the tundra north of Perdition.

His son didn't survive the crash intact.

Fleet Commander Robert Elision carried his son ten kilometers through the blackest ashblown Stygian night, in a broken environment suit, making it to Perdition only to discover that his son had been dead even before he'd picked him up.

In one sense, it was nine years ago.

In terms of Ivor's own personal history, it happened twenty years ago.

As far as the universe was concerned, it never happened at all.

The food riots, the six years of civil unrest, the bloody military push into the Citadel, his son's death in an aircar crash—all existed only in Ivor's memory.

Styx was an old colony. It was founded in the middle of the twenty-second century, nearly a century before the first human use of a tach drive. A remnant of the founders hung in a trojan orbit between Styx and Sigma Draconis, the engineered wormhole that had brought colonists, equipment, and raw material from the even older human base at 61 Cygni.

The wormhole was technically one-way. The separation between the points the wormhole connected wasn't only 11.3 light years in space, but nearly twelve years in time. Travelers from 61 Cygni would suffer a time lapse.

Anyone entering from the Sigma Draconis side would enter their own past.

In a way, what Fleet Commander Robert Elision had done was more final than death. He had left Styx in secret and had piloted his scout craft down the wrong end of that wormhole. His piloting skills allowed him to avoid destruction by the automated defenses at the 61 Cygni end—barely.

In surviving, he became a ghost from a future that was changed simply by his presence in his own past.

He'd wanted to change the course of events on Styx.

That he had done.

But not for the better.

Ivor Jorgenson established himself on Bakunin, where it didn't matter if he were a ghost, a side effect from a wormhole bleeding excess mass.

He should have stopped there. But he had contacted Commander Robert Elision, warning his earlier self. That warning had set in motion the attempted coup that had led to the

TEC laying waste to the entire city of Perdition—except for the government in the Citadel.

That was fifteen years ago, something he and the universe agreed upon.

Things were worse than he could've imagined on Styx now, and he hadn't even managed to save his son. He'd managed to cut his son's revised life even shorter.

Now he was caught again in large events, and he had lost Tetsami as well.

"Damn it!" Ivor slammed his fist against the control panel, cracking the cover on one of the holo displays. He dipped the contragrav and flew a few meters above the dunes. "She has to be out here somewhere!"

It was a plea of denial as much as anything. She *didn't* have to be out here. She didn't *have* to be anywhere. But he needed her somewhere. The only allegiance that mattered to Ivor after the last two decades was the allegiance of family. Tetsami *was* that family. Blood didn't matter, she was his daughter by any meaningful measure of the term.

She's not in the hands of the TEC. They'd question her— all hell would have broken lose at Dominic's mountain.

But then, he'd been gone for over thirty-two hours. The whole base could be overrun and he wouldn't know about it.

The contragrav slid away from the remains of Ashley, zigzagging across the desert. Ashley was his base of operations, the only place that he was sure Tetsami had been. He had managed to find signs of her presence there, things like stripped-down radios where she was checking the EMP damage.

Don't let her get hit by an EMP. Don't let her die like her parents did.

Ivor was an atheist. He didn't know whose help he was asking.

The little contragrav hugged the onyx dunes. According to the locator in the dash, he was ten klicks away from Ashley when he saw something flash in the mountains.

What?

The flash happened again, near a saddle in some peaks to the north of the pass. Without looking at the control panel, he tapped controls on the computer that would save the data collection from the forward cameras.

"That's a laser," Ivor said. The fact he saw it at this distance, from air-scattered light, told him that it was a damn powerful one.

The beam of light died, leaving a faint white smudge. Ivor couldn't make out any details. He turned to the comm display, and had the computer enhance the video he'd just recorded. For once he was glad to have this semi-luxury contragrav rather than a real exploration vehicle. This car, at least, had all the electronic bells and whistles.

The computer showed him a magnified view of the scene.

It was a laser, the beam was unmistakable. In its wake, after it had flashed out, it left a cylindrical white cloud billowing up from the ground. The cloud lasted a few seconds before the wind tore it to shreds. He couldn't get any sense of scale from the video.

That wasn't a military laser. Military combat lasers were either invisible or polychrome. Not a comm laser either. Those tended to be infrared or—

"Comm laser?"

Could that be a signal?

Even if it wasn't, it was something worth investigating. Something rotten was going on in this desert and—despite his arguments with Dom Magnus' priorities—Ivor wanted to know what that was as much as anyone.

Ivor aimed his contragrav at the pass while he had the computer cook up a terrain map, giving him a set of possible locations for that laser.

He was close to a hundred klicks closer to the Diderot Range before he noticed something odd on the contragrav's radar. With all his attention ahead of him, it had taken Ivor a while to notice.

The radar on this little scout was designed for airborne use, and at his ground-hugging height it was nearly useless. All the screen would show was a lot of reflected trash from ground clutter—

Except for a massive blank spot forty klicks away and behind. The blank covered half the radar's scope and was moving toward him.

The blank spot kept moving, an invisible amorphous line erasing the ground clutter. The area that Ivor was looking at, the area erased, now covered nearly two thousand square kilometers. It was moving toward him at close to a hundred klicks an hour.

It had to be the Proudhon army, advancing behind stealth and ECM craft. Even as Ivor accelerated the contragrav he knew that, if that was the front line of an advance, then he was already well within the range of their scout craft. There was a good chance he was surrounded and had only escaped a confrontation so far by luck and flying close to the ground.

As the little contragrav accelerated, he hugged it even closer to the ground. Close enough to set off the proximity alarms.

As he flew, he killed the radar. If he were to get out of this, he had to offer as low an EM profile as possible. That meant no radar, no radio. He had to get away from the advancing army as fast as possible. In a small aircar like this, if anything armed actually saw him, he was dead.

What about that laser? Did they see it?

He pushed the contragrav near the limit of its ability. Once his velocity passed two hundred klicks he no longer had time to think about anything but flying the craft. The car rode barely three meters above the surface and it took all of Ivor's attention to avoid slamming the craft *through* a dune. Even so, the craft sporadically threw up sheets of sand in its wake when it came close to kissing the ground.

The distance between Ivor and Ashley steadily grew, but not fast enough for Ivor's taste.

Through the gray haze of a sand-covered windshield, the only stable part of Ivor's world was his destination, the pass in the Diderot Mountains. He angled the craft north, because the pass would be an obvious target.

The pink-capped peaks wrapped his horizon, immobile while the desert around him was an accelerating blur.

The mountains and the sky both remained fixed.

The desert changed around him.

Soon it became too dangerous to hug the surface. As he closed on the mountains, the terrain became more uneven and rocky. Also, the desert plants grew from small ground-hugging globes into three-meter bushes like giant purple broccoli. Ivor punched the altitude to four meters, and he still had to skirt occasional fingers of wind-sculpted rock.

Even though he was ahead of the advancing line, and diverting north of it, Ivor had no illusions. Advance craft would be scouring the desert, and probably the pass ahead. In the open, in a civilian contragrav, he was much too exposed.

The ground below the contragrav was rising, and had turned from sand completely to rock. Ivor had to give the ground even more clearance as it became more irregular.

Plants died out around him, giving way to the naked mountain side, and shortly afterward, snow sheeted across the nose of his craft.

His altitude climbed as he aimed through a pass much higher than the one he'd avoided. He aimed through it, and toward a saddle between two high peaks further away. Above him and ahead, the saddle offered him possible cover.

It became even more of a chore to control the contragrav, forcing it into an unnatural upward angle. He no longer had the option to hug the surface. All around him was chaotic mountain terrain.

As he closed on his goal, a shuddering thunderclap rocked the little craft. Ivor was thinking sonic boom even before he saw a turquoise arrow slice through the sky above him and to the south, above the great pass.

As he tried to push the contragrav to get even more acceleration, another multiple thunderclap almost threw his contragrav into a mountain wall. It was only Ivor's piloting ability that kept him from losing control. The snow seemed alive below him now, and much too close, and he had to raise his craft higher to avoid being swamped.

Three more arrows sliced by, in formation.

All Ivor could do was hope the fighters didn't see him. The next five minutes were agonizing. Warning lights were telling him that the contragrav was overheating, that he was flying without radar.

Five minutes deeper into the mountains, and the fighters didn't return. Peaks rose on either side of him. If a fighter found him here, he would be trapped.

It was nearly ten minutes without the fighter's return before Ivor could breathe again. Then he began to realize his mistake.

That saddle he was aiming toward, was passing over— even now—had been the source of that first laser flash. Either the source of that flash was Proudhon, or they were going to send scouts to investigate.

Without warning, a shadow passed in front of the craft. Ivor was pulling the craft into an evasive dodge to starboard, up the side of the northern peak, even before he realized what he'd seen.

Even so, he was too late.

A beam of coherent energy sliced through the body of his contragrav as he turned. The beam was perfectly aimed, straight through the contragrav generators, totally disabling. Ivor slammed the emergency eject.

The cockpit pod was thrown from the body of the scout as the contragrav blew itself apart in a flower of plasma. The explosion shook the pod, sending it tumbling, giving Ivor a facedown view of the slopes speeding by, twenty meters away.

Ivor hugged his crash harness as the pod arced downward and slammed into the Diderot Mountains.

CHAPTER THIRTY-THREE

Debriefing

"Half of knowledge is knowing the questions."
—*The Cynic's Book of Wisdom*

"Beware your allies' secrets."

—LI ZHOU
(2238–2348)

Tetsami drove the *Lady* in a bucking, sliding climb up an ice-lined tunnel. The *Lady*'s progress up the steep slope was accompanied by cracked and falling ice. Every time Tetsami goosed the drive, the *Lady* bucked forward in a shower of snow.

She'd tried to have the hole widen as it went, to keep the edges from collapsing under their own weight. The *Lady* climbed the shallowest angle of an irregular cone whose far edge was near vertical, and it *still* felt like she was driving up an avalanche. When the car finally bucked itself out of the hole, the sudden stop was a shock.

No longer in danger of sliding backward, Tetsami pulled the car around to face the hole. She could finally see where the *Shaftsbury* had landed.

They sat in the bottom of a saddle-shaped formation between two knobby white peaks. The *Shaftsbury* was nothing more than a hump in an otherwise smooth curve of snow. Not even the tail section, five meters taller than the remaining craft, showed above the smooth drift.

The wind was fierce. It roared against the side of the *Lady*, blasting it with loose snow. The hole she'd excavated with the laser seemed to fill even as she watched. The purple-tinted glare off the drifts hurt her eyes. Occasionally the whole landscape would white out.

Of the trench that *Shaftsbury* must have left upon landing, there was no sign.

A hundred meters or so beyond them, the saddle opened up into a larger valley and then dropped away, leaving a view of the rounded Diderot Range. Rounded white peaks carved a sky too blue for Bakunin.

I'm looking at the sunrise. We're facing east!

Either Jarvis or the pilot had the *Shaftsbury* turn completely around during its flight. It made some sense, getting out of the mountains. Had they managed a little more altitude, made it past that saddle a hundred meters away, they would have ditched in the desert not the mountains.

She didn't know if that was good or bad.

Tetsami watched the snow-whipped landscape and wondered, *Where to now?* She'd never felt so isolated. Even the near panic attack she'd felt in the desert was trivial compared to the bone-numbing aloneness she felt right now. She looked at an environment that wasn't only unmoved by her presence, but was actively hostile.

Well, we're out, damn it.

She drove the *Lady* toward the edge of the saddle formation. Near one edge, there was an outcrop of rock that would shelter their craft from the wind. As she drove the vehicle, she watched the rear video. Their tracks vanished under the snow as soon as they were made.

Search party's going to have a hard time finding us. Again, she didn't know if that was good or bad.

Once she was parked in the lee of the rock outcrop, Tetsami glanced at Kelly. He sat next to her, watching the view out the windshield. As his attention was occupied, Tetsami got out of the driver's seat and moved to the rear of the *Lady.* She gave the three wounded men a nominal check before she picked up the one matte-black Dittrich HVE they'd liberated from the wreck. It wasn't something she'd want to fire inside the *Lady,* with its overcharged electrostatic flechettes, but it was the one weapon they had besides the mining laser.

She pointed the HVE down the length of the *Lady* and cleared her throat.

"Nice view—" Kelly said as he turned to face her. He saw the gun leveled at him and froze, half-turned in the chair.

He swallowed and said, "You don't intend to fire that weapon. Do you, miss?"

"I need to ask you a few questions, Kelly."

"The gun isn't nece—"

"Humor me."

Kelly looked up at her. His expression was all boyish innocence, and the more she saw of it, the less she trusted it. Apparently he didn't like what he saw in her face, because the disarming smile he wore collapsed into a weak nod.

"What the hell are you?" she asked.

"I defected from the Occisis marines—"

"Not who. *What.*"

Kelly looked up at her, expression blank, and said, "I don't know what you mean."

"You know damn well what I mean. Your breath doesn't fog. Your body temperature's somewhere around freezing. The wreck tossed you as bad as Gavadi, and you don't have a scratch. You don't sweat. The stun field didn't affect you at all. I'm half convinced this gun won't work on you." Tetsami looked at the gun in her hand, and up to Kelly. "Explain yourself, or I'm going to find out if it does."

There was a long silence as Kelly stared at her.

"I'm waiting," Tetsami said.

"Please, I must think—" Kelly's voice had lost its Occisis accent. It was flatter, not quite emotionless, but close to a monotone. His tone of voice was naggingly familiar.

"What's to think about?" Tetsami asked. The change in Kelly's expression was disturbing. It was as if the human expression had been sloughed off and he was still looking for a replacement.

"I should have anticipated this." Kelly's expression was back, but it was much less the boyish con man. In less than two seconds, his whole manner had shifted from aggressive gregariousness to ironic worldliness. "I wasn't undamaged in the crash. And some of the damage is functional."

"Stop stonewalling."

"I'm answering you." Kelly sighed and shook his head. "And that gun *would* do me serious damage. You might want to sit. This will take a while."

He started by telling her about Kelly, the *real* Kelly. The man calling himself Michael Kelly had been officially dismissed from the Occisis reserves for a number of profiteering charges—a capital crime on Occisis. Kelly managed to escape to Bakunin, outside the jurisdiction of Occisis and the Centauri Alliance. Ever since his arrival on Proudhon, Kelly had been a visible fixture in the sanctioned rackets within the spaceport. This had been the case for nearly five years standard.

None of that official story was quite true. The identity of the man called Kelly had been a fiction created by the Occisis intelligence community. Michael Kelly was actually one of Centauri's best covert operations specialists. Kelly had been put in place on Bakunin to be Centauri's contact with Gregor Arcady, the security chief of the Proudhon Spaceport Development Corporation.

Shortly after Kelly's arrival, Gregor Arcady had secretly assassinated the Proudhon Board of Directors and used the Proudhon Security Force to cement himself as acting CEO and de facto dictator of the Proudhon Corporation.

Kelly had facilitated Arcady's coup. Kelly helped funnel money from the Alpha Centauri Alliance into Proudhon Security. Kelly financed Arcady's military buildup in the desert.

"You're responsible for all this crap!" She nearly shot him.

Kelly must have seen her tense, because he violently shook his head, "No! You don't see. I'm *not* Michael Kelly."

"What the fuck?"

"You asked me *what* I am. I'm a cybernetic reproduction of Michael Kelly's body and a computer record of most of his memory."

Tetsami backed up to a crate and finally sat down. "Christ hardboiled in an Easter egg."

"Our crash didn't affect me cosmetically, but I'm suffering a lot of internal systems damage. You mentioned sweat and fogging breath—losing that's an automatic response to conserve power. I'm running at thirty percent."

"You look fine to me."

Kelly shook his head. "No, I'm not. I'm losing power at a steady rate. I'm eighteen hours from a complete shutdown."

"What the hell is the point of all this?"

"I'm a double agent. You could say I was programmed to infiltrate the conduit between Centauri and Arcady. Contaminate the data flow and so on—"

Tetsami felt a knot in her stomach as she thought about

what Kelly was saying. She asked him, "Are you an AI, Kelly?"

Kelly nodded.

She looked at him and saw something whose *mind* was a construct, a computer program that thought it was alive—

She realized that her gun was pointing at the floor. She raised it to point at Kelly again. "It's not the flechettes in this electromag that'd hurt you. It's the charge they carry, right?"

Kelly nodded. "In my state, the shock to my power systems would—"

"Who do you work for?"

There was a long pause before Kelly said. "I can't tell you."

"*Don't fuck with me!* I want to waste you just because of the way you make my skin crawl. Don't give me an excuse!"

Kelly raised his hands, and Tetsami thought the expression of fear he wore was very human. "You don't understand—"

"Tell me, you wirehead bastard!" *God, did I actually say that word?*

"—security. I don't know! The information was erased before I replaced Kelly."

Tetsami looked at Kelly and wanted to shoot. But it made too much sense. If she was using an agent and had the ability to selectively remove any memory that could implicate her, she wouldn't leave her name in there for the opposition to find.

"How'd you report to your employer?"

"I don't."

"What?"

Kelly shrugged. "I was sent out with Kelly's memories and a core program to follow—"

"Can you access the program?"

He shook his head. "After the crash I don't even know if it's still there."

Tetsami lowered the gun. She felt a wave of self-loathing on top of the creepiness she felt about ersatz-Kelly. She had never used the word "wirehead" before. It was the kind of term that East Godwin maggots used for *her.* Her hand went to the base of her skull and felt the biolink there.

Wirehead.

"Arcady's people found out you were a double agent, right? That's why they locked you with us."

"No."

Tetsami looked up. "No?"

"Arcady wanted to feed me to his TEC allies as a good-will gesture. Terran Executive Command recently took over the operation here. Alpha Centauri is no longer officially a part of things here—"

Tetsami snorted at the word, "official."

Kelly went on. "Ever since Executive Command took over the operation here, Centauri has been elbowed out of the way. The Executive is paying for Arcady's army now."

Great, Klaus is in charge of all this—are we really surprised? "What the hell is going on here, Kelly?"

"Do you want the long or the short version?"

"I don't think I could take the long version."

Kelly sighed. "Simple version. The two 'closest' arms of the Confederacy, the Centauri Alliance and the Sirius-Eridani Economic Community, have economic problems. Bakunin is a huge drain of potential tax revenue to them—something equal to triple the gross product of a well-off Confed planet. That's just in lost taxes."

Tetsami nodded. Most Bakuninites were proud of statistics like that. It was an objective measure of how the planet was giving the finger to the rest of the Confederacy.

"Centauri and Sirius conceived of a plan to impose a State on Bakunin. That's what Arcady's army is for. Centauri simply chose the largest central authority on the planet and financed it until it was large enough to take on the role of conqueror."

"The takeover of Godwin Arms. What's that got to do with this?"

"That's the TEC's hand in all this. In order to arm Proudhon's swollen ranks, Proudhon needed its own factory. Taking it over itself would raise more suspicion than having the TEC land."

"But why? The Confederacy has plenty of its own weapons."

Kelly sighed. "The Confederacy Charter will only recognize a government imposed by domestic arms and domestic forces."

"Of course," Tetsami said, as if it made sense.

"The Confederacy Charter has to be signed by a power

that's in charge of the planet. Sirius and Centauri are backing Gregor Arcady and the Spaceport Company for that role. According to the Charter, the force has to be domestic—which is why we haven't had an extraplanetary invasion."

"What about the ships hanging in orbit?"

Kelly smiled humorlessly. "One of many loopholes— If Gregor *requests* aid, Sirius and Centauri can land as many troops as they want."

"He hasn't," Tetsami said. "Or else Arcady wouldn't have imprisoned his pet Centauri spy, right?"

Kelly nodded and pointed toward Gavadi. "In fact—"

"What the fuck?" Tetsami jumped up and ran to the front windows of the *Lady*. Something had flashed by the horizon, and as she reached the window she heard thunder rattle the sides of the vehicle.

In less than a second, the image repeated itself fourfold. Above them and to their right—south—a quartet of aircraft shot by. They had gone by the time she had a chance to register the image.

"What the—"

"Raptors," Kelly answered. "High maneuverability ground attack aircraft. The first one must have been some sort of spotting plane."

"The shit's about to hit the fan." Tetsami winced. "The mining laser! That had to be seen all over!"

"If they knew where, we'd be dead by now." Kelly's expression belied the assertion.

At least he acts *human.*

She was about to say something along the lines of, "Why me?" when a small contragrav craft shot over the lip of the saddle. It looked close enough to touch, and it was traveling fast enough that it was gone before Tetsami knew what she saw.

"That was civilian," Kelly yelled as something with hideously loud engines erupted from around the peak to their north. There was a subsonic rumble, shaking the *Lady*. Tetsami thought they'd been hit.

But then she saw a weapon discharge and she knew they'd been nowhere near hit.

A bright flash illuminated the mountainside, polarizing the front windshield despite the fact that it was to their rear. Half the *Lady*'s cameras were buried in snow, but one backward camera showed the shot. Tetsami only saw one brief tableau; a knobby ground attack craft—not a Raptor—racing past them, a flying tank whose drives could engulf the civilian contragrav it attacked; a beam firing from the midst of the armaments bristling the craft's nose, invisible but for the vapor trail left in its wake; the contragrav, pierced by the beam and blowing out a ruby ball of flame.

Then the camera was buried under more snow.

Tetsami waited, unmoving, for that beam to turn upon them.

She waited, as the echoes of explosions and engines receded. Until even the wind was muffled.

After a long time, Tetsami said, "We should be dead."

She looked out the windshield, and only saw flat white. She looked at Kelly and screamed, *"Why the hell aren't we dead?"*

She clamped down on the panic that gripped her. She was shaking.

Kelly looked nearly as bad off, but that could have been mimicry. He shook his head as if he couldn't quite believe it himself. "They're predators," Kelly said. "They're attracted to movement."

"Huh?"

"At the speed they go, they're relying on radar and energy profiles to pick out targets. We're too close to the ground and too low-powered to be a threat." Kelly looked at the whited-out windshield. "And we're buried again."

"Let's hope they keep thinking of us that way," Tetsami said. "Let's also hope that this avalanche isn't deep."

It took a long time for the *Lady* to rock out of the snow. Eventually, Tetsami managed to drive her out in the open.

Sheesh, she thought, as she emerged.

The landscape had changed, there wasn't a sign of the drift covering the *Shaftsbury,* now, or of the hole from which they'd emerged. The smooth white snowscape was now a collection of dirty, clumsy, drifts. Between sonic booms and explosions, the near mountainside had shed a lot of accumulated snowfall. The outcrop that the *Lady*'d been next to had prevented her from being buried impossibly deep. There was at least one place where the snow looked piled at least five meters above and beyond what had covered the ground beforehand.

Far past them was a pillar of black smoke. It had to be the civilian contragrav they'd seen.

She asked Kelly, "How long you think we have?"

"Before the army follows? A while. Hours. Those are only the first sorties, there's going to be a lot more."

"And they aren't going to clean our clock?"

"With this thing's RF profile, unlikely. They'll be concentrating on the pass to our south."

"That contragrav crashed only five klicks away—the enemy of my enemy, right?"

After a short debate within herself, she held out her hand.

Kelly took it. She avoided shuddering at the touch of cold flesh.

"Enemy of my enemy," Kelly said.

It took nearly a half-hour to maneuver the *Lady* down the slope toward the wreck. They were halfway down when Tetsami knew that they'd committed themselves. With the damaged wheel, there was no way that the *Lady* was going to make it back up. She almost wished for a contragrav, but every time she heard the sonic boom of another sortie of Raptors passing by she knew that, if the *Lady* was a contragrav, the energy spike would've gotten them blown apart before they'd seen the first enemy flyer.

They half rolled, half slid, down the slope. It was an effort to keep it pointed in the right direction. When they finally hit bottom, the *Lady* was plowing a two-meter-tall pile of snow ahead of itself.

Tetsami was a better driver than she suspected. The *Lady* came to rest only a few dozen meters away from what appeared to be the landing site of the contragrav's escape pod.

She drove the *Lady* toward it. A steaming groove in the snow had melted down to the rock beneath, ending at a heaped crater of snow. Tetsami circled the crater until she could see the crash pod clearly.

"I don't see anything moving in there," Kelly said, stepping up next to her.

Tetsami stopped next to the steaming crater. "How're our passengers?"

"Gavadi's still doing badly. I don't think the ride helped—"

"Damn."

Kelly shrugged. "There's no easy way out of these mountains, and if we stay put—without a doctor—we'll lose him. The good news is Jarvis and Baetez are probably going to make it."

Tetsami nodded and stared out at the pod. "I don't see anything moving out there either. At least this guy has the decency to crash in the direction we need to go."

She stood up, and winced. The drive downhill had managed to irritate her battered legs. She took a step and would have tumbled to the ground if Kelly didn't catch her.

"Maybe I should go," he said.

"I'll be all ri— *shit!*" Tetsami pulled away from Kelly and tried to move forward. Her leg collapsed underneath her. The painkillers she'd doped herself with had allowed her to reduce her right knee to gelatinlike wreckage that even the bandages couldn't help.

"Father, Son, and Holy-fucking-Ghost!" Tetsami slammed her fist into the floor, more in anger than in pain. "Christ, all I ever wanted was to get off this fucking planet."

Kelly helped her back into the driver's seat. "I'll go check the pod, okay?"

"Yeah, sure. You can handle the cold better anyway."

Kelly picked the HVE from between the seats. "You can cover me though the door." He handed her the weapon, butt first.

Tetsami took it.

Kelly grabbed a shovel and opened the door, letting in a burning wind and fragments of wind-blown ice. *If something goes bad out there,* she thought, *the best I could do is empty the gun and close the door.*

With the bum knee, she felt useless.

The open door let Tetsami see only a slice of the pod, and much of that view was hidden by a mound of snow. Kelly's movement was slowed by the wind and thigh-deep snow. On her that snow would be up to her waist.

The farther away Kelly walked from the *Lady,* the more nervous Tetsami became. Visibility wasn't great. Even with a cloudless sky, snow was constantly whipping through the valley. Sudden gusts could totally white out the landscape. The only sound was the wind ripping around the edges of the door.

As Kelly made his way around to a scalable part of the crater, Tetsami lost sight of him four or five times. Each time she tried to pull herself to her feet, and each time Kelly came back into view before she could get her damaged leg to work.

Come on, I was walking around all over the place before—

That was probably the problem.

Kelly slid down a slope of dirty snow to land on a partially hidden side of the pod. After a few seconds he waved his shovel in the air and yelled something. Covered by the tearing wind, she could barely hear that he'd made a sound. However, from the gestures, she thought it a good bet that he'd found someone.

Another gust blew by them, turning the view out the door into a blank whiteness. Even through her driving gloves, her fingers were starting to numb. The wind from the door bit into her face. Her eyes burned and watered.

She was getting sick of snow.

The gust died and she could see Kelly's head nodding up and down. Occasionally she could see the shovel. It looked like he was digging out part of the pod—

Whoever it is, just don't let him be another physical wreck. Tetsami would almost prefer to dig up another corpse than deal with more injured.

After what felt like an hour—though it couldn't have been more than ten minutes—Kelly stopped digging. He waved his shovel and yelled again.

All Tetsami could hear was, ". . . pilot . . . you . . ."

Being barely able to hear him was more frustrating than being immobile.

She could see the pod door open, and another powerful gust of wind whited out her vision. This one didn't die out over a few seconds, like the previous ones. The wind razored by, shaking the *Lady* back on her suspension. After nearly a half minute of blindness, Tetsami yelled, *"Kelly?"*

She could barely hear herself over the wind.

"Kelly!"

She could feel her hands again. Her grip on the HVE was tight enough to feel like she was driving needles into her fingers.

Outside, the wind began to pick up. Swirls of snow and ice danced across the floor of the *Lady.* A drift was building up inside the door. She couldn't even see the sky any more.

"Kelly, damn it!" She reached out and grabbed the back of the passenger seat. She pulled herself upright. The pain in

her knee flared all the way up and down her right side. She managed to hold herself upright.

What the hell was she doing? She was in no condition to be on her feet. She certainly couldn't go out and look for him.

Alone, I just don't want to deal with this alone— "Kell—"

A shadow huddled itself through the open door, cutting her off. It wasn't Kelly. The man was much too big. He was also dressed very badly for the snow. He wore a V-necked shirt, and khaki shorts and was hugging himself to keep warm. That barely registered on Tetsami because she was staring at his face.

"Tetsami?" Ivor said.

"Shit," she whispered.

CHAPTER THIRTY-FOUR

Silent Majority

"When in doubt, duck."
—*The Cynic's Book of Wisdom*

"We enter the world with pain, blood and screams—
too often we leave in the same manner."
—WILLIAM IV
(2126–*2224)

The Proteus guest apartments were built along more conventional lines. They could have been part of a luxury hotel in Godwin. Eigne had led Dom to the room and told him to expect a more formal interview tomorrow.

Dom had collapsed on the bed, expecting to fall asleep immediately. Instead, he remained awake, thinking.

He had come here intending find a new identity, a final escape from not only his brother, but the rest of his past. It had seemed a simple proposition when he had first thought of it. The people here would allow him to shed this body like so much excess skin, they could even give him a body that was fully human, they could even give him a new life. . . .

If he was a true pilgrim. If he paid their price.

Could he allow anyone to see inside his mind when he could barely look in there himself?

That raised another, more troubling problem. The chains of his past life weren't anchored in his body, they were sunk into his mind. He could be restructured down to the molecule and none of that would change. He could hide from his brother—

But would that solve anything?

He would still have to look over his shoulder, even if the alteration was perfect. Klaus would still be part of his psyche. And, even if the stigmata of his cybernetics was replaced with living flesh, he would still be an automaton, following its program and unable to think deeply without puncturing a tenuous sanity.

He could sever his ties to the Confederacy, to Klaus, to Bakunin, to Tetsami even. . . .

Could he sever his ties to himself?

Was he only running because he could picture himself doing nothing else? Perhaps he had done what anyone else could reasonably ask of him, but what about what he asked of himself?

Eventually, Dom slept.

He dreamed of Tetsami.

Eigne came the following day.

Her mirrored form was incongruous in the traditionally-styled apartment. Her appearance forced a sense of illusion to the entire scene. Dom sat across a table from her, eating a fairly normal-looking breakfast.

"Everyone has these doubts," she said.

Dom shook his head. "I don't know. I believe I came here to escape something that I cannot escape."

Eigne nodded. "You haven't told me much about this weight you're carrying."

Dom tried to ignore the silverware shaking in his hand. "I'd rather not."

"Everyone has demons, Dom."

He shook his head. "Not like these."

She smiled, and though the mirrored surface made it hard to read, Dom thought the expression somewhat condescending. "I chose my name, do you know what it means?"

"Eigne . . . no."

"First born."

Dom slowly lowered his fork to the table and looked at her.

"Two hundred years ago, people thought differently about the technology we use here. We were terraforming Mars, Venus, Titan even. I'm the only remnant of that project who has opted for continual existence."

"You're that old?"

Eigne laughed.

"Sorry."

She shook her head. "It's all right. After two-hundred and

fifty-one years standard, age becomes irrelevant." Eigne's voice became serious. "I'm the caretaker of Proteus. I contain and drive our efforts. I interface with the outside. I do it to atone."

"Atone for what?" Dom asked, even though he was beginning to expect the answer.

"I was in charge of the project on Titan."

The Titan terraforming project, when it had gone wrong, had gone wrong in the worst possible way. Titan was why Proteus would be destroyed if it was in any part of the Confederacy's jurisdiction. The Titian disaster was directly responsible for the death of over a million people. In the end the numbers might be incalculable.

Dom was about to respond to her, but she interrupted, answering a question Dom hadn't thought to ask. "It *is* an article of Protean faith that as long as the information survives, the individual doesn't die. I managed to save copies of the casualties and escape before the purges began— But I'm still human. And the Change that came with the disaster was without faith, without consent."

There was a long silence.

Still human, Dom thought.

"The gray goo problem," Eigne said.

"What?" Dom looked up into her mirrored eyes.

"That's the name for what happened on Titan," she smiled weakly. "They named the problem long before they ever had to deal with it." The smile left. "Sudden uncontrolled replication. The nanotechnological equivalent of cancer. The Terran Consul thought the machines were trying to take over, when the problem was, they were sick."

"Uh-huh— Are you sure you should tell all this to potential pilgrims?"

"It's mandatory, in fact."

If you couldn't escape something like that after two hundred years, what chance did he have? He had run, and run, and run. It had never gotten him anywhere. Yet he still kept on running. Out of habit.

Coming to this place was beginning to seem more and more a pointless exercise.

"I think," Dom said, "that I shouldn't go through with this."

Eigne nodded. "Most people believe the price for this is too high."

Dom shook his head. "That isn't it. I just came here to buy the wrong thing." A new identity was pointless when his previous life was still so unsettled. He had disposed of his life on Bakunin, but he still had everything before that.

He had his brother.

"Thank you for your hospitality anyway." Dom held out his hand.

Eigne took it, the chromed hand still surprisingly warm. "Visitors are rare here. Perhaps you can stay a while as our guest."

Dom didn't think so. It would be another escape, an attempt to escape his brother, an attempt to escape his past, an attempt to escape what happened to Tetsami.

Some of his careful internal reserve crumbled at that. *She's gone, damn it, because of my damned brother and his vendettas.*

Worse, Dom doubted Klaus even knew what he'd done.

"Are you all right?" Eigne asked.

Dom shook his head. Internal structures of denial were crumbling inside his head. As they fell, Dom saw huge blind spots that had clouded his thinking.

I am a fool, Dom thought.

"Dom?" Eigne said uncertainly.

"Your people are in serious trouble," Dom said. He had allowed his own provincial concerns, his Bakunin-bred prejudices, to blind him to the obvious. Proteus was a prime—maybe *the* prime—military target for the Proudhon invasion. The TEC, Klaus, would want this place *crushed.*

The complete story took Dom an hour to tell.

Eigne looked disturbed, yet she said, "Thank you for this information. But you have to understand our priorities here. The primary mission of Proteus is not just our survival, but the billion minds we represent. We can't involve ourselves in a greater conflict."

"This is the Executive Command we're talking about, they've destroyed one planet—"

"Dom, we cannot act belligerently. You have no idea how fragile a balance we have here."

"Don't you see? The Confederacy's about to force a de facto jurisdiction on this planet. Any day now, Proudhon will—"

"They'll destroy us. I know. We know."

Dom stared at that flat assertion and tried to come up with an argument. He couldn't. *They know they're doomed. How can she take it so calmly?*

In the chamber, by the egg, Eigne mentioned over six thousand of those black ellipsoids. Maybe, as long as those "seeds" were out there, they didn't mind dying.

Before Dom spoke again, he was interrupted by a low whistle that reverberated through the entire room. It died to a supersonic buzz, then became audible again.

Like the omnipresent voice Dom had heard inside the contragrav, the whistle seemed to come from everywhere.

"Preserve us," Eigne whispered.

"What—"

Eigne grabbed his arm and pulled him toward the door. "You must leave. Now."

"What's going on?" Dom asked as she dragged him, running, through a logarithmic corridor.

Eigne was nodding at something Dom wasn't aware of. As they ran—toward the Spire, Dom could tell—they dodged other Proteans. All seemed to be running somewhere. Black tumbleweeds were rolling everywhere, flowing between the less dexterous runners.

"What's happening?" Dom repeated.

"Supersonic fighter aircraft, passing through the Diderot Mountains. Turning north. You have to get out of here before our shields go up."

Eigne was nodding again, at nothing.

Dom realized that she was probably networked into the entire Protean city. She had heard and disseminated his story, even as he told it to her. He had been talking to everyone, through Eigne. That was probably why the alarm had been raised. He had primed them to expect an attack—

Just in time, it seemed.

They ran into the archive section of the Spire. Dom was surprised to see what must have been a dozen tumbleweeds clumped onto the black egg-thing that was on the central workbench. Before Dom could ask why they were here, Eigne said, "Traveler, we have a request. If you help us, we will lend you our aid when and if we can."

"What?"

"Take our seed to safety."

Dom looked at the black object, near-invisible under a cloudy blur of tumbleweeds. "Can't you launch it?"

"The drive isn't charged for orbital capability. The sails are being replaced by as many minds as can fit. Please give us an answer. We have little time, and you are our only route Outside."

Dom only thought about it for a moment, thinking of potentially a million minds inside that egg, and nodded.

Immediately, the tumbleweeds dropped to the ground and the three-meter egg rolled on top of them. The seamless black egg floated out of the archive on the backs of the tumbleweeds, who showed no strain from moving what had to be a massive weight.

"We need to get to your contragrav. The fighters will be here in ten minutes." Eigne pulled Dom up and slipped an arm around him under his armpits. Before he could object, his feet had left the ground and Eigne was running through the halls at a frightening pace. For the first time her grip felt like the metal it resembled.

Dom wondered just what her body was capable of.

They reached his contragrav in less than fifteen seconds. The egg was already wedged where the passenger seat had been. Of the passenger seat, there was no sign. The crash harness was there, seamlessly modified to slip over the egg and hold it in place.

"Thank you," Eigne said as she put him down inside the contragrav. "The survivors of this attack will help you, Dom."

"Yes, but—"

"The screens go up in half a minute. You must be outside the perimeter by then or else you cannot leave."

"What do I do with . . ." Dom tried to continue, but Eigne had left. He was alone on the landing pad.

He started to power up the contragrav, wondering what he was supposed to do with the egg once he got it to safety.

CHAPTER THIRTY-FIVE

Downsizing

"You cannot escape the interconnectedness of events."

—The Cynic's Book of Wisdom

"There are no small changes."

— BORIS KALECSKY
(2103–2200)

Shane silently followed Random's robot back to the inhabited part of the mountain.

Hougland wasn't with them; there was no real way for Random and Shane to carry the body through the kilometers of caverns. Shane was too weak, and Random's contragrav wasn't charged enough.

Hougland's body rested in a rocky alcove a short distance from the pyramid, waiting for Shane to return with the equipment to dig a grave.

Shane marched back to civilization, despite her exhaustion—driven by a hard kernel of anger. Anger at Random, anger at Hougland, anger at the forces that placed her on this world in the first place.

On top of it all, Hougland had dropped into Shane's hands a truly disruptive piece of archeology.

The Confederacy linked power directly to the control of planets. Planets, population, and a baroque seniority system defined power in the Confederacy. Wars had nearly broken out over strategically placed planets—more often because of their seat in the Congress than intrinsic value.

The search for new planets was an expensive matter of long-distance surveys and fleets of scout-craft, with the Protectorate of Epsilon Indi the only arm of the Confederacy with an ongoing scouting project. Establishing a base on a marginal planet was expensive, the relatively few earthlike planets were foci of political power. A disproportionate number of those were remnants of Dolbrian terraforming.

Foreknowledge of a dozen Dolbrian planets, gleaned from a small shard of an ancient starmap had helped make the Centauri Alliance one of the richest and most politically powerful arms of the Confederacy. In the century since universal employment of tach-drive starships, the Confederacy—especially the teeming populace of the Indi Protectorate—had grown far beyond the perimeters of those shards.

Now, in the heart of the Confederacy, was the most pristine example of Dobrian architecture to have ever fallen into human hands. And the bounds of *this* map reached as far beyond the borders of the Confederacy as the Confederacy had reached beyond that single Centauri shard.

And Hougland had died to find it.

Shane found herself torn between wonder, anger, and a deep sadness that she was no longer a part of her own culture. If she were like Hougland, if she still had her belief in—at least—the marines, then she'd relish the prospect of delivering this to Occisis. Bring a second golden age for Occisis and the Centauri Trading Company.

With this complete starmap, a single arm of the Confederacy could have leads on *hundreds* of Dolbrian-terraformed planets. Whether they hoarded the information or sold it, the government that controlled that cavern could dominate the Confederacy for centuries to come. In the short run, the information had the potential of reinventing the entire political landscape of humanity.

And, right now, it was only between her and Random.

God, take this cup from my lips.

It was too much responsibility, even if she did share it with Random. Too much to realize that she didn't trust her own people enough with this information. She trusted the Confed central government, the Executive Command, not at all.

It was just as well this structure was on an anarchist planet. She didn't want anyone to have a proprietary claim on it. Just as well to be forgotten. But . . .

Random had planned this discovery, and had seen the map. Random was a computer, and his memory was as good as any other physical record. It was quite possible that Random had already compensated for the passage of time and had calculated coordinate sets for each of the planets listed on the sides of the pyramid down there.

But . . .

Hougland had died finding the map. That called for some sort of recognition on Shane's part, even if it didn't involve the marines. That room transcended politics, it involved humanity as a species.

How many hundred earthlike planets?

Too many to visit in a single lifetime. Shane felt guilty for the tiny tug she felt at her heart. A tug that had nothing to do with guilt, or anger, or alienation from her people. The tug had more to do with what she had felt when she first decided to go off-planet.

The tug she'd felt when she'd first seen Occisis from orbit.

The siren of the infinite. There was a lot more to see out there than her own petty bickering slice of the universe. It seemed grotesque to feel that when she had to bury the corpse of a one-time friend.

However, remembering the mural on Hougland's cell, Shane thought her comrade might understand.

It had taken them a full day standard to find Hougland. Shane pushed herself, all the way back up the now-familiar path. Their time was cut nearly in half. When they pushed into Dom's underground warren it was a little past seventeen, local Godwin time. Just an hour after midday. They'd been gone for four or five hours longer than a Bakunin day.

What a difference a day made.

Random warned her that the place had been evacuated as soon as he came within the umbrella of RF communications. Shortly after, she saw what evacuation meant.

The whole mountain had bugged out. What had taken nearly two months to build had been stripped to the bone in less than thirty-two hours. "There are people here," Random said. "Here to take down the computer system."

Shane nodded and looked at the robot.

"I can find my way, Random. Make sure they leave some mining equipment." *So I can dig a grave.*

Random nodded and left her.

Shane found herself alone in a deserted cavern. As she walked up to the conference room, she passed doors opening into rooms emptied and scattered with garbage. Every once in a while she passed a vacant niche carved in the wall, a place for equipment now vanished.

She passed a window that opened over a vehicle bay. The bay was empty except for a single battle-scarred contragrav van. The echoes and emptiness of the caverns that had once been inhabited reinforced her own exhaustion.

She reached the conference room and found it a final refuge of human activity. Mosasa and Zanzibar were there, as well as a half dozen uniformed and armed men. Shane noted the uniforms had a new detail—a shoulder-patch with a stylized "BD," and in smaller type, "Bleek-Diderot, Weapons and Weapons Systems."

That was quick.

The room was awash with partially dismantled equipment and open shipping crates. The floor was a tangle of optical fiber and other cabling. The circular conference table had been dismantled, revealing the electronic guts for a number of holos.

Something had interrupted the breakdown, though— before she'd arrived.

The uniformed men were standing off to one side of the hemispherical chamber, leaving the floor to Zanzibar and Mosasa, each of whom were bent over a separate holo display. Zanzibar was watching the main display, that had been the center of the table, while Mosasa sat to the side working on a portable model jury-rigged into the heart of the electronics.

Shane stepped into the room and one of the uniformed men tapped her on the shoulder.

She looked to the man, who gently shook his head— *Don't interrupt.*

She nodded and stood back by the door.

Zanzibar was saying, "We can get a medic to your location. We're loading the transport now."

Faintly, Shane heard a voice on over the holo, "—zzz— long befor—zzz—expect the—zzz—bad way here—zzz—"

"A fast scout from Jefferson can be there in an hour."

"—n't know—zzz—have that long—zzz" The voice was familiar, but through the static it took Shane a few moments before she realized it was Tetsami.

Zanzibar slammed the side of the console. "Damn it, Mosasa! Can't we get better reception on this thing?"

"Lucky," Mosasa said in clipped tones, "to have *any* audio. Their comm is damaged badly."

"—ee casualties—zzz—losing Gavad—zzz—n't any faster?"

"We'll try," Zanzibar said. "We're trying to find a commune closer to you."

"—od. Any—zzz—damn aircraf—zzz—north?"

"I couldn't get that."

"—tor fighters—zzz—ing *north* of—zzz—ve ideas why?"

"Mosasa?" Zanzibar said.

"I think the question is if we have any ideas why the sorties they're watching are flying north."

North? Shane thought. *Sorties?*

It had started already.

"I've got Flower netted into this conversation," Mosasa said. "It wants to know what type of aircraft."

"Flower wants to know about the aircraft," Zanzibar said into the holo.

"—vor says—zzz—ptor ground attack aircr—zzz—leet of armored Royt cont—zzz—nd Kelly thinks—zzz—ily defended ground targ—zzz—where north of us now—"

Zanzibar looked at Mosasa.

Mosasa nodded at his own holo, which was oddly silent. *He's probably picking up the data directly through Random,* Shane thought.

Mosasa said, "Flower confirms that the description is consistent with a mission to take out a hardened ground target."

"But they're north of just about everything useful—"

"—lso a pair of marine scout—zzz—rom GA&A running a search—zzz—n't notice us. Look—zzz—thing different—"

Suddenly, all the fragments of information began to collapse into place for Shane. Tetsami had just described a typical marine search-and-destroy deployment. The kind Klaus was excessively fond of. Combine that with a heavy attack on a hardened northern target . . .

"*Proteus,*" Shane whispered.

Zanzibar was talking. "Flower says that the marines were a search-and-destroy deployment. They didn't attack you—did they see you at all?"

"—zzz—height they'd be blind, dea—zzz—umb not to—"

Shane stepped up to the comm Zanzibar was running.

Strangely, her oddly arranged loyalties didn't seem to matter much. What mattered was that people she knew were in serious trouble.

"I know what they're targeting—" Shane said.

Zanzibar whipped around to face her. "What? Oh, Shane—"

"—zzz—me again. What—zzz—"

Shane stepped up to the comm and said, "Tetsami? This is Shane. Those attack craft are after the Proteus commune. It's a high tech target, they want to incapacitate it before they progress any further."

"—zzz—mn. That's got to—zzz—dred klicks from us—"

Mosasa said, "Flower's looked up Proteus on its database. It confirms that probability."

"—zzz—at about the marin—zzz—ith the others, Shane. You're th—zzz—arine expert—"

Shane swallowed. "They have to be looking for Magnus."

"What?" Shane heard from several places at once.

Shane told them. "He was going to head for Proteus when he cleared things here. He'd almost certainly be there by now. Klaus must have sent the marines out on his trail."

"—zzz—it, shit, shit—zzz—"

CHAPTER THIRTY-SIX

Civil Defense

"Even a saint has ulterior motives."
— *The Cynic's Book of Wisdom*

"We would often be ashamed of our finest actions if
the world understood all the motives which produced them."
— François duc de la Rochefoucauld
(1613–1680)

"Damn it, are you sure that Dom went there?" Tetsami said
into the *Lady*'s comm.

"zzz—ffered zzz wit zzz—oteus—zzz—"

Tetsami slammed her fist next to the small console.
"Damn it, Kelly! We're losing them again!"

Kelly's voice came down from the roof of the *Lady*. "I
can't do anything more. The antenna array is shredded."

Tetsami turned back to the holo comm. It hadn't been a
great piece of equipment to start with. Now it was almost
useless.

"Say that again. I'm not getting you clearly."

"—zzz—ng up—zzz—ar any—zzz—"

"Shane? Zanzibar? Anyone?"

"—zzz—zzz—zzz"

Tetsami sank back in the driver's seat. it was getting to be
too much. "We had them. The transmission was crystal clear
a moment ago."

Ivor sat in the passenger seat next to her and fiddled with
the frequency controls on the comm. He only managed to
find more dead air. "We're relying on one of the comm ar-
rays at the mountain. Diderot barely has enough sensitivity
to pick up our signals. Any atmospheric interference could
have wiped out our transmission."

"Yeah, yeah." Tetsami put her face in her hands. She added her elbow to her list of pains.

To top things off, the *Lady* was losing it. *Two* wheels were without power now and there was a steady decrease in maximum velocity. According to Kelly, who was showing a sudden and unexpected technical aptitude, the problem was damage in the power storage systems. It wasn't something that could be repaired. The *Lady* was going to suck power at fifteen times its normal rate until it was dead. That gave them maybe five hours, and at their crippled velocity, that wouldn't even be enough time to get to the nearest commune. According to Tetsami's database, which was still in the *Lady*'s memory, they were over two hundred kilometers from *anything*.

And looked it.

They had made it out of the mountains, the right side of them, too, bucking the *Lady* down grades Tetsami never wanted to see again. They'd finally had to join up with the pass and race west, ahead of the invasion. Once out of the hills the accumulated mechanical difficulties had made themselves felt.

They were in the middle of a rolling plain of purple moss. The landscape was dotted with clumps of fleshy bushes, but none even reached the height of the *Lady*'s windshield. Empty hillsides with no trace of cover. Broad daylight. And soon there would be a ground invasion force spilling through the pass, less than forty klicks behind them.

"You all right, Punkin?" Ivor asked.

"You know damn well I'm not. Why the fuck are *you* in this? Isn't it enough to worry about my own hide?"

Ivor gave her an ironic smile. "Now you know how I've felt ever since you were six."

Tetsami realized the truth of that, even if she didn't feel it. "You went out, alone, looking for me?"

Ivor nodded. He had already gone over the story of his search once.

"You used to have brains," she told him. "What the hell were you thinking?"

"Someone had to."

She shook her head. "That's crap and you know it. How many times have you told me to weigh the risks versus—"

"Hey, down there," Kelly said from the roof.

Tetsami turned so she was looking out the open door of

the *Lady*. It was pointless. Since Kelly was on the roof all she saw was rolling hillside. "What is it?"

"I think I might have the radar antenna back on-line. Try and boot the system back up, will you?"

"Okay." Tetsami bent across Ivor and started fiddling with the controls that commanded the radar array. In a few minutes she had a screen of contacts coming on-line. "I got it, Kelly, it works."

She shook her head. The—AI, android, whatever he was—was exceptional with dealing with electronics. He was almost as good at it as . . .

"Ivor?"

"Yes?"

"Kelly remind you of anyone?" There had been a nagging familiarity about Kelly ever since she'd confronted him out of the con man persona.

"No, not offhand—"

"Come on, who else you know is this good with electronics?"

"What, you're comparing him to Mosasa?"

"There's something I can't put my finger on—"

Ivor nodded. "Sure. I see it. If Mosasa was white, a head shorter, had hair—"

"Never mind," Tetsami said. She closed her eyes and tried to ignore the pain.

Tetsami opened her eyes and realized that she had dozed off.

She bolted upright to look at the radar screen.

Unlike the comm, the radar setup on the *Lady* was decent, if not up to military specs. While Tetsami saw damage—a blind spot wiping out about half of the southwest quadrant—she could get contacts out to the horizon.

Unfortunately, with supersonic aircraft flying around, it wouldn't be much of a warning. If the antenna array weren't so damaged, they could have tapped into an air traffic satellite and have gotten a view of the air traffic for hundreds of kilometers . . .

Then again, Proudhon runs those air traffic sats. Maybe not.

She turned around to look behind her and saw Ivor watching Kelly fiddle with her personal field generator. She automatically slapped her hip, where it usually went. Of course it wasn't there, her captors had taken it. Kelly must have found it somewhere in the *Lady,* stashed like her biolink interfaces.

"Hey, Kelly, what're you doing with that?" she asked.

Kelly looked up. He knelt on the floor between the bunks, surrounded by every electronic tool the *Lady* had on board. Open, next to the small box that contained the generator, was a small computer screen that seemed set up to dump data into her generator. The small Emerson field generator was opened on the floor, so Tetsami could see the small high-density battery array surrounding the small chromed sphere—the size of a ball bearing—that was the generator itself.

That box was the only defense she had.

"Let me explain—" Kelly started.

"Damn well better," Tetsami almost levered herself out of the driver's seat. But she couldn't put weight on her injured knee without a massive stab of pain. She had to settle for swiveling the chair around to face the back.

"I let him," Ivor said. "He modified mine as well, listen."

Kelly nodded. "Ivor described the damage to Ashley."

"So?"

"We are excessively vulnerable to any EMP-based attack. You, me, and Gavadi may be injured or killed by a pulse that isn't even directed at us."

That sobered Tetsami. A pulse—supposedly an attack that targeted equipment and not personnel—had killed her parents. A refined EMP could fry most all electronics, and it didn't stop only because those electronics were wired to a nervous system. Someone with a cybernetic limb could find themselves paralyzed by an EMP. Someone with a biolink could find themselves lobotomized. She felt at the base of her skull where her flesh dimpled for the biolink socket.

Even raw EMP from a dirty little micronuke could fry her skull beyond the range of the blast itself. . . .

"What're you doing with that, then?"

"Making a pulse shield," Kelly said. "I have to reprogram the control system on this."

"How—" she started to ask.

"It's just a matter of making the absorption band on the field wide enough. Unfortunately, that lowers the duration from the limited power supply—but it only needs a few microseconds to damp the effects." Kelly waved back to the rear of the *Lady* where she saw what had to be Ivor's field generator nestled in a mass of wires hanging out of an open maint panel.

Kelly noticed her gaze. "That one is for the whole vehicle. It's tapped into the *Lady*'s power system."

Tetsami felt a familiar wave of suspicion. She wanted to resist it, but she knew little about Kelly, and what he'd revealed about himself didn't exactly inspire trust. She felt that deception was part of his nature.

She hoped it wasn't prejudice on her part.

Ivor trusted Kelly, but she knew it was only because she appeared to.

Tetsami saw the mining laser back there and asked, "What'd you do with the laser?"

"Recalibrated it for military use. I don't know how useful it will be, but it has an adjustable frequency and it's the only energy weapon we have."

Ivor was looking at her now, his expression was hardening somewhat. "Tetsami? What—"

She was still looking over the electronic debris scattered around Kelly. She could see a pile of restraint buckles, dull metal toroids that had come off of her, Kelly, Gavadi, and Jarvis. She had thought most of those were left back on the *Shaftsbury*. Those were the same thing as the personal field generators, right? They were just programmed differently, so they'd interfere with a nervous system rather than a laser—

Kelly anticipated her question. Without again looking up from his work he said, "Cannibalizing those for parts, reprogramming the controllers would take too long—the software is much too different." After tapping a few controls on the computer he said, "There."

He began disconnecting cables and shutting the case on Tetsami's field generator. *Damn it,* she thought. *What are you really doing, Kelly?*

Ivor was still looking at her, and seemed about to say something when an alarm began sounding from the *Lady*'s control system. Tetsami spun the driver's chair back around. Her knee slammed into the control stick and the pain nearly made her pass out.

She grabbed her knee and looked at where all the flashing lights were. She saw, through watering eyes, the radar. The lights and alarm were contact warnings. Three aircraft had just passed into the twenty klick range.

"Three aircraft," she said through clenched teeth. "Twenty klicks. Small."

"Northbound?" Ivor asked. "The medical transport?"

Tetsami shook her head. "Southbound, right toward us."

She shut off the radar's contact alarm and silence wrapped the *Lady*. After a few moments she said, "Eighteen klicks. No transponder reading yet."

Behind her she heard Kelly say, "Help me get the laser set up out there."

Like that is going to do us any good.

"Sixteen klicks." Tetsami looked up. The craft were flying low, but she could probably see them by now.

We're dead. The moment they see us, we're dead.

CHAPTER THIRTY-SEVEN

Search and Destroy

"Anything can appear to be worse upon further reflection."

—*The Cynic's Book of Wisdom*

"In the fight between you and the world, back the world."

—FRANZ KAFKA
(1883–1924)

Dom flew the contragrav south, low to the ground, trying to avoid detection. He was doubly aware of the fact that it was broad daylight and he was flying toward the incoming aircraft. Objectively, daylight shouldn't matter—any hostile force would see Dom's contragrav on their instrumentation long before they had any visual contact. As far as flying toward the hostiles, Dom had little choice. The charge left in his contragrav wouldn't carry him to Godwin. It would barely take him to Jefferson City, where he was heading.

His black ovoid passenger remained mute.

Dom headed almost directly south. He hoped that whatever aircraft were heading for Proteus were hugging the mountain range and would pass him a fair distance to the east. He might avoid being taken as a threat, even if they saw his contragrav at this altitude.

As he hugged his aircar to the hilly ground, Dom thought about what he had to do. He had warned people of a potential attack, but it was coming too damn soon. There was little chance that Godwin was ready for this. No chance at all that the communes were. The only chance Godwin had was Proteus. If Proteus could hold out long enough for Godwin to get its shit together, there could be a chance to slow the invasion.

As if in response to Dom's thoughts, a thunderclap resonated the windshield of his contragrav. As he looked up, he saw the turquoise arrows of ground-attack craft rocket through the eastern sky, between him and the mountains.

More thunderclaps.

More aircraft.

He counted a half dozen, headed toward Proteus.

Defended as Proteus was, he knew it was going to be overwhelmed. All the Proudhon forces would need was a small breach in the external screens and a micronuke. Considering the technical expertise that Proteus represented, any invasion would throw maximum force against it until it was no longer a factor in the war.

Another cascade of sonic booms rocked his contragrav. None of the aircraft took notice of him.

Hours, maybe less, before the invasion force turned back south. He didn't know what contact Proteus had with the rest of Bakunin, but he doubted it was adequate. Dom also doubted that any orbital sats remained to broadcast the invasion. Those would've been the first thing to be taken out.

He *had* to risk a transmission.

And beaming a transmission in this situation was almost guaranteed to draw the wolves down upon him. The Proudhon air traffic sats would still be up there, feeding the enemy command with his location as soon as his radio lit up. Even now, on some computer, he was probably tagged as an unidentified civilian contact—

To hell with it.

Dom turned on his comm to send a transmission to whatever remained at Diderot. He hoped a tight-beam transmission in that direction had less chance of giving him away. He could only hope that someone was still there.

The holo snapped into focus and suddenly he saw Zanzibar's face saying, "—zzz in. We have the medical transp—" Zanzibar's eyes widened at him.

"Zanzibar. Good. The invasion—"

"Dom! You're alive? *Where the fuck are you?*"

Zanzibar? Dom thought.

"Sir," she added, apparently an afterthought.

Dom shook his head. "The Proteus Commune. They're under a massive attack by Proudhon forces."

Zanzibar nodded. "We know."

What? "They can only hold out for a few hours, at best. Then the massed force is going to turn south."

She continued to nod. "Random is trying to ready the people you contacted."

"How . . ."

"Tetsami," she said.

The world around him did a little lurch and he wasn't sure he was hearing correctly. "What?"

"Tetsami. She escaped out of the mountains with Ivor and—"

Everything swelled inside him. Suddenly, the invasion, Proteus, his brother, all meant precious little to him. She was *alive,* alive and not in Klaus' hands.

"God. Is she there? Can I talk to her?" *I've needed to talk to her for weeks.*

"No. Her vehicle's stuck—zzz—forty klicks out of a huge pass in the mountains. We've got a medical—zzz—heading there from Jefferson."

Medical team? Please, not when I've just had my hopes raised. "Is she all right?"

"—zzz—alive— "

"Where is she? What's wrong?

Dom was already turning the contragrav southeast as he asked for Tetsami's location. It became more and more frustrating talking to Zanzibar. The signal was inexplicably degrading.

But he was lucky. Damn, he was lucky. He was actually closer to them than the medics. Dom would beat the Jefferson ambulance by a quarter-hour at least.

The fact that she was alive was shaded over by the fact that she was much, much too close to the action for Dom's comfort. Once Dom knew where they were, he told Zanzibar that he would be heading back with the medical team.

"Mr. Magnus—zzz—one more th—zzz—"

"I'm losing you."

"—zzz—two—zzz—mar—zzz—you—zzz—"

"Zanzibar?"

"—zzz—"

"Damnation and Taxes!" Dom slammed the side of his comm.

Whatever happened, he wasn't going to lose Tetsami again. He promised himself that.

Dom scanned the comm's entire spectrum and felt his

stomach begin to sink. Only white noise on all of the channels. The comm on this contragrav was in perfect condition. The only explanation was he was being jammed.

He was heading toward Tetsami, but he was also heading for the mouth of that mountain pass. The pass the invasion was going to spill through. He began to accelerate the contragrav past its design specifications, suspecting all the while that both he and Tetsami were in serious trouble.

Despite the ECM that washed out his radio, he could still make out the first faint contacts on his radar. The radar's output was fogged with spurious contacts, but Dom could definitely make out two contacts flying an intercept course. All he could tell from the contacts was range.

Twenty klicks and closing.

His contragrav had hit over three hundred per, and it was becoming hard to control. Vibrations rippled through the chassis that Dom didn't like at all.

The two contacts were subsonic, closing slowly. They weren't the ground-attack aircraft he'd been seeing, and they weren't large enough to be airtanks. If they had been, he'd have been dead already. Tetsami's vehicle was supposed to be fifty kilometers from him now. His tail had closed the gap by another kilometer.

Another ten klicks toward Tetsami and the contragrav was going slightly faster. However, now it was shaking violently and Dom had to pull up from the ground because it was becoming difficult to maneuver.

He had to pull away from his present course. He couldn't lead his escort toward Tetsami.

As he started turning, the readout on the defensive field on his contragrav registered a dual hit. The contact was momentary, but even so it had pumped the field halfway to the failure point. The field in this thing was a military-grade model, but not very heavy. A few more shots like that, and the charge would go over the top and he'd be dead.

Dom flipped on the rear video and tried to decipher his attackers from the ECM interference. Two small dots banking after him, fifteen kilometers away. They fired two more lasers and missed.

Their ECM must interfere with their targeting system. At this range they shouldn't be missing.

As they closed, both the video and radar began to fuzz into uselessness.

Targeting or not, he was unarmed and in a civilian contragrav. He was dead. It was only a matter of time.

With the radar and the locator fuzzed by his pursuit he had no clear idea of where he was. He estimated that he was within thirty kilometers of Tetsami's location.

Two more lasers fired. One hung onto his ass long enough to make the contragrav's field shimmer and raise the temperature in the cabin. Dom managed to jerk the contragrav up from under its stare before something exploded.

He was facing a pair of marine scouts. The scouts were designed to hang from parasitic hardpoints on an orbital drop-craft in lieu of bombs. He had seen ten of these things under the wings of the *Blood-Tide,* the ship that had attacked GA&A. The scouts were landing craft, only designed to get ten battle-suited marines to the ground. If he'd had any sort of armor or weapons, he might have had a chance.

He began to pull his contragrav into a climb.

There was no way he was going to escape these marines. That realization allowed the cold part of his mind to take over. There were only a few advantages he had in this fight.

They had speed, but he had less inertia and, therefore, a slight edge in maneuverability. Most of his body was artificial, especially his circulatory system, and he could take about twice as many Gs as the marines could, even in their suits.

He was taking those Gs right now as he boosted the contragrav into a near vertical climb that slammed him into his seat. The climb was becoming a tight-radius vertical loop that threw the horizon around him. The forces pulling at him made it impossible to move anything short of the fingers on his left hand—the one on the control stick.

His right hand, the one part of his body that was still fully human, was crushed against the armrest. It felt as if it were being compressed under a blanket of needles.

If not for his reconstruction he would be suffering tunnel vision and would have probably blacked out by now.

But at the top of the arc his vision, and his thinking, were still clear and ice-fine. Through the arc of the windscreen he could see the two scouts below him.

There were two other advantages he had.

The first was that the scouts, because of engineering constraints and the fact that they were built to defend against ground-based attack, had very little topside armor.

The second was that no one in his right mind would do what he was about to do.

He maneuvered the controls so that the left scout was directly under his nose. As it got larger, he could see the details on it. A T-shaped aircraft with a bullet-shaped nose and a tapered narrow body. It was about ten meters long. Through window slits in the armor he could see movement inside.

The scout only had the laser mounted in the nose. The marines inside couldn't fire back at him because their personal weapons weren't tied into the scout's defensive field. Without communication between the weapon and the force field, the field wouldn't care if the energy were going out or going in.

Dom gave the scout a hard little smile and glanced down to see that his crash harness was on.

They expect me to pull up at the last minute.

"Surprise," he whispered as the contragrav plowed into the top of the marine scout.

CHAPTER THIRTY-EIGHT

Dirty Tricks

"Worry when the man with the gun is smiling."
—*The Cynic's Book of Wisdom*

"The impossible is simply the untried."
—AUGUST BENITO GALIANI
(2019–*2105)

"Sixteen klicks," Tetsami repeated.

She could see them—dots in the distance. She could see flashes that had to be lasers striking something.

What's going on out there?

Kelly had gotten the mining laser set up in front of the *Lady's* nose. Tetsami could see only one of Kelly's jury-rigged modifications. The casing over the laser's frequency control systems had been removed. Wires ran from the hardware inside to the palmtop computer that had been taped to the back of the laser, next to the targeting control panel.

He works as fast as Mosasa, Tetsami thought. *Maybe even faster.*

Of course he wasn't human. Kelly was some sort of artificial robot designed to look human. Still, more and more, he kept reminding her of Mosasa—and that made her wonder about Mosasa.

She glanced down at the radar and saw that the three aircraft were holding at sixteen kilometers. Tetsami breathed a little easier. They weren't after them or the *Lady*. The two moderate-sized blips were chasing the smaller one, and the smaller one had begun turning away from an intersecting course.

There was another flash of laser fire out by the horizon and Tetsami looked up. *Oh, no!*

Those were the two marine scouts that had been can-

vassing the area earlier. The ones Shane had said were a
search-and-destroy team. The ones that were supposed to be
hunting Dom.

"Kelly, Ivor, that's Dom out there!"

"What?" She could barely hear Ivor. Kelly remained bent
over the laser, typing commands into the targeting system as
well as his addition.

"Two marine scouts firing at the unarmed civilian
contragrav— That's Dom out there, shoot already."

Tetsami stared at the horizon, watching the tiny dot of the
contragrav begin climbing.

"Are you kidding, at this range? A mining laser might not
be enough if they were on top of us—"

Kelly interrupted Ivor, "Temperature, atmospheric pressure."

"What?" Tetsami looked down. Kelly's hands were mo-
tionless over the keypad of his computer, waiting. The laser
was moving on its own, the servos run by the targeting computer. It had to be locked on one of the scouts.

Why doesn't he fire already?

"I need those figures, Tetsami. *Now!*"

Tetsami looked down at the control panel and had to hunt
down the environmental display, something she hadn't even
glanced at since she bought the vehicle. "Fifteen degrees,
point-nine-eight atmospheres."

Kelly nodded and began typing on his keypad. Tetsami
looked up to watch the trio of aircraft in the distance. For a
second she couldn't quite understand what she saw. The
small one was above the two others and flying backward—

Then she saw it was looping around.

"Christ is coming and he is pissed," she whispered as the
small contragrav looped downward and accelerated into the
scout below it. The contragrav impacted the larger craft and
the two became a single chaotically tumbling mass. Even
from this distance she could see the wreckage shed pieces of
metal, and possibly bodies, as it fell. Tiny black motes won
the race to the ground—the crumpled mass of metal, the
body of the wreck, was falling slowly, fighting a pair of failing contragravs.

She heard Ivor say, "Shit."

"Three hundred klicks an hour. They were going nearly
three hundred klicks an hour—" She was interrupted by a
buzzing from in front of the *Lady.* As the buzz reached its

apex, a white light enveloped the second, undamaged scout. For a half-second, Tetsami could see the scout's defensive field outlined in white light—a blindingly clear ellipsoid. Then the field collapsed as the rear of the scout exploded in a ball of yellow flame.

This scout did no slow contragrav tumbles. It plummeted straight into the ground, trailing smoke.

Tetsami could almost smell the smoke.

Then she looked down and saw that she *was* smelling smoke. The mining laser had caught on fire and was shedding sparks. Kelly and Ivor had backed away from it.

It was nearly half a minute after the laser's flames had died down, before Tetsami said. "What the *fuck* was that?"

Kelly climbed back inside and went to the rear, checking wounded.

Ivor followed. "I've never seen a laser do that before."

Was that a trace of a smile she saw on Kelly's lips? "Of course not. What I did is impossible."

"What'd you *do?*" Tetsami asked.

Kelly finished checking Gavadi and must have found him satisfactory.

He straightened up and looked at her and Ivor. "A defensive Emerson field is dynamic. The controlling software has to change the peak absorption band based on the field's own feedback. The software has only a few hundred nanoseconds to match the field's absorption band to the biggest delta-E crossing its surface."

Tetsami shook her head. She barely understood what he was saying. Suddenly it wasn't Kelly talking, *any* of the Kellys she'd seen so far. It was like Mosasa, but a *different* Mosasa.

She was becoming afraid of Kelly again, and she was out of reach of the gun.

Ivor seemed to have noticed the change in Kelly's voice as well. "That doesn't explain—" he began.

Kelly shook his head. "Of course it does. Just look at the process. To change the dynamics of the field, you have to get into the software—but because of the feedback, you can get into the software from the outside."

Ivor froze. "You're kidding."

Kelly shook his head and started looking over Jarvis. "If you know what you're doing."

Tetsami turned the driver's seat full around so she could

see what Kelly was doing. "You reprogrammed their field by shooting at it?"

"Not exactly. But I did manage to reset the field's peak absorption wavelength."

"To what?" Ivor said.

Tetsami was remembering the time she had first met Mosasa. He'd been experimenting with a huge toroidal field generator. He had been shooting small quantities of matter into the field, which promptly turned it into energy. . . .

"Particles have wavelengths, too," Tetsami said.

Kelly nodded. "Right. The specific band I reset it to was the DeBroglie wavelength of a nitrogen molecule of average momentum out there."

Ivor sucked in a breath, and stayed silent.

Kelly bent to check on the still-sedated form of Marc Baetez. "A significant quantity of the air around their field was converted to energy. Their defenses suffered a catastrophic overload—"

Ivor stepped up next to Kelly. Tetsami noted that Ivor was heading toward the rifle. *Good,* she thought. She didn't trust this situation at all. As Ivor moved, she asked Kelly, "How the hell do you know all this, Kelly?"

"A gift from my creator."

To hell with this, Tetsami thought. She turned the driver's chair around and began to power up the *Lady.* There was still a wreck out there that might have survivors in it, and one of them might be Dom.

There was still enough charge left to get them there.

Maybe.

"My turn for a question," Kelly said.

"What?" Tetsami said. She looked over her shoulder. Behind her, she could see that Ivor had reached the gun. That made her feel a little safer.

"What are you intending to do?" Kelly asked.

"We're going to see if anyone survived that—"

"Especially Dominic Magnus, correct?" Kelly was between her and Ivor. He held two things in his hands. One was her modified personal field generator. The one he said was to protect against an EMP.

Tetsami nodded.

"There may be marine survivors, hostiles," Kelly said. It was like he was reading from a script. "We only have one rifle."

"Yes, but—" Tetsami began. Then she saw what was in his other hand. It was the dull metal form of one of the restraint buckles. The ones with the stun field.

A stun field that wouldn't affect Kelly at all.

Kelly shook his head. "I cannot let you endanger the wounded."

He did something to the restraint buckle.

Tetsami saw Ivor collapse as she felt the pressure of a stun field washing the world away.

CHAPTER THIRTY-NINE

Preemptive Strike

"Superior technology is not a panacea."
—*The Cynic's Book of Wisdom*

"The next dreadful thing to a battle lost is a battle won."

—ARTHUR WELLESLY
(1769–1852)

"Do we have an ETA on the linac?" said the tech to Klaus' left.

"Thirty-three minutes at . . . *mark*," responded another tech.

Klaus' command center was a hive of activity. Around him worked every ranking TEC officer here on the ground, all coordinating the attack with Proudhon command. The fact that their command was being funneled through Proudhon Security grated on Klaus, but only a little. Through mutual agreement, even though Gregor Arcady was theoretically in command, Klaus ran the invasion.

As it should be.

Above Klaus' seat rose the massive holo display. It showed a realtime terrain map. Force positions were outlined, the data points fed in from the forces on the ground, from Proudhon's air traffic sats, and from the orbiting TEC Observation platforms. Even as Klaus watched, the resolution improved as recon craft dropped intel pods over the battle area.

The intel pods were photographic cluster-bombs, dropping thousands of pea-sized holo cameras over the terrain. The cameras were multispectrum, redundant, and each was a small part of the computer net that turned the battlefield into a fully mapped realtime virtual universe.

"Third Artillery, you're drifting off-course. Turn fifteen degrees north-northwest," one of Klaus' techs said, too far for him to hear the response. The glyph for the Third Artillery began turning to its left on the giant holo above.

Klaus called up a magnification on his own small holo. Intel on the battle zone had reached saturation about ten minutes ago, Klaus could now call up an image from any arbitrary point within a fifty-klick circle around Proteus.

The scene Klaus called up showed a division of heavy artillery. It was one of three that was moving in to provide support for the assault on Proteus. The mobile guns moved quickly out of frame. Most of the guns were tracked fifty-centimeter electromags—they were tracked because a contragrav couldn't handle the recoil of the massive gun that formed ninety percent of the vehicle's length. Flitting along with the guns, insects compared to the huge fifty-centimeter artillery, were contragrav missile craft. They were small disks, stacked with pyramids of missiles. Somewhere, inside that fast-moving group, would be hidden the mobile supply depot, tactical HQ, and the target acquisition system. All the light craft hiding behind the heavy guns.

Klaus switched his perspective to see the target.

Proteus emerged on the screen, all distorted crystalline angles, like a gigantic blob of molten glass had dropped on the Bakunin plain.

Klaus smiled.

"Current ETA on the linac?"

"Twenty-four minutes . . . *mark*."

Unlike the web of restrictions that constrained Operation Rasputin everywhere else, here, in this hive of heretical technology, Klaus had leave to do as he saw fit to sterilize this "commune." It wasn't only a strategic necessity, but a moral one.

Above, on the holo, glyphs of the three artillery divisions halted. They were in position, on three separate flanks of the Proteus commune. A wing of ground attack craft flew in, between a pair of artillery divisions.

A flash caught Klaus' eye, and he looked down to his own holo.

Artillery was raining down on Proteus. It was aimed at presumed air-defenses, the crystalline spires at the perimeter—all tiny mirrors of the giant central spire. Shells rained across the commune, and as Klaus watched, the explosions spread across an ellipsoid surface covering the whole of Proteus.

The shells hit some invisible horizon, and when they struck, blew all their energy out, away from the shield. The surface, when struck turned from transparent, to ruby trans-lucence, to a redshifted mirror sheen. The explosions, fire, smoke, debris, all blew outward, sliding across the ellipsoid whether it was visible or not.

Klaus could see the fire-pattern in the useless explosions rippling across the surface of the Protean shield.

"Advise," the tech to Klaus' left said. "The defenders have a mass-capable Emerson field."

No shit, Klaus thought, fascinated in spite of himself. The things you could do with something like that.

The aircraft wing flew into frame, diving at Proteus. The diamond formation of Raptors broke apart to saturate the surface below with everything they carried. Plasma waves crashed into the reddening shield like hell's own tide. The attack-craft pulled up at the last moment, some needling through the flame and smoke of their own plasma backwash. On three of them, Klaus saw the rainbow ellipses of the Raptor's own fields soaking up radiant energy.

Suddenly the techs around him were yelling over each other.

Klaus couldn't make out individual commands, but he could see what they were yelling about. On the screen, as the Raptors broke away from their first attack wave, some-thing came out of the Protean shield.

Multiple somethings.

Klaus manhandled the controls to his holo so he could follow the progress of one of the somethings. Even in the intel-saturated site around Proteus, the computers had prob-lems keeping up with the object. It was a small metallic sphere about a meter in diameter. It confused the computer by continually changing color and moving near the speed of the Raptor.

Actually, this sphere was faster.

Klaus saw the sphere race ahead of an accelerating Raptor and park itself in front of the attack-craft's nose. As intel struggled to keep up with the data, a small red point of light emerged between the sphere and the craft. The Raptor's pilot began maneuvering frantically, firing plasma cannon and the laser in the craft's nose. For a moment, Klaus thought the nose laser had shot a hole through the sphere. The laser hit dead center on the sphere, and it obligingly blew out into a hoop of blue-tinted metal.

The red dot of light remained where it was, relative to the Raptor, as did the remains of the sphere—this, despite the fact that the pilot was pulling ten-G looping maneuvers to shake the object from in front of him.

When the laser was fully discharged, Klaus watched in amazement as the metal flowed back into the center of the hole. In less than a second, the object was spherical again.

Then the light flashed and the computer lost contact with the Raptor.

Klaus punched controls on the holo in a frantic search through all the incoming data. It took him nearly half a minute before he found the time-lapsed record of what happened.

When the red light had flashed, it had englobed the Raptor with a ruby field all too much like the one covering Proteus. In response, the sphere, the field, and the Raptor inside, all *stopped.*

It didn't decelerate, didn't maneuver, simply stopped there, dead in midair. It was an impossible maneuver that made the intel computer blow its ability to follow the action.

Where did all that momentum go?

When Klaus saw the ruby field drop from the Raptor, there was no longer an aircraft inside. Instead was a thick black cloud of particulate matter and, Klaus noted on one of the subordinate readings, a burst of radiation.

Klaus glanced up on the big holo and saw that there were no glyphs left from the ground attack craft. "They took out a whole damn wing," Klaus said. "Keep our aircraft out of there from now on," he yelled at the room.

"Yes, sir," responded several techs from various stations.

Klaus switched back to Proteus, where artillery still rained down. The shield was still holding up.

"How long until the linac's in position?" Klaus asked.

"Thirteen minutes . . . *mark.*"

"Tell artillery," Klaus said, "they have nuclear authorization. Aim at the edge, ground bursts. They can't shield the shockwave." At least it would be damn irritating if they could.

The rain of conventional artillery ceased. Klaus watched on the holo until a flash whited out the scene.

Unfortunately the use of nukes tended to lose intel saturation. While the troops were EMP-shielded, it wasn't economical to do the same to thousands of pea-sized holo cameras. Multiple nukes would damage their intel for a hundred-klick radius at least.

Klaus switched the holo to the orbital feed from the TEC observation platform. The resolution wasn't as good, especially with the flashing explosions blanking Proteus' part of the scenery, but the overhead view could resolve the surface down to a few centimeters.

The barrage ceased. As Klaus waited for the kilotons to clear, one of the techs said, "What's the problem? Third Artillery, repeat, are you under attack?"

Klaus switched to a view of the Third. He had a ground based view, the intel cameras might be fried, but he could tap into the Third's own cameras.

The scene defied understanding for a moment. The Third was deployed on a ridge overlooking Proteus, Klaus could see the giant combined mushroom cloud in the distance. In the foreground, Klaus saw what had to have been one of the fifty-centimeter guns. It wasn't more than a pile of component parts. Not an explosion, everything was neatly stacked, from the bolts and washers, to one of the giant electromagnetic coils that fired the rounds. Even the treads had been disassembled into hundreds of rectangular plates stacked in pyramids in front of—

God, that's the crew.

Neatly lined up, next to one of the three-ton axles, were three polished skulls. Then, sorted neatly, were piles of vertebrae, ribs, the long bones of the arms and legs. All were neatly polished. Then, next to all that, were less neat piles of steaming debris. Klaus stared at part of one neat stack and watched part of it move.

Everything neatly disassembled, down to the circulatory system. Not even any blood. One of the crew's hearts was still beating.

Klaus only took a moment to absorb the scene of wreckage, there was still a battle going on. Klaus had the computer shift his viewpoint, and he saw what remained of the Third.

Black cotton balls, that's what they looked like. Dozens of the things rolled over the vehicles of the Third. Soldiers were fighting them, firing into their midst, but the weapons didn't have much effect. Projectiles passed through the black things as if they were so much vapor, and when energy weapons were used, part of the blackness would fold and curve into a mirrored collector, sucking up the energy.

Klaus watched one of the big guns collapse under a hundred of the things. The outline of the gun shuddered and dissolved, and as the black things rolled away, they left neat piles of the gun's component parts in their wake.

"This is bad," Klaus said. He looked up, and saw the flashing indicators of combat in the other two artillery divisions. He'd stationed them too close to Proteus.

"Time to linac?" he asked.

"Five minutes . . . *mark*."

Time to cut losses. "On my mark," Klaus said. "Nuke our forward artillery positions."

"Sir?"

"That's an order, we're dealing with an infection here. Look at your damn screens."

"Yes, sir," said the tech. He passed the order on to their more rearward artillery.

Damn waste, but it had to be done. Klaus couldn't let those black things run amok.

Klaus switched to the orbital view of Proteus. Klaus was amazed at how little damage he saw. He'd nuked the damn place. Even though he was theoretically aware of the possible Protean defenses, actually seeing a city survive a multiple nuclear blast was something else.

"Forward artillery targeted, sir," said one tech.

"Linac position in three minutes . . . *mark*," said another.

"Both fire on my signal," Klaus said.

That Protean shield might survive a few tactical nukes, but there was very little chance that it would survive what Klaus was about to throw against it.

"Two minutes . . . *mark*."

The linac was a piece of Proudhon Security's orbital ordinance. It was one of the weapons that helped the Proudhon spaceport maintain its monopoly. Right now, though, the linac was pointing down, toward the planet.

"One minute . . . *mark*."

The linac was a huge gun, a one-and-a-half meter version of the ill-fated electromags of the Third Artillery Division. The linac's barrel was nearly a kilometer long, and, in the vacuum of space, it could fire its projectiles at a velocity nearly half that of light.

"Twenty seconds."

Klaus had persuaded Arcady to allow him to co-opt the linac for his own purpose. Arcady was leery, with foreign spacecraft in orbit, but Klaus had made a very convincing argument.

"Fifteen."

Then it was simply a matter of timing and orbital mechanics to get the linac in sync with their attack on Proteus.

"Ten . . . nine . . . eight . . . linac has target acquisition."

"Confirm target acquisition."

"Four . . . three . . ."

"Linac charged."

"Two . . . one . . ."

"Fire!" Klaus ordered.

At Klaus' order, a series of three projectiles were fired down on Proteus from low orbit. The first struck the atmosphere at half-C and vaporized instantly into a wave of plasma and hard radiation. By the time the plasma shockwave had rippled halfway into the atmosphere, the second projectile followed in its wake. The second projectile didn't vaporize until it had caught up with the bow-shock of the first—the atmosphere had been blown away in a percussion wave from their paths.

Just as the plasma wave of the first two projectiles reached Proteus, the last one hit, blowing through the near-vacuum wake all the way to the ground.

Klaus knew the process, but it all occurred in a fractional second. To his eyes, it just looked like someone firing God's own plasma rifle down on Proteus. The flash of light hurt his eyes.

Before Klaus opened them again, he felt the rumble of impact, a faint seismic shockwave passing by the GA&A complex, traveling south.

When he opened them, Proteus was gone. The battle site was now opaque to visible light, but the TEC observer had obligingly switched to radar imaging. Where Proteus had been, was now a crater that looked about four or five kilometers in radius.

It was probably a good thing that Proteus was so isolated. The percussion wave and firestorm had razed the ground for fifty klicks in every direction. The most surreal image was the face of the Diderot Mountains—all the snow facing Proteus was gone to the bare rock.

Their first battle was a success.

Klaus looked up at the holo and saw a tally on the side, glyphs marking a wing of Raptors and three artillery divisions, close to twenty-five hundred men in total. It had been an *expensive* success.

But, to have cracked Bakunin's most advanced defense, it was a price willingly paid. From this point on, Klaus' army should have little trouble.

CHAPTER FORTY

Damage Control

"Dangerous is the man who accepts his own mortality."

—*The Cynic's Book of Wisdom*

"The death of a nation is less moving than the death of an individual."

—BORIS KALECSKY
(2103–2200)

The contragrav plowed into the top of the marine scout.

The sound was of someone balling the universe into a fist-sized chunk. The windscreen was replaced by crumpled metal and flying glass. The impact slammed every joint in his body together. Most of the pain was cut out by the processors monitoring his rewired nervous system—

The processors couldn't mediate the parts of him that were untouched by reconstruction. His right leg felt the full impact of the forward chassis giving way, bending inward, trapping his legs in a crushing embrace. His right hand felt the laceration of the exploding window.

The world tumbled.

The contragrav and scout-craft had become one inseparable object. The scout enfolded the smaller vehicle like a ragged hand. Dom could feel the fist tumble through space, slowly, gravity still partly canceled by the scout's contragrav.

Dom knew it was the scout's. Smoke from his own contragrav's fused engines filled the cabin.

The tumble was slow, but Dom knew that the combined velocity of both craft must still be over three hundred kilometers an hour. Dom lost consciousness when the ground finally reached up and slammed him out of the sky.

* * *
Pain woke him.

Dom opened his eyes and only saw darkness.

He upped the gain on his photoreceptors and was greeted with tiny white glitches all the way to the right in his field of vision. The more he increased the gain, the more they spread across his vision, little white electronic motes.

His right hand was in agony, and he couldn't move it.

He tried to move his legs, but they were trapped.

When he could finally see, he was effectively blinded in one eye by electronic snow.

The first thing he *could* see was the egg. It was still an intact black ellipsoid; wreckage had wrapped itself around it. Moisture shimmered on its sides, and Dom briefly thought the egg was bleeding. Then he realized that the blood was his own.

The right side of the cabin, where the egg sat, was sprayed with the viscous translucent fluid that his body used for blood. He looked down at his pained hand and saw why.

His hand wasn't there any more.

He could feel it, still being crushed, shredded. . . .

But he was looking at a ragged stump. A few shards of bone stuck out from the end. The blood had slowed to a trickle. Thanks to the capacity of his artificial circulatory system he wouldn't bleed to death. The veins and arteries had shut down at the next major junction.

Unfortunately that was about the same as applying a tourniquet just below the elbow.

The pigment on that arm had faded, leaving a look of flayed skin on top of darkened muscle. The muscles were the dark natural ones he'd been born with. With the blood shut off they were slowly dying.

Dom looked away.

No telling what condition his legs were in. His lower body was covered with wreckage. The chassis should have prevented his legs from being totally crushed, but he remembered seeing the chassis bend.

He wasn't dead, but he was pretty damn close. With all the machinery in his system he'd probably be able to catalog every failure as it occurred.

According to the chronometer in his skull he'd been unconscious barely ten minutes.

He wondered where the marines were.

He couldn't move his right arm. It was numb except for his missing hand, which hurt as if it was being ground under someone's foot. His legs were trapped.

His left arm and hand, the fully cybernetic ones, were free to move and seemed undamaged.

The first thing he did was release the crash harness on his chair. Doing so, he realized that he was more damaged than he thought. He pitched forward, and suddenly realized the whole contragrav was nosing into the ground. His balance circuits were screwed. He hadn't felt the pitch of the floor. He kept from injuring himself by hanging on the chair with his undamaged hand.

He found a stable position to sit in and realized that it was much too quiet in this can.

He raised his left hand to his head and felt around. The right side of his head was wet, he could feel lacerations in the pseudoflesh around his ear.

Damn.

He upped the gain on his audio, and like his eyes, interference began washing out his senses. To his right he could only hear the roar of white noise, to his left he could hear some of the world around him. At least Dom *thought* he was hearing the world.

It only took a few minutes of inspection to discover that freeing his legs with his one usable arm was hopeless. He couldn't get any decent leverage in his position, and even though the cybernetic arm was stronger than its biological counterpart, Dom doubted that it was anywhere near strong enough to bend the metal surrounding his legs.

The electronics in the contragrav were dead, no power ran through the systems; there was no way of calling out, even to the enemy. He would have to wait to be found.

For the second time in his life, Dominic Magnus—who'd used to be Jonah Dacham as well as half a dozen other names—was forced by immobility to contemplate his own mortality.

He closed his eyes.

The last time he had seen his brother face-to-face, not through some electronic medium, was a decade ago, ten years in time and eighteen light-years from where he was now. He had been conducting business with the nomadic people on Facion.

At least that's what he'd thought.

The conclusion of the arms deal proved that assumption wrong.

The meeting was held at the edge of one of the massive waste farms that ringed Facion's towering, overpopulated cities. He was supposed to meet a liaison for the nomads.

Instead he'd met Klaus.

A Klaus who had become obsessed with revenging himself upon him. His twin brother had fired between three and a half-dozen shots. The impact had carried Dom over the guardrail and into the waste tank, a waste tank that was a ripe green sewer brimming with engineered algae and bacteria that were intended to reduce the megatons of organic waste produced by Facion's tower-cities.

He fell directly into the city's digestive tract.

Acids burned his skin, blinded him, started dissolving his extremities. He had floated on his left side, giving the organisms the chance to fully consume his leg and arm. By the time his allies had fished him out and begun extraordinary measures to save him, he had lost sixty percent of his skin, had lost two limbs and crippled a third, most of his face was gone down to the bone. By the time the medics had stabilized him, the bacteria had found its way inside him, destroying a lung and most of his heart, liver and kidneys.

He had been in that tank for only eleven minutes.

It took them another five minutes to stabilize him and kill the remaining bacteria in his body.

He had taken six minutes to lose consciousness.

Dom opened his eyes. He was still greeted with static fuzzing the right side of his vision.

"Klaus," he whispered in a voice that he couldn't hear over the static in his ears. He no longer needed to ask the why of Klaus' obsession with killing him. He was beginning to understand.

There was a sound behind him that even he could hear. He turned as much as he could, to look behind him.

The space behind him didn't look like the contragrav any more, it was a surreal open space made of twisted metal from both vehicles. It formed a rough dome above and behind him, nearly two meters in diameter. With the intensity nearly maxed on his photo-receptors, he could see a light source back there. A spot on the back wall, above him, was glowing near white.

The sound he heard was metal warping.

Dom's first thought was that the scout's contragrav had slagged and that molten radioactive metal was melting its way down to him. But that made no sense, since the scout—mostly—was below him.

Someone's found me.

Dom would have readied a weapon, since it was probably the marines looking for him, but his sidearm was one with the wreckage below his waist.

He watched the glow and waited.

He had to scale down his photoreceptors twice, as he watched the back of the wall being cut away. With the increased light, the static in his right eye got worse and worse. Eventually, all that eye would produce was static.

The metal warped away from him, leaving a glowing-edged hole about a meter in diameter.

Dom waited for the marines.

Instead, he saw an unarmored head looking in at him. A young man with red hair and freckles. The man held a laser with all the maint panels removed.

The young man stared in at him and grimaced.

Behind the man, Dom could see sky.

The man wore overalls that looked like military issue, and it also looked like he had seen combat in them. The overalls were dirty, blood-spattered, and in one place had a charred laser track across the chest.

The man, however, showed no sign of injury.

The man said something inaudible beyond the static in Dom's ears. Dom shook his head and pointed to his ear with his good hand. "Mostly deaf," he said.

If this was a marine, would he kill him, or save him for Klaus?

What if you finally get me, brother? Would that force you to examine yourself?

The young man cast a worried look off at the sky and said something that sounded like ". . . take this . . ."

The man reached in and gave Dom a box—a personal field generator. "I have—" Dom began.

The man was shouting. ". . . d's sake keep it! . . . ose you . . . egg . . ."

"I don't understand."

The man passed his laser in to Dom. ". . . fied for cutting . . . free . . . itues before—"

Then Dom heard a very distinct word.

"Shit!"

Then a flash of light washed out the man's image and triggered the emergency cutoff on his eyes.

For a few seconds he was blind. After that pause, his left eye came back on. The right one stayed black.

The man had collapsed over the edge of the hole.

Dom only had a moment to register that when the wreck was washed with sound that even he could hear. The wreck shook back and forth, and Dom felt an evil dry heat washing in from the hole.

The young man stayed draped over the hole, unmoving. The laser the man had handed him had been stripped and modified for use as a cutting tool. Dom noted that it had once been standard Occisis issue. He was glad it wasn't a plasma rifle.

Dom was twelve minutes into freeing himself, when another flash whited out his vision. The reflection of the console in front of him was blinding. He smelled smoke.

Then the wreck rolled and shook as if it was on a breaking surf. It felt and sounded as if he was smashing into the marine scout again. The heat became worse, much worse. It felt as if he was much too close to a plasma backwash.

When his vision cleared, the world had settled.

And, between him and the egg, the field generator the stranger had given him lay in a smoking ruin.

Dom returned to freeing himself.

The laser cut through the chassis pinning his legs and Dom found that his biological leg—while sprained and lacerated—was unbroken. Once he had freed his legs, he had to put down the laser. He had to pull himself out of the wreckage with only one arm.

He stuffed his wounded, and still pained, arm inside what was left of his shirt and climbed out of the hole. It was an ordeal. A number of times he had to stop and let the pain recede. When he got to the hole and maneuvered around the young man's body, it was clear his benefactor was dead.

When he was fully out of the hole, and in the open air, he began wondering if his benefactor had ever been alive.

The red-haired corpse was smoking from quite a few laser holes in its torso. There was no sign of blood and the smell was a burning chemical smell. Dom examined the wounds and could see—even with his damaged vision—that this man's insides were metal and ceramic.

The smell from elsewhere was all smoke and burnt flesh. The sky was hazy, and Dom could see the wreck's shadow outlined before him. In the shadow of the wreckage the moss was a normal purple, outside the shadow, it was black.

Smoke rose from a half-dozen exposed corpses.

Dom looked in the direction of Proteus. The sky had turned muddy, and smoke rose from everywhere on the plains. Above it all, a hazy shadow within the smoke, he could see the remains of a massive cloud rolling up into the stratosphere.

To be seen at this range, megatons worth, maybe more.

Dom closed his eyes. He could see what happened. This robot-man had handed him a personal field generator. It was probably modified like the laser. Modified to protect the wearer from a severe electromagnetic pulse. Unfortunately for the samaritan, the radius of the field wasn't wide enough to protect *him* from the EMP.

This stranger had just given whatever life he had to save Dom.

With the reconstruction wiring Dom's nervous system, without the protection of that field, even a low-level EMP would have been unquestionably lethal.

Dom stared at the towering cloud on the horizon.

A billion minds were in that archive. They've just wiped out the equivalent of an entire planet. And none of them even know what they've done. Not even Klaus.

Especially Klaus.

Dom looked around the scene of the wreckage and studied the marine corpses. He began to reconstruct what looked like a skirmish that had occurred on a hill maybe fifteen meters away.

The good samaritan had managed to kill off all the survivors even before the blast.

Dom felt his good leg giving out and he slipped against the side of the wreckage. As he slid to the ground he could see another, closer, pillar of smoke. He guessed it to be the other marine scout, though how one man—construct or not—could take out a flying scout all by himself . . .

It was probably the blast.

Dom looked south.

Tetsami was out there somewhere only fifteen or twenty klicks away.

She might have been only fifteen or twenty kilometers away, but in the condition he was in, they might have been on the other side of the planet. Dom doubted if he could make it twenty meters. His good leg looked like hamburger and felt like jelly. In full daylight he could barely see.

And twenty klicks farther would still be too close to the EMP. Dom sagged as he realized that Tetsami was as vulnerable to an EMP as he was. He lost any real desire to retain consciousness.

He stayed, collapsed by the wreckage, for maybe half an hour before something caught his attention on the southern horizon. Something was moving out there.

It was an aircar flying in his direction.

At first he thought it was part of the invasion force. But then he saw the red, white, and blue markings of Jefferson City. Jefferson had to be far enough away to avoid the EMP.

It was the ambulance.

SECOND EPILOGUE

Mid-Season Corrections

"The contest for ages has been to rescue liberty from the grasp of executive power."
—DANIEL WEBSTER
(1782–1852)

CHAPTER FORTY-ONE

Lines of Secession

"Forget enemies. Be afraid of friends with something to gain."

—*The Cynic's Book of Wisdom*

"The best government is a benevolent tyranny tempered with an occasional assassination."

— VOLTAIRE
(1694–1778)

Gregor Arcady paced in an office near the top of one of Proudhon's white skyscrapers. The sun had long since set. The mobilization had long since begun.

He had been waiting for this moment for five years standard. Ever since the agent from Alpha Centauri had contacted him. In those five years he had risen from Chief of Security to the head of the entire Proudhon Spaceport Development Corporation.

He poured himself a brandy as he waited for orbital traffic control to call him back. The brandy was old, and from Earth. It was an expensive indulgence bought by Arcady's predecessor in this office, the former CEO of the Proudhon Spaceport.

That man had died in this office. Arcady liked that thought, it lent an otherwise sterile room some atmosphere.

He drank, watching the mountains out the window. Proudhon huddled at the base of the Diderot Range, and from his high vantage the mountains' silhouette carved an impressive chunk out of the sky.

He shouldn't be worried.

But he was.

He had begun this whole project by having an understanding with Alpha Centauri. Two arms of the Confederacy, the

Centauri Alliance and the Sirius Community, wanted a State formed on Bakunin, and the Proudhon Spaceport monopoly had been the perfect foothold from which to launch such a takeover. Gregor Arcady, the man in charge of the massive Spaceport Security Force, was the man to lead it.

So it would seem. Arcady agreed. He had always had an attraction to power, and had long ago planned to eventually take over the whole Spaceport Corporation. And here he was.

In charge.

Arcady shook his head, smiled, and took another drink.

Off-planet financing had allowed him to build a mercenary army of unprecedented size. He had built an army capable of conquering the planet—but the money made him beholden. He had allowed his lusts to overcome good sense. He was now at the mercy of Confederacy politics.

First, the Terran Executive Command supplanted his contact with Alpha Centauri. The TEC took over the financing of the entire operation. Then, the TEC dropped a military presence on the planet, and forced Arcady's timetable.

If that were all, it wouldn't be worrisome. It mattered little to whom Arcady owed allegiance, as long as he received what was promised him—control of Bakunin. Control of one of the richest planets in the Confederacy.

Arcady was beginning to suspect that the TEC Colonel across the mountains didn't see things that way.

Then, there were the Sirius warships in orbit. They were technically allied with Arcady, but he didn't trust their intentions. The Sirians were much too eager to assist him on the ground. All it would require was a word from him.

That word would be a tacit agreement of formal allegiance, and would mire Arcady, and the planet, within Sirius' sphere of influence—perhaps permanently. Money was one thing. Troops were quite another.

Now, simultaneously with the long-awaited offensive, had come news of yet another off-planet fleet taching into orbit. Things had gotten out of hand, and Arcady was starting to regret his own ambition.

The holo on his desk buzzed for his attention.

He sat down, activating the holo. Facing him was one of the many officials who had the job of manning the orbital traffic center. Proudhon's orbital traffic center was now Bakunin's communication center and only defense. Any competing satellites had been blown out of the sky in the first hours of the operation.

"Arcady here," he said.

"We've a positive ID on the incoming contacts, sir." The man looked to a small palm-held readout and read off of it. "Fleet of twenty-seven ships consisting of the scouting vessel *Red Sun* and escort. They've tached in directly from Dharma."

"Drop the euphemisms. This isn't the Confederacy—" *Yet.* "What kind of firepower are we talking about?"

"The *Red Sun* is one of the most advanced carriers in the Indi Protectorate. The ships accompanying it range from planetary attack craft and fighters to interplanetary battleships. In numbers, they're double the force accompanying the *Daedalus*."

"Travel time from Dharma?"

"Minimum ninety days standard."

"Has there been any contact?"

"They identified themselves and 'suggested' that we don't interfere. They've fanned out in a confrontational stance with the SEEC ships—neither fleet has talked to us since."

"Any shooting?"

"Not yet."

"Thank you," Arcady said and cut the connection.

Now he had reason to worry. Not just because two arms of the Confederacy seemed about to go to war above Bakunin. He had to worry because the *Red Sun* left Dharma over three months ago. That was before the TEC's ground team had even left Earth. It had left at least a month and a half before the *Daedalus* had left Khamsin, and the Indi fleet was acting as if it expected to find the Sirius fleet here already.

And Indi had come in force. Enough force to maybe take the planet, if need be.

When Arcady had found an Indi spy in his ranks, he had sent him over to the TEC. Confed politics was Colonel Dacham's problem. Now Arcady wished he had kept hold of Gavadi. Then at least the spy would still be alive.

Arcady needed to talk to his opposite number across the mountains.

He activated his holo again, and was about to route the call—when his office plunged into darkness.

Arcady's hand drifted to his sidearm and he backed to

the window. The position would be exposed, but the windows were so armored that anything getting through them from the outside would also succeed in taking off the top of the Proudhon Tower.

At the moment, Arcady was more worried about what might be in the building with him.

His fears were confirmed by movement in the far shadows of his office. Whispering, subliminal movements that his eyes couldn't track.

Where the hell is building security?

Arcady drew his weapon, a gamma laser. The GA&A Gamma 505 was a brute force weapon, sucking more energy than a plasma rifle and costing three times as much, but it was much, much more compact.

Things moved.

"Show yourselves," Arcady said in an even voice. He aimed the Gamma at the densest area of moving darkness.

The darkness resolved itself, seeming to coalesce into a flat black humanoid form. Facing the black-on-black form, Arcady found it impossible to resolve depth, as if he faced a two-dimensional cutout of a man. The black form walked toward Arcady, right in line with the Gamma.

Every guard in this building is going to be looking for work after this.

"gregor arcady." The voice was a monotone as black as its silhouette. Flat, unaccented, devoid of any character whatsoever.

Arcady had decided that he faced a man dressed in a form-fitting black leotard. Something in the weave of the black suit was causing visual interference. The voice was probably modified by the suit as well.

"I suggest you leave," Arcady responded.

"we represent lucifer contracts incorporated."

What?

Arcady felt the first twinge of fear. Lucifer was the most shadowy and feared of any native corporation. Lucifer's purpose was to witness and enforce contracts between—anyone. With no legal system on Bakunin, Lucifer was a necessary evil. Few people bucked a LCI contract—no matter the money involved—because LCI only observed one method of enforcement.

"I've never signed anything with you people!" Arcady said.

It was true. None of the "legal" documents that Arcady had signed had ever been witnessed by Lucifer. LCI required a hefty sum to file a contract, and neither Arcady, nor his former employers, had filed such a sum.

"we have been retained to rectify a breach of contract."

The shadows around him were moving. Arcady kept the Gamma facing the speaker. "What are you talking about?"

"your contract with the board of the proudhon spaceport development corporation."

Arcady felt the window pressing into his back. "My dealings with the corporation have nothing to do with you." He leveled the Gamma at the silhouette. "Last warning," he said.

The silhouette kept talking, like an automaton. "your assassination of the proudhon board of directors was a willful breach of your contracted duties as security director."

Arcady fired the Gamma.

The only sign of the beam was a slight heat shimmer through the area between him and the apparition. The beam shot through the figure and fire exploded out of the opposite wall.

The figure didn't move.

What?

"lucifer contracts incorporated has been hired to enforce this contract after the fact."

The fire illuminated the entire room, showing Arcady more shadowy black forms. Arcady systematically fired the Gamma through each of them. No reaction.

"Holos, damn prerecorded holos."

The one in the center of the room kept talking. It was an obvious holo now that it was illuminated by the half-dozen fires that Arcady had ignited with his Gamma. "the heir to the former chief executive officer has provided adequate documentation and capital for lucifer contracts to act on his behalf."

Arcady shook his head and walked up to the image. He passed his hand through it a few times. No reaction. He had to talk to security about this.

He walked to the door of his office.

It wouldn't open.

"any final words in your defense, gregor arcady."

Without the inflection it took a moment to realize that a question was being addressed to him. He tried the door a few times, but the mechanism was fused. He turned and found himself facing a dozen of the matte black silhouettes.

"any final words in your defense, gregor arcady."

Arcady looked at the figures, and at the useless Gamma 505 in his hand, and realized that he was trapped.

Oh, hell.

He turned back and tried the Gamma on the door. As the door began to bubble and melt, Arcady heard behind him the toneless voice say, "plaintiff waives final statement."

Arcady thought he could see light through the hole in his door—

—then the top three floors of the Proudhon Tower evaporated in a tide of light and wreckage.

Colonel Klaus Dacham got word of Gregor Arcady's demise while he was sequestered inside his command center.

Klaus hadn't moved from the room since the attack began. Above his chair, the giant oversized holo was graphing force distributions in glowing lines over a topographical map of Bakunin's one continent. Proteus had been the site of their heaviest losses. Since, the invasion had progressed with impressive speed.

In front of Klaus was a smaller holo that showed a schematic of the immediate space around the planet, out to one AU. It showed everything that the TEC observation platforms saw—mainly the forces from Epsilon Indi facing off with the smaller fleet from Sirius.

A third holo showed an image of a severe man in his midtwenties, it was that man who was receiving Klaus' undivided attention at the moment.

"This is certain?" Klaus asked.

The man—the last surviving heir to the former CEO of the Proudhon Spaceport Development Corporation—gave Klaus a cruel smile. "Not that I don't trust Lucifer, Colonel, but I had observers monitoring Arcady inside my father's office. I can provide you with a video record."

"No need."

"I, myself, plan to watch it often." The smile shed a little of itself as the man asked Klaus. "Now, your end of the bargain?"

"Proudhon is yours. You can be assured that its monopoly will continue."

The man on the holo nodded slightly and said, "Here's to a profitable alliance."

The holo disappeared into static and then invisibility.

Klaus steepled his fingers and smiled a little. Unlike Arcady, the man he had financed to take Arcady's place had no unanswered questions about his loyalty. The CEO's son had no ties to any arm of the Confederacy. And, unlike Arcady who was motivated by power, the CEO's son was motivated by money and simple revenge. Klaus knew that the CEO's son thought little beyond Proudhon itself, and would be easily manipulated by his own greed.

The CEO's son was as much a mercenary as the troops out there.

And now that Arcady was out of the picture, the mercenaries could be funded directly from GA&A, and Klaus would be in direct control of the operation.

Even as he stared at the vanished holo, techs and intel people moved around the command center, rerouting the chain of command so that it ended here, in this room. Around him, his TEC people were excising the bloated form of Proudhon Spaceport Security from the body of the Spaceport Development Corporation. Within a few minutes, the army spilling over Bakunin would officially be a sovereign enterprise, not a subsidiary of some corporation.

Within a few more minutes the official would become the real as the last of two hundred and fifty of Gregor Arcady's loyalists would be silently eliminated from the command structure of the army, to be replaced by people picked by Klaus.

As far as Operation Rasputin was concerned, the coup would be painless, if not bloodless. And, as a side-effect, the CEO's son would find himself totally dependent on Klaus and his army for the security of the spaceport and his own continued power.

Klaus turned to the holo transmitted from the TEC observation platforms.

Only two things muted Klaus' pleasure at a near flawless operation.

The first was the presence of the Confederacy here. The fact that a fleet from the Indi Protectorate had come to face off against the SEEC vessels meant that things could get ugly.

However, as long as there were no calls for intervention

from any legitimate planetside authority—a fuzzy definition that may only have included himself and Arcady—things could still go smoothly. Klaus had eliminated Arcady just to prevent such a debacle. If there was a call for some sort of intervention, it would almost certainly pit two arms of the Confederacy against each other. Against each other in a shooting war that could spread into an interstellar conflict inside the Confederacy itself.

The two fleets were like a weight pressing down everything on the planet.

The other factor tempering Klaus' latest victory was the absence of his brother. Jonah—Dominic—was almost certainly dead. They had finally tracked his single contragrav to Proteus. It had left, but there had been two marine scouts to intercept it. That meant that Klaus' brother was either in Proteus during the preemptive strike, or he was in an unarmed and unarmored civilian contragrav to be attacked by two marine scouts.

Dead, almost certainly.

But between the EMP from the Proteus strike and the electronic countermeasures from the scouts themselves, they had lost track of the scouts. The last word had been the two scouts targeting a civilian contragrav. But after the static had cleared the battlefield, there were no signs of any vehicles—scouts or contragrav. *If it just wasn't for the pulse.*

And, because of the scouts' ECM, there was a hundred kilometer search radius from the last contact. In that area—Klaus had seen from satellite surveillance—there were at least fifty individual wrecks. Contragrav neutralized by the invasion force, preinvasion wrecks, vehicles wiped out by either the pulse or shockwave from Proteus.

Even with all this networked electronic military intelligence gathering, once the war began, things still fell through the cracks.

The marine scouts he sent out there had probably gone down after the blast on Proteus. They would have been EMP hardened, but they weren't the most stable aircraft for riding out a shockwave.

What worried Klaus was the fact that he had no beacons from the scouts. They could still be flying out under their ECM, but that was doubtful after several hours. They could have landed and powered down their defensive screens, and the EMP would've fried all the electronics in their craft. Or, they could have been very close to Proteus when it went.

Why am I worried? Klaus thought. *An EMP would fry all those cybernetics. A pulse is as good for brother Jonah as a bullet.*

His brother was certainly within the lethal range. But Klaus still worried. Worse, Klaus wondered if the worry was that his brother was still alive—or whether his brother was finally dead.

Anxiety over his brother's *death* was such a repugnant sensation that Klaus immediately shut away any more thought on the subject. His brother was a closed chapter now, no questions.

He looked up at the strategic holo map.

This was his future. The army had passed south of the equator and was surrounding Troy and Godwin. Little red dots marked communes of little value that had been neutralized, blue dots marked the cities that represented 90 percent of Bakunin's huge economy.

Two of the larger blue dots—Troy and Godwin—were being wrapped in the green of Klaus' forces.

The siege was beginning.

Fifteen light-years away from Bakunin, the man calling himself Jonah Dacham looked into the Australian night sky. He redid the calculations in his head. Even though he knew, intellectually, that simultaneity was as much an illusion over interstellar distances as causality, he still thought, *it has begun.*

His hand began to shake.

In seven Bakunin days he would lose everything he cared about.

CHAPTER FORTY-TWO

Restructuring

"Of forgiving and forgetting, the latter is infinitely easier."
—*The Cynic's Book of Wisdom*

"I can pardon everyone's mistakes but my own."
—MARCUS PORCIUS CATO
(254–149 B.C.)

Dom spent at least two drugged days of intermittent consciousness before he realized that he was in a hospital in Jefferson City.

He spent most of that time dreaming of his brother. His twin. Klaus.

There had been a time when they had been close, closer than many twins—a united front against their mother. He had defended Klaus against some of Helen's uglier rages.

They had served together, even when rank began to separate them. They were practically the same person.

Until Styx.

Until Helen Dacham's death.

Dom, for once, could see through the layers of guilt surrounding the two of them like a twin-hearted onion. Helen wasn't just an unfortunate woman who was at the wrong place at the wrong time.

She was *all* of their victims. Everyone who had fallen under the twins' actions for the TEC.

The two of them, Dom and Klaus, were still twins. They still thought alike. Dom realized that his actions on Styx, and their result, made him carry the guilt for both of them.

While Dom had pulled all the crimes upon his own head, Klaus had projected his own guilt upon him. Dom became numbed and suicidal. Klaus, obsessed and murderous.

Dom had been asleep for a long time. Since Styx itself. It felt like he was finally awaking. It had taken the destruction of Proteus to wake him.

I was what he has become, and that is why I should die.
Why we both should die.
Why the TEC should die.

When Dom opened his eyes, they were working.

He lay in a hospital bed in an antique-looking room. Ivy covered part of the one window, cutting Kropotkin's ruddy light into random uneven blotches. Sitting on a wooden chair, at the foot of the bed, was Tetsami.

Dom sat up and found himself surprised that he could. His voice caught in his throat. Then he stopped trying to talk. He had no idea what to say. He stayed sitting upright, sheet bunched around his midsection. He barely noticed that there was a shiny-new glint of chrome from where his right hand should be.

"Dom," Tetsami said with a half-smile that made her look like an Asian Mona Lisa. "You have more lives than a cat."

Dom stared at her as his hands found each other. The right one was now fully metal. *I always heard that Jefferson was somewhat backward when it came to reconstruction.*

Dom realized that he was feeling the same metal around his right leg. It didn't disturb him as much as he thought it should have. For years he had seen his humanity as something that had been blown away with the tattered shreds of his original biology.

Something about Proteus, and its destruction, had driven that idea from him. He realized that if he still denied his own humanity, he denied the Proteans'.

"You should be happy to know, everyone's accounted for. Ivor has some clout here and got them to let us use a tightbeam comm. Flower's running Bleek with Ezra and your GA&A people. They're arming Godwin. Zanzibar, Random, Mosasa, and Shane are stuck in the mountains, but safe."

"Tetsami," Dom said finally.

"For the moment," she went on, "we're safe. The army's invaded, but they're just surrounding the major cities. They've ringed Jefferson, blockaded everything, and broadcast terms of surrender. The city fathers here've been debating since, and the Jefferson City Congress has been in continuous session."

"Tetsami," Dom repeated.

She waved her hands, her voice sounded far away. "They used an orbital linac on that commune, Dom. *An orbital linac!* Scorched the ground for kilometers. Communes dropping right and left—those bastards razed Shambala, what the hell did a bunch of bald monks do to anyone?"

"Tetsami," he said, a little more forcefully.

She looked at him and folded her arms. She was short, dressed in black, and—the first time Dom had realized it—beautiful. "You keep saying that, Dom."

His mouth dried as he formed the words. "Tetsami, I'm sorry."

She stared at him as if he had spoken a foreign language.

He tried to go on, but there wasn't really any more he could say. He could try to justify his actions, explain himself, but that would be pointless.

There was a long pause before Tetsami said. "You just apologized."

Dom nodded.

She gave him a suspicious look. "For what?"

He sighed. "For everything. Taking you for granted. Never saying what I felt."

She hugged herself tighter and walked to the window. Dom noticed that she was limping, and there was a padded bandage on her right knee.

"How are you doing?" Dom asked.

"Me? Oh, fine considering. Considering—" she shook her head and stared out the window. "What do you feel, Dom?" It was nearly a whisper.

What do I feel?

"Too much. Not enough." Dom paused before he finally said, "Love?"

All motion in the room seemed to cease. Motes of dust hung in mid air, caught in ruby shafts of light. The silence was a solid thing. Dom felt much too warm.

It was too much of admission, especially to himself. *Love?* Someone like him shouldn't even be capable of such an emotion. It was hubris to believe that he could actually care for someone, and it was a travesty to ask her to believe him.

The fact that it was the truth didn't help at all.

Tetsami turned to face him, slowly. As if he were caught in a nightmare, Dom found himself unable to move. Even the tightness he felt in his hand and cheek, the normal prelude to a nervous tic, stayed frozen. Immobile.

Her eyes were wet, and tears had begun to trail down her checks.

"You bastard," she whispered.

She stepped to the bed, reaching for him.

"You Christ-fucking asshole."

She placed her hands on his shoulders. He didn't resist. Dom allowed her to pull him to the edge of the bed, spilling the sheet around his ankles. He was naked underneath it. Other than the chrome-sheathed arm and leg, he looked human.

Their faces were only centimeters apart now. "I tried to give up on you," she said. "You hopeless unemotional fuck."

He felt her breath on his face, and, when he stared at her eyes, he saw a reflection of himself looking back. *No scars,* came an idle irrelevant thought. *The benefits of a pseudoflesh skin.*

"You wouldn't let me, you sadist." She covered his mouth with her own.

"Do you have any idea how pissed off I am?" Tetsami said as she gently pushed Dom back on to the bed.

From the tone, it was a rhetorical question.

It was the first time in over fifteen years that Dom had made love to anyone. Because of both their injuries, it took a long time. Fortunately, his reconstructed anatomy looked and behaved like his original equipment, and as a rule, it was more durable.

When it was over she said, "Damn you, Dom. Damn you straight to hell."

Eventually, as the sun faded, she told him what had happened. She told him about her escape from captivity, about the crash of the *Shaftsbury,* about finding Ivor, and about the enigma of Kelly.

"He was the man who saved my life," Dom said. "He died doing it. Fought the surviving marines and gave me the field that saved me from the EMP."

Tetsami nodded, rubbing her bruises. "He probably *made* that thing just to do what he did. He was expecting, or was programmed to, save you—"

"Any idea why he stunned you?"

"He said he didn't want to risk the people in the *Lady.*"

"Considering the remains of his firefight with the marines, he was probably right."

Tetsami told him of the time since the demise of Proteus. The ambulance from Jefferson collected everybody living. By the time it had returned to Jefferson City, it was flying only a few minutes ahead of the invasion. The Proudhon army had been a tidal wave racing south, but it hadn't overrun Jefferson as it had the communes.

Instead of invading Jefferson, the army had ringed the city, blockaded it. Within hours, the invasion had done the same to Godwin, Troy, Sinclair, and every other major city between the three.

"It's been two days," she said. "And the news is they've gone as far south as Rousseau."

"They've stayed out of the cities?"

Tetsami nodded. "As far as my tightbeam conversations with Flower go. It's a blockade, nothing gets in or out of the cities without having Proudhon roast it. They've spent most of the time broadcasting the terms of surrender."

Dom nodded. "They want the planet unified, with the economy intact—not a bunch of burnt-out cities. It won't be long before people start giving in."

"Huh? This is Bakunin, Dom. We've been giving the finger to collective authority for a century."

Dom nodded. "Sure, the idealists will hold out. The idealists run the communes. The communes are burning. Who runs the cities?"

"The corporations," Tetsami said slowly.

"And they'll nod wherever they see their bottom line tilting. Also—it's the communes that produce most of the food on this planet. How long do you think Jefferson, for instance, can hold out?"

There was a long pause before Tetsami said, "I talked to Flower."

"Yes?"

"It suggested two or three weeks. Godwin maybe a week longer if the city gets its shit together."

"Not that long," Dom said.

After a while, Tetsami said, "You're going to have to do something."

"Me?"

"According to both Flower and Random, you're the token head of the resistance now."

"How—" Dom suddenly remembered all the comm calls he had made before he had left the mountain. What had Random said? *"They're going to need a leader here."*

Dom shook his head. *Why not? It gives a neat symmetry to the whole enterprise. Klaus on one end, me on the other.*

"How are things in the mountain?" Dom asked.

"They're cut off from Godwin by the blockade, but they aren't under any direct threat. And, apparently, they've found something."

"What?"

"No one trusted the tightbeam enough to give me specifics. But they were pretty damn excited about it."

"Did they say anything about it?"

Tetsami stayed quiet.

"Well?"

After a long pause, she said, "You have to understand, this is from Random, and I don't quite trust him."

Dom nodded.

"Random says that what's in the mountains might render this war—his words—*'insignificant.'* "

"Random said that?"

"Yeah." She stood up and gathered her clothes. Her limp was more pronounced than it was earlier.

"I'm going to have to talk to them."

"And the people in Godwin. At the moment you're the only central authority we've got." She walked to the window and said, "Now I get to ask you a question."

"Go ahead."

"Tell me, what the fuck is that?" She pointed out the window.

Dom pulled himself to the edge of the bed, sat up, and peered out the vine-covered window. The window overlooked a courtyard that was ringed by the wings of the hospital—all red brick and ivy.

In the center of the courtyard, ringed by warning flags and temporary barriers was a black ovoid that sucked up all the dim evening light, reflecting back none.

"Who brought that here?" Dom asked, surprised to see the Protean egg. He wouldn't have thought anyone would have salvaged it from the wreck, especially when they were about to be overrun by an invasion.

"No one," Tetsami said. "It followed the ambulance in."

"Followed . . ." Dom started, then he remembered that the egg was a probe. It had its own contragrav, and probably some level of intelligence. "Not the ambulance," Dom said. "It followed me."

Tetsami stared at him and asked, "but what the fuck is it?"

"An egg," Dom said, answering everything and nothing. "An egg I'm supposed to find a nest for."

"Uh-huh."

Dom leaned back into the bed, feeling his injuries again. "I need to rest."

As he closed his eyes he heard Tetsami say, "God, you can be frustrating."

"What do you expect?" Dom whispered. "I'm only human."

APPENDIX A

Alphabetical listing of sources

Note: Dates are Terrestrial standard. Where the year is debatable due to interstellar travel, the Earth equivalent is used with an asterisk. Incomplete or uncertain biographical information is indicated by a question mark.

Lord Acton
    (1834–1902), English historian.
Agathon
    (*ca.* 448–*ca.* 400 B.C.), Greek poet.
Beecher, Henry Ward
    (1813–1887), American clergyman.
Bonaparte, Napoleon
    (1769–1821), French emperor.
Cato, Marcus Porcius
    (254–149 B.C.), Roman statesman.
Celine, Robert
    (1923–1996), American lawyer, anarchist.
Cheviot, Jean Honoré
    (2065–2128), United Nations secretary general.
Cicero, Marcus Tullius
    (106–43 B.C.), Roman statesman.
Colton, Charles Caleb
    (1780–1832), English clergyman.
Danton, Georges-Jacques
    (1759–1794), French revolutionary leader.
Galiani, August Benito
    (2019–*2105), European spaceship commander.
Hamilton, Alexander
    (1755–1804), American statesman.

Harper, Sylvia
(2008–2081), American civil-rights activist, president.
Heracleitus
(*ca.* 540–*ca.* 475 B.C.), Greek philosopher.
Herbert, George
(1593–1633), English poet.
Hippocrates
(*ca.*460–*ca.* 360 B.C.), Greek physician.
Jay, John
(1745–1829), American statesman, jurist.
Kafka, Franz
(1883–1924), German writer.
Kalecsky, Boris
(2103–2200), Terran Council president.
Kropotkin, Prince Pyotr Alekseyevich
(1842–1921), Russian writer, revolutionary.
la Rochefoucauld, François duc de
(1613–1680), French writer.
Lenin, Vladimir Ilyich
(1870–1924), Russian political leader.
Li Zhou
(2238–2348), Protectorate representative.
Machiavelli, Niccolo
(1469–1527), Italian political philosopher.
Madison, James
(1751–1836), American president.
Michelangelo Buonarroti
(1475–1564), Italian artist, sculptor, architect.
Montesquieu, Charles
(1689–1755), French philosopher, historian.
Plato
(*ca.* 427–*ca.* 347 B.C.), Greek philosopher.
Rajasthan, Datia
(?–2042), American civil-rights activist, political
leader.
Shakespeare, William
(1564–1616), English dramatist.
Shane, Marbury
(2044–*2074), Occisian colonist, soldier.
Stone-by-water
(*ca.* 2288), Voleran ambassador, first contact.
Tacitus, Cornelius
(*ca.* 55–120), Roman historian.

Voltaire
        (1694–1778), French writer.
von Treitschke, Heinrich
        (1834–1896), German historian.
Walpole, Horace
        (1717–1797), English writer.
Webster, Daniel
        (1782–1852), American statesman.
Wellesly, Arthur
        (1769–1852), Duke of Wellington.
Wilde, Oscar
        (1854–1900), Irish writer.
William IV
        (2126–*2224), Monarch of United Kingdom in Exile.
        *(Note: Also "William VI" before the English revision
        of 2294.)*

The Cynic's Book of Wisdom is an anonymous manuscript
        that first appeared on Bakunin in 2251. Since then, it
        has seen innumerable editions, many with substantial
        additions or modifications. The generally accepted text
        is credited to "R. W."

APPENDIX B
Worlds of the
Confederacy

The Alpha Centauri Alliance:

Number of member worlds: 14	Number voting: 13	Number prime: 10
Capital:		
Occisis—Alpha Centauri	founded: 2074	a
Other important worlds:		
Archeron—70 Ophiuchi	founded: 2173	c
Styx—Sigma Draconis	founded: 2175	b

The People's Protectorate of Epsilon Indi:

Number of member worlds: 31	Number voting: 17	Number prime: 15
Capital:		
Ch'uan—Epsilon Indi	founded: 2102	a
Other important worlds:		
Kanaka—Zeta' Reticuli	founded: 2216	a
Shiva—Delta Pavonis	founded: 2177	a

The Seven Worlds:

Number of member worlds: 7	Number voting: 7	Number prime: 5
Capital:		
Haven—Tau Ceti	founded: 2073	a
Other important worlds:		
Dakota—Tau Ceti	founded: 2073	a
Grimalkin—Fomalhaut	founded: 2165	x

The Sirius-Eridani Economic Community:

Number of member worlds: 21	Number voting: 14	Number prime: 12

Capitals:

Cynos—Sirius	founded: 2085	x
Khamsin—Epsilon Eridani	founded: 2088	b

Other important worlds:

Banlieue—XI Ursae Majoris	founded: 2146	c
Dolbri—Cl	founded: 2238	d
Paschal—82 Eridani	founded: 2164	a
Thubohu—Pi³Orion	founded: 2179	a
Waldgrave—Pollux	founded: 2242	d

The Union of Independent Worlds:

Number of member worlds: 10	Number voting: 2	Number prime: 1

Capital:

Mazimba—Beta Trianguli Australis	founded: 2250	b

Non-Confederacy Worlds:

Bakunin—BD+50°1725	founded: 2246	c
Helminth—Zosma	discovered: 2277	c
Paralia—Vega	discovered: 2230	d
Volera—Tau Puppis	discovered: 2288	e
Windsor—Altair	founded: 2146	x

Notes:
a = habitable earthlike planet
b = marginally habitable planet
c = possible site of Dolbrian terraforming
d = definite site of Dolbrian terraforming
e = site of Voleran terraforming
x = planet uninhabitable without technological support

S. Andrew Swann

HOSTILE TAKEOVER

☐ **PROFITEER**   UE2647—$4.99

With no anti-trust laws and no governing body, the planet Bakunin is the perfect home base for both corporations and criminals. But now the Confederacy wants a piece of the action—
and they're planning a hostile takeover!

☐ **PARTISAN**   UE2670—$4.99

Even as he sets the stage for a devastating covert operation,
Dominic Magnus and his allies discover that the Confederacy
has far bigger plans for Bakunin, and no compunctions about
destroying anyone who gets in the way.

OTHER NOVELS
☐ **FORESTS OF THE NIGHT**   UE2565—$4.50
☐ **EMPERORS OF THE TWILIGHT**   UE2589—$4.50
☐ **SPECTERS OF THE DAWN**   UE2613—$4.50

Buy them at your local bookstore or use this convenient coupon for ordering.

PENGUIN USA P.O. Box 999—Dep. #17109, Bergenfield, New Jersey 07621

Please send me the DAW BOOKS I have checked above, for which I am enclosing
$_____ (please add $2.00 to cover postage and handling). Send check or money
order (no cash or C.O.D.'s) or charge by Mastercard or VISA (with a $15.00 minimum). Prices and
numbers are subject to change without notice.

Card #_____ Exp. Date _____
Signature_____
Name_____
Address_____
City _____ State _____ Zip Code _____

For faster service when ordering by credit card call **1-800-253-6476**

Allow a minimum of 4-6 weeks for delivery. This offer is subject to change without notice.

Science Fiction at Its Best

Karen Haber
☐ **WOMAN WITHOUT A SHADOW** UE2627—$4.99

Kayla, a gifted telepath, is about to be caught in a struggle between two deadly forces determined to use any weapon to secure total victory.

Betty Anne Crawford
☐ **THE BUSHIDO INCIDENT** UE2517—$4.99

So Pak, seeking the path of freedom, launches a mission on the starship *Bushido*. But someone is determined that neither So Pak nor the *Bushido* will ever return to Earth.

Daniel Ransom
☐ **THE FUGITIVE STARS** UE2625—$4.99

The tail of the comet held more than just harmless space dust. It also contained the seeds of an alien invasion . . . Only one man could sense what was happening, but could he prove it before it was too late?

DEBORAH WHEELER

☐ **JAYDIUM**　　　　　　　　　　　　　　　UE2556—$4.99
Unexpectedly cast adrift in time and space, four humans from different times and universes unite in a search to find their way back—even if it means confronting an alien race whose doom may prove their only means of salvation.

☐ **NORTHLIGHT**　　　　　　　　　　　　UE2639—$4.99
Kardith found a home, family, and purpose among the Rangers, patrolling the borderlands known as the Ridge to protect the people of Laurea from invasion by the norther barbarians. So when Avi, her closest comrade-in-arms disappeared into the badlands, Kardith set off on a search to find her, thus beginning a dangerous odyssey which would take her into the heart of enemy territory to uncover a secret beyond her wildest imagining . . .

KAREN HABER

☐ **WOMAN WITHOUT A SHADOW**   UE2627—$4.99
A fugitive in a galaxy wary of anyone with mind powers
and all too willing to turn her in for the bounty on her head,
Kayla, a gifted telepath, is about to be caught in a struggle
between two deadly forces who will stop at nothing for total
victory.

☐ **THE WAR MINSTRELS**   UE2669—$4.99
Kayla has been on the run since she used her mind powers to strike out at another human. And in a solar system
where her only allies are pirates and aliens, and her enemies have sworn to see her enslaved or dead, how long
can even a triple empath such as herself hope to survive?